THE CHRONICLE OF THE DEWNAN

Tbis
SACRED
LANd

PART 2, FIGHT FOR FREEDOM

TIM
BAGSHAW

I AM SELF-PUBLISHING

@iamselfpub
www.iamselfpublishing.com

contents

Maps:

Chapters:

Ocean And The Pretan

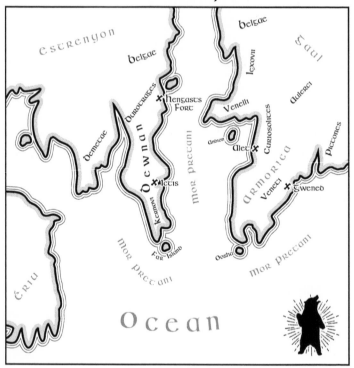

Estrenyon

belgae

belgae

Saul

Iexovu

belgae

Durotriges

✝ Hengasts Fort

Venelli

Auterci

Demetae

Dewnan

Mor Pretani

Anbion

Alet ✗

Curiosolites

Armorica

Pictones

✗ Aletis

Kernow

Veneti ✝ Gwened

Mor Pretani

Far Island

Oosha

Mor Pretani

Eriu

O c e a n

Tamara in the land of the Dewnan

Run Houl

Tamara

Dowr or Ronni

Dynas Dowr Teyl

Ker Tamara
Menlint

Dynas Kazak

Marthros

Iccis

Nowyth Iccis

Mor Pretani

Killas

Casworon

Menicriel

Meneth Nev

Foye

Dynasdore

Kammel

The Sanctum

Ker Kammel

Mor Pretani

Kernovi

Porthmetern

Menluit and the Twin Forts

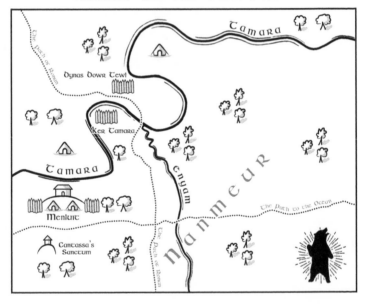

The Moons of the Dewnan

Loor Bleydh	*Wolf Moon*
Loor Tewedh	*Storm Moon*
Loor Plansa	*Planters Moon*
Loor Tevyans	*Growing Moon*
Loor Skovarnek	*Hare Moon*
Loor Golowan	*Midsummer Moon*
Loor Medh	*Mead Moon*
Loor Barlys	*Barley Moon*
Loor Trevas	*Harvest Moon*
Loor Helghyer	*Hunter's Moon*
Loor Owrek	*Golden Moon*
Loor Derwenn	*Oaken Moon*

For Penny, together in endeavour.

*Absence of Evidence is not
Evidence of Absence*

Even supposing events did turn out contrary to their expectations, still, they had great seafaring strength, while the Romans had no skill with ships and no knowledge of the waters, harbours, or islands in the areas where the campaign would take place. They also knew that navigating the great-unbounded ocean was quite a different matter from sailing in land-locked waters.

These plans were adopted. The Veneti fortified their towns and gathered in the corn from the fields... They also summoned assistance from Britain, which lies opposite those regions.

Julius Caesar, *Commentarii de Bello Gallico*

passion rekindled

Artur awoke from a fitful sleep. He and the Company had stood long by the funeral pyre, in homage. Marrek had sung a series of laments as the fire had slowly consumed the bodies of their fallen comrades. Finally, long after Sira Howl had gone to his walk in the Underworld and as the fire dwindled, they had all lain down and slept a last sleep with the three lost warriors. Soon, they would commit the ashes to Tamara, so that their earthly remains would be washed clean into Ocean's embrace.

As Artur looked around, bleary-eyed, the rest of the Company stirred. As he stared into the last of the embers, Gwalian, who had been lost from his thoughts during the act of lamentation and a restless sleep, came rushing back into his growing consciousness. He wanted, needed to talk to her. In the heat of the battle, and then while releasing her brother's slaves, he had been determined and confident, angered and spurred on by the loss of Casvelyn and Brengy and his desire to overcome Anogin. The look of disgust she had given him, however, had undermined all of that; a hard, cold face looked at him in a completely different way – with contempt. He did not like it. Somehow, he had to make amends; and then there was Morlain. She was unexpectedly prominent in his thoughts also, confusing his intention. She had risked everything to help him, fearlessly challenging the giant Anogin, even in the face of such an obvious mismatch.

He jumped to his feet. 'Maedoc, will you make my excuses for me? I need to be alone and to think. I am going to walk through the woods downstream for a while. I will meet you all back at Pendre later.'

'Artur, Aodren will return soon. I am sure he will have heard of events by now. We will need to ensure a balanced explanation when he does return and you will need to be there.'

'Yes, I know. I will not be long. I will be at Pendre by midday.'

He walked away from the clearing, through the port and past the slave pen. The Belgae, awake and alert like caged hunting dogs, scarred but undeterred, looked keenly towards him, leering, mocking with their eyes despite their incarceration. One rose with a wicked black-mouthed grin, his moustache rippling provocatively on his upper lip, and spoke out.

'Off to find your girly, Prynsling? Wonder if she'll give yer the same tongue-lashing as yesterday? What do we make of the men of Dumnoni, sub-standard and controlled by harridans, eh boys? Bet he wishes he'd been born a Belgae!'

Blistered lips parted and more toothy grins appeared.

'Our womenfolk know their place and it is on no battlefield or dictating terms!'

Others joined in.

'You need to tether that young hussy, or she's going to run you ragged.'

'Let us out boy; you can trust us to help you overcome your little problem! We'll be your guide!'

At the far end of the tethered line, the largest of the group, perhaps the most senior of this remnant, spoke next while the rest looked to him.

'Mind you, we saw she again this morning.'

All of them smirked wide-eyed, nodding their heads.

'And not alone either, no, comforted in her distress, as she should be, poor little thing. Is it you, Prynsey, do you think? Not good enough for 'er, eh? Not enough to satisfy 'er? Bet she's a bit of a goer, eh? You can tell us!'

The man next to him quickly joined in.

'Pretty minx, isn't she? I'll bet she shags well! Send her down here to some real men and we'll have her in turn and tell you what we think, where you might improve things!'

Artur's hand gripped firmly on his sword hilt, while gruff, cackling, raucous laughter broke out behind him, but he controlled himself, ignored them and carried on.

Now he wanted to see her and explain his actions; how he had felt them to be necessary from the leader of the Company. Would she understand? He would try to apologise for the way he had dealt with Ewan and be grateful for the way that she had raised support and rushed, with Lancelin, to his and the Company's aid.

Quickly, he came to Enyam, walked upstream and crossed at the stepping stones that Gwalian had led him across, not that long ago, at the wax of Loor Tevyans. He strode across and pressed on now, knowing where he was going. *Would she be there?* If not, he would return to the Company, look for her at Pendre later, but he had to check. Desire and a tightening within his belly drove him forward. He had to speak to her if he could.

***

'We should never have parted, you know that. We had made a deep and passionate commitment to each other, but I was a fool and I let you down badly. I allowed a mad impetuous impulse to take me. Dearest Gwalian, you must believe me when I say that I regret my actions bitterly and I would do anything to change what I have done and prove to you, as before, that you are the love of my life and the most beautiful woman that I have ever met.'

Lancelin sat beside Gwalian on the small bed in her hut in the woods. He held her hands in his and gently squeezed them. She looked back at him, exploring his face, searching for truth.

'I don't know. You say you have changed, but how can I really be sure? I thought we were best friends, lovers. I believed in you. Foolishly, I now see! I would have followed you anywhere, loyal to you in whatever you did, or wanted to do, but you chose instead to betray my trust. Not through a small transgression with one of the whores in Porth Ictis, although that would have been bad enough; no, instead, it was with the trader's daughter, thin and tall with her cascading hair, the colour of autumn leaves. She turns up here, in my father's hall. Did you and she contrive it to cause me maximum shame and embarrassment? "Where is my Lancelin, I must leave and he must come. Where is my love?" I was humiliated and made to look a trusting fool by you, who I thought I could trust most of all!'

She threw his hands off, stood up and walked towards the open window. The dappled light of the morning sun caused her to recall her archery contest with Artur. The hint of a smile passed across her face. Quickly, Lancelin was by her side and turned her around to face him.

'I can prove myself again. I will honour you, cherish you, protect you and love you if you will only forgive me.'

She looked back at him as he stared intently into his eyes. Could she ever trust him again?

'Besides, you have had your lover too and yet the Pryns of the Dewnan has shown his true colours now. He lusted for you, but I know that you did not feel the same level of passion, even if you enjoyed his company for a while. He is not one of us, Gwalian, and we know each other so well. He can never truly be one of us and he would not have acted in the way that he did yesterday if he really cared for you.'

'Lancelin, you are of the Dewnan and he is your Lord. Do you show the same level of disloyalty to him as you showed to me?'

'I will fight with him, go into battle with him and, if it is needed, I will defend him. Already, I have had to rescue him twice, but I am for the Veneti! Many men of Tamara are; it is not just us. I hear of discontent along Foye also. The so-called King of the Dewnan and his lately arrived son have done nothing to protect us and advance our interests. No, we are Veneti in all but name. Gwalian, I am for you and I will fight for you and love you with all my heart, and I will never look at another woman again!'

She smiled in spite of herself. *He was much more direct, said what he thought, but then, they had been friends since childhood.*

'You see the way that he looks at the Priestess, of course. The way that she looks at him?'

Their eyes met again and now he knew that his words had hit their mark. He continued with a hint of exasperation in his voice: 'I have made a massive mistake and you have justifiably sought consolation elsewhere, but Gwalian, we were meant for each other, were always meant to be together. Let's put what we have done behind us and look forward to what we will do!'

Briefly, imploring her, he stared into her eyes. She was wavering and he knew it. She felt let down by Artur; he had been harsh, unkind and Morlain undoubtedly had used her brief trip downstream to maximum advantage. Seizing his opportunity, he leant forward and kissed her. Those old familiar lips full of passion; perhaps she had missed them more than she knew, their reassuring warmth in the face of uncertainty. She kissed him back. He needed no further encouragement. Oblivious to all around them, their rekindled passion consumed them.

***

Artur stumbled along the path. Somehow, despite his conviction as he crossed Enyam, it all looked different today and he grew increasingly agitated at his failure to locate the hut. Then, as Sira Howl broke briefly through the canopy, he saw it. Stained dark green with the drip of trees and an infusion of airborne algae, it was camouflaged by the angle of the light, blending in amongst shades of brown and green from tree and woodland bush. He strode forward with new purpose, a smile returning to his face.

As he approached, he caught a glimpse of movement through the gaps in the side panelling. She was here. His walk had been worthwhile; now he would explain and then, he hoped, they could return to Pendre, justify his actions to Aodren and agree on the next steps of preparation for the crossing to Armorica. *Rowing practice*, he briefly thought, *was the next important piece of work for the Company*.

He made at first for the door of the hut, but then noticed that the shutters were open on the window. He walked towards them now. He would surprise her and laugh, show that he had not changed and that a grave series of events had chastened him, but now the normal Artur, her friend and lover, was returning.

He looked in through the window.

The shock of what he saw utterly overwhelmed him, and he stood completely still. In an instant, everything changed. He had thought it, but never really believed it; and yet, there it was, irrevocable, irrefutable. Gwalian was passionately kissing Lancelin and he, in return, caressing her, moving his hands all over her body, that lithe, beautiful body that he, Artur, had so recently enjoyed, while, eyes closed, lost in each other, murmurs of indisputable pleasure came from both of them. Lancelin, who had not seen him, turned his back to Artur and in so doing, turned Gwalian to face the window as their embrace continued. Gwalian, breathing deeply, opened her eyes as her lips, malleable and warm, mixed with Lancelin's commanding and passionate riposte. Her shock too was instant.

Looking straight back at her was Artur's face, rapidly turning to anger; his eyes moist with disbelief and his body beginning to shake as he remained rooted to the spot for a brief moment longer. Then, with no thought of direction or purpose, except to get away, he turned and walked quickly, before breaking into a faltering run. He headed back down the path along which he had come.

Gwalian broke away from her lover and burst out of the hut door. 'Artur, come back. Don't go, don't run, come back!'

It was too late; he was gone and she would not catch him now.

ancestors

At the wax of Loor Skovarnek

His nose wrinkled, causing his long white whiskers to twitch as he sat upright; sideways on to her view. He sat quite still, watching and questioning with his big round eye; a wide, dark pupil in a narrow ring of light-brown iris that was alert and focused on the girl. Most of his winter coat had moulted, apart from a narrow band of thicker fur across his snout, ruffled by a gentle breeze. As the light of early morning filled the air, his long ears pointed rigidly to the sky, listening intently in the centre of the field. He had been feeding when he noticed her, surrounded by new shoots of tender grass and green-leafed plants. He missed little, wary of predators and threats, so how had he missed her?

She sat equally still, matching the intensity of his stare. Briefly, they looked at each other. Despite her young age, she did not waver in her concentration. He meanwhile, looked and calculated. *Stay still or turn and run?* If he did, she would not catch him; but humans could not be trusted, it was not just about whether they could catch you. Still she sat, watching and holding him in her gaze. It unnerved him and his rear hind leg, strong and powerful, flexed as he began to waver and prepared to bolt. Then, her mouth began to make slight soundless movements and her eyes and eyebrows flickered expressively. The hare shuddered slightly, as if surprised at this unexpected turn of events. Next, he visibly relaxed, as if she had given him reassurance. His ears loosened, lost their rigidity and collapsed. He tilted his head and while one ear pointed broadly upwards, folding gently in the middle, the other pointed sideways to his right. It was slightly comical and you would almost believe they had shared a joke, if she was not a girl and he was not a hare.

Watching the scene unfold from the corner of the field, a woman, tall, elegant and finely dressed, looked on with amusement. Suddenly, the hare saw her. It was too much. He turned and was gone, his large raised and rounded bottom moving with speed toward the far side of the field and safety of the low hedgerow.

The girl rose from her seat and casually walked towards the corner of the field.

'Hello,' said the woman

'Hello,' the young girl replied, smiling politely. She would have left it at that and carried on walking had the woman not spoke again. 'He was a fine example of his kind. Do you like hares?'

She was trying to start a conversation.

'Yes, I do.' For a moment, the girl stared up at the woman. 'Why?'

Again, the girl paused, looking up at her before looking away and replying casually, 'Because they are tall and wise and they walk nobly across the land.'

'Wise?'

The girl looked back at her. 'Yes, wise.'

The woman nodded her head thoughtfully, holding the girl in her gaze and said, 'They came with the Greek traders to Ictis, noble and strong like the travellers. They are special to the land of the Dewnan. They are a symbol of hope and possibility.'

The girl nodded casually and the woman said, 'What is your name?'

'My name is Morlain.'

'And how old are you?'

'I am seven springs old, ma'am.'

'And who are your parents? Where do you live?' The woman had a gentle tone of command.

'My parents are dead, ma'am. Taken in their prime, my aunt says. They did not honour the spirits of the water and fields in the way that they should, or make enough offerings, my aunt says.'

'And what do you think?'

'I think they got ill and died, nothing could be done. They could not be cured.'

The woman could not help but smile. 'Yes, that sounds more likely.'

'And I live over there, ma'am, at the round with my mother's family.'

A conical roof with smoke drifting lazily upwards from its tip peeked above the already abundant hedge growth, a few fields distant. Collective munching and grunting from the adjacent field drifted through the wall top growth. One of the sheep bleated sharply and broke the pastoral calm. The woman looked down again at the girl.'

'My name is…'

'I know who you are.'

'Oh, do you?'

'You are Heulwen, Queen. I have seen you, watched you.'

Heulwen narrowed her eyes and considered Morlain. Had she finally found her, here at this remote round, away from the main settlements and royal centres of the Dewnan lands? Could the girl and her extended family have actually travelled to a place where they had seen her before? It seemed unlikely as few, beyond warriors of fortune and the royal household travelled far, and yet she did not doubt the girl's words. She knew that she was Heulwen.

'Morlain, we have only just met, but I wonder, if we spoke to your aunt and your family, would you like to come and live with me for a while? I think you are a very special little girl, and I think I can help you to make the most of what makes you special. Although, we perhaps will not mention that to your aunt. What do you think?'

The girl looked up at her, a little more wide-eyed now and nodded her head.

'Good, then let us go and talk to them and, as we walk, I will tell you about my daughter; she is tall and clever like you. And about my son. He is only four winter's old, but I know that he will grow up to be strong, brave and handsome like his father, and as you grow older, I think that you and he might be good friends…'

***

A sudden impulse jolted her and Morlain sat up quickly. Too quickly. She clutched her side as pain shot through her still very sore ribcage. She had been dreaming, asleep in the late afternoon sun, seeing again the day that changed everything, years ago now, or so it seemed. She sat high on Marghros, the hill of the horse, facing towards Ictis, where Tamara embraced the Mor Pretani. Quickly, her mind returned to the present and to the deliberations that had occupied her before she had succumbed to tiredness. All seemed peaceful in the mellow fading light, but it was an illusion. Above, the vanguard of this year's martins, newly returned from distant lands, swooped low over her head, catching food, fly and midge on the wing and reacquainting themselves with their summer home. There was no threat from these invaders from the warm lands who were, instead, an irrefutable and ancient indicator that winter was over for another year. Then, without warning, another spasm convulsed her. She clutched her side, her face contorted as the pain pierced through her body.

Behind her, a rustle of grass, a gentle cough and Wenna stood forward.

'Madam, we have watched you while you slept. Lady Cantassa has arrived and is preparing a bath of hot water and herbs. We should begin to work on those wounds if you are to recover quickly. Is it difficult to stand? Taran is here. He will lift you.'

Slowly, she raised her upper body again and turned towards them.

'No, Wenna, Taran, all of you, I am fine, thank you. I can walk to the bath, I am sure.'

They helped her up and together they walked steadily to the large and distinctive roundhouse, Dynas Kazak, home of the High Priestess at the summit of the hill. Visible across all the land, on Menitriel, from Menluit and from Ictis, it crowned this distinctive feature in the landscape, a gentle curvature in the surface of Mamm Norves; circular and less conical in shape than the typical roundhouse, the building brought succour to the people of the valley. It stood proud, a symbol of the Dewnan, and the Ocean People. Around the hill, sunken, small but intimate deep valleys spread out, undulations in the land that delved deep between Menitriel and RunHoul, seeking the treasures of Mamm Norves and giving life to the people and their farms. Shaped at first by Tamara and her acolytes, Ocean's spirits had also penetrated the land, shaping it. They had been driven in by Sira Howl and his twelve gille Loors, the masters of the days and the seasons, who created the heartland of the Dewnan.

On a tall pole attached to the side of the roundhouse was a large pennant, embroidered with a crudely-shaped but prancing white horse. It rippled gently in the breeze and, away to the left, the beacon was lit; denoting, near and far, that the Priestesswas in residence.

As they approached the door, they saw Cantassa inside. She turned, saw them and walked towards Morlain, her face full of concern. 'Dearest, you are more hurt than I think you allow.'

Morlain, stooped from the walk, looked up at her through her hair, which had fallen across her face, lank and dishevelled. 'I slept and then, today, I have considered events and our next move, but I will confess I fell asleep again. Perhaps I am more tired than I thought. Should have taken action earlier? Suddenly, I do not feel so great again, very stiff and aching… Cantassa it is good to see you!'

Only the swiftness of Taran's actions stopped her from falling forward at the feet of her friend. He held her and gently turned her around before lifting her into his arms and carrying her into the house.

Steam rose from a large iron bath, enhancing the pungent and varied smell of infused comfrey, lady's mantle, mint, linden flower, yarrow and lovage, all intended to soothe her bones, ease her pain and relax her mind. Mildly intoxicating and very aromatic, the smell greeted her senses and gently called to her as she undressed, helped by the female acolytes. All gasped at the extent of her bruising. Cantassa and Wenna examined her body quickly while the others supported her so that she could stand.

'You have been lucky,' Cantassa concluded. 'It is going to hurt for a while, but I do not feel that anything is broken.'

Morlain, drowsy and semi-conscious, looked back at her with a half-smile and said, 'Good, I thought that too.'

They held her hand as she slowly ascended a placed step and carefully got into the bath. It was very hot at first, so she carefully lowered herself down into the depth of the water, feeling the tingle, pleasure and adrenaline of the heat surge through her, while the aroma of the herbs rushed up her nose, permeating her head and body, curing, restoring and relaxing – and, at least for the duration of her bath, banishing her troubles. Her whole body submerged apart from her head. Her legs stretched forward to touch the end, holding her in position in a bath that had been specially made to fit. She put her arms down beside her, closed her eyes and dozed, letting the herbs and the heat do their work, while the acolytes stood in attendance.

When Morlain awoke, she gently opened her eyes and raised her chin out of the water. She could hear a whispered conversation beyond the screen that shielded her from the view of the rest of the roundhouse. Wenna, with an occasional furtive glance towards the bath, spoke to Cantassa. Morlain breathed in deeply, raised her head further and turned towards them.

'He comes. I know.'

She stood carefully and as she turned towards them, fronds of sodden lovage draped languidly across her bosom.

'Can you help me out and can someone find a clean robe? Cantassa, can you stall him until I am ready?'

***

Abandoned for the day by the King and his warrior followers, the hall was quiet. In the distance, the cry of gulls could be heard and an onshore breeze moaned morosely around the building, at the join of wattle, daub and thatch – the lament of the spirits, blown in from Ocean, tugging, searching for an entry and muttering bad news. Occasionally, the breeze got through, blowing gaps in the rushes and straw newly laid for the evening meal, and in the far reaches, in the smoke and gloom, a handful of servants busied themselves, preparing the table for the King's return that was expected before dark.

At the centre of the hall, a small group of women sat talking quietly as the fire spat and crackled in front of them. Most spun threads with stone whorl weighted spindles and each had small piles of newly-provided fine under wool, separated that morning in a nearby roundhouse, having been plucked, sheared, cleaned and combed and brought from the fields of the King's land the previous evening. They prepared it for dyeing and, as they did so, took it in turns to put down their spinning and re-plait each other's hair in anticipation of the King and his retinue's return.

At the head of the group, Andras sat sullenly glowering, sensing ill-tidings. One of the women stood up to adjusted her line of combed fibre. As she did, the wooden doors to the hall creaked slightly and a crack of outside light began to widen between them. All turned their heads. Andras, who had been lost in thought until then, focused all of her attention to the opening door. As the gap widened, a slender, hooded figure slipped in and removed the hood. Once fully through, an unseen hand from one of the guards pulled the door shut again. In the restored gloom, it was hard to see the newly-revealed face, but then Zethar's distinguishing pale complexion and short black hair emerged as she cautiously approached the centre of the hall. Her normal confident and disdainful expression had gone and her erstwhile piercing green eyes had an uneasy, nervous look that foretold her bad news.

'Zethar, I had hoped to see you before now. What news?'

Andras stared coldly, unflinchingly preparing for what she knew was coming. Zethar glanced cautiously around her at the other women, before looking back at Andras, anticipating her first words. Suddenly, realising her reticence, Andras clapped her hands.

'Just leave all of that. Leave us. I will talk with Zethar alone.'

Hurriedly, the women placed spindles and combs aside, rose and walked away to the far side of the hall.

'Madam, I bring bad news. Your brother has won a victory, the Belgae are routed and,' a hint of emotion came into her voice, 'Lord Anogin is dead, slain by your brother.'

Andras nodded slowly, expressionless, as she continued to look across the hall.

'And my gold? What chance of its retrieval now?'

'Madam, I…'

Andras, her father's daughter, turned sharply, grabbed and gripped Zethar's wrist, her voice bristling with bitterness and anger. 'No, I am sure you don't know. This was a fool's errand. I should never have listened to you and you will be blamed if any word gets to my father.'

Her eyes sparked with rage as she continued under her breath.

'I will not mourn for that Belgae lout, no loss to anyone, but we have helped my brother, though your folly, to build more repute. I trusted you, Zethar, but we move backwards and my gold is gone. Go! Leave me.'

She thrust Zethar's wrist back and almost spat at her as she said again between her teeth, 'Go! Do not bother me again until you have news worth telling.'

Zethar turned and walked slowly and sullenly back toward the doors.

Andras breathed in and out deeply, growled and then let out a piercing cry of anger as she kicked several of the spindles, sending them clattering across the floor in the direction of the departing Zethar. She breathed in again. Fate, it seemed, was against her. As she exhaled, Andras sat back down on her chair and buried her head deep into her hands.

***

Artur opened his eyes slowly. The flaxen-haired priestess had asked him to wait here, take refreshment. He must have fallen asleep. He rubbed his face with both hands before smoothing back his hair. There was a quiet cough behind him.

'My Lord, I am Taran. My Lady asked me to stand in attendance to you when you awoke.'

Artur turned quickly to see a tall man standing back from the bench, slightly concealed by the fug of the smoke.

'Where is the day? Have I slept long?'

'You have slept all night, my Lord. Sira Howl shows his light but has not yet appeared above RunHoul.'

'Where is the Lady Morlain? I have come to Dynas Kazak to talk to her. I did not intend to fall asleep. There was mead. Did it include a sleeping draught?'

'I know not, my Lord. I did not prepare your refreshment. However, my Lady has slept soundly also, which will have helped her recovery. She has risen now and asks you to join her when you are awake. She has had breakfast prepared for you both.'

Outside, all was alive with activity, animals tended to, water carried, clothes washed and the sound of food preparation from within one of the buildings. In another, there was the sound of metal on wood, metal on metal and the flash of sparks from the blacksmith's anvil.

They passed the large roundhouse on a path that continued along the crest of the hill. The view was immense, taking in all of the surrounding landscape on this side of Marghros, a panorama mixing all shades of green, interspersed with brown and the distinctive lines of wall and hedgerow, demarking a patchwork of fields and lanes. The long grey line of RunHoul, distant and large, defined one side of the valley while in front of them was the widening of Tamara as she approached the Mor Pretani, sparkling grey, white and silver as the first rays of sunlight spread across her.

On the far side of the roundhouse, in a paddock marked by a low fence, the distinctive and substantial form of Steren Uskis grazed on fresh spring grass. His mane ruffled in the breeze and his tail swished idly while he ate. As Taran and Artur walked by, he raised his head, gave a gentle whinny and returned to his grazing. The low fence would not retain him and instead, it indicated clearly a piece of ground that was for his exclusive use. As they walked on, there was a copse of tall trees with thick girths a little lower down on the slope. These were remnants of a noble line going all the way back to the Great Wood that had once covered all but the summit of Marghros. As they walked, two distinctive black and white birds gave flight from these trees. Iridescent blue, green and purple wings shimmered in the early morning light, with what looked like white fingers at the end, feeling the air. At first, they dipped and then soared higher on the breeze. Their pointed black beaks opened to emit an occasional "chacker, chacker" as they called to each other while they sailed along the hill together. Then they rose up, using the breeze as a break to their flight, and landed a short distance apart from each other. Something had caught their eye and now, with a distinctive gait – shoulders and feet moving forward in exaggerated style – they walked on to investigate.

'Pies, I do like the way they walk! They are a pair and nest at the top of the oldest tree in the copse over there. They are full of curiosity and attitude and I think they are here because we are. Their ancestors have been here for many generations.'

He had not seen her approach. Perhaps the birds had distracted him.

'Morlain, it is good to see you. How are your injuries? Forgive me, I fell asleep last night. I have come looking for you in the hope that we can talk.'

Words were tumbling out of his mouth. With a gentle rise of her right hand, she indicated that he should pause and said, 'I am pleased to see you too. For my injuries, I think my chest is going to ache for a while, but there is no lasting damage. I will mend,' she smiled warmly back at him, 'and do you know I was very tired too. A good night's sleep has made me feel much better.'

Now she paused and looked past Artur to her gille.

'Taran, thank you, I will speak with Pryns Artur alone now, please.'

Taran bowed, took one more look at her and walked back along the path.

'Now, I have some cheese, bread and eggs. Will you join me for breakfast?'

'I would like that. I do feel very hungry.'

They sat on a large woollen blanket with breakfast laid out in the middle. Beneath them, the sponginess of furze, heather and moss brought extra spring and comfort. At the centre of the food were two sprigs of yellow furze flower, specially picked and placed for the meal. The breeze, unusually light today for this lofty position, gently played with their hair and rippled at the corners of the blanket as they ate, while across the sky small clouds ambled towards them from the Ocean. On the slopes below, cattle grazed, occasionally lowing to each other or to nothing in particular while they prepared the ground for next year's planting, and in between the bovine bluster and the bubbling warble of alauda, the hovering lark began again his search for a mate.

She finished eating first, turned, wrapped her arms around her drawn up legs, and looked out towards Ictis and the Mor Pretani beyond. He continued to take food, prevaricating, sensing the inevitable first question. She could wait no longer.

'So, I am pleased to see you, but you are here alone and looking a little despondent, what has happened? Have you seen Aodren?'

He chewed a final lump of cheese and took a long gulp of cool fresh water, wiped his mouth on the sleeve of his tunic and raised his head to look at her.

'Yes, I have seen Aodren. He returned late yesterday morning. It was a difficult discussion. Ewan was determined to undermine me. He can be very strident in his argument.'

'Yes, he can be, but Aodren is a sensible man, I am sure he saw that you acted wisely?'

'Well, I think so. It was difficult for him to be supportive with his son so vociferous in his other ear. I can see that. I said that a decision was required and I had taken that decision. Others in the Company supported me.'

'And you were strong and assertive with him? He will respect that.'

'Yes, yes I was. You would have been pleased, I am sure.'

'Good and now you prepare for war. You will all depart very soon. Yet, you are at Dynas Kazak, having breakfast with me, alone, atop the hill of the horse. There is something you do not say, it is obvious.'

'Maybe, but I have not come to discuss that. I too slept well and feel differently this morning, but I need a day away from the preparations and I have come to see you. Maedoc knows where I am, encouraged me and will make my apologies. I followed your beacon and I have come to talk of this ring,' he touched the hilt of his sword, 'why it is so significant and I want to know more about the story of the Dewnan and our shared destiny? Hints are all I have this far, but now I want to know everything. We go to war, as you say, and I do not know if we or I will return.'

He looked away and then with renewed enthusiasm, turned back to her.

'See! Sira Howl clears RunHoul and begins his journey. We have the whole day; and then, when he heads beyond Ocean to his walk in the Underworld I will return to Pendre and make ready for departure. Maedoc has organised rowing practice for tomorrow!'

She smiled, whatever had occurred, there was a natural optimism within him. 'Very well, the moment has come. There is much to tell, but I will only give you the shortened version before Sira Howl completes his journey. It would take much longer than a day to tell you everything; the stories and the tales across countless lives, but I believe...' To his surprise, she took up his hand and looked warmly and determinedly back at him, '...that you will return and that your story, our story, will then be told in full.'

His eyes widened, and for the briefest of moments, squeezed her hand. The complexity of his feelings now both confused and intoxicated him. Only a short while ago, his passion for Gwalian had been intense. Despite his chance discovery of her with Lancelin in the woods, he could not forget that passion and the hurt that he now felt. But there was something here that was genuinely different, something he was not sure how to respond to. It kindled as he had struggled to get up the bank and come to Morlain's aid in the fight with Anogin. Awoken from a place deep in his heart as he had seen her suffer at the evil giant's boot and his consequent overwhelming desire to rescue and protect her. She had saved his life, she had fought for him and then he had saved hers. Deep down, he knew he could trust her. Whatever happened, she would stand beside him, help him, guide him, and this morning she looked as fine as she had ever looked; battered and bruised, but fresh, clean and alert, ready for the next challenge, indomitable.

'You know the story of our beginnings, from the warm lands after the age of cold.'

'Elowen has told the story since my return, and I have heard it before, of course.'

'Well, Ocean did flood the land, and all before us, and much more was created. From Tamara's broad waters over there to the Foye and the Kammel and the Falla in Kernovi – creating harbours, islands for trade and bringing Ocean closer to the Dewnan. The world of the Ocean People had been created.'

'The land was created for us by the actions of Sira Howl and Mamm Norves? We are favoured above others, as the story tells?'

'How else are we to think? But not just the Dewnan. The Ocean People border Ocean. They live alongside her, with her, and on her and through generations, they have travelled across many different lands, but always Ocean is there. From what is now Olissipo, where Venetia came ashore, to wherever both deep harbours and productive land exist, through the lands of the Gallaeci to Armorica. On to Demetae, land of the dragon slayer, to Ériu and Epidii, where the horse people live, until finally coming to the Orcades and the High King of the cold lands, resplendent and defiant in his mighty tower of stone, where Sira Howl stays longer in the summer. At the very centre, is the land of the Dewnan, and at the centre of the land is Marghros, hill of the horse and here, Artur, you and I sit, now and always, at the centre of the Ocean People. If we fail, if we fall, the Ocean People will fall with us; that is what I believe, as did your mother. I was to be her protégé, until the evil giant intervened, to work with you to defend all that we hold dear and is special.'

There was a pause as he looked back at her and then he said, 'I do remember you before I went away. Not clearly, but I do remember. You looked different then!'

He laughed before continuing more seriously.

'What could my mother tell you that she could not tell her own son?'

'I am at least three springs older than you, and I could tell in the way that she spoke to me, that if she had lived, she would also have spoken to you when you were old enough. She saw the potential for great things in you, and as the storm clouds gathered around us, believed in you, the man, her son, as being able to turn the tide. Artur, so much has already fallen! Olissipo and Gallaeci have faded from the Ocean People. Now, these cruel men sweep through Gaul and only the Veneti stand between them and total dominion. We must defend them with everything we have. These men of the land must fight on Ocean, and even if they succeed, they must cross her to reach the land of the Dewnan. This is our chance! The blood of the Gaul, the Celt and the Ocean People spills across the land, but when it can go no further, Ocean will staunch and cleanse the wound, and in its place, the blood of the aggressor will flow freely, all of the way back to Rome!'

She was agitated, her eyes intense with determination, and he said, 'What of the other lands you mention? When we need them, will they come to the aid of the Veneti and Dewnan? Surely, they must see our collective peril.'

'If only it were that simple! Look at Gaul; no proper confederation there and instead tribe conspires against tribe.

Only when it is too late, I think, will they come together casting off self-interest, but by then the Romans will be ensconced and victory impossible. As for the free Ocean People, to come to our aid, they must first receive a call from your father and he, as you know, refuses to accept the magnitude of the threat. The Roman army sweeps all before it across Gaul and yet he refuses to believe that they will try to come here! Only after a long discussion, argument and much searching for that deep inner realisation, did he agree to send Maedoc for you. Your sister tried everything to prevent it. I am not sure even now what Meliora did to secure his agreement, but when he changed his mind back again, brave Maedoc had already sailed beyond the horizon.'

'What motivates Andras against me? I have done nothing to offend, as far as I know.'

'No, you have done nothing, but you were your mother's favourite, you see, and she did not always disguise it well. Then, when Andras and I were seven years old, I joined your household. Andras did not like it. Before you and I arrived, she had been the only child with the full affection of her mother and father and then, as you grew, and through the four springs that I had with your family, the affection faded away, or at least so she thought. I think your mother had other plans; a strong leader supported by two strong advisers was her intention, a powerful triumvirate to take on our enemies. Andras, however, does not like being anything other than first. I do not think she had any part in your mother's murder, but she has sought advantage from it ever since, to regain and retain what she believes to be her rightful position.

'I had forgotten any enmity towards me before I went to Demetae. Perhaps I should have been closer to her, supportive of her. But I was only a boy.'

'Yes, you were, but maybe if we had all realised – if your mother had realised – the extent to which your sister was prepared to go for her revenge, we would all have acted differently. Artur, she has strong powers; she is your mother's daughter and I am sure that she and her associates tried to influence Ocean's spirits in your crossing from Demetae. I do not approve of human sacrifice in any way, but perhaps it was only Meliora's last act that saved you from oblivion. Whatever affection Andras had for you went long ago and she works against you.'

'Does she think that if something happens to me, my father will acknowledge her as his heir? Will he? Would the Lords of the Dewnan acknowledge her as Queen when he is gone?'

'Maybe, if she could command a sufficient force after his death. She has her supporters in your father's hall and even the Estrenyons, who see their women as being lesser than men, have had Queens, I am told.'

He reached again for the bread as he continued to consider her words.

She continued, 'Artur, that day will never come while you and I are here to do anything about it. You are your father's heir. The Dewnan view men and women differently, as we have discussed, but even we do not accept a daughter should succeed ahead of a son, and your sister knows it. I should sympathise with your sister, but in this case, it works in our favour!'

'Then let us hope I return. My sister would not suffer you here long if she were Queen.'

'No, it would be difficult, but you will return, so it is not an ending that I am considering.'

He turned back to Tamara.

'I am flattered by your belief in me.'

'Don't be, I am only saying what I see. All you have to do is prove me right!'

He smiled as he looked across the valley. 'I will try.' There was a short pause in the conversation before he continued, 'Is that Porth Ictis I can see? There are boats, so it must be…'

'Yes, Tamara finds her way to the sea, bending right and then left before opening into the Sound of Ictis, where she and her sisters gather before the ocean. The original port and fort are on the left side of the Sound. It is the citadel of Clesek, Lancelin's father. He is a close associate of the Veneti and other traders. This Ictis is the original settlement; the fort and port connect at low tide and goods are brought, collected and transported along the coast to Hengasts Fort, the markets of the Estrenyons and across to the port of the Curiosolitae. However, Ictis has diminished significantly. This angers the Curiosolitae, in particular, hence the conflict between them and the Veneti in recent years. When Aodren's grandfather established the Veneti colony, to take firmer control of the metals and other trade, in agreement with the King and Lords of the Dewnan, he built Nowydh Ictis on the island where Tamara meets the Sound. There is deeper water there and the larger ships of the Veneti can dock more easily. A small settlement has also developed on the shore that faces it. The Veneti build their boats well, can sail further and control the Mor Pretani. All they gather here, they transport to Burdigala in the land of the Biturges and the great river, Garumna. From there, the trade is upriver, across land and downriver to the ports of the warm sea. It is in Caesar's interest then, and the marauding horde of thieves and prospectors that support him, to control the trade. They will stop at nothing to get it.'

He said nothing but then smiled and said, 'Tell me about the Pretani! They crossed Ocean and spread to the lands you describe, and King Ronan came here too?'

'Yes, although here the Pretan Lords were never more than a small but very influential ruling elite. Little remains, apart from our blood and our faith in Sira Howl and Mamm Norves. They came to explore and take advantage of the metals that we still gather today. Copper first, then tin and silver, and then they found gold to match what they had brought across Ocean. Their intention was always to travel towards Sira Howl and his returning light. The Ocean People were already here, spread over many lives of men, as I have described, connecting and trading with each other along the Ocean's seaways, praising Sira Howl, honouring Mamm Norves and building temples of stone and monuments in honour of the dead.'

'What was different about the Pretani, then? Why do we revere them?'

'They embraced what already existed and made much more of it, and brought gold, lots of gold! Few had seen it in the Ocean lands before then and people could not fail to be impressed and influenced by the way they wore it, shining brightly in praise of Sira Howl in the morning light. Their skills in metalworking, in copper and gold, then with tin, and making and shaping bronze that was strong, and their distinctive pottery and temple building, added much and brought a new beginning – and Artur, they were confident in their own ability. Sira Howl led them across Ocean, gave them a clear purpose. Now they would go towards Him; Venetia had decided in the earliest days and there was no going back. The sons and daughters of Aleman and the children of Thurien were destined to meet again, as foretold, on high ground at the centre of this land that bears their name. Even now, many lives after the incursion of the Estrenyons and the wretched Germani, they call it Pretannia. Even the Romans call it that, I hear! The legacy of the great Pretani hegemony lives on!'

'It is a noble story.'

They looked at each other for a moment and then she continued the story.

'The Pretan lords went toward Sira Howl after that first encounter with Orsa, Lord of the Crossing, through the great wood to RunHoul, and there Ronan met Ailla and wandered no more but consolidated his position as Lord of all Nanmeur. Sawkerdh weaved between the trees and people travelled freely from Menitriel to RunHoul and back, fording Tamara at Orsa's crossing. On the slopes, and in the streams of RunHoul, they sourced and traded even more metals; copper, gold, tin and silver for the smiths to work with. Still, though, the zeal for conversion and expansion lived within the breast of the Pretan and their journey continued, looking for the day when the children of Thurien would meet the sons and daughters of Aleman again.

The great road wound on into the land of the ancestors of the Durotrages and then to the wider land. Albion, the people called it. Readily, these people embraced the Pretan ways, and the road went on to a high place in the middle of the land. Here, at last, was a perfect position to welcome Sira Howl, to sing out in praise each day on His return in the summer and, in the winter, to exalt His brilliance and encourage His return the following day.

Others had been there before them and a sacred land of praise and honour, resplendent on the face of Mamm Norves, was established, but now the Pretan and their followers brought much more. They built in stone across a wide area, creating new temples and places of ritual and worship. They used the Dragon Stone, brought from the Ocean lands, and built two great temples that were a day's walk apart, specially shaped and positioned for praising Sira Howl and honouring Mamm

Norves. News spread across all Albion of the golden Pretani and their temples of stone. Emissaries from many lands came to see these wonders, and they too wanted to call themselves and tell all who asked that they were "Pretani".

'This is many, many lives of men ago, I think? How do you know all of this?'

Now it was her turn to look across Tamara toward the distant Ocean.

'From an early age, young acolytes, future priests and priestesses learn the story of our people. We use it to help us interpret and guide all that is yet to come.'

She paused and then said, 'I think I might have a little more cheese. Could you pass the bread? I am feeling hungry again, and that is a good sign!'

They ate a little more and looked across the fields of the lower slopes, while Sira Howl climbed high in the sky. After a while, Artur turned to Morlain and said, 'Are we descendants of the Pretan Lords then? You and I carry their blood within us; the last defenders, in a long line, of this diminished land that you have talked about before.'

'Yes, we are certainly descendants of the Pretani, as are many of the Dewnan – and there is a purity to our Pretani blood that the Estrenyons do not have, as many have come and gone since those ancient days. In the beginning, they were few but, over many lives, their blood spread through the Dewnan.'

'But there is more than just the Pretani and the Dewnan… the Ocean People within us?'

'Yes, at first the Pretan hegemony, begun here, ruled across Albion all the way to a meeting with Ocean again. Others replicated what they had seen in the great temples to Sira Howl in their own lands and gave homage to the High Pretani King. The Ocean People engaged with the people of the interior and people traded ideas and skills in making things for generations, in healing and in leadership, based on their shared faith in Sira Howl and Mamm Norves. The great temples became the centre of all the land and many came to live, worship and praise there.'

She paused and took a sip of water.

'Word spread beyond Pretannia. Finally, the sons and daughters of Aleman, who had traversed the land from those original words of Olian all those lives before, crossed the Mor Pretani and brought new people, new skills and ideas to the great temples in the land. The heirs of Venetia spread across both land and Ocean, speaking the words of the original Ocean People. The Pretan hegemony now covered the great centres of the children of Aleman in what is now Gaul and across the great mountains and back into what are now the lands of the Lusitanians and the Celtiberians, from whence it had come, although they had other names then, and our kin the Gallaeci. For many lives, there was a balance and a great network of trade and ideas, exactly as Venetia had intended.'

She paused, guffawed ironically and then sighed.

'It could not last. Other forces, deep within the soul of the sons and daughters of Aleman, born from their delving far into the forests, where those whom Mamm Norves had banished still lurked, waiting for their chance to return. From the beginning, Aleman's heirs were greater in number and they brought with them these Estrenyons, converts supposedly to the Pretan way, but they were ever liars and thieves for deep within them, infiltrating the sons and daughters of Aleman, was a desire for control and domination waiting to emerge. They wanted all of the fine things – gold, bronze, pottery and extended their control of production and output of goods substantially – but they also wanted control of the land and its people. So the Estrenyons asserted that they, the most recently arrived, were the true heirs of Venetia, not the Ocean Peoples, who they said were inferior. They sought revenge for that original banishment, claiming that they should rule in Venetia's name and all should submit to their edict and revere them, as they were now the masters of the great temples at the centre of the land. Quickly, they asserted authority across Pretannia, in the land that once was ancient Albion. We, the Ocean People, gradually retreated to whence we had come and all that Ronan had initiated, slowly faded away. Worse was still to come, and has continued to come. Once unleashed, once the gate was open, many followed and the Belgae are just the latest to threaten our last great bastion of the Pretan heritage, which will be diminished again if the Veneti fall! Artur, we must stand firm!'

She had raised herself on to her knees. In her determination, she held his attention with a firm, unyielding stare, but then her fervour subsided and she relaxed, still kneeling back on her bottom.

'I will drink some more water!'

He was enthralled by her and by her story, but before she could speak again, he said, 'So here we are, clinging on to our last foothold in Pretannia and in Armorica, with the slow push of the Belgae and the rapid approach of the Romans squeezing us tightly. In the end, is their approach insurmountable?'

'I do not underestimate the scale of the challenge that lies ahead, but I have not yet finished my story – there were checks to the persistent spread of the Estrenyons.'

'Then please, return to a positive story and let us have some hope!'

She wriggled her bottom on to the ground, removing some of the numbness from kneeling too long, before turning to him. Sitting cross-legged, she continued, 'The peace of generations was shattered. The fallibility of the Estrenyons, however, is their willingness to fight each other and forcefully mark out and fight over their own pieces of land. I told you on Menitriel, our greatest defence is their inability to be coordinated. They have what they came for, control of the rich central lands of Pretannia, the Veneti still provide them with tin and it is only the adventurers and chancer exploiters who attempt to enter our lands. Theirs is a martial culture, whose rise has led to the great glory of the Pretani Hegemony being lost forever. Strong leaders came and went on both sides. New defensive structures and hillforts appeared all over the land and a long period of regular war ensued. The ordinary people returned to a simpler way of life, only affected if a raiding party came through or if they lived on the dividing line between Ocean People and Estrenyon; but still the Estrenyons, who had a zeal for it, gradually pushed towards us.

When hope had nearly gone and it seemed that all trace of the true Pretani heritage would be lost, new people came from the warm lands. Clad against Ocean's wind and spray in heavy dark cloaks, there was nothing about their arrival that gave a hint of what was to come. Just three small but sturdy boats come to the land of the Dewnan at the end of a very long journey. When they removed their cloaks, the men and women in each boat were of noble appearance. Twenty-four per boat, they travelled from a distant land by the shores of the warm sea.

Ictasus was their leader, tall with long dark hair and a distinctive moustache. He and his followers came ashore in armour made of bronze, copper and leather, and a simple helmet attached to their heads by three metal straps, with short swords and daggers at their sides. He said they had come in search of "Kassiteros" and had been sent by their King in distant Achaea to trade and secure their supply; adventurers at the furthest most limit of their world. Quickly, these good men established themselves, founded Porth Ictis, where Tamara met the Mor Pretani, traded and collected kassiteros, their word for tin, and sent it back to their King. At first, this was done by using a single boat, but then through a network of contacts in Armorica. They used a downriver course and crossed the land back to the warm sea and on to their homeland – and a strong bond was formed between the land of the Dewnan and the land of the Achaeans, far away.'

Artur was also sitting cross-legged now.

'So our link to the warm sea goes beyond traders like Gyras and the threat of the Romans?'

'Yes, much further back. Ictis has brought traders from the warm sea or Mesogeios, as Gyras calls it, from the days of Ictasus, and many different peoples have used the port since then. They were often linked to the Veneti, but occasionally, like Gyras and the men of Achaea, they came all the way from the warm sea themselves.'

Artur looked at her and nodded slowly as he took in what she had said.

She continued, 'When they came to the land of the Dewnan, Ictasus and his family wore rings as a sign of their togetherness, binding them on the journey to the edge of their world. These were no ordinary rings, wrought as they were in a fabulous lost city, raised resplendent from the sea, but then destroyed by *Runoul* fire when burning rock belched out from deep within Mamm Norves. Who knows what the people of that city could have done to offend the Earth Mother, but the rings escaped the devastation with the goldsmith who had created them. He had intended them for the High Priestess who had been lost with her city under the waves.

"'Take them and go quickly," she said to him as fire and mayhem gave forth. "I will not leave this city, no matter what its fate. Take these rings with you and from the devastation. May the rings bring all who wear them luck and serve as a reminder of what we had and all that we achieved." The goldsmith left the city and sailed to a new island home. He never married, but continued his trade and lived a long and happy life.

'As he lay dying, he was visited again by his friend, a metal trader from Achaea who bought and sold the items that he made. "My friend," the smith said, "we have served each other well, you and I, and I have led a long and productive life, but I have no one to pass on my precious items to. Take these rings on your journeys to distant lands. Tell all who you meet of the glories of the great city, lost beneath the waves, and may they bring you and your descendants the same good luck that they have brought me."

'The trader had a son and the rings passed to him. He, in turn, had a son, called Ictasus, and the rings passed to him. Like his father and his grandfather, Ictasus was a trader in metals and a voyager to distant lands. One day, the King of the Achaeans called for him and said, "Ictasus, as King, it is my role to ensure a constant supply of kassiteros for our bronzesmiths and for making wonderful things for all of my followers. You are a traveller to distant lands. I command you now to seek and secure new supplies of kassiteros for Achaea. Take men and build a colony. I will pay for the journey from the royal treasury and then, when you find the kassiteros, send it back to me."

'Diantha was the wife of Ictasus and they had two daughters, Eupheme and Kaliope. Knowing that it would be a very long voyage, he said to his family, "I will not leave you behind, uncertain of my return. We will travel and share all that our voyage may find, and each of us will wear one of these rings bequeathed to me. May they bind us and bring us good luck on our journey ahead."

'They searched for the source of kassiteros, beside the great Ocean on the edge of the world. The weather was warm and winds favourable and it seemed that luck shone upon the family, as well as their small flotilla and company of followers. Eventually, they reached the lands of the Ocean People and turned away from the warm sea. The weather turned colder and the waves grew higher. Out of all of them, Diantha was perhaps the least prepared. A fever came upon her and it was soon clear she was dying.

'"What luck is this!" lamented Ictasus. "My beautiful wife, these rings are an indulgence. I will throw them into Ocean's vastness and then, perhaps, the gods will see fit to look favourably upon you and on us again."

'Diantha lay upon her bed of animal furs and smiled weakly back at him. "Husband, dear Ictasus, do you not see? These rings have brought us luck and much more! They unite us in our resolution to succeed and have brought us this far. You did not leave us behind, and instead, bound us together with these rings to voyage, explore and wonder together. Lament my passing if you will, but then sail on, take our daughters to new lands and build new relationships. Pass these rings on as a symbol of strength, unity and purpose for all our descendants. I will always be with you, even though I walk in the Underworld; and then, one day, my love, you and I shall meet again".

'Her eyes held Ictasus to her, but she said no more. He held her hand until gradually her eyes closed and her spirit passed beyond the horizon to the land of the ancestors.'

Morlain paused and turned her head to the Ocean horizon.

Artur said, 'I am surprised I do not know this story. Is my ring one of Ictasus's rings?'

Morlain looked back, her eyes moist and slightly reddened. 'Yes, it is. As I have said, I do not know why your mother did not tell you. The detail of the story has faded from memory for many of the Dewnan, but we keep it alive in the priesthood and one day, maybe, the rings will bring renewed unity and resolution to our people.'

'So, do you know where all of the rings are?'

'I know where two of them are.' Their eyes met and she said, 'Let me complete the story.'

He nodded his head and she continued.

'When they came to the land of the Dewnan, Ictasus now wore two rings, his and the ring of Diantha, one on each hand. His was in the shape of a double-headed axe, in gold with an inlay of deep blue lapis lazuli; a symbol of resilience and determination to work towards their common aim. Hers was a gold band with a meandering pattern of worked gold around its edge, again with an inlay of lapis lazuli, evoking the warmth and wisdom of its most recent bearer.'

Artur reached for the catch on his sword hilt. 'That is my ring?'

'Yes, but do not reveal it yet. Keep it safe and out of sight. Its day is coming.'

He took his hand away from the hilt and she continued.

'His daughters, Eupheme and Kaliope, each wore a ring of the same design, gold and lapis lazuli, but these were in the shape of a knot, symbolising the bond between all four of them and their followers. The rings and their bearers impressed all of the Dewnan, and soon the deep blue lapis lazuli came to represent Ocean they had crossed and the bond between these new arrivals and the land of the Ocean People.'

Struck by sudden inspiration, he raised himself up onto his knees. 'Morlain, do you think that these rings could inspire our people again in the battles ahead?'

'Maybe I do, but we must use their power to inspire carefully and only, I think, as the beginning of a new order and new hope for the Dewnan.'

He looked at her quizzically. She glanced away and then back again quickly.

'What I am trying to say is that when it is revealed, it must be the right moment, not too early, and we must believe that we have a chance of success. You see, Artur, there are other forces at play, not just the Romans and Estrenyons – and here I must return to your sister. She knows about your mother's ring, the ring of Diantha, perhaps the most powerful of them all, the bringer of wisdom and foresight – but she does not know where it is and it vexes her greatly. Those who knew of your mother's ring assume that it was lost in the raid that took her life and this adds to their despondency and sense of quickening decline for the Dewnan. Andras, however, knows that her mother would not have left for that final journey without first having a plan for the ring if she did not return. She knows also that, with the ring in her possession, it would greatly strengthen her position to regain all that she believes she has lost and the opportunity, she thinks, to inherit your mother's position. That must not happen, Artur. She is an appeaser of the Estrenyons. We know that she talks to the Belgae, and with Andras in full control, they would rapidly enter our land, which would be the end of the Dewnan.'

'Morlain, I will follow your guidance, but what of the other rings? The other three, what has become of them?'

'One of them did not stay long in the land of the Dewnan. Loyal to her father and her family, Kaliope had joined them on their voyage, but with great sadness, had left behind in Achaea her lover Polydorus, youngest son of the King. Few at the King's Court expected Ictasus and his company to return and so when the first ship of kassiteros arrived from the land of the Dewnan, Polydorus wept for joy. He and others suspected the King had chosen Ictasus for this quest with the intention of also removing Kaliope, who he deemed an unsuitable match for his son.

'Polydorus, regretting his previous acquiescence, petitioned his father to go in search of Kaliope and the King, impressed by the achievement of Ictasus, agreed. Polydorus travelled to Ictus and asked Kaliope to be his bride and return to Achaea and live with him in his palace by the warm sea. Saddened though he was by the departure of his daughter, Ictasus saw her joy with Polydorus and gave his consent for their marriage.

'"Daughter, you go with my blessing and my wish that you and Polydorus will live long and happy lives together in Achaea. Send me word when you can to let me know that you are well, and take the ring that I gave you when we set out on our journey. Keep it as a reminder of the bond that we will always share. Take also a ship of kassiteros, your dowry and a gift from you and this outpost of Achaea, on the edge of the known world, to Polydorus and his father, the King of the Achaeans".

'Then, he turned to his gille and turned back to reveal a large, luxurious necklace that was light, charged to the touch and the shape of a large flat collar worn across the breast. It was created of multiple shaped beads of descending sizes and metal plates were used to space them.

'"Take this from me as a mark of my love for you. Wear it on the finest occasions and in the presence of the King when he is holding court. It is a fine ornament of quality and great craftsmanship and will mark you, wife of the son of the King and daughter of Diantha and Ictasus, as a woman of note and standing."'

Morlain paused and looked at Artur as if she expected him to ask something, but he did not, so she said, 'Our achievements with the Achaeans lasted for many generations and the Lords of the Dewnan and the priesthood are their descendants – a small group who are leaders of our people, and not gaudy, ostentatious nobles who constantly seeking reassurance from the gods, like the Lords of the Estrenyons. Instead, we endeavour to be refined, dignified and wise amongst those that we lead and care for. Of course, not all achieve this, but even your father, I think, would say it is what we broadly aspire to.'

'I am a descendant of Ictasus.'

She smiled warmly back at him. 'You are, through Eupheme, and it shows in the features of your face, your height and your long flowing hair, although its colour must come from somewhere else!'

'And you?'

'Well, yes, probably, although I am not of an obvious line of kings or priestesses and my immediate parentage is less certain. However, I think it is clear to you, and to many others, that there is something about us that we share, that distinguishes us from our fellow Dewnan, even if it is less clear where I get it from!'

She burst out laughing and he laughed too.

'I don't think you need a line of kings or noble Achaeans behind you to give you self-belief. I think you do that perfectly well on your own.'

Her eyes grew wide with affection, as she looked back at him.

He was about to ask who Eupheme had married and about her ring when Morlain looked up and back along the path. 'Here is Maedoc, he looks concerned.'

Both of them stood and faced the gille as he came hurriedly along the path.

'My Lord, Lady Morlain, I am sorry to disturb you both. Pryns Artur, you said that you would return this evening, but I felt I must come to tell you of word that has newly arrived from Armorica.'

'Maedoc, yes, of course. What is it?'

Maedoc caught his breath and took in a deep gulp of air before he spoke.

'We hear that General Caesar heads for Armorica with a new army to add to that of the boy Crassus. They spread word about their intention to annihilate the Veneti and all who stand with them. Lord Aodren is full of agitation. He now says we must be ready to sail at the full moon at the latest. Artur, already Skovarnek's waxing crescent is three days old and full is only days away. The shipwrights have worked quickly and our boat will be ready tomorrow, but we must practice our rowing.'

He looked anxiously at both of them.

'Oh yes, and then, in the upheaval of recent days, it seems no one has thought of Gyras the Greek. He has escaped and Aodren, to add to his vexation, is convinced that the Greek carries intelligence to Caesar. We must act Artur, we cannot wait.'

Morlain spoke next. 'You must go.'

As they walked, Artur spoke to Morlain, 'I have enjoyed our conversation, learnt a lot and there is more I would like to ask about the matter we have just been discussing. Can we meet again before we depart?'

'It is my intention that we should. Come to the sacred stones as Sira Howl dips below the horizon ten days from now and bring the Company, all of them. Maedoc will guide you. Between now and then, come back to Dynas Kazak, if you can. You are always welcome, but only if the Company can spare you.'

Quickly, they had come to the horses. Maedoc led both his and the Prince's horse to them. Artur took the reins and turned to Morlain.

'Morlain, thank you. We will meet again very soon.'

'I look forward to it.'

Artur and Maedoc mounted, turned about and rode out of the yard. Cantassa came to the door of the main house.

'A better day?'

'Yes, a better day.'

'And is he suitably informed? Does he know what he needs to know?'

'Well, he knows some of what he needs to know and some of the rest, perhaps, he is better off not knowing.'

She laughed. 'It will only confuse him!'

Cantassa laughed with her. 'Come in now, dearest, darker clouds approach from Ocean. It will rain soon. You must not get cold and you still need rest. There is much to do before they depart.'

***

The drizzle had started as the evening came on. Wrapped from head to knee in a cloak, Gyras quietly watched the port. A large boat that was moored on the far side of the Sound particularly drew his attention. *Not Veneti, but Curiosolitae*, he thought. It had come in on the early morning tide, just before full, and dropped its stone anchor. Given the disputes he had heard of at Menluit, it seemed likely the boat would leave quickly on the evening ebb tide. He just needed to get across to it. With the Gaulish gold staters hidden on his journey to Menluit and retrieved on his return, he would have enough to pay for his passage to Gaul, back to the Pro-Consul. *Information imparted, mission accomplished and then on to Massalia!*

In front of him, jutting into the Sound, were two piers of roughly-hewn wooden planking from the straggled landside settlement of simple buildings serving the new port. They were four planks across and supported by three cleaned and evenly-spaced cross-frame tree trunk piles. Log boats and coracles were everywhere, plying their trade, ferrying people and goods over the water to the island of New Ictis, to boats anchored in the sound or to the original port.

Halfway along one of the piers, two boatmen stood discussing the activity on the water.

'More of 'em Curiosity's cum then. What ee make o'that? Old Aodren'll be fumin' wen 'im finds out. Them's ignorin' im no matter wat ee does. Soon as one's gone, more takes 'em's place.'

The other, looking across the water to the Curiosolitae boat, nodded his head thoughtfully, rubbing his tongue around his teeth and then replying gravely, 'Ole world's changin', thas wat I make of it. Romins fightin' Veneti, Curiosity pushin' Veneti. I rekon 'ems day's done 'fore much longer, make no mistake.'

The first boatmen nodded his head vigorously before saying, 'Yer right, I had sum o'them Curiosity sailors in me bote 'fore noon, bort em over ere. Yerd em tell that Caesar bloke gwain gi'those Veneti a darnd good thrapin.'

His companion looked directly at him with wide eyes and a furrowed brow. 'Ee's a scary one id'n ee. Oid gi'm a wide berth, mezel. Don't be vules, do as ee asks!' He paused for effect before continuing, ''Em not a-veered tho', thas the problem, Aodren an 'is kin. Think 'em superior. Walkin' to their demise I zay and then, yule see, uz'l copit too by sociation.'

The first boatmen nodded his head in grim confirmation, 'Zackly, cursed foriners, baint right. Go 'ome, Veneti. Fight yer own war, ee bring no good ere now.'

A cough behind cut into their conversation and both turned slowly around to see Gyras standing on the pier. The first boatman looked him up and down while the second watched nonchalantly. The light was fading and Gyras was about to say something when the first boatman spoke.

'Yer a long way from ome marster, if ee don't mind me zaying. Ow can we 'elp ee?'

'Can you take me to that large boat over there?' Gyras gestured toward the Curiosolitae ship.

'Appen, thing is tho…'

'I have the means to pay.'

'Oim zure you do. No foriner's goin to be ere without gold, zilver to take im out again.'

He exchanged the briefest of glances with the other boatman. 'What with 'em Romins on the warpath, that boat might be th'last for a while. A bloke could get forgot ere if ee's not careful.'

For a moment Gyras said nothing, weighing the boatman's words and then said, 'Alright, four pieces of gold, but I need to go quickly.'

The second boatman spoke up now. 'Make it five marster and the ol' bote'll be vauchin across the Zound like a blowy wind!'

'Very well, five it is, but I need to go now.'

'Right yer are!' The second boatman replied with sudden animation. 'Jump ee down there in the mid,' he gestured to the moored log boat. 'Oil untie er and uz'l be off.'

When they were all in the boat and had pushed off, the second boatman, who faced Gyras while his companion rowed, spoke again, 'Dimmet's comin' on now, good an proper; be dark soon an tide's about vul. Ship'll leave no doubt on the ebbin' tide, bin loadin' all day.'

Gyras nodded guardedly uncertain of his meaning. 'Yes, she will sail this evening. I am sure.'

'Wher'ee from then, marster?'

'Massalia, by the middle sea. Mesogeios, my people call it, or the warm sea.' He smiled palely at the boatman before saying, 'Warmer than this one, anyway.'

'Is tha'right?' The boatman nodded with a feigned look of interest. 'Quite the traveller then.'

Ahead a tallow candle flickered on the transom of the Curiosolitae boat, indicating its position as dusk came early with thickening cloud cover. The second boatman spoke again.

'No'so long ago uz zee lots of Emmets, like ee, plenty o'work then for a fore-right boater, but tha's all gone now. Romins and their plunderin' seen to that and taint right – and no doubt 'em got plans for it all dreckly when 'ems cotten Ol'Veneti, but now it's hard zee, an uz uncertin of future work.'

Gyras looked directly into his eyes, trying to look concerned. As he did so, the boatman reached under his tunic and produced a crude dagger. Gyras breathed in deeply and flexed his fingers on the side of the boat. Behind him, a deep swirl of the oar brought the boat to a stop.

'So, marster, no offence, but us is gwain ask nicely for all yer money in that big pouch. Otherwise, oi might need to get fitty wi'this knife zee and hend ee in to the Zound!'

He gestured forward with the dagger.

'Come on, 'and it over!'

They were halfway from the pier to the boat and it was clear that they had at least planned for this possibility. Although, by the nervous look on the boatman's face, Gyras sensed they were not habitual muggers. Would they take him to the boat even if he gave them the pouch? He could not be sure and he quickly calculated his response.

'Very well, if you put it like that, I can see I have no choice.'

He untied the pouch from his waist belt and threw it midway between him and the boatman. With arm and dagger still outstretched, the boatman looked suspiciously towards the Greek. But then, with the pouch of gold coins before him, he could not resist and leant forward to retrieve it. In an instant,

Gyras was up and at him, grabbing the boatman's arms as he leant forward to take the pouch, and with a strength that belied his height and build, he tumbled the boatman into the water.

Frantically, the impromptu mugger scrambled for the side of the boat. He clearly could not swim and his pathetic, desperate cries and grasping were in stark contrast to his attempted malice only moments before.

With the dropped knife in his hand, Gyras turned to the other boatman. 'Give me the oar, come on! Give it to me now!'

The first boatman, shaken by the sudden turn of events, thought about tackling the Greek for a moment, but then thought better of it and handed him the oar. As the boatman in the water came up for one last desperate gasp of air, Gyras lent over the side of the boat and shoved the oar towards him.

'Grab this!'

He shoved it in between the boatman's flailing hands who, grateful for something to cling on to, grabbed it while Gyras slowly pulled the oar towards him. As the boatman transferred his grip to the side of the boat, coughing and spluttering, the Greek stood up, turned and threw the oar and the dagger as far as he could out into the Sound. Then, he carefully bent down, picked up his pouch and took from it two gold coins. He threw them down into the boat and then slipped the rest into his leather, water-resistant flat body pouch that was laid across his chest and belly, beneath his heavy tunic, where he concealed the majority of his coins.

'The halfway fare, I think. It has been an interesting conversation, but I won't trouble you any further from here. I had hoped to stay dry, but it seems it is not to be – and please, if you are going to call yourself boatmen, do at least learn how to swim.'

With that, he walked to the end of the boat and dived into the Sound. It would be a hard swim, but this was not the first time that he had needed to escape potential robbers. He had swum from an early age and had the strength and determination now to complete his journey.

The boatman, in the water, arms resting on the side of the boat, coughed and spluttered again and then, sodden and exhausted, looked towards his companion in the boat.

'Darn fitty foriners, more twily than 'em's worth, I zay.'

'Zackly… ockerd buggers!' he shouted in the direction of Gyras, but the Greek by now had disappeared into the gloom between them and the Curiosolitae ship.

***

Morlain sat at a simple table in the small roundhouse that was her bedchamber, built on the side of the main large house of Dynas Kazak. Opposite her was a large bed with multiple animal furs and several linen pillows filled with goose down. A fire crackled on a small hearth in the centre of the room. Cooking would be the only need for a fire soon, as spring filled the air and summer came on. But this evening, under clear skies and Skovarnek's filling gibbous, it was cold and damp from the earlier rain and she felt the need for warmth.

Between the table and bed was a small freestanding loom with its two principal uprights dug into the ground. The warp was weighted and held firm with baked clay weights, and at the top of the frame, combining warp and weft, was the first stages of a new woven cloth in red and blue yarn.

From the table, she picked up a small bronze mirror. The reflective surface, illuminated by the firelight, enabled insight and contemplation. On its reverse were two circles, detailed with inner swirling motifs and created by hatching in the bronze. The motifs were irregular and uneven but the overall design, with its two encompassing circles, provided balance, stability, togetherness and were perhaps, she had thought, illustrative of the constant change and flux all around her, contained within the twin certainties of the conjoined realms of Sira Howl and Mamm Norves. It was one of her most prized possessions.

'Madam, I am sorry; may I disturb you?'

Wenna cut in to her thoughts from the door. Morlain turned and smiled tiredly at her.

'Wenna, yes, of course, what is it?'

'Madam, the Pryns is here, diverted from the Company, en route to Menluit with Maedoc, and asks if he may see you.'

She breathed in deeply. It had been eight days since their breakfast and conversation on Marghros. She had heard word about him and the preparations in the Sound, but this was his first return to Dynas Kazak.

'Yes, thank you. I will come into the main hall...' Wenna nodded and turned to go. 'Actually, no Wenna, show him in here, and Maedoc too, if he wishes to join us.'

'Madam, are you sure?'

'Yes I am, but give me a moment to tidy myself, if you would.'

Wenna left and pulled the heavy curtain that served as a door back across the entrance to the room and then, after a suitable pause, returned with the Prince.

'No Maedoc?' she said when Wenna had left again.

'No,' Artur replied, 'he has gone on to Ker Tamara. There are items that he feels we must have for our sailing, more rope in particular.'

'Well, it is good to see you at least – and the preparation, it goes well?'

'Yes, I think so, there is little more that we can do now, saving Maedoc's rope. We row strongly and the boat sails well; our swords and sword arms are prepared; our shields are loaded. Aodren proceeds to Menluit, stopping at all the Veneti mines, and then on to settle his affairs at Pendre. The Veneti flotilla is ready and we sail on the morning tide after the full moon. He and I and our immediate followers ride together from Menluit to the sacred stones two nights from now, to meet you – and then to the boats and departure.'

He took a deep breath and seemed about to say something else, but then he held back and looked towards the table instead.

'That is a fine mirror. My aunt had a similar one, although simpler than yours, I think.'

'Oh, really? Yes, I am very lucky. It came to me from an old priestess in Kernovia after I had nursed her when I was fifteen springs old. She was the daughter of one of the Tin Lords. They are wealthy and she and her sister had a matching pair made for them by one of the bronzesmiths, I believe.'

Artur nodded his head but said nothing. He was somewhat interested, but she could see he was here for something else.

'And what is this?' He picked up the item with both hands; there were several of them spread across the table. His fingers rubbed and felt the texture as he held it. 'It is animal skin, but what are these strange patterns? What sort of animal has these markings?'

She stood beside him, her arm rubbed gently against his as they both looked at the patterns.

'They are not markings but a collection of symbols. The symbols are called letters which indicate sounds and the sounds go together to make up words, marked or written on animal skin, as you say, or parchment to give it its proper name. Do you see how there are groups of letters and then gaps before another group of letters, so each group of letters makes a word.'

He raised his head and turned to her, and her eyes penetrated deeply into his, waiting for what he would say next.

'So, these symbols, letters, make words, words that we speak, like I am speaking now?'

'Yes, although, actually – not the words that we speak, but in fact Greek words.'

'Greek? Gyras is a Greek. Are these his… parchments?' A different emotion was growing in him now. 'Do you have a connection to Gyras that I do not know about?'

'Artur, Gyras is not the only Greek in this world and no they are not his. They are mine. If he had had the chance, he probably would have been able to understand or "read" the words; and very interesting he would have found them too, I am sure. But, thankfully, he has not had that chance.'

'If they are yours, can you… read them?'

'Yes, I can, and more than that. I made these symbols, formed these words. Artur, I "write" or I have "written" these words on this and that, and that piece of parchment,' she gestured across the table. 'I do it to tell a story.'

Again, their eyes met. Would he now ask her the question that she expected?

He did not.

'And, why do you make, write these symbols for Greek words and not for the language of the Dewnan, the Ocean People?'

'Well, because the Greek speakers developed their symbols, their letters, many years ago. They have an established group of letters that help them to write their words and it is easier, perhaps, to learn to speak and then write Greek than to develop new symbols for the language of the Dewnan. Besides, it was part of my training to learn Greek, and with traders coming regularly to Ictis, it has proved useful to be able to speak in that language. I have learnt much by doing so, speaking to those who travel far and who bring news of change.'

'Can all of the priestesses speak and write Greek?'

'There are only a few of us who have an interest, an aptitude maybe. Much of our learning is retained in our memory only, as has always been the way.'

'I did not think there was anybody in Demetae who could… read.'

'No, and as far as I know, there are few amongst the Estrenyons. We have the longer-established link here, you see, Artur; the connection with the warm lands and the middle sea. Our tin has attracted them for many generations, from the Acheans onwards. Many lives have gone by since those first Acheans, but in some of us, in you and me, Greek blood still flows, however distant.'

'Should we then have made more of Gyras being here?'

'No, I think Aodren's sense was right on that. He was up to something. I am not sure what, but I am sure we will find out soon enough.'

Artur nodded his head and then said, 'You are writing a story?'

'Continuing a story…'

'About brave rheidyrs; battles, quests for glory? Or do you write the stories of the Dewnan?'

'Both!' She paused for a moment. 'Artur, it is my duty to tell and record the story of the Dewnan. My sisters, brothers and I learn and tell stories to understand where we have come from, uphold what we stand for and spread that message to the ordinary people. Then a few of us write the story of our people on these parchments. I am only the latest to do this in a long line, a special skill used by only a few since the first Greek traders came amongst us.

'How many of these parchments do you have?'

'There are many, and some very old, would you like to see?'

'Yes, I would.'

She led him out of the bedchamber and across the main roundhouse. Several heads inclined slightly to watch them go. Outside, she crossed the open yard to a roundhouse on the far corner of the compound. It had a strong, thick wooden door mounted on simple, sturdy iron barrel hinges. An elderly guard stood to attention as Morlain approached. Taking the door handle with both hands, she pushed hard against the door and it slowly swung open. Inside, tallow candles gave a dim light, and there was another guard standing just inside the door.

'Thank you, Bacun. You may step outside if you wish, while I show Pryns Artur around.'

'Thank ee, ma'm.'

'There is always someone here,' Morlain explained, 'day and night, watching over the parchments. Bacun is particularly attentive; he has guarded the parchments for many years.'

As his eyes adjusted to the light, Artur looked around. There were parchments everywhere; rolled and stacked on shelving that spread across the floor and around the building.

She said, 'The traders tell of a great collection of writing, a library they call it. There the wise and the learned come together in a city on the far side of the warm sea where a mighty tower shines its light to guide the ships to its harbour.'

She paused and looked around her and then turned to him.

'How I should like to go there one day!'

'And what now? Will you write about us and record all that happens, as we go to meet the Roman aggressor?'

'Yes,' she smiled gently in the soft light. 'I will write of bravery and rheidyrs and a battle to defend all that is important, and about you and me.'

For a moment, they held each other's gaze, and then he looked away. Quickly, he looked back, stood forward, took her hands and said, 'Morlain, I have thought of you often in recent days, although in truth I don't know what to think. I am strong and determined with the Company and we go to our battle well equipped and determined to fight hard for the Dewnan and the Veneti and all that we hold dear. And yet still, I think of you… '

'Well,' her voice faltered slightly at the implication in what he was saying, 'we have become good friends in recent days and I have enjoyed speaking to you, but what of Gwalian? You have seemed inseparable. Have you quarrelled?'

He looked to the floor. Even in the dim light, the change in his countenance was obvious.

'Gwalian has made her feelings very clear. It appears that I was misled in her regard for me.'

'And so now you have come to me?'

He looked up and shook his head and took her hands again. 'No, it is not like that. Morlain, I see how the people look to you, with the highest respect and you are beautiful – but it has taken me a while to see it. I cannot fully explain it; my feelings have grown stronger. You saved my life, but it is more than that, you know and understand so much. Look at all of this!' He gestured around the building 'And, I did so enjoy listening to you.'

Now she held his hands and looked back at him.

'Artur, I like you as well and believe our destinies are entwined, in whatever form that takes, but let us focus on our tasks in the remaining days you have here. I will look for your return and will it with all my power – and then, well, then we can think about you and me in a different way. You should be sure of your feelings before you say much more and only a proper passage of days will allow that.'

'Wait and see if I return, very sensible.'

'Artur, it is not like that. You will return and when you do, we can talk more, and I look forward to that.'

His smile was fleeting.

'Yes, of course, you are right. I will go know and see you at the stones, two nights hence.'

He bowed, turned and walked out of the door.

As she watched him go, a fleeting vision of Heulwen, her childhood mentor and his mother, entered into her consciousness.

'Only you Morlain can guide him, truly. He will be strong. He will need to be. But he will need wise words and insight. It is clear to me that fate has chosen you for this task. You and he to approach this great challenge together. You will guide our people, but above all, you will guide him and to do this, you too will need great strength...'

Morlain tidied several parchments on their shelf, sighed briefly and called for Bacun to return to his post.

***

Two evenings later, horses and rheidyrs, supported by their mounted gilles, milled around the lower yard, just before the main gate of Menluit, waiting for the signal to move out.

In the hall of Pendre, a small group stood before the central fire. Prince Artur was prominent, flanked by Drustan, Kea, Nouran and Gourgy on one side and Gawen, Silyen and Maedoc on the other. All listened to Aodren, flanked by Ewan, Winoc and the senior members of the colony. A little apart from the rest, uncommitted to either side, stood Lancelin and behind him was Gwalian, sat on a chair of the roundtable.

Aodren drew his sword. 'Pryns Artur, this is the Sword of Menluit, an ancient sword, heavy and dense, and all who attempt it, find it unwieldy. All, that is, save the Lord of the Crossing, Tamara's servant and guardian. To him, it is light, strong and sharp, and the grey tint tells of the special ore, dug from workings hereabout. This sword dates back to a different age, long before the Veneti came, when the ancestors of the Dewnan came down from RunHoul and Menitriel to the land around Menluit and began to clear the Great Wood, open Nanmeur for farming and search for metals. Through some strange power, magic even, the sword will only respond to the acknowledged Lord of the Crossing. He who resides at the very centre of the Valley, where Orsa once trod, is honour-bound to wield the Sword of Menluit, the gift of Tamara, bringer of life. The sword will bring strength and purpose to his task. It is a sword of leadership and inspiration and should not be used lightly, but if ever there was a need it is now and I am proud to wield it alongside you in our great battle ahead.'

'Lord Aodren, we are honoured to fight with you, the Veneti and the Sword of Menluit in defence of our people. We will take the fight to the aggressors, and whatever the end may be, they will know they have been in a fight when we have finished with them.'

There were murmurs of agreement from the Company and the older man grinned.

'Well said, young man, and now let us away to the stones. Lady Morlain awaits us with the blessing of the ancestors. Then to the ships; we sail on the morning tide. Already Skovarnek rides high and full!'

They turned and moved towards the door. Gwalian quickly walked to the side of Artur.

'How has it come to this... and all this misunderstanding? Is there no way back? Can we not begin again? Forget all that has happened since the wane of Loor Tevyans...'

He stopped and turned to her.

'Gwalian, I saw the passion in your embrace of Lancelin. There is no misunderstanding and there can be no new beginning. Your affection lies elsewhere and you are not helping yourself by denying it.'

Her eyes held him to her, no matter how he felt he could not look away. She saw it and raised herself to her fullest, proudest height.

'My Lord, all are ready to leave, you must come now.' Maedoc stood anxiously by the door.

Still those eyes held him. After a short pause, she spoke. 'Go then, but go wisely and carefully. Do all in your power to smite the oppressor and return to Menluit and to Pendre so that I may see you again. We will wait for you and think of you and all who sail with you – and know this: no matter what you think now, it will not just be the Lady Morlain who looks for your safe return.'

His face softened (how could it not?) and he took her hands, smiled, but said no more, and turned and walked toward Maedoc and the open door.

***

Sira Howl had sunk from view, but his light still straddled the horizon, a thin line diminishing quickly, casting gold, black and yellow-red fiery and tempestuous shades on a billowing and developing cloud mass, forging, shaping and heading towards them.

Three circles of upright stones, each the size of a man, stood adjacent to each other, ancient stones raised by the ancestors of the Dewnan and Pretan lords, close to Menitriel, that aligned with the tombs of long-dead kings and their followers, built while the Great Wood still covered Nanmeur and deep reverence for Orsa lived in their hearts. Within the middle circle, the rheidyrs of the Company and principal men of the Veneti colony each stood with their back to a stone and with swords drawn. They watched as Morlain, wrapped in her great cloak and flanked by Elowen and Cantassa, raised one hand to the evening sky while she held with the other firmly to her great staff of oak. The breeze freshened, tugging at cloaks, tousling and tangling hair. They all looked to the High Priestess, silently urging her to proceed quickly if they were not all going to get very wet. Perhaps sensing their plea, she spoke, imploring the sky and the brightest stars, still discernible in the remaining moonlight.

'Sira Howl warms us. He is the light that gives life and guides us. Mamm Norves has reared us. She provides for us and nurtures us, the Ocean People; but you, mighty ancestors in the heavens, our forebears, we honour you and all that you have achieved – and thank you for all you have done to bring us here to our place in Mamm Norves! We come to the sacred stones, symbols of those that have passed, to be with you, who have gone before.'

She lowered her eyes, and with staff tilted forward slightly from upright, turned around the circle with eyes of determination and authority, earthly stars shining fiercely like jewels set within the pale light of her countenance, taking in each man's stare, speaking loudly and clearly.

'Together, we are strong in the face of aggression. We shall draw strength, knowing that all who have gone before fight beside us in the struggle ahead.'

She spun again and pointed her staff skyward. At its tip, it shone with iridescent light.

'See! As darkness falls, the great bear, mother of Orsa, shines brightly in the sky. Her son was sent down to walk amongst us, inspire us and is now back in the heavens from whence he came. He forgives our betrayal and bestrides the sky too, with his great guiding star, friend to our people as we sail on Ocean's broad expanse. Mother and Son watch over us!'

Slowly, her arm came down and her head bowed to the ground. Gradually, her head rose again and she began to walk around the circle. Artur knew that she would stop before him.

'Here, beneath the great celestial mother, made real again on Earth is Orsa's heir!'

She stood beside him and turned to face the circle, commanding and authoritative. After a short pause, she walked away from the Prince again.

'Through him, we can return to the great days! That is what we fight for and Artur will lead us in this great quest!'

She turned again and looked towards him, determinedly, but with the hint of a smile. She had not warned him or prepared him for this. It was a test perhaps, but now he was clear of his role and increasingly of his relationship with Morlain. He smiled back with equal determination.

Now Elowen and Cantassa both took a beaker from the acolytes. These were distinctive with rounded flat bottoms, before rising to a prominent lip.

'Come, drink your fill from these pots as our ancestors did; be inspired because Artur, heir of Orsa, has come amongst you.'

The beakers began to pass around the circle, and although large slugs and swigs were taken by all, each pot never needed refilling. After the fifth or sixth man, everyone began to notice and exchange glances. Morlain, impervious, silently watched the beakers go around until they finally came to Artur and Aodren on the opposite sides of the circle. When they had taken their swig, emptying the beakers, she spoke again.

'We fight for our homeland, for freedom, and with the blessing of our ancestors. We will prevail!'

All had drunk fully and the liquid, whatever it was, enlivened and emboldened them. She drew to her conclusion.

'Hold your swords aloft, all of you, and come forward together. Touch my staff as I raise it to the sky and then each other's swords.'

They did as she asked, and as the sound of metal clashing with metal rang across the land, a strong gust of wind wrapped around them and a crash of lightning broke the sky. The light it gave shone on all of their faces as they shouted battle cries to the night, to their ancestors and to great bears in the sky. Fuelled by all that she had said and the liquid in the beaker, they cheered in their belief of impending victory and their triumphant return.

Then, it was all over and the rain began to fall heavily.

Aodren spoke first, shouting above the rapidly increasing wind. 'We passed old Casworon's hall on the way up. He foresaw the rain and the storm as he greeted us and offered us shelter, let us make for there. It is only a short ride.'

***

'Skinniest bear Ize ever zeen!'

Gourgy smiled his toothy grin at Artur as the Company and all of the Veneti squeezed their way into Casworon's modest hall.

Casworon's voice carried above the pushing and the hubbub as they all sought a place in the hall. Some, who were still outside, shouted to others to move up as the rain still pounded down on them.

'Tis a great 'onour my Lady, Lord Aodren you visitin' uz ere and the Pryns, 'im that the ole valley is talking about. I zee 'im with Lord Lancelin and Tinos and others of ee's Company. Fine lookin' young man, idn't ee!'

For a moment, the old man fell silent, perhaps in reverie at the thought of his own youth. A back shoved into him, jolting him to the present.

'I should like to pay my respects when ee finds 'is way over – an offer my support. If I wuz not so shaky on me legs, Oid be askin' go with him, no mistake!'

Aodren smiled at their host. Short and stocky with faded-brown hair and white flecks, he was a descendant of the original Dewnan Lords. His clothes had seen better days and the hall had a ramshackle appearance, but the warmth of his welcome was genuine.

'Casworon, old friend, the Pryns will make his way across shortly. I am sure, but for now, we are grateful to be warm and dry. A flagon of mead each would be very welcome. It has come on quite a blow out there!'

'Aye, aye, I told ee when ee passed by earlier, storm's comin.'

His reply was slightly distant. Another thought had entered his head.

'My lady, t'would warm us all if ee could tell a story of the old days? It would bring great repute to my hall, as war approaches and you bein' the finest storyteller in the whole Valley o'course. T'would be a great privilege for uz all!'

Morlain laughed. In his day, Casworon had built his own reputation as a brave and compassionate warrior, fighting with the Veneti against the incursions of the Estrenyons while caring for his small group of tenants and followers. As his reputation and stock had grown, their wellbeing had increased with it.

Although advanced in years now, his poise and confidence still held true.

'Lord Casworon, I would be very happy to do that; perhaps the story of the Dragon's Stone?'

'My Lady, t'woud do very well, indeed.' He turned to his wife and the two house attendants standing behind him. 'Mead for all and cake. Come, let uz serve these brave souls quick now. Keep em topped up!'

Morlain smiled at the attendants. Elowen and Cantassa offered to help with the pouring and soon all were inside. Then, flagons in hand, they looked towards Morlain, who was stood at the centre of the hall. Her appearance was softer, warmer in the glow of the firelight, less dramatic than it had been by the stones; but still, all listened intently for what she would say next.

**

Pryns Piran and the Dragon's Stone

A son was born to King Ronan and Queen Ailla and they named him Piran. He was strong and determined like his father, and handsome and wise like his mother.

Tall and valiant, he grew to yearn for the chance to emulate the ancestors – Venetia, Thurien, Ronan, and all who had gone before – to continue the celebrated progress of the Pretan towards the great Father.

'Patience my son,' Ronan said to him. 'Your chance will come. Gather followers to you; the young men of Menitriel and RunHoul who share your zeal for adventure and for spreading the influence of the Pretan.'

Pryns Piran waited, as his father advised, and gathered good men around him – brave Clesek, loyal Bronek and Madern the bold, amongst them. They practised swordplay, grew accustomed to each other and prepared for the anticipated challenges ahead.

Then one day a traveller arrived, even though the winter winds blew harsh and cold, and Ronan and his court gathered around the great fire in the hall at Menitriel.

'I seek King Ronan of high fame and repute,' the traveller beseeched as he entered the hall. 'I have journeyed far in the darkest of days, and tidings of danger and calamity I bring.'

Dishevelled and weary from his journey, he stood before Ronan and Ailla. The light of the fire revealed a deep scar that ran from the centre of his forehead, around his face and down to his chin. All who saw it were dismayed. How had this brave stranger received such a mark?

'Great King and Queen of the Pretan, my name is Cadan ap Gruffudd, he who is King of the Mata, Ocean People like you. He has sent me to appeal for your help. This is no season for Ocean traversing and so I have travelled over hills and mountains, through deep valleys and across great rivers with the harsh cold of winter all around. The reputation of the Pretan and the good you have done has spread across this land – in Cymru and ancient Albion and now, when all hope seems lost, I come to ask for your aid.'

'Brave and heroic Pryns,' said Ronan, 'What foul deed has afflicted your people that you seek our aid in this frantic manner? Sit by the fire, rest first, let us bring you refreshment and dry clothing and then we will hear your plea.'

'Great King,' said Cadan, 'you are very good, but I must eat and drink quickly, tell my story and prepare for my return to the land of Mata as soon as I can.'

Quenn Ailla signalled for meat, broth and mead and implored him, 'Honest Pryns, rest a while; it will do you no good to hurry away so soon.'

Cadan smiled and bowed before her. 'Fair Queen, your beauty and wisdom are of equal repute. I thank you for your care and attention.'

He took a great swig from the pot of mead and ravenously tore chunks with his teeth from the meat taken from the plate before him. Whispers all around speculated on what might have happened to bring Cadan ap Gruffudd before them in this manner. Pryns Piran, in particular, sat by the fire and studied the Pryns of Mata with great interest. Then, when he had eaten and drunk his fill and a warm, dry cloak had been brought for him, Cadan wiped his mouth with his sleeve and said with renewed urgency, 'Please, good King, will you allow me now to tell my tale?'

King Ronan nodded his head and Cadan began.

'The land of Mata is green and fertile. Forests and pastures fill our river valleys and Ocean and the mountains surround us. We live on the hills and, in the spring, our sailors trade with the

Dewnan, across to Ériu *and the lands of the Ocean People. We take our lead from the light and vigour of Sira Howl and the wisdom and generosity of Mamm Norves. We honour our ancestors and take care with the spirits of the land and water, and over many lives, we have built great monuments of stone, high in the hills, where the spirit of our ancestors and the joining of Sira Howl and Mamm Norves is rekindled.'*

He paused and drank more mead. Ailla smiled softly in encouragement and Ronan said, 'Cadan, it is the way of all who live beside Ocean and in the presence of great hills and mountains, and was even so with my ancestors on Ocean's far side.'

Cadan inclined his head in acknowledgement and continued, 'And yet in one thing the Mata are different: the stone we use, "I Main Brith". It is said to be forged in the fiery and productive belly of Mamm Norves and cut from the sacred hills above the fertile plain, which makes it distinctive. Hard and dark, it is littered with white colouring and glittering with countless tiny sparkles, twinkling like the stars in the night sky. It symbolises our ancestors, as it matches their appearance in the heavens!

'The fame of our glistening stones has spread far, beyond our borders and yet we do not seek fame. The Mata are farmers – we fish and hunt and are content to live a simple life, seeking no conflict with man or tribe; and so it has been for as long as anyone can remember and maybe, in this, we grew complacent in our contentment.'

The faces in the firelight all listened intently as he continued.

'Then, last summer, a terrible curse fell upon us from the sky. From the remote mountain fastness of Gwinid an evil, covetous dhreic came, not seen since the giants walked this land. She had been awoken by whisperings of glittering treasure after sleeping for an age of men."

The eyes around the fire widened and many shifted at this unexpected development in the tale.

'Umgras was her name and she showed no mercy, seeking the sacred stones of Mata, which she desired for herself. Breathing fire, many lives were lost and homes destroyed in the devastation she wrought.

'Quickly, we gathered a company of warriors, brave and true, and I led them to meet the odious dhreic in battle, but Umgras had no desire for a fight and sought the stones instead. So we went to the very thing she sought; the sacred valley in the hills below Cadair Breentin, the ancient seat of the Kings of Mata. Atop the royal hill, we spied her, shouted her vile name to bring her to us and made our way to Cylchau y Seren, circle of the stars, in the sacred valley.

'Umgras sped towards us, her great wings spread wide like the sails of a mighty airborne vessel, bearing down upon us and darkening the sky with each flap of those immense and powerful extremities. She encircled the Company, considered our strength and visibly drooled in her greed and desire for the stones. She dwarfed us, with her impenetrable skin of grey, green and brown scales, and spikes like mighty impaling thorns crowning her spine to the tip of her long and ruinous tail, a mass of slimy meat and muscle that guided the dhreic forward like an enormous rudder at her rear. The sinews of muscle in her wings and in her legs pulsed with ruthless intent. Then, at the end of each front leg were fearsome, piercing and grasping claws. She had three talons at the front, each the size of a young oak tree with one slightly smaller at the back for gripping her prey – and all as black as night.

'Astride the stones, we stood and called to Umgras to engage us. At first, she appeared to pay no heed and retreat, but we knew better than to cheer. She circled Cadair Breentin, swung around and came straight at us, breathing fire with manic, ravenous eyes, full of evil intent, digging deep into our fear, becoming more dreadful and terrible the closer she came. A forked blood-red tongue flickered in her open mouth, eager and ready to pounce, and set within her upper and lower jaw were teeth like you have never seen, sharper than the finest sword's blade.'

'"Hold your ground," I shouted. "Wait until you are sure of your shot and on my command."

'Many trembled and rightly so, as those fearsome eyes, boring into our souls and striking dread in our hearts, drew ever nearer.

'"Prepare to meet your end, Cadan ap Gruffudd and all your paltry followers," she cried as she raced towards us. I am Umgras the Impaler, Umgras the Devourer, and I shall have my stones!"

'"Let loose your weapons!" I cried when she was almost upon us.

'All the shots were true! Yet none hurt the dhreic or penetrated her scaly skin. We stood our ground heroically but Umgras picked us off, one by one. Screams of terror filled the valley as she burnt *her victims alive or pierced them on her mighty claw. It was a terrible sight.*

'I was the last man standing, and her malevolent eyes narrowed in contempt as Umgras turned to face me. She then sneered and rolled her great forked tongue around her upper lip.

"'How fitting, Cadan ap Gruffudd, that it is you that I must remove last of all," she said. "Soon, I shall rule this land as one day you had thought you might."

'Her voice crackled and she spat sparks of singeing fire. "Think of what might have been before your end. Your people will be my slaves and you nothing but a charred pile of bones!"

'She rushed at me and I fell to the ground. She caught my face with her talon and gave me the wound you see upon me, but it was a cut and no more. Then, as her momentum carried her, unable to stop, I thrust my sword into the soft place at the centre of her underbelly. It went in, but not all of the way. It was certainly not fatal, but it did hurt her. I heard her grimace.

'Livid with anger, she turned to me with fury and hatred. I got to my feet and staggered backwards. I knew I had to get away, find a stronger weapon, come back and fight her again. Slowly, but deliberately, she came towards me, her mouth dripping with relish and intent as it seemed the end was near. But then, Sira Howl broke through the clouds and shone his light in my moment of need and the stones began to sparkle all around us. The dhreic was distracted. I turned and ran as fast as I could and when I reached the valley top, back at Cadair Breentin, there was Umgras still amongst the stones wallowing in her pleasure at their sparkle.'

King Ronan spoke for all in the hall as they sat silently, shocked, watching him eat and drink.

'Cadan ap Gruffudd, you have been brave against this fearsome beast and now have travelled on a great journey in search of aid. How can we help you in your struggle?'

Pryns Piran stepped forward into the full glow of the fire and said, 'Father, I think I can anticipate the request of the Pryns of Mata.'

He bowed and introduced himself to Cadan.

'He comes for the strength and hardness of our swords and our arrows. The skill of the Pretan smiths is of wide renown and our copper and tin alloy is the strongest available, strong enough perhaps to pierce this dhreic's underbelly. He will only get one

more chance to skewer the beast. He must be sure of his weapon before he returns to the quest."

Cadan bowed to Piran.

'Pryns Piran, Umgras is a formidable, cruel and heartless opponent. She will strike me down if she gets the chance, but I know where her weak point is! I need a weapon that will readily cut deep into her underbelly and end the vile and wicked life she leads.'

'You do, brave Pryns of Mata, and you need a Company to support you in this daunting task. My Company and I will join you if you will have us. Let us proclaim the unity of Pretan and Mata and bring with us our newest weapons to take the monster down!'

"Pryns Piran, I thank you, but we cannot delay. Umgras has returned to her mountain lair for the winter, taking the stones of the Cylchau y Seren with her. Soon, the new shoots of spring will emerge and she will return. We must strike before she even sets out. Will you join me, brave Pryns, with your warriors, in an assault on the mountains of Gwinid!"

"We will, Cadan ap Gruffudd. We are ready and together we shall be triumphant!"

They set out the next morning, wrapped in warm clothes and with their best weapons at their side. Slowly, they made their way across the land of the Dewnan, through icy wind and rain, over hilltop and through deep valley. Then, the land became flat and they forded a great river. Guided by Cadan, they crossed more mountains until, finally, they came to Cadair Breentin and Umgras's devastation was clear for all to see. The people of Mata rallied and new warriors joined the cause on seeing their Pryns returned with new friends and allies, and the people cheered them on as they set out on the final leg of their quest.

The first shoots of spring were in the valleys as they began to climb into mountainous Gwinid, but snow still lay all around in the high mountains and the walking was heavy and difficult here, but then, as they approached the dhreic's stronghold, on the highest of peaks, all the snow had gone and the earth was barren and charred. Bones littered the ground and, ahead in the still unseen lair, Umgras could be heard snoring and grumbling. Carefully, they put their packs aside and drew their weapons: sword, spear, bow and bronze-tipped arrow. As they crept around a large rock, there she lay in a large cave, sleeping. Great wafts of air were being sucked in and blown out of her nasal passages and slimy green slobber hung from her mouth and draped across her chin – and there, by her side, stood the stones of Cylchau y Seren. Stealthily they came, spreading to encircle the dhreic and inflict the maximum number of wounds, but then, and without opening her eyes, Umgras spoke. Her voice, grating and harsh, struck fear into all of the Company.

'Hmm, what's this, I smell man flesh. Who dares approach the lair of Umgras the Devourer! Only a fool would expose themselves here, where there is nowhere to hide.'

Her great wide eyes opened and she looked straight at them.

'Ah, yes, of course, Cadan the foolish and some fresh new meat. What business have you here, spawn of Gruffudd? What has led you to this folly, only to end up as my new spring breakfast?'

The giant dhreic was on her feet in an instant and she swung her head around breathing fire.

"Get back!" yelled Cadan.

"The stones are mine!" Umgras bellowed as she burned and scorched and her eyes flickered with resentment and hate.

Quickly, she came upon them. Some were swift to get out of the way, but others hesitated just a little too long. Her mouth engulfed them, biting their bodies in two. The legs and lower bodies that remained convulsed pitifully for a short while afterwards; while muffled, fading cries came from the poor souls inside her mouth as they disappeared down the dhreic's gullet.

'Yummm, that feels better after a long sleep; I feel veerry hungry!'

She turned one way and then the other and then another, looking for warriors to eat.

Breathing heavily, hiding behind a rock, Cadan spoke to Piran and a group of his closest warriors.

'We must distract her, draw her out into the open and expose her underbelly. I know my mark, but I must have clear sight.'

Prince Piran looked to his comrades, shocked by what they had seen; but with determined faces, they nodded back.

Piran said in a hushed voice, 'We will do it, but use the arrows we have given you and strike true, Cadan ap Gruffudd, or we shall be dead men and a dhreic's breakfast!'

Slowly, Piran and his warriors edged around the rocks, out of sight of Umgras, and found a way to climb up and above the dhreic's lair. Bronek, who was the last in the line, suddenly he lost his footing as he climbed, and his sword fell from his hand, clanking and clattering down amongst the rocks. Umgras turned in an instant, and through the gap, saw the exposed warrior, terror in his eyes, frantically trying to regain his footing. With a wicked smile, Umgras calmly opened her mouth and her forked, stomach-churning tongue, glistening wet and sticky, rolled out. It shot forward and wrapped around Bronek as he scrambled madly backwards.

'Piran, Clesek, Madern, help me!' he called out in desperation as the dhreic, gurgling and rasping her hideous laugh, drew poor Bronek towards her gaping mouth and scything teeth.

Piran charged back down the path, followed by the others, swords above their heads and slashed cuts into the dhreic's tongue.

'Aaaargh!'

Umgras's cry of pain filled the sky and the warriors fell to their knees, clutching their ears. Piran was again quickest to recover, and grabbing Bronek by the shoulders and dragging him away from the receding tongue as the others followed.

'Aaaargh!'

The dhreic cried again and raised herself up in anguish – now Cadan released his strengthened bronze arrow and it pierced Umgras in her soft underbelly. Again, she cried in pain.

She stomped around and the mountain shook beneath her. Then, unexpectedly, she stood still, turned and darted out of sight into the cave.

Stumbling and banging sounds came from within and Piran and the Pretan above, and Cadan and the Mata below, edged forward cautiously to see what Umgras was doing. As they peered, there came a mighty whoosh and she flew out of the cave, extending her gigantic wings and quickly gaining height, clutching the stones of Cylchau y Seren. Out of range of any arrow, she hovered in the air for a moment, showering fire down on them all, before turning and heading across the mountains.

'Quickly,' cried Cadan. 'Keep track of her; we have unleashed her on unsuspecting lands and must now hunt her down.'

Across the mountains, they went and into the heart of ancient Albion. Misery she caused as she fled, laying waste to trevs and gorging on unsuspecting farmers and their families. Many more warriors and the lords of Albion joined Piran and Cadan in their quest to slay the dhreic. Umgras flew, until she came to Ocean again, but sensing her own frailty, declined to cross the water and instead turned back. The distance that she flew reduced each day as the arrow buried in her underbelly festered and ate at her body until, finally, Piran, Cadan and their followers caught up with the dhreic as she came to a stop on the Hill of the Sacred Spring of Albion at the very heart of the Sacred Land. Umgras was exhausted but she still would not give up the stones. With caution in their step, the two Pryns approached the dhreic.

Cadan spoke with grim determination. 'Umgras you are a wicked dhreic and a disgrace to your kind, give up the sacred stones of Cylchau y Seren right now and think of what might have been before your end.'

The dhreic raised her head from the ground and now it shook in her frailty, but still she managed to sneer her defiance.

'I will never surrender to you, Cadan ap Gruffudd. If you want the stones, come and get them!'

With one last surge of strength, Umgras got to her feet, flapped her colossal wings and took flight across the sacred landscape, but Piran and Cadan, anticipating the dhreic's reaction, took up their mighty bows and fired their strengthened arrows. Each gleaming cursor sailed true to their mark, piercing the monstrous dhreic all the way to the centre of her rotten existence. Umgras let out a deafening wail of capitulation and came crashing to the ground in the midst of the Sacred Land, with the stones of Cylchau y Seren scattered all around.

When they were sure she was dead, the people and priests of the land approached the body of mighty Umgras, devourer no more, and marvelled at the dhreic and those who had hunted and brought her down.

Many said that the fabled ancestors, who had hunted the mighty beasts when giants walked the land, and who wandered the skies at night, had returned to Albion once more. With them came the dawning of a new age, embodied in the magical stones, glittering like the stars in the sky. No longer would they build their temples in wood but instead in stone, and at their heart, would be the stones of the stars brought to the Sacred Land by a mighty dhreic. Piran and the Pretan came from Menitriel and RunHoul and became the leaders of the land – and the

sons and daughters of Cadan the Dhreicslayer, the acclaimed
stonemasons of Mata, rebuilt Cylchau y Seren at the heart of the
sacred landscape.

***

The hall remained silent as Morlain finished speaking and then
Casworon said, 'Lady Morlain, we iz 'onoured by yer tale of
bravery and perseverance. Tis a fine send-off fer brave souls,
an reminds uz all great deeds are possible even in th'face of a
fearsome foe.'

Morlain looked back at the old man with a gentle smile. 'It
does indeed, Lord Casworon.'

Aodren spoke next in a loud commanding voice, looking
towards the Prince, who confidently nodded his head in
agreement, 'Come, to the boats, we must depart!'

'Let's be at 'em!' Gourgy could not contain himself, sparking
much cheering and shouts of encouragement. Aodren went to
the door and Artur was about to follow with the rest of the
Dewnan when Morlain said, 'Artur, before you go, could I speak
to you alone, briefly?'

He looked back at her, searching her eyes for what she
might want to say. 'Yes, of course.' He turned to Drustan and
Kea. 'Wait for me outside; I will not be long.'

They watched Veneti and Dewnan file out and then Morlain
said, 'The day has come and much hangs in the balance. Travel
safely and think wisely, not rashly, be brave and not foolhardy –
and do not let the dhreic have an easy strike!'

A weak smile faded to a look of concern that she could not
hide, but quickly, conscious of this lapse, she rallied and stood
tall.

'I will think of you and try to support you every day until
you return. Listen for me; my words will come in unexpected
places, but they may help.'

She looked at him, her eyes softening again. He was about
to reply, but she spoke again. 'Artur, I shall miss you. Come
home safely, to me.'

She kissed him, gently, unexpectedly. Forgetting all else,
he responded. Wrapped in the warmth of her lips, her sudden

passion stirred his adrenaline – and roused hope within him. Then it was over, and she stood back and said her final words.

'Go now! The Company awaits!'

He was going to say something, but instead smiled, turned and walked out of the door.

***

Julius Caesar sat astride his horse surrounded by legates and tribunes, watching as twenty cohorts of infantry held their own standard or signa prominent above the mass lined up before him. There were lines of maniples and centuries within each cohort, stretching back as far as he could see, all following the parade instructions of their centurion. Watching over all of them was pilus prior, the senior centurion and designated commander of their cohort for this campaign.

The most experienced men in the two legions present, the first cohort, lined up directly in front of him. For all their experience, they dressed similarly to the massed ranks behind them and wore body armour, a mix of metal and leather, as well as a cassis with protrusions on the front and back to protect their heads against sword blows. Each carried a shield or scutum, and for fighting, a gladius, or a pilum for throwing.

At the front of them all, the aquilifer, resplendent in his lion-skin headpiece, carried the Silver Aquila, the Eagle of the Legion, and alongside him were the horn-playing cornicerns in their wolf-skin headpieces with their G-shaped cornu. These were the signal givers and directors of signals to the cornicines of the centuries.

The infantry was ready and the attack on the Veneti senate and their stronghold would commence at first light the following day. This final show of strength, organisation and control showed his intent and the futility of continued resistance.

Not that he expected the Veneti to concede now.

He had arrived on the border of the Venetic territory on Kalendae Maius. It had been a wet spring; travelling had been difficult and still, here on Pridie Kalendae Iunius, a cold wind blew across the nearby Ocean, bringing dampness and a chill to the air.

Initially, he had taken the time to take proper stock of the situation, discussed all that had happened with young Crassus and heard from others who had valuable information to impart from spies, reconnaissance and defectors from the Veneti and their allies. His plan was taking shape and the tribes, in their belligerence and response to his overall strategy, were helpfully playing their part.

Around the Ides of Maius, he had directed Titus Labienus against the rebellious Treveri at a key crossing of the Rhenus and a potential renewal of the Belgic hostilities that needed controlling. Meanwhile, he had allocated Crassus new duties and sent him and a strengthened VIIth Legion as a reward for his handling of the Veneti provocation. This would secure the coastal flank and prevent any support for the Veneti amongst the Aquitani tribes. Finally, Quintus Sabinus was deployed with three legions to deal with the other Armorican tribes and Viridovix and the Venelli, in particular, who had made a pact to support the Veneti. Decimus Brutus had also reported that the fleet was ready for deployment when the Pro-Consul was ready. Caesar would lead the infantry in the land-based assault on the Veneti and, in doing so, hoped to capture the Venetic navy largely intact.

In late Maius, they had advanced, meeting only token resistance, but he knew from all the reconnaissance that, to be victorious, he had to defeat the Veneti in their coastal stronghold and capture or destroy their navy. If his deployments worked by summer's end, he would have a firm grip on the coastline facing Britannia, ready for his intended crossing, which he had decided would be in the next campaigning year.

Stern-faced and maintaining his stature in front of the men, his mind wandered back to Julianus whilst he waited for the formalities of the parade to conclude, his.

Nobody loved women and sexual conquest more than Gaius Julius Caesar! His desire for supremacy and triumph over others featured in all parts of his life. Power, control and proving that he was better than other powerful men was what he craved – triumphing on the battlefield and in the political arena, and seducing their wives and mistresses as well gave him great satisfaction and drove him forward. Of course, he never let a pretty slave girl go by either, and courtesans and his own mistresses had featured too. Yet, despite his multiple conquests, only a handful of women had been of particular significance. In the last fifteen years or more, Servilia, clever, beautiful and so like him, had been a regular companion in the bedchamber, particularly since the death of Cornelia, his respected first wife and mother of his daughter Julia. Pompeia had come and gone since then as a second wife and now shy and retiring Calpurnia was his third official wife, but before all of that, his first real love had been Flavia.

After Julia's birth, he had felt a growing sense of purpose and built his legal reputation. He was back in Rome after the Sulla dictatorship and the threats and confiscations that had been endured and, for a couple of years, Flavia had shared this and his passion. She had been his regular mistress alongside his official marriage and partnership with Cornelia. From this sense of purpose and desire had come Julianus.

Then, cautious of the reaction of some of the powerful men he had spoken against, Caesar had felt it prudent to leave Rome again. He had gone to "study" in Rhodes but had ended up challenging and defeating the Pergamum pirates and fighting in Pontus, young, daring and determined to build a reputation.

On his return, he had found Flavia dying from an outbreak of malaria and promised to provide for Julianus. Now, twenty-three years later, the boy had grown into a young centurion, deployed with Decimus Brutus and the new Oceanus fleet. He was confident and assertive, like his father, and ready to step into the unknown in pursuit of glory and reputation.

The young man had come to him the previous evening.

'Father...'

'I have told you not to call me that away from the most private of locations. I am your commanding general, address me properly.'

'Pro-Consul, Dominus,' he lowered his voice and looked at the General with a hint of appeal. 'I have done as you have directed, served my apprenticeship, now I am ready for action and responsibility, to emulate all the deeds that you have told us about. It is in my blood!'

Caesar looked sternly back at him. He had indeed made sure that the world, the Roman world, knew about his exploits and achievements and continued to let them know – but this was an unintended consequence. Frankly, he found the boy irritating, but he had promised Flavia; and despite his ruthless and womanising nature, he retained a soft spot for that passionate early love. Even so, the young man pushed him to the limit of his tolerance.

'And so you shall, as trierarchus and centurion on your bireme. You have complete command, and it is a mark of mine and of Legatus Brutus's faith in your ability. You also have a crew of legionary rowers, not all have this. They are the elite of the navy, as you know. This is an important engagement, Julianus. We must remove or bring under our control the Veneti navy, as I am sure the Legatus has told you.'

The young man contemplated his father for a moment. He clearly had more to say.

'It is in your power to award where the senate would not. All know that Legate Crassus is only that to his men. His status is not an official one. I have earnt my chance and my men will follow me as readily as Crassus's will follow him. Did I not serve with distinction with the XIth last season against the Viromandui, when all of the officers had failed, helping you to rally the situation?'

The Pro-Consul considered his son for a moment. He had Flavia's eyes; soft, warm and appealing. He could see her now, even after all of these years; but with that distinctive nose and high forehead, he was undoubtedly and – perhaps unfortunately – also a Julii Caesare.

'Julianus, the command is set, we engage the enemy tomorrow and you need to return to your ship. Serve with distinction again here and then we will see. That is all.'

Julianus was not finished. Despite his dismissal, he looked sternly back at Caesar, and in the manner of his father, inclined his head to acknowledge the command, but then continued, 'Dominus, let me tell you one more thing. Intelligence has reached me of a secret nature.'

Caesar raised an eyebrow but said nothing.

'We know of the treasure of the Veneti, of course, the possession of the ruling elite and their priests of ancient provenance and from some mystical land, they say, across the ocean. Many in these parts talk of it, along the banks of the Liger, in the countryside. It is the talk of the men and I wonder that Crassus has not done more to acquire it for the glory of Rome.'

He let that linger for a moment while Caesar, expressionless, waited for him to continue.

'My men picked up a defector three days ago. He maintains that the treasure and the fabled great statue, the Venetia Teg, is to be removed to Britannia and that a boat comes especially for this within a contingent of support for the Veneti from that country.'

The Pro-Consul breathed in deeply and intensified the sternness of his stare. He knew this. Gyras the Massaliot had returned from Britannia to the Curiosolitae port and been escorted to Caesar by Marcus Trebius Gallus, stationed in his secret posting with the Curiosolitae tribe. The Massaliot, it seemed, had faced no little tribulation during his reconnaissance. He had spoken to him and received a detailed debriefing eight days back. Already he and Gallus, transferred from Crassus's command and attached now to the Pro-Consul's small special-forces unit, had begun to prepare a plan to capture the treasure and the boat from Britannia; a secret mission, with the support of the Curiosolitae chieftain, or King, as he called himself.

Now the General spoke. 'Who else knows this?'

'The informant was brought to me and I alone interrogated him. I have told no one. Pro-Consul, Dominus, give me responsibility for identifying this ship and ensuring that it does not escape. I will play my proper part and support my Legate in battle, but give me responsibility for securing this ship and its contents for Rome!'

The general considered the young man, the beginning of an idea was in his mind that might serve several purposes.

'I will consider this, go and brief your Legate, allow him to come and brief me as is the proper chain of command and then come back to me two nights hence.'

***

Sira Howl poked his head above the watery horizon of the Mor Pretani. The wind was favourable and the oars stowed as Prince Artur's boat, thirty-five men in all, pulled out of Ictis

Sound. All around them the Veneti flotilla of twenty boats sailed confidently forward. They were larger and taller and each held sixty men. In the midst of the Sound, he saw the twin harbours of Ictis diminishing quickly as they gathered speed and the distinctive curve of Marghros in the distance, and upon it Dynas Kazak, the house of the High Priestess. No flickering beacon this morning. The Priestesswas not at home.

Artur stood in the stern and looked to the hill. Maedoc guided the ship forward and above them, a new pennant of the great bear with sun rising fluttered in the breeze. Artur thought of her kiss. Where was she now? Doing something supportive somewhere, he was sure.

'Pryns Artur,' Maedoc touched his arm and he turned. The coxswain pointed away to the right. 'The light shines in the sanctum on Penn an Hordh.'

Artur looked towards the headland and the flickering light. Skilfully, Maedoc steered the boat so that it was the furthest right in the flotilla and there, standing in front of the main house, the acolytes and attendants were waving banners. On the wind, the sound of a song floated across the water and the men began to cheer on the Veneti boats – and there she was, astride the unmistakable Steren Uskis. All of the other faces seemed blurred and indistinct, but Morlain's he saw clearly, smiling broadly, and then they were round the headland and sailing forward. Artur looked back to where she had been and where the morning sunlight created a glow around the receding headland.

'Pryns Artur, Lord Drustan.' Maedoc called to them both and they walked over to listen to him. 'I was with the Veneti captains at first light this morning. We will sail to the mouth of the Foye, and then swing toward the tip of Armorica and follow the coast at a safe distance around to Gwened.'

Drustan smiled wistfully. 'Cousin, let us both view the Foye. I hope we will come back again in better days.'

They walked to the right-hand side of the boat. Others stood there also and collectively they watched the coastline go by. After a while, the mouth of the Foye approached. They saw a number of small boats before two larger sails appeared and headed to the flotilla. Drustan looked keenly, as if he wanted to be certain before he said anything.

'It is my brother, Lord Hedrek! I am sure of it.'

One of the boats moved ahead of the other. As it drew closer, it swung around and drew alongside the Prince's boat. A distinctive looking man stood out from the others, wearing a cloak of blue and gold. Swarthy and weather-beaten in appearance, he stood gripping the gunnel and the yardarm stay.

'Brother! Pryns Artur, I assume. Greetings from my father Idrus, Lord of Dynasdore! We come to join your fight, if you will have us. Eighty of us here, across two boats, and the best men of the Foye. For the Dewnan and for our Veneti friends, we stand with you!'

More cheering broke out across the boat and rippled across the Veneti flotilla. Prince Artur leant forward, gripping the stay of the yardarm. 'Lord Hedrek, you bring us strengthened hope for our journey and the battle ahead. You are very welcome!'

The new arrivals fell in line with the rest of the flotilla, while the lead Veneti boat, with Aodren visible in the stern, swung away to the left. It went away from the coast and away from the home of the Dewnan, across the Mor Pretani and to the fight to come.

***

αt the end of all days

King Mael dejectedly surveyed the table and makeshift hall around him. The fire burnt low and the last of the wood was gone. The stormy summer had kept the Ocean-inexperienced Roman fleet in harbour; but Caesar held virtually all of the land and the Veneti position was increasingly desperate. Two moons ago, before midsummer, the land-based Roman legions had deployed. The tribe had retreated to the coast, but Caesar had stormed several of the coastal towns. On each occasion, the Veneti fleet had come in as danger approached, rescued the inhabitants and taken off all of the important goods. In this, the stormy weather had served the fleet well. They were used to it, knew how to handle it and met no opposition, while the bulk of the Roman fleet cowered in port and Borrum, spirit of the wind, was with them. Some of the Roman galleys had tried approaching the towns but run aground in the shallow water and then the defenders had made them pay for it. Gradually though, over the summer, many of the people had drifted away into the countryside and away from the Roman army and immediate danger. Slowly, the legion had closed in and then, seven days ago, he, Rozen, and their council had decided to abandon Gwened. Again, the navy served them well, but the sheer numbers and overwhelming force of the Roman legions had finally breached the walls and stockades. The boats had taken them all off as the legionaries and Roman auxiliaries swarmed through. *How long could they keep running?*

Now, here they were on a piece of land at the entrance to the small gulf that lay before Gwened. It was almost an inland lake of salt water that was full of islands and, according to the priests and priestesses, there was an ancient land half-sunk beneath the water. Beyond here were other islands, refuges to sail to perhaps, but this was where Ocean proper began. This last stronghold was not a promontory town or sanctum, as such, it was larger than that, but still surrounded by water and inlets, several of which harboured the ships of the Veneti navy. A narrow piece of land joined it to the mainland, spanned by a battlement, and before it, Perig and his men mounted a last-ditch defence against the vanguard of the Roman force in the darkness.

The fleet, led by the lords and their sons, remained loyal and there was still hope while it sailed, even if the Romans controlled the land; but their position was precarious. A decision was imminent, this small piece of land would not hold for long. Where would they go then? It seemed that few in Gaul and Celtica supported them and those that did succumbed to Caesar's legions. Pryns Artur suggested that they take the navy, sail to the land of the Dewnan and regroup, and Lord Aodren had been supportive. They would abandon the ancient land of Venetia, maybe forever. Some had even talked of abandoning it all and sailing towards the declining Sira Howl in search of Venetia's homeland and far from the reach of any Roman legion.

Queen Rozenn sat beside the King, then Prince Artur, others of his Company, and the captains of his three ships. Three moons had passed since their arrival and Mawgan, he mused, had indeed been cautious in his contribution to the fight. At least his son and companions had fought bravely as they had sought to hold their position. To the King's left were Veneti lords and other members of his household. Lord Aodren and his son Ewan had been here, but they had now gone to join their respective ships. The defining battle was coming.

While the King considered their position, the Queen spoke quietly and resolutely to the Prince.

'Pryns Artur, your ships are prepared, ready to leave? It is imperative that you get away before the final onslaught. It comes quickly now and no doubt there have been defectors, informers; the Romans may know of our plan by now and it is only their caution in the heavy seas that holds them back. Nothing motivates them like gold and plunder, I understand, and the weather has changed. Their confidence will be building. It will not pay to linger.'

'My Lady, all is loaded and spread across the boats, and all three are at secure anchor. Lords Drustan and Hedrek will oversee two boats of the Foye, while my coxswain Maedoc and I will oversee the third.'

'Your coxswain seems a most able man.'

'He is. If anyone can guide us back across the Mor Pretani, he can.'

The Queen looked on his face with soft, motherly eyes. Sira Howl had felt unable to raise her sons to adulthood and so Mael stood as King and Perig as heir, at least for a little while longer. This young man, however, reminded the Queen of her husband when she had first known him. He had so much yet to give; but then, so many had already given and many more would before this was all over. He and his Company lingered for the fight, to stand in solidarity with them but they had to get away and take the inheritance. If the light was going out in the land of Venetia, they had to rekindle it in a new place and continue the fight!

Her eyes hardened a little and she turned and gestured to a man on the far side of the hall. He had clearly been waiting for a signal.

'Pryns Artur, this is Bran. He is a pilot and a guide for boats that sail under our protection along the shores of Armorica. He is one of our best and knows the coast intimately. You need to go now with great speed to your homeland. Some may chase and others may try to intercept you, enemies of the Veneti. Maedoc will know how to get the best from your ships, but occasionally, it may also pay to a have a good understanding of the coast. Bran will come with you and assist you in this.'

'Queen Rozenn, thank you, we will be glad to have Bran with us.'

Maedoc stood and took Bran to the far side of the hall. After a pause, Artur said, 'Queen Rozenn, my Company has formed a strong bond with the brave Veneti people. We do not want to leave ahead of the decisive battle.'

'No, I am sure, and all of your courage and the support you have given for our fight has been of great service to the Veneti. We shall not forget you, but leave you must. Is your Company all present? Artur, the fight must go on; however, it ends here. It is vital you get away.'

'The boats are ready, but we await the return of Lancelin, Tinos, Ryol, Silyen and their gilles. They volunteered to fight with Lord Perig on the outer defences, some days back. We have sent word and will not leave without them – good men all of them and, as Maedoc has made clear, our boat must have its full complement if we are to make good our departure.'

The Queen stared deeply into his eyes for a moment before saying reluctantly, 'Very well, but I hope that they come quickly.' She rose and turned to him. 'Pryns Artur, will you excuse me now? I must attend to some other matters, outside of the hall. I will see you again before you leave.'

The Prince, quick to his feet, bowed before her. 'I look forward to that.'

***

The Pro-Consul had established his new position atop a high point that the Veneti called Penharth. It afforded both a fine view of the sweep of the great outer bay and also the small promontory opposite. The Veneti senate held out on it, surely increasingly desperate and ready for the taking, now that the weather had turned and Brutus and his men were ready. A short way beyond the promontory was the Veneti fleet. Since the start of Junius, he had taken command of all of the land action, but whenever a decisive victory seemed to be close, the Veneti navy, expert at sailing in shallow waters, had come in and rescued the leaders of this rebellious tribe. Meanwhile, the weather had been very poor and the fleet, ready at least six weeks back, had been stuck in harbour. Well, now the weather had changed and the constant manoeuvring had brought the Veneti senate to this narrow strip of land. The advantage was his, if they could just finally deal with their fleet.

The centurion of the guard pulled back the flap of the small tent that served as the field command centre. 'Dominus, a messenger is here from Legatus Brutus.'

'Very good, send him in.'

The messenger ducked beneath the tent flap and strode confidently in, as he knew the Pro-Consul would expect. A bit dishevelled from his journey over sea and land, he nevertheless stood tall and delivered his message.

'Dominus, I bring the compliments of Legatus Legionis Brutus. The fleet is ready and holds its position offshore, five mille along the coast. I come for your final command. We stand ready to serve you!'

Caesar breathed in deeply. The defining moment had come. He knew it.

'Come with me.'

He walked out of the tent and stood on the headland, looking across to the Veneti position.

'Do you see over there, the promontory? There is still a little glow from their fires. On the far side, my informants tell me that there is a narrow inlet where their fleet waits. Tell the Legatus I want the promontory surrounded by water, so send in the smaller boats to the inlet. We will take responsibility for the land. This time, no one must escape. Do you understand?'

His eyes and voice had a hint of menace that the messenger understood only too well.

'Yes, Pro-Consul. I will depart immediately.'

'Good, do not delay. Return my compliments to the Legatus. He must proceed immediately; and tell him, if the Venetic Navy comes out, the Legatus is to engage it and take it or destroy it and all who sail in it. I shall watch from this vantage point here and I shall see everything. I am looking forward to our final victory. Be on your way.'

***

The night was nearly over and the half-light of dawn spread across the land as Artur peered into the gloom.

'Where are they? We serve no one by delaying.'

'Kea, we cannot go without them; you know we need all the strength that we can gather to pull that boat.'

Drustan looked grimly out from the stockade. The battlement stretched across the narrowest part of the promontory. It was an earthen, stone bank and stockade fence with a narrow walkway on the inside that enabled sentries to watch the land and to mount a defence.

'Cousin, we know that, but it still rankles many of us that we wait again for Lancelin to pursue his own agenda before we can act.'

'Drustan, we also know that when the fighting is most intense, whether we like it or not, Lancelin adds significantly to our capability; but let me tell you this also, if only he were out there, we would be on our way by now.'

'What is that?' Kea had continued to peer into the half-light. 'Someone is running. There is another, no, hang on, oh no, they are all coming!'

The advanced defence force was in full and frantic retreat. As the first men approached the battlement, many more appeared out of the gloom and the noise and the panic in their voices grew in intensity.

'Open the gate!' somebody called along the battlement.

'Where are they?' Drustan shouted. 'I cannot see them. Have we waited for nothing as the enemy closes in?'

Then, a little way forward of the retreating mass, a fighting group was coming backward towards them, holding the advancing force at bay, out of sight, at least for the moment. Lord Perig was there and close to him the very recognisable forms of Lancelin and Silyen, and then on one side of the rearguard, Tinos and Ryol, perhaps.

'Should we go to them?' Kea shouted above the din of the retreat.

'No, we stand firm here.' Artur was grim but determined. 'You said it yourself only moments ago: if we go out, then we are certainly doomed. Let us trust in their ability and wait...'

The Roman force began to appear and all three stared in disbelief. Drustan put into words what they were all thinking at that moment.

'I have heard it, but I am not sure that I ever believed it. There has not been that many before, or have we always left before their full force came up?'

'Drustan, I do not know, but now we must go. Direct your gille to take word to Hedrek and Maedoc, prepare the boats. Kea, direct your man to gather all the Company that is still on land. Be ready to leave as soon as I give the word. Come on, there is still a way out of this!'

Across the promontory, less than half a mille in Roman terms, the combined infantry legions had spread out as directed. They were four men deep in the first line and there were four further lines behind them, cutting off any land-based chance of escape. Slowly and determinedly, the front lines advanced, shields locked together. Force of numbers and meticulous organisation would carry the day. The infantry moved steadily and relentlessly forward, despite the irritation posed by the remaining Veneti defenders, and irritation was all they were to the Romans, who acted like a great beast swatting the bite of an insect. Inside the compound, the hopelessness of their position was clear and panic and terror had quickly taken hold.

Drustan went with his gille while Artur and Kea watched in increasing despair. Slowly, the rearguard came towards them and then, unexpectedly, everything stopped. The Roman front line prodded back, responding to the lunge and parry of the Veneti and Dewnan, and closed shields completely. Behind them, the three subsequent rows of the front line raised their shields above their heads and then closed them tightly. Isolated clanks of metal on metal interrupted the silence as Lancelin and several of the Veneti ran forward and struck their swords against the closed shield wall. It had no effect. Lord Perig, Silyen and most of the Veneti and Tinos and Ryol's gilles were heading for the gate. However, Lancelin, Tinos, Ryol and several of the Veneti, still faced the Roman mass as they retreated backwards, hurling abuse.

Kea muttered angrily under his breath. 'He should just come back. He has made his point. We need him, but no, it is all about him. I'm not going out there to get him if they charge, that's for certain.'

As he spoke, a building crescendo of noise broke the forward silence. The noise of the legionaries banging on the inside of their shields, getting louder and faster, reverberated around the promontory; a death knell that defied the levity and promise of a late summer's morning, coursing through earth and stone, threatening, menacing, terrifying. They were here to capture, kill or worse and no defence offered would withstand them when they were ready to act.

Lancelin, inexplicably, ran towards them again, shouting. Tinos and Ryol followed, but then a loud, harrumph! The shield wall and covered front line moved forward quickly toward the men of the Valley.

'What is he doing?' Kea was beside himself. 'Come back you idiots!'

'Lancelin, Tinos, Ryol, come on!' Artur shouted.

Lancelin, it seemed, also felt he had taken a step too far and abruptly stopped, turned, and ran back toward the battlements. His sudden change of mind, however, caught Tinos and Ryol by surprise and as they turned to follow, both slipped in the mud churned by the retreating bulk of the Veneti force.

'Harrumph!' The front line moved again to within paces of the Dewnans as they scrambled to their feet. Now they were up and alongside Lancelin who had stopped to wait for them. All three ran, but as they did, a company of pilum throwers standing behind the advancing legionary line took their mark and launched their deadly cascade.

'Run!'

Artur and Kea were both shouting now. Lord Perig was now at the gate and had run through with most of the Veneti, Silyen and the gilles quickly following.

Tinos stopped and turned, was about to shout something, but then, instinctively, looked up at the sound of the gentle rush of wind that accompanied the spear's deadly descent. It went straight into his open mouth and split his skull in two. He was dead and pinned to the ground in an instant.

Now, another line of legionaries ran forward several more paces and released another volley, reaching their majestic apex before dropping like daggers from the sky.

Artur and Kea watched in horror as the spears came down towards Lancelin and Ryol. Then, at the last moment, for a reason they would never know, Ryol ran behind Lancelin. The spear that would have been his struck harmlessly into the ground, while Lancelin's entered Ryol's back above his shoulder blade. Lancelin stopped, turned and went back but it was too late, the piercing sharpness of the spear had penetrated body and heart. Ryol was quite dead. Lancelin turned again and ran, less urgently, for the gate. Once through, they shut it behind him, in the vain hope that it would keep the legions out.

'You're a bloody fool!'

Kea could not help himself. Lancelin sat panting and dejected on the edge of Lord Perig's contingent.

Silyen was quickly up and in front of him.

'Lancelin fought very bravely. We have been on the run for most of the night. They broke through just after the peak of the moon. We had no chance, but kept them at bay for a short while to get all our people back. Lancelin was instrumental in that.'

Perig looked up, older than the rest, weary and worn by the retreat. 'It is true; Lancelin has fought bravely.'

'Hmm, and yet we lose two men, good men, through unnecessary bravado.'

Lancelin looked up as he breathed heavily, with a barely disguised sneer. 'Well, man of tin, at least they died fighting. None of us gets out of this alive, you know. I would rather go down with bravado than be killed standing and watching.'

'Right, stand up!' Kea was incensed.

'Kea, leave it now, it serves no purpose.' Artur spoke resignedly, 'Lancelin, we have a task to deliver and we need to stand together. If we work for each other, maybe we have a chance.'

Lancelin was on his feet. In the heat of the moment, his veneer of support failed and contempt filled his eyes. 'I don't care about the task! We are finished, can you not see that? Let us fight as the warriors we should be; give these Romans a real scuffle before they overwhelm us.' He then partially recovered himself and said, 'Come on, Artur, the Company is breaking up, good men lost and we lack direction. Let's you and I take on the foe together for one last fight.'

No one spoke around them and all looked to Artur. He looked emotionlessly at Lancelin.

'I am done with you. Fight your fight if you must, if it is what you want. All who stand with me have a task to deliver that is essential for the Veneti, the Dewnan and all that comes after this day, and I shall not give in until there is no hope left – and there is still hope.'

'*Well said! Who said anything about giving in? Be resolute and brave. Look for the opportunity! Maedoc will know.*'

He had not expected to hear her here, no matter what she had said.

From the gate of the inner compound, Gawen shouted, 'Artur, Kea, you must come!'

Artur took one further look at Lancelin and then nodded to Kea and they both turned and ran towards Gawen. Silyen looked towards the man of the valley, shook his head, got to his feet and he, his gille and Tinos and Ryol's gilles ran after the Prince.

Gawen ran into the inner compound as Artur, Kea and Silyen approached. They followed him to the seaward battlement. Here, there was a full view of the sweep of the great bay and across to the headland of Penharth. From there, and coming towards them at great speed, spreading out across the sea with the clear intention of surrounding them, was the Roman fleet, rapidly closing in on the promontory.

Gourgy with Nouran had walked up behind them as they stood and stared. 'Got ar work cut out to get off, tha's for certain.'

'All those oars and sails, how can we outrun them?' Gawen spoke what the others were thinking.

'I don't know, but we must try.' Artur looked around him. 'Are the others gone to the boats?'

'Yes, Drustan and Hedrek led them down earlier. Only the men of the valley are missing.'

'Tinos and Ryol are dead and Lancelin will make his own way, if he wishes.'

As the Prince looked back toward the Roman fleet, there was an exchange of glances around the group. Then he spoke again.

'Those ships come too fast. We will not get out unless they are distracted. Where is the Veneti fleet? Silyen, with your gille, go quickly to the boats. Tell them to conceal themselves. Let us hope the Romans only intend to cut off the inlet and not enter it.'

All around was chaos and then the doors of the hall at the centre of the inner compound swung open and the King and Queen strode confidently out. Erwan, Jodoc, Judikael and Perig, returned from the outer compound, flanked them a few paces behind. A servant stepped forward and blew a horn. The shouting stopped and gradually all those within the inner and most from the outer compound, save those on the battlements watching the Roman force, gathered to listen. King Mael stepped forward.

'Friends and proud Veneti, we are the heirs of Venetia! Ours has been a long and celebrated story. We stand here today as the proud inheritors of all that has gone before. No one, no Roman or any other aggressor, can ever take that away from us – and we are not finished yet! Soon the fleet will enter the bay. Let us see then how able these Romans are in engaging the Ocean People. Stand firm, Lord Erwan will lead the defence of the outer compound, and I with the Lord Perig, who has already led our defence with distinction, will command the inner compound. All not engaged in the defence should move to the inner compound. Listen for the sound of the horn and for further instruction, and be ready to evacuate when we have taken command of the bay.'

Nobody cheered; instead, faces of grim resignation looked back at the King. They now all dispersed in a more orderly way as both Erwan and Perig began to organise those around them, men and women. Others, the older women, young children and the oldest men, went back towards the seaward battlement to look for the arrival of the Veneti fleet.

***

'Dominus, the latest report. The legions are in place before the insurgent's barricade and signallers are positioned around the bay. We are ready to act on your instruction.'

Since before first light, Caesar had stood on the vantage point atop Penharth. The lanterns of the advancing legions had progressed slowly around the bay. Eventually, they had reached a point on the promontory, across the water directly opposite to where he stood. Then, with the first light of morning, the fleet had come up under oars and passed him into the bay. At its head, the ship of Decimus Brutus saluted him and many that followed did the same. Now, he watched as they closed in, in an arrowhead formation, towards the last stand of the Veneti nation.

Carried on the breeze, a cheer of many voices could be heard coming from the direction of the promontory, and then a sail was seen, the first of the Veneti fleet. Sailing closer to the shore than any of his captains would dare, the lead ships sailed around the promontory, forming a protective cordon, but also around, on its shoreside flank, the oncoming Roman fleet. Others detached from the main group and made to do the same, but on the seaward flank.

He had known, of course, that they would respond, but he watched with some trepidation as the Veneti ships swung in from the shore and engaged at close quarter. Stoutly built, and taller than the galleys, they had no fear of close, side on engagement, scattering and snapping oars with the strength of the ship's structure. From their elevated position, the Veneti crews, unhindered by rowing, hurled missiles down on the surrounded fleet. The galleys on the outer flanks were now taking a pounding, several were burning and all forward movement had been lost. Then came signals from Brutus: withdraw and regroup. Thankfully, the galleys at least had the edge in manoeuvrability and speed over the Veneti ships, helped by the experience of the oarsmen brought from the Province. He watched as the rear galley became the lead and the fleet began to pull back out towards the open sea. He breathed in deeply. It had not been a good first encounter. Sternly, he looked toward the galleys. They knew he was watching them. They would do better next time.

'Centurion.'

'Dominus.'

'Send word to Primus Pilus Avilius. He must ensure that no one gets off that promontory and I want the Senate, and as many of the others as possible, to be captured alive.'

'Yes, Dominus.'

***

Some cheered and others watched intently as the Roman fleet withdrew.

Gawen, his great bow strapped across his back, and his lithe, long body twitching with an intensity of feeling, said to Artur. 'They will come back. We need to go. Our best chance of escape is while the fleets distract each other with their engagement.'

'Yes, Gawen, go to the boats. We will follow very soon. Tell them to be cautious about revealing themselves, but be ready to go as soon as we arrive. Maedoc, Drustan and Hedrek will be ready, I am sure.'

Artur looked to Kea and then along the sea battlement.

'Gourgy, Nouran, come on; the boats are waiting. Let's go.'

Shouts and the sound of metal on metal came from the outer compound. As they passed the hall, the Queen stood in the doorway, looking to the gate of the inner compound, belt and sword strapped to her waist. She looked at all of them quickly.

'Safe journey, brave friends. Your battle is crucial to us all. Go and I hope that one day we will meet again. Farewell.'

She turned and walked back into the hall. On they ran, along the barricade of the inner compound. To get to the anchorage of the boats, they had to cross the edge of the outer compound and so, cautiously, they looked around the end of the inner barricade. Roman soldiers had entered the outer gate, spread across the outer compound and now fighting raged around the inner gate. Lord Ewan and his men stuck doggedly to their task in the face of daunting numbers. Shouts and screams came from the inner battlements, around the gate, and women and men called down damnation on the slowly advancing Roman forces, hurling any missiles they could find at them.

Artur turned to the other three. 'I think we just have to run for it. They all seem focused on the gate.'

From the barricade, they ran and, seemed to be getting away at first. Then up ahead, at the start of the path down to the boats, they found Roman soldiers and a fight already in progress.

'No use – got er take em on!'

Gourgy was at the forefront now, but all of them recognised there was no avoiding it.

Taking the Romans by surprise, they surged into them, removing the first four with ease, slashes to the neck and straight thrusts into the sides of their ribcages. Below, on the path to the boats, Artur caught site of Drustan, Silyen and Gawen and their gilles. He swung again as two legionaries came at him, parried one and struck hard through the abdomen of the next. Gourgy and Nouran were men possessed and took out three more, while Kea dealt with all that he parried. The shouts from behind were getting louder; they had to get through to Drustan and the others before they were overwhelmed from behind.

Kea pierced the gut of another Roman soldier and slowly they worked their way down the path. Then, another warrior, who came from nowhere, his approach unseen, barged into the remaining Romans, cutting and slashing. It was Lancelin, his hair tangled and face covered with mud and blood.

'I told you, one more fight together!'

'Not one more,' Artur said, breathing heavily from his exertion. 'We can still get out of this, you and me together.'

He turned and gave a thin smile to the man of the valley before turning back and parrying a further thrust.

Lancelin returned a brittle smile and swung strongly at two advancing Romans. 'You haven't seen what's coming down the compound. These aren't much good.'

He swung again and Artur parried a further lunge from the dwindling numbers of Romans,

'But those are.'

He gestured towards the main gate before swinging, parrying again and catching his breath.

'If there were twice as many of them, we could take them, but they are more by tenfold, at least – and then there's the fleet. We have no chance.'

He moved to one side, swung up the arm of the Roman he fought, and swiftly planted his sword in his midriff.

There were only two Romans left who both backed away and ran up the path towards the compound. At the top, they stopped and turned to look down to the Dewnans and then more legionaries began to appear. With no word from the small party sent previously, the cohort's Pilus Prior had sent a full centuria to ensure that this side of the outer compound was secure.

The Prince turned to all who stood around him. 'This is what we will do. Drustan, go to the boats. You and Hedrek depart and agree with Maedoc where we will meet, beyond the long peninsula on the far side of the bay. Tell him to make ready to depart the moment that we arrive. We will follow shortly.'

'There are too many, cousin, you will not hold them. This is reckless.'

'Drustan, go! You need to ensure that you and Hedrek are clear of the jetty and out into the inlet, pulling towards Ocean when we depart.'

Drustan held his cousin's stare before slowly beginning to nod his head. 'Very well, but do not linger any longer than you need to.'

'We won't, and Drustan, one more thing, and please be clear with Maedoc on this. If the first person he sees coming down the path, once you have departed, is a Roman soldier, he must depart immediately, even with a depleted compliment, and he must have no further thought for any of us on this path until he has rounded the peninsula.'

Artur looked back up the path. A more dominant voice rose above the others. Some form of leader had arrived and was giving instructions. He looked down straight into Artur's eyes and then led the legionaries towards them. Drustan and his gille were already on their way. Artur turned to the others, Kea, Silyen, Nouran, Gawen, Gourgy and their gilles.

'Where is Lancelin?'

None of them seemed to notice him disappear, too engrossed in the conversation with Drustan perhaps. Momentary exasperation passed across the Prince's face, but then the pounding of feet coming down the path grew louder.

'We can be as wide as the path and we have to hold them up. That is all. They will not pass until the first two boats launch. Alright!'

All nodded their heads, stern-faced and determined. They liked a good fight, but all knew the challenge that was about to engulf them and steeled themselves for the impact of the revenge-driven legionaries that approached them.

Gourgy spoke next, hurriedly and with unusual tension in his voice. 'I reckon six of uz can old this path, least ways for long enough. Send the gilles as well, Pryns Artur, I zay. Elp get the boat ready for a flyin' departure when we come runin'. Man the oars, yer know. Otherwise, these vermin'll be on top of us before we're gone.'

Quickly, Artur looked to the others, who all nodded back.

'Yes, do it.'

The gilles hesitated and then, to a collective shout of 'Go!' turned and ran down to the boats.

Around the corner of the path came the centuria. The centurion and tesserarius led the way at a fast walking pace, but stopped as soon as they came around the corner. The impression they had got from above was that there were more rebels than this, but only six men stood before them, blocking their way. None wore a helmet, some carried gladius and scutum, others just a gladius. There was no other armour and all were dressed in their woollen trousers, tunic and leather boots. What was most noticeable was their long tangled hair and the variety of beards and moustaches. One of them, with no beard or moustache, looked no more than a boy. As they stood and looked at each other, one of the six said something.

'Unless weez goin' to fight, we might as well turn tail an run fer it. Or iz we to have a starin' competition to 'old these Romins up?'

Several of the company smirked at Nouran and it took a little of their nerves away. The Centurion, uncertain about what had amused them, slowly raised his sword and then, to his surprise, the boy initiated the fighting.

'Come on, we don't have all day; are you going to fight or not!'

The Dewnans charged fearlessly into the narrow front of the centuria column. Artur went straight for the centurion, while Kea charged at the tesserarius. Taken slightly unawares, the legionaries quickly recovered and responded strongly. The Prince took a knock to his shoulder and Silyen a glancing blow to his left leg. He staggered backwards, while Gourgy fighting next to him raged into the legionary who had delivered the strike. They fought on, but the path was almost too crowded. Although it was clear behind the Dewnans, the press of men behind the lead Romans made it difficult for full combat. The centurion continued to engage with Artur, but once it became clear that none of the defenders understood Latin, he shouted a message to his optio at the rear of the column.

'Take some men back and find a way across the rocks. We need to come at them from the rear as well. It is too narrow here to overwhelm them quickly.'

The message, acknowledged, passed back along the line. The centurion responded with his scutum to another blow from the Prince's sword and as he parried the blow away, he saw coming towards them very quickly, behind the fighting six, a man screaming and bellowing. He had a very large piece of wood. It looked like an oar. Darker-skinned than the rest, and with shorter hair, he had seen this one before, up in the compound. A number of good comrades had already lost their lives to him.

'Brace yourselves!'

Artur and the rest heard Lancelin before they saw him. 'Get out of the way! Now!'

They all instinctively fell back as he charged through the middle of them with the oar, and with force and momentum, ploughed straight into the centuria, dislocating shoulders and battering helmets. Now, he lifted it up and swept the oar across the front of the column. He made to do it again and turned to them all.

'Run!' and then, with eyes of iron, 'It's now or never!'

The surprise, the shock of the unexpected, rooted them to the spot, but then they looked to the Prince. Gathering his wits and gulping, he began to push them, 'Yes, yes, go. Come on!'

The six turned and ran down the path, but Artur stood his ground as the man of the valley swept the oar again, ferociously and with every ounce of strength he could muster, across the centuria line.

'Lancelin, one more swing and then go, come on.'

The oar swung across the front line battering those that couldn't get out of the way in the narrow space, and its length meant that they could not reach him. He was a man possessed, as he had been before the gate, all over again.

'Lancelin, come on!'

He threw the oar at the legionaries, turned and followed the Prince down the path. Almost instantly, the legionaries were on their feet, stepping over those who were on the ground and after them. As Artur and Lancelin ran, the path narrowed and then widened as they descended, before turning a corner. It came out onto the jetty and there was the boat, unmoored, waiting to go. The other five were clambering aboard and Maedoc was at the stern, anxiously looking for him. Breathing heavily, Artur turned, expecting to see Lancelin, but he wasn't there. He was about to go back when there were shouts from the boat.

'Artur, no, we have to go now.' Maedoc's voice was loud and clear, no deference, just clarity on the pressing need.

The Prince breathed in deeply, shook his head and turned back, ran down the jetty and summoned just enough energy to jump on board the boat.

'Oars at the ready, heave.' The Coxswain's voice rang loud and clear. As they began to gain movement, around the corner of the path and down onto the jetty came Lancelin. As they pulled on the oars, all in the boat could see him. Some started to call.

'We have to go back.'

'Come on, Lancelin!'

'We are not going back. It will be the end of all of us.' Maedoc was unequivocal.

Artur was in the bow as Lancelin ran down the jetty.

'Come on, you can do it, get ready to jump, we will catch you.' Gourgy and Nouran were by his side.

At the lead of his men, the centurion stopped as the centuria reached the start of the jetty. He turned to his optio who had managed to find a way around on the rocks.

'Pass me a pilum.'

Lancelin was running, and as the boat's momentum built, his moment was upon him. He altered his steps and leapt in the direction of the boat. Up into the air he went and for all in the boat, in that moment, everything slowed as they watched the familiar swagger fade as he rose. Even before he had reached the top of his leap, his eyes and arms, sensing he had not done enough, reached frantically, forlornly for the side of the boat. As he reached the peak, the perfectly weighted flight of the pilum, thrown by a trained and experienced soldier of Rome, struck him straight between his shoulder blades, diverted his direction of travel, pierced out through his chest, and sent him crashing back down on onto the jetty.

'Got him! Come on, the fleet will get the rest of them, back up to the siege.' The centurion turned and urged the rest of his command back up the hill.

Briefly, the boat stalled as all looked on.

Maedoc brought them back. 'Come on, pull hard. This is only the beginning; we have a long, long way to go.'

Gradually, mechanically, they all did as he instructed.

Lancelin's eyes held Artur's as the momentum of the boat began again.

'Farewell' and 'Gwalian' he seemed to mouth. Then his eyes and his mouth moved no more.

***

Julius Caesar watched as the fleet renewed its approach to the promontory. Now, there were four lines of Roman ships with good spacing between them, sufficient to allow the Veneti ships to pass between them, which they readily did. Once again, coming in close, they hurled missiles down on the Roman galleys from their superior height.

Brutus and his captains were allowing the Veneti ships to sail alongside, and in a different way, surround them and infiltrate their formation! A protective covering of scutums shielded each ship from the worst of the missiles flung by the Veneti, but surely, the Legatus hadn't contrived a different version of the same failed manoeuvre?

Then, Caesar smiled as he recognised the plan. Of course, Brutus had mentioned the long poles. It was an idea from one of the centurions, developing their previous use to pull down land walls in sieges. They had waited until they had a full line of Veneti ships to engage on either flank and between the lines, before revealing their new weapon – *stealth and innovative thinking, the mark of a good Roman!*

The poles had sharpened hooks fixed into their ends. As they sailed by, the Roman soldiers used the poles and hooks to reach up and grab the ropes securing the yardarms of the Veneti ships, while the galleys continued to row forward strongly. Pulled taught by the opposite motion, the ropes along the Veneti line began to snap and the yardarms fell or tilted sideways. In the ships nearest to him, panic was quickly setting in. The same would be happening across the Veneti fleet and now he looked on the scene with increasing satisfaction.

Chaos and confusion built and without the ability to sail with the wind, the primary manoeuvring advantage of the Veneti fleet had been lost. Now it depended on the Roman fleet engaging the enemy and he was confident they would not fail, particularly while their commanding general watched on.

***

'Release the sail, there's a drop of wind still in the air, tie it off and we'll use the oars to give us maximum speed in the shelter of the bay. Come on lads, big effort now, pull!'

Maedoc barked instructions and tried to distract their attention from what had just happened.

He took one last look back at the jetty. The Romans did not follow and so he indicated to Marrek, the nearest rower to him, who took the steering oar, while Maedoc worked his way down the boat.

'My Lord, Artur, we remain in real and mortal danger. If we do not pull together now, with all the strength we have, we will not see our homes again. I cannot speak more plainly.'

Artur leant disconsolately on the wale of the bow as the boat pulled away from the jetty. Nouran and Gourgy, normally so ebullient and pragmatic, sat looking sombrely to the rear of the boat and Silyen, Gawen and even Kea pulled on their oars but without conviction.

Then he heard her voice in his head again.

Maedoc knows; follow his advice, his moment of great strength has come. Remember, you promised to come back to me; we have so much left to do, you and I. What has gone is in the past and you cannot alter it. Stand tall. Lead your men home!

The Prince looked to the coxswain, nodded his head and breathed in deeply. He stood, gave the disappearing jetty one last look and walked briskly to the stern, with the briefest functional smile of thanks. Maedoc followed.

The sight of the Prince beside the steering arm alongside the coxswain changed the mood of the boat. Grim, but focused, the oars began to pull with strength and they built up speed. Ahead, now well out into the bay, Artur could see Drustan and Hedrek's boats. They could all hear the clash and cry of battle, on or beyond the promontory; but no Roman galleys challenged the Dewnan boats ahead. Perhaps then, he thought without real conviction, their escape would be easier than he had anticipated. Up to the mouth, they came and the noise of the fighting significantly intensified. The rock of the promontory had shielded some of the cacophony but, despite all they had seen, nothing could have prepared them for the devastation that now emerged before them. The Veneti fleet lay in ruins. All of the ships they could see had lost their masts, while Roman soldiers swarmed over the disabled vessels. Several of the ships were ablaze.

At first, it was hard to take in. Then it was clear; there was no future here. This was the final defeat for the Veneti, a nation of great antiquity, but now at the end of all days.

They looked to the promontory, where people were running, shouting and pointing. In the midst of them all, Rozenn stood and watched them leave. She raised a cloth of many colours to the sky in a final salute and then, in the last great gasp of the diminishing wind, let it go. The cloth drifted lazily away on an uplift towards them before it descended amidst the destruction of the fleet. Artur watched it, and when he looked back, she had gone.

'Come on, pull for home! Bring as much strength as you have to bear now.'

He was about to take his seat and take up his oar when Maedoc said, 'My Lord, there is something in the water, it looks like…' He hesitated and Artur joined him at the steering oar while the rest rowed and the sail billowed despite the decreasing breeze.

Ahead, ignored now by the galleys, part of a ship bobbed above the water, capsized and sinking. A man sat on the upturned hull and he seemed to be looking towards them. As they approached, he jumped into the water and grasped and splashed rather clumsily, perhaps exhaustedly, in the water as he tried to swim to intercept them.

'Swing closer, Maedoc. Ambros, Marrek, I think I am going to need your help.'

When they were virtually upon him, Maedoc shouted, 'Oars out of the water.'

The swimmer held something. It was hard to see through the raised oars. He floundered now and would not swim for much longer.

'Ambros, Marrek, space yourselves down the boat and grab hold of him if I miss.'

At the front of the boat, Artur leant over the side. The swimmer disappeared under the water, but still held aloft with one hand what was now clearly a sword.

'Somebody hold my legs while I lean over.'

The rise of the sea brought the sword up to him. He grabbed it and then, with his other hand, grabbed the upper arm of the man in the water.

'Pull me up. I have him… we need more help.'

Ambros and Marrek held Artur's legs and others leapt up to help and to pull the man in.

It was the Sword of Menluit and many recognised it. Sat on the deck, sodden but alive, was Aodren's steward Winoc. For a moment, he coughed, spluttered and shook his head and looked down at the strong oak planking of the deck. Then, he ran his hand through his long, dripping hair, pushed it back and looked up at them, speaking slowly.

'Lost my Lord, all lost. On this day of immeasurable sorrow, my Lords Aodren and Ewan, killed, defending each other from the murderous horde and our ship was one of the first to be overwhelmed, captured and destroyed, sinking over there. All gone!'

His eyes were wide with distress and agony. He paused before speaking again, answering a question he felt might be in their mind.

'And I? Well, like a miserable coward, I hid in the bowels of the ship, as instructed – the strongest swimmer on board, despite my years. Then, when I was sure they had left, and as the ship sank around me, I scrambled out in the desperate hope, if the spirits were with me, of seeing you, as Aodren hoped to see you, to bring you the Sword of Menluit. Two boats rowed past at speed and away as I tried to gain their attention. With great effort, I clambered up on to the keel. The sword is so heavy for a non-bearer! But they were too distant now and bitterly I sat, thinking how I had stayed too long in the bowels and that my absence from my comrades and their brave last fight had been for nothing. Despair rose within me, but then, there you were.'

Suddenly, he was animated.

'We will take it home while we still have a chance; it is a sign and will keep their brave memory alive in Tamara's valley. We will find a new wielder of the sword and help assuage the guilt of an old man who should have been there, with his friends, alongside them, when they died.'

The whole boat had paused, even Maedoc, to listen to the steward.

The Prince spoke. 'Winoc, we grieve for Aodren and Ewan, and for all of our Veneti comrades. They have died bravely and as warriors fighting a monstrous enemy, but you too have been brave and determined. Because of your actions, we will fight again and we will beat them and have our revenge. I give you my word.'

Galvanised by the recovery of the ancient sword, symbol of the Dewnan and the valley, and despite all the losses, the Company pulled strongly on the oars now and distance quickly built between them and the sea battle.

Maedoc regularly looked back to check their progress, and as he did so, the last of the breeze died, as it had threatened to do all day, and a complete calm descended.

He called from the stern. 'Furl the sail. Rowing only now lads, wind's gone, but we're making good progress; tip of the peninsula approaches, round that and we're on our way.'

He looked back again sadly, realising the implication. With the wind gone, the ships had no response and now, in the distance, like insects around a rotting corpse, the Roman galleys surrounded them. The last thin thread of hope of the Veneti nation had gone. Now he faced forward, resolute, ready to guide the boat for home, concentrating and not looking back until they had rounded the headland of the peninsula.

Everyone had their heads down and were pulling hard, so neither he, nor anyone else in the boat, noticed that three of the distant galleys did not engage with the Veneti ships and, instead, pulled away from the final stages of the battle and followed in the direction of the Dewnan boats.

***

Caesar sat on his chair on the promontory, flanked by his senior commanders. In the end, once the wind had dropped, the Veneti senate had realised the futility of their struggle and surrendered themselves and their property to him. A very satisfactory conclusion and the braveness, tenacity and ingenuity of his men had once again shone through.

Before him, the members of the Veneti senate, nobility they called themselves, were being marshalled, having been marched out by the centurion of the prison guard, from the wooden building at the centre of this inner compound for an audience with Pro-Consul. In the distance, just discernible on the headland of Penharth where he had watched the sea battle unfold, a series of wooden uprights stood, with single horizontal beams, positioned three-quarters of the way up the vertical pole. He had given orders for their construction to begin as soon as they had capitulated.

At the centre of the group in front of him was a tall man with long grey-flecked hair and matching moustache; he was battered, bruised and with one deeply swollen black eye. He had torn clothing from a struggle, but defiant still, he looked grimly back at him. Next to him a woman, perhaps forty years old, tall also, with darker hair that still had streaks of grey coming through. Of course, his men had had their reward with the captured women and this one, the supposed queen, had been a particular prize, so that now she stood before him bruised and scratched and her dress torn and muddied. It was a shame he had come later; she would have been a bit of a beauty at the beginning and he probably would have indulged himself.

The centurion, happy with the line, walked forward and saluted the Pro-Consul.

Caesar stood up, acknowledged the centurion, and looked down on the motley line of prisoners and at the tall grey-haired man in the middle of the line.

'Well, your rebellion is over, have you anything left to say?'

King Mael stood tall.

'We are the Veneti, the sons and daughters of Venetia, proud descendants of the Golden Pretani who came over the Ocean, and of a heritage and line that far outstrips that of any Roman. You have laid waste to our land and destroyed our people, but you will not escape justice in the end, you are a wicked...'

Caesar was reasonably conversant in the common tongue of Celtica and Gaul, but the broad, slightly odd accent of this man made it difficult to understand what he was saying. He had heard enough.

'Silence, I do not want to hear any more. You and your senate are agitators and rebels. You have broken Roman law and the law of nations. You are the enemies of the people of Rome, criminals and, as such, you will receive a criminal's punishment. Tomorrow, at first light, you will be taken from here, and atop the hill of Penharth, suffer death by crucifixion. Let that then serve notice to all others to abide by the law of nations or feel, instead, the full force of Roman justice. Centurion, take them away.'

Few of the Veneti nobility understood what he had said, but all reckoned that their fate had been decided and knew their end was near. Tall and defiant, they walked away, staring darkly at Caesar. It had no effect. Consumed in his own importance and assured of the ascendancy of the Roman world, with one more vanquished Gaulish tribe, one more stepping stone towards his ultimate ambition, he cared nothing for their opinion. They were pawns in the game, his game, to win the biggest prize, to lead and dominate the greatest city and the greatest empire the world had ever seen.

The Centurion of the Pro-Consul's guard walked forward. 'Dominus, there are many more in the outer compound. How shall we deal with them?'

'Are the slave dealers at the gate?'

'Yes, Dominus. Of course, as always.'

'Good, sell them all.'

'All of them?'

'Yes, centurion, all of them – and I want the best prices, do you understand?'

'Yes, Dominus.'

'Let it be known throughout Gaul, once again, that death and slavery are all that awaits those who defy Gaius Julius Caesar.'

'Yes, Dominus. I will send out the proclamation riders in the morning.'

'Good and send word to Prefect Gallus with the rider that goes to the Curiosolitae. Simply say, 'The bird flies and the eagle chases'. He will know what I mean.'

For several seconds, the centurion held the Pro-Consul's gaze and then said, 'Yes, Dominus, I will organise it right away.'

Flight across the ocean

First light revealed a low, early morning mist across the water. As the day grew across the land behind them, Artur, Drustan, Maedoc and Bran, crouching behind a rock on the low summit of the headland, peered into the gloom, listening to the distant sound of oars.

Maedoc had guided the boat away from the battle, around the peninsula to the rendezvous with Drustan and Hedrek. Then the three boats rowed hard in open water through the night, following the land to the next prominent headland. The next morning, they had seen ships behind them, not close at first, but drawing nearer as the day went on. Eventually, as darkness fell again, they had reached the next headland, rounded it and turned toward Orsa, resplendent in the night sky. The ships were coming closer and Bran suggested rowing to this hiding place under the cover of darkness, whilst the ships had yet to round the headland.

'What do you think?' the Prince asked.

'Master, I think they move away,' Bran replied.

Maedoc agreed, 'Yes, I think so too. They have gone, for now at least. But who are they? Are they following us specifically?'

'Roman galleys,' said Drustan, 'what else from that direction? They follow us, I'm sure.'

Artur nodded his head and spoke directly to Bran. 'Do we wait until they have travelled a sufficient distance, even though we cannot be certain that they will not come back? Or do we move now? Strike out onto Ocean and use the mist to hide. How long will the mist last Bran, do you think?'

'Once Sira Howl shows is face, eel 'ave it cleared before he's halfway to his top, I reckon. Maybe afore.'

The Prince nodded his head and turned to the coxswain. 'Maedoc?'

'We should head for open water. The Romans are in waters they do not know, so mist or no mist, they will not want to follow out of sight of the land. Make for Enez Isel and the nine priestesses where we watered on our journey from Ictis.'

Bran looked to Artur. 'Out on Ocean serves uz well, master. Lose the Romuns, pick up a breeze an sail beyond Enez Isel – Senez, as some call it – and the sacred Gallizenae, who cures disease and changes shape inter diffent animals ter suit ther purpis, watchin' Ocean's spirits, elpin' those who wants their elp and asks fer it. The island'll shield uz from view and take ee away from Lin Manawydan, consumer of souls!'

Until now, he had been quiet and authoritative and so this sudden rush of animation was a surprise. He felt compelled to say more.

'Across the bay from ere, the land rises to Penerevant afore descendin' cruelly into the sea, jagged and pointed like a great aerouant's tail. Dhreic, I believe uze call em; great 'orrid beast, with grey an brown, ancient and 'orny weather-beaten scales. When the aerouant swings is tail, then men beware. Many have lost their lives through lack of care and respect. Tis said the spirits, Manawydan fab Llŷr and is people placed the aerouant there. Tis their creature, permanently tethered to the land, guiding the foolish and weak into their graspin' arms as they reach through the tumult of Lin Manawydan, a writhin', envelopin' pool of gurglin' water, draggin' you down, where only the most able and blessed pass through. The Gallizenae look to great Ocean and stand watch over the entrance to the spirit world, doin' battle with the mighty serpent, but they do not alays triumph and men are lost, dragged down to a miserable death!'

The three of them sat and stared at him. Drustan was the first to speak.

'Well, we'll give that a wide berth then, and I do not think we can delay with a visit to the priestesses, as useful as their blessing might be.'

'Yes, yer lordship.'

Bran returned to his plain authoritative self. 'I think it best. I'll guide ee to the far side of Enez Isel. If the mist lifts, the people of the island will see us and come to us. They'm fisher folk but also pilots an guides in these difficult waters. They'll try to elp us if they see the Romuns. They'ze renowned defenders of freedom. Tis in their blood.

The Prince jumped to his feet.

'Good, come on then; let's get back to the boats and get under way. We should be able to make good headway once we have found our way through the mist.'

***

Gyras stood miserably on the galley deck. He should have been halfway to Massalia by now. She was a bireme with a full complement of one hundred and seventy legionaries and officers on board, specialists who combined the ability to row and fight. Of those, about one hundred and twenty were doing the rowing at any one time; thirty men in two rows either side of the galley. He listened now to the rhythmic chanting and pipe playing below that helped the rowers to coordinate the gentle sweep of the oars as the galley moved forward at a cautious speed. Somewhere in this clinging mist were the two other ships of Flavius's little squadron. Gyras could hear them, but could not see them. *Surely*, he thought, *however capable they are, they should remain in sight of each other in unknown waters?*

They had left the battle with the Veneti two days ago and that, at least, was a relief. He had kept out of it, of course, but the blood, carnage and death were unbearable. He would not have called himself squeamish before he had gone to war with the Romans, but they lived up to their reputation: organised, efficient and ruthless. Make peace while you can, remained his advice.

At first, they had made good progress, gradually catching the Dewnan boats and the Nauarchus Julianus Flavius had seemed to be content, talking and joking with him. Then they had somehow lost them in the dark last night and now the mist shrouded everything.

Gyras was sure that Flavius should not style himself Nauarchus. Certainly, in the Greek world, the title implied at least ten ships in the squadron, but he was not about to challenge the volatile commander and, it seemed, nor was anybody else either. Although, he had to admit the crew and centuria seemed very ready to follow their commander, no matter how he styled himself.

As he dwelt on Flavius, his thoughts drifted back to his last audience with Caesar.

If he got out of this alive, he would never engage with the man again, he had decided that. He would remove his family from Massalia and find somewhere, anywhere, that the Pro-Consul's men would not find them, cash in his assets and lead a simple life, hidden away. He had done what had been asked, at great risk and expense to himself, and overcome a series of barriers and threats to get the intelligence through to the General, but it wasn't enough – no. Now he must do it all again and face even bigger danger, and for what? Some promised share of the spoils from this, in his view, highly risky venture. He was wary of Flavius and his men. They pursued the gold and the treasure. All on the three galleys were aware of the prize, Flavius had made sure of that, and he was sure they would end up doing something foolish before the end of this in pursuit of their aim, and that was fine, as long as he wasn't involved!

Involved, however, he unavoidably was because Caesar had sent him to be the Nauarchus's guide and Flavius, it was clear, expected much from him. It filled him with a dark foreboding.

***

Cautiously, the three boats pulled into open Ocean. Their oars cut softly into the water, while a man was placed at stern and bow, listening for the sound of oars that were not their own. The warmth of the day grew behind them, and with it, the distance they could see increased. Suddenly, there was a shout from Hedrek's boat on the left and pointing. Sira Howl broke clear of the land behind them, the mist evaporated and there, just across the water beyond Hedrek, was a Roman galley and a few lengths beyond it, another. Maedoc swung around, where was the other one? There, beyond Drustan's boat, and about six boat lengths away. They had managed, unseen in the mist, to row between the Roman galleys. Artur and Bran were up beside him.

'My Lord, I don't want to shout. Can you pass the word, 'full speed now and full effort'. Hopefully, we can get a few pulls head start.'

For a moment, the men in the galleys didn't appear to notice the new arrivals in their midst.

'Come on, Come on.' Maedoc was glaring back down the boat, quietly urging the rowers.

The boat picked up speed quickly, but there were splashes from misplaced oars in the rush to get going and now the galleys had noticed them, removing the need for stealth.

He shouted down the boat. 'Pull hard!'

They had good momentum, and looking in both directions, he could see that both Drustan and Hedrek's boats pulled well. They had to try to outrun them. Their speed was good, but the galleys had turned and were making towards them. They were big, compared to the Dewnan's version of the Veneti ships and carried more weight, but with much greater pulling power, and they began to gain on them.

'We have to give more, they have the edge on us, pull hard!'

It was all hands to the oars and only Maedoc remained standing. He was not in the habit of calling for storms, but they could do with one now. A calm, flat Ocean worked in the pursuers favour. Maedoc shouted and Bran left his oar and joined him.

'We need something to distract them, hold them back. There seems no prospect of the weather changing in our favour. What can we do, Bran?'

The Veneti pilot looked towards their direction of travel, thought for a moment, and said, 'There iz one-way. Tis difficult and not fer the faintarted, but may put things back in our favour and confound the Romuns, stop 'em even, for a while at least.'

He explained his plan to the coxswain, and then made his way to the front of the boat and to his baggage. When he returned, Artur stood listening to Maedoc while the mighty heave of the oars continued around them.

'So, we will take the Lin Manawydan and Drustan and Hedrek must take their chance with the islanders. It's desperate my Lord, but we have to try it, and with luck, we will get through and away while the Romans are delayed.'

Bran stood alongside them and steadied himself as the boat continued to race forward. 'The lords should blow this 'orn ter signal their need fer assistance and the Gallizenae. The islanders as a special way of respondin' zee, stoppin' those who refuses the toll. Don't matter who you are, they treats all as equal in that regard.'

All three Dewnan boats were coming tighter together as the galleys now began to close in. Maedoc signalled to Drustan's boat, which came in as close as it could with all of the oars still pulling hard. Bran shouted instructions across as the Prince watched on. Drustan, standing atop the wale and holding on to the backstay, stern-faced, looked back and nodded his head. Finally, on the end of a long rope, they threw the horn across and the man of Dynasdore caught it, acknowledged them again, jumped down and walked back along the boat to his coxswain.

***

'Dominus, the right-hand boat is coming around the back of the middle boat, but they all head for the rocks. We should proceed with caution. Their draught is shallower than ours. Shall we slacken the pace; allow them to stay in deeper water?'

Flavius looked forward, towards the small boats and quickly approaching cliffs, considering his options. *Why had they changed places? They had just been shouting between boats, what did it mean?* When he spoke, he didn't answer the optio's question.

'Where is the Greek? You there, Gyras, come here. Those boats and the men within them, you are certain they are the rebels? Come on, I need quick answers!'

'Of course, Nauarchus, it is them. The two men conversing a moment ago, one is the Prince and the other his cousin.'

'Hah! Prince, he is nothing but a boy. Where will the statue be, in which boat?'

'Nauarchus, I cannot tell you. I was not there when the boats were loaded.'

'Who is most likely to have it, do you think? The Princeling or one of the other boats?'

As Gyras hesitated, the powerful, rhythmic and relentless pounding of the oars drove them forward. In the open sea, half an hour would be enough to overhaul the boats ahead, but on the current course, in less than twenty minutes they would be on the rocks. Flavius needed to make a decision.

'Nauarchus, I cannot be certain. The Prince has charge of bringing it back, that I know.'

'Dominus, if I may interject.' It was the optio again. 'The other two boats are larger and seem lower in the water and there are probably fewer men on the Princeling's boat from what we have observed so far. It is perhaps then unlikely that they are carrying and pulling the heaviest weight, if we assume that is the statue? If it was me, I would put it in one of the support boats.'

Flavius looked across to the optio.

'So, you've considered this.'

'Yes, Dominus, as we have chased at close quarter.'

Flavius continued his steely glare, before turning quickly to the rest of the officers.

'Very well. Tesserarius, send word to Trierarchus Rufinus. He is to follow the Princeling's boat and must not let it get away. Trierarchus Longus and I will pursue the other two boats.'

***

Artur briefly caught the eye of Drustan as his boat reduced oar speed, slowed and came around the back of the Prince's boat.

'Good luck, cousin,' he shouted, as the practised men of the Foye worked at the oars. They resumed speed and his boat was off and away, drawing Hedrek's boat with him and veering toward Enez Isel, parallel but still at some distance from the descending rocks of Penerevant.

Maedoc steered for a gap beyond the rocky protrusions of the dhreic's tail and gave instructions.

'Ease the speed, gentle pull, enough to give us steerage and make it look as if we are still rowing. We want to draw them in, lads. Be ready to pull hard again on my word.'

The Company breathed hard as they slackened the pace of their rowing, a form of rest after the exertion of the chase this far. All looked to the coxswain and Gourgy grumbled at the front of the boat.

'Knackerin! Not sure I wouldn't rather just turn and take 'em on. See ow far that got 'em.'

Still, he pulled gently along with the rest of them, waiting for the next instruction. As they did so, all became aware of a growing rise and fall to the boat.

Holding firm to the steering oar, Maedoc looked behind him. As they had intended, two of the galleys went in pursuit of Drustan and Hedrek, but the third rapidly gained on them.

'Hold it steady lads, as slow as we can make it.'

The current, created by the narrow passage between the rocks, was slowly hauling them in. Pulling hard, Maedoc adjusted the steering oar to keep it straight.

The Prince had returned to his oar and only the pilot stood, with the coxswain gripping the wale firmly. He spoke with tension in his voice. 'Line of the distant headland, that's where we're aimin' for. That's it, nice an' straight now.'

Both of them looked back again. The galley was no more than four boat lengths behind and closing in fast. Maedoc turned back to the boat.

'Alright, oars ready and… pull hard!'

Even in their seated rowing positions, all could see the approaching galley. It focused their actions and the boat built momentum quickly.

***

'We are gaining on them, Dominus. It looks like they are tiring. We will be alongside them before they have reached the rocks,' the optio reported to Trierarchus Rufinus.

'Good, detail some men to the front with grappling hooks, we will come up behind and then alongside. We need to be firm, but take the boat in one piece before we get too close to the rocks.'

Rufinus allowed himself a moment to look away to the two galleys still racing towards the small island beyond them. He would be the first to capture one of the treasure boats. The Nauarchus, he hoped, would be pleased; although, with him, you could never be quite sure. He had already been on the receiving end of that in the past, but in this instance, he had been clear – do not lose the rebel boat. Rufinus did not intend to do that.

'Dominus, they are picking up speed again!'

A final desperate attempt to evade us, Rufinus thought. It wouldn't work, of course, the difference in manpower made certain of that; a large rowing boat, really, against a ship of Rome. The end was inevitable. His optio looked to him for his command.

'Hold our speed then, let's draw them in now. They will not be able to build sufficient speed in time, we are nearly upon them.'

The optio lent over the side of the stern to get a better view and spoke back with urgency to his commander. 'Dominus, the sea is getting more agitated ahead. We should proceed with caution, I think. There may be unseen rocks.'

Trierarchus Rufinus stood resolutely at the centre of the stern deck. 'Maintain speed, optio; we must have that boat before it is through the gap and evades us. The turbulence will affect them more than us. A final push now and we will take it.'

Several of the junior officers looked nervously to the optio as he gave the instruction, stepping across and looking anxiously over the side. Unexpectedly, the sound of running, gurgling, chortling water came rushing up towards him. The sea began to roar and what he saw next confirmed his worst fears.

'Dominus, their boat has sunk into the waves. The pull of the current turns us. More men to the rudder, we must slow down!'

***

'It's going to get a bit choppy! Hold on tight and whatever happens, keep rowing. Forward movement is everything.'

Maedoc barked out his instructions. Two powerful currents met under Penerevant, the perfect ingredients for malevolent, wicked spirits to take their toll. Into the heaving mass, they went and Ocean opened in a great chasm, tipping the boat forward. Water cascaded over the bow drenching the rear-most rowers, but they still kept driving them onwards, shaking their heads, removing the water from their hair and eyes.

'Hold tight, keep rowing! The boat will right itself and we'll come back up. The water will come out at this end.'

Maedoc held his nerve, as well as the steering oar. They just had to get through the rocks to the calmer water; if they kept going, they would be through very quickly. The boat rose at a steep angle in the water, which ran the full length of the vessel, washing around his boots and out of the deck drain holes. Spray from the white crest of the wave filled the air. The confluence of waves from different directions and currents battered and buffeted the boat until it slowed as they reached the peak of the wave. They looked out to the rocks that surrounded them and then plunged into the next deep valley.

'Keep going, three or four more of those and we're through!'

Down they went and quickly up the other side. As the boat slowed again, Maedoc looked back. The Romans had followed and he watched, gripping his own steering oar, as the galley pitched first down and then up in the air before slapping on the surface of the water, scything its way through the next wave. This unsettled the lower set of oars and probably knocked them out of their seats. They were clearly having trouble keeping it straight and this blow to their forward movement only impeded them further. The benefit of their small size was their flexibility and ease of movement, he quickly thought, as he looked forward and they plunged into the next valley of water.

Down they went and then, suddenly, he heard an agonising scraping noise along the bottom of the boat as they came through the valley and up the other side. Whatever it was, they had skimmed the top of it rather than struck it clean. Maedoc tried to look down the centre of the boat, but could not see any damage to the internal structure. Up to the top of a huge wave, they went once more. He looked back again. The galley was getting closer, the oars had righted and the ship began to rise on the wave behind them.

The Dewnan boat had reached the centre of the confluence, at the heart of Lin Manawydan, and a heaving, churning mass of water enfolded them, drawing its victims in. They pivoted on the top of the wave and sped down into the next valley. The water began to spin, sucking at them. Despite the strength of their rowing, the water held them back. Conscious their movement had slowed and that they were on the point of going backwards, the rowers frantically tried to restore their forward motion.

'Harder lads, harder, you can do it!'

Even Maedoc was concerned. The water gurgled and giggled as they pulled hard up the other side of the wave, but it just… would… not… go.

Wicked laughter filled the air.

You're ours now! Fools and drunkards are our normal fare. Who else would enter these waters? And yet you are sensible men and come to us willingly. We will not let it pass!'

The rowers were drenched and exhausted. Maedoc, stalwart and unwavering, sought to rally them once more. Wiping the spray from his mouth, he called down the boat, 'One more go lads; one more mighty effort, then we're over and we're out. Come on!'

Trying hard, excellent! It's not worth it though, you know. Give in now and let us take you.

Howls of mocking laughter filled the air and all around them seemed to stop as the forward wave crashed down upon the boat and the water cascaded around them, blurring their vision and drowning any sense of purpose. The oars swung loose, buffering and clumping in the water, while the Company slumped over them and their vessel slid backwards, into the heaving, claiming mass and gateway to oblivion.

As they reached the bottom of the valley, when all appeared to be lost, Sira Howl, climbing steadily across the land, appeared above the peak of Penerevant. The angle of His light, at the last possible moment, shone in on their peril. Then, other voices could be heard on the breeze and coursing through the water all around them, arguing and forceful, and within them, getting louder, an urgent voice that they all knew.

'They are not yours, Manawydan fab Llŷr or whatever name you go by here! Do you know who this is? Careless and impetuous spirit, it is him; yes, him and his brave and faithful gille!'

The voice built to a determined and commanding presence all around them.

'You made a promise, on my friend's life, and you will honour that promise or I will bring damnation down upon you, and you know that I can!'

Moaning and grumbling filled the air, but Maedoc was on his feet, rallying the boat. Heads began to rise, her message of hope pulsed through them, hands drew through sodden hair and gripped oars and the coxswain roared through the din of the tumult, 'Get ready. Just the right side first, that's it, straighten her up, good. Now, all together, pull!'

The boat slowed as they crested the wave and Maedoc turned to look back. The site that greeted him could not have been more shocking. The galley had struck the rock they had scraped and holed badly under the water. It was listing to one side and sinking. There were bodies in the water, while others were trying to launch several small boats. He saw no more as they went on into the next valley. When they came up the other side, the last before they reached calmer water, all that was visible was the galley's stern sticking out above the water and the remaining crew clinging desperately to the stern deck wale.

***

'Blow the horn, Ridik!' Drustan called to the prow, to the youngest member of the crew, with the least battered and most flexible, pursed lips.

The two boats approached Enez Isel side by side. Drustan looked back, while before him the crew continued to row strongly. He was a Lord of the Foye. Unlike his cousin, he was used to holding a position of authority, directing to achieve the best from sail, oars and vessel, but never to get involved with the rowing. It did not occur to him to do so now, even in this increasingly desperate situation; and they, the men of the Foye, sailors and boatmen all, did not expect him to.

The galleys were about six boat lengths back and closing. He and Hedrek had hugged the line of rocks projecting out from Penerevant for as long as they could, but now it was a straight chase and the greater Roman pulling power was telling. Something needed to happen or the galleys would overhaul them.

A muted, stuttering blast came from the horn. The boy was nervous, but this was no place for nerves.

'Blow it again. Concentrate!'

Now the horn rang out and, almost as if they had anticipated it, boats were beginning to emerge from the little harbour ahead. A small flotilla headed towards them and then behind them, two pairs of much larger rowing boats, about the same size as the Dewnan vessels with a similar number of oars, and they appeared to trail some form of line behind and between them in the water. Two of the flotilla approached the oncoming Dewnans, waving arms, calling for attention.

The first boat came as close as it could alongside, shouting as they quickly passed by.

'Row between the big boats, make sure the Romuns follow ee!'

***

The optio surveyed the approaching flotilla from the left-hand wale of the galley and then looked across to Nauarchus Flavius.

'Dominus, no doubt these small craft attempt to hold us up. How shall we deal with them?'

'Ignore them! What harm can they do? Sink anything that gets in our way. Concentrate, optio. Keep close to the rebel boats; we nearly have them and must not lose them.'

The optio looked over the wale again.

Four larger craft had come out from the island into the rear of the flotilla. They had split into two pairs and each of the rebel boats now intended to row between their selected pair in a widening gap between them. Perhaps they intended to pick up supplies or exchange men in some way. Although they would need to slow down to do that, so it seemed unlikely. *There was some purpose, but what?*

The optio turned back to the stern deck.

'Prepare the sagittarii, position them the full length of the galley and be ready to shoot at my command as we go between the two larger boats ahead.' He turned to the Nauarchus. 'Dominus, with your permission, I will signal Trierarchus Longus of our intention to do this and that he should do the same with the other rebel boat.'

***

The larger island boats approached, with sufficient width between each pair to allow the Dewnan boat and pursuing galley to pass through. Drustan looked across and could see that Hedrek's boat did the same towards the second pair of island boats. The galley pursuing Hedrek was little more than two lengths behind, while the galley pursuing his boat seemed to have increased its speed. It loomed now behind him. It was desperate.

'Come on, lads. One last big pull to get rid of these bastards.'

He touched the hilt of his sword. A boarding seemed likely now and it would be a fight to the death.

Between the island boats they went, and there was a slight bump as they did, followed by another along the bottom of the boat, and then another. Drustan stepped to the right and saw, slowly rising to the surface, fixed firmly with stout iron shackles onto iron bollards bolted to the deck at the rear of the island boat, the thickest iron chain he had ever seen. Quickly, he crossed to the left and there was the chain again, coming out from under the Dewnan boat and running to the second of the two island boats, where again it was attached equally firmly to the rear.

He looked back. The commanders of the galley would not see it, at the rear of the boat.

They were through, over the chain and past the island boats, positioned now to pull against each other, poised and ready. Their oars entered the water smoothly and the boats pulled away strongly, practised over many such instances when passers-by refused to pay their toll. The chain rose out of the sea and the approaching galley had no chance to stop or begin a reverse manoeuvre. The island boats rowed away in a 'v' shape, but then drew slightly closer together and, in doing so, ensured that the chain narrowed its 'v' shape and secured itself to the prow of the galley. The galley's oars were strong, but the strength of rowing from the two island boats served to equalise the pull in the opposite direction and the galley came to a juddering halt. The island boats could not pull it back while it continued to row, but equally, it could not move forward, and so the island boats cancelled out its pull in the opposite direction.

In a normal action, the small boat crews, heavily armed with knives and swords, would now board the avoider's boat and politely ask for the appropriate fee. The islanders knew better than to try that with two Roman galleys, but this was not about the toll. Their purpose was to hold up the Romans for as long as they could, without coming into open conflict with the Roman soldiers.

***

The galley stuttered violently and rose out of the water, its forward movement checked as the long chain became taut and the island boats rowed strongly in the opposite direction.

The stern deck was in chaos and the Nauarchus, on his knees, jolted forward with the rest as the impact of the chain had reverberated along the structure of the ship. The optio was the first back on his feet, bellowing instructions.

'Keep rowing. We need to pull those two forward! Sagittarii, fire at will! Take out any of the miserable shits that you can!'

Nauarchus Flavius got slowly to his feet. All those around him felt his bristling anger. 'Why bother with a lookout,' he roared, 'when they don't look? What is the damage? I need a report, now; and prepare the boats. We'll board those bastards and make them pay, and then we'll return to our chase of the rebels who, no doubt, are disappearing into the distance as I speak! Well, are we rowing or not!'

Red-faced and fuming, he continued to lambast those around him, before continuing, 'And what of Longus and his galley? Yes, of course, look: the same outcome for him and there they go, small and smaller specs in the distance – the boats we were about to capture and would have captured if we'd had a better lookout! Come on, sort this mess out, Optio, and present your assessment.

***

'Ha, that is amazing!'

Drustan took in the chaos behind them for a moment. 'Better not let themselves get caught,' he thought out loud.

He looked across to Hedrek's boat, also now free of its chasing galley's attention, and his older brother standing on the wale and gripping the yardarm stay, shouting something, but also urging them forward.

Drustan turned back to the crew. 'We're away! This is our chance, come on! Coxswain, I think… yes, that is Pryns Artur's boat ahead, so they have made it through too.'

He shouted down the boat again, 'One last big row across this bay; got to be some wind soon!'

'Lords Drustan and Hedrek approach, my Lord. Both seem intact and there's still no sign of the Roman galleys, perhaps sunk also.'

'Yes, for the moment we have escaped. I am sure that is not the end of it, though.'

Maedoc nodded as he held firmly to the steering oar and looked back again toward the slowly gaining boats.

'No, but at least the immediate danger has passed. We move on, helped by our friends and supporters.'

For a moment, their eyes met as he turned back. Artur allowed himself a brief smile.

'Yes, we are watched and supported here and from distant places. We are lucky.'

'We are. My intention now, with your approval, is to steer for the larger island over there. Oosha, the locals call it. We sailed in close to it on our journey out. We will round it from Oceanside and then, with continued luck, finally pick up a breeze that will carry us back to Ictis and away from any recovering galley that might be coming up behind. If Borum is with us, the breeze will see us back in the Sound of Ictis before Sira Howl descends tomorrow.'

Artur nodded his head in return now as he looked towards Drustan and Hedrek's boats. 'No more rowing would be good. The oars have saved our lives, but the Company has rowed enough, I think, for one journey.' He looked to the coxswain. 'Take us home, Maedoc.'

***

Marcus Trebius Gallus stood in the mid-afternoon on a small bluff above the beach, waiting with his centurions for the arrival of King Brice and his Senate, watching as goods and men were ferried to the largest Curiosolitae ships, anchored in the deeper water. The tribal port of Alet was alive with activity as the Curiosolitae prepared to take advantage of the fall of the Veneti. Events, it appeared, were working in their favour.

On his arrival, the Pro-Consul had despatched Quintus Titurius Sabinus and three legions to the Venelli and Curiosolitae to ensure that these tribes did not interfere in his engagement with the Veneti. Legate Crassus, however, had given a full briefing before departing for Aquitania and Caesar had then sent word of his support for Gallus. The Curiosolitae, of course, did not intend to aid the Veneti and had quietly submitted to the Roman advance, as Gallus had advised.

Sabinus, therefore, had focused his attention on the Venelli and their leader Viridovix. Emboldened by the support he had received from the Aulerci, Eburovices and Lexovii, Viridovix now claimed that he led on behalf of all of Armorica, and had put a large force into the field. By all accounts, it had been a difficult engagement, but through further subterfuge, ill-judged actions by the Gauls and the bravery and skill of the Roman force, Gallus had heard that the Legions had prevailed. In the end, through the effective use of cavalry, victory had turned in to a rout. The Venelli and their allies were utterly defeated which, no doubt, further bolstered the Curiosolitae in all of the activity Gallus saw before him.

As he watched, Gallus thought how curious it was that they took such pleasure in betraying the other Armorican tribes. They not only congratulated themselves, but were also ready to profit from the defeat of those around them. Disunity in the face of the Roman advance had been a feature of the Gallic campaign and Gallus mused how more commonality of purpose would have done much to hold back the Roman force. He knew the Pro-Consul secretly encouraged the sowing of seeds of division away from the battlefield and provoked fights to further his aim, and the Gauls were taken in too easily by this and so appeared to be the aggressors. Despite this and his own part in the deception, Gallus felt an empathy born of a distant Gallic heritage, as his name suggested, which led to a distaste for the Curiosolitae's duplicity and a sympathy for the other tribes.

Of course, he would allow none of this to undermine his orders or his mission. He was a Roman citizen, military commander of distinction and his career, at the age of thirty, progressed well for a man of his beginnings. Further success here would add strongly to his reputation and show the range of his ability.

The King's approach brought him back from his reflections.

'Honoured King, you have returned from the island and our preparations are nearly complete. Are the Curiosolitae ready to sail?'

The King, who had been in Rome in his adolescence, could speak Latin in a formal way. Gallus's fluency in the common language of the Gauls and the Maritime tribes, however, meant that he spoke in the King's tongue to ensure that there was no misunderstanding, real or contrived.

The King, with a reputation for avarice, hoarding, and manipulability for financial gain, had sailed the previous morning to Andion, a large island close to Alet, and held directly by him. Before first light, his men had loaded large amounts of coin and jewellery onto the boat. The word was that he had ordered the burial of these coins, of various denominations and source, at secret sites on the island – insurance, should their forthcoming action fail. The King assumed then that he, at least, would return, should that happen; but it wasn't going to happen. The mission would be a success.

'Praefectus Gallus. Yes, the final preparations have been made while I have been away. Your ships are prepared and await you alongside the middle jetty. My own fleet is at anchor, before you. We sail on the morning tide.'

'Very well, we will begin boarding this evening.'

His men, strengthened by the maniple of specialist legionary rowers sent to the King by Caesar, now made up two full cohorts, nine hundred men. This was enough to crew twelve adapted Curiosolitae ships, with lowered sides and two tiers of added oars on either side. An experienced trierarchus and centurion took command of each ship, who had supporting officers and an additional group of legionary marines at their disposal, able to deploy quickly to secure a landing position. With a retained mast, each ship also carried a Curiosolitae sail master and a handful of riggers, should the weather call for it. Each ship had undertaken manoeuvres in the last month, as Legate Sabinus had distracted the Venelli, and were now ready to depart. In addition to the legionaries, the Curiosolitae auxiliaries, or Cohors alaria as he had begun to term them, provided another four cohorts. Each of these was a milliaria, around eight hundred men each, with ten of the smaller, taller Curiosolitae ships per cohort and each cohort with senior tribal commanders and several Roman officers; adjutants or adiutors intended to facilitate and support the coordination between Roman and auxiliary units. This was, effectively, a full legion, along with whatever Flavius had contrived to bring with him. He would have liked more men, but if the King stuck to the plan, it would be enough. Gallus spoke to him again.

'As you know, this is a difficult mission. Capturing and holding our position through the winter while we wait for support will take concentration and determination. We will rely on your supply line and the skill of your sailors to cross the Ocean in winter. Honoured King, I have said it before, but I will say it again, the secret of Roman success is in organisation and control, so I will run through our plan again before we depart.'

The King's eyes narrowed into a hard stare. They had been through the plan on many occasions. This constant repetition was patronising. He was the King! He gave the orders, not this middle-ranking Roman officer. The Curiosolitae would control the trade to Pretannia, control the ports of entry, starting with Ictis, and the wealth of that trade would flow back to Alet and to him. That was the plan. After the destruction of the Veneti, a new power was rising, aided by this Roman force, that added legitimacy and security to his position. Soon, he anticipated, he would have increased engagement with the Pro-Consul, rather than his emissary. He had taken precautions with some of his wealth, you never could be too careful, but he had plans and a big vision and so, reluctantly, but necessarily, he nodded as the Praefectus ran through the plan, again.

'We will cross to the port called Ictis. Your men know it well. Following the Pro-Consul's victory, the men of the Veneti will not return. We understand from your men, confirmed by the reconnaissance of the Massaliot trader, that without the Veneti the defence of the port is poor. It is ready, with swift action, for a new controlling force to take over. The trade in metals is of great interest to Rome and to the Curiosolitae. The Massaliot travels with Trierarchus Flavius in pursuit of the three Ictis-based Veneti boats that managed to escape. We will rendezvous with him and his flotilla offshore and then move to secure the port and build a defendable camp. Your men, using your river craft, will secure the principal routes and then we will settle down to defend our position over the winter. When the weather allows, your ships will run supply lines and we will open discussions with the local tribe to agree the provision of additional supplies. When the season returns, we will await further instruction and direction from the Pro-Consul to support his wider plans for Rome in Britannia. Success for us all depends on coordinated action, not rash and impetuous pursuit of advantage. Is that clear?'

The King was perhaps around forty-five summers old. He was the King, so who was this younger man to give instructions to him? Over the summer, he had tired of Praefectus Gallus, but he was necessary, at least for the moment. As soon as they had successfully taken the port, and he had a much larger force of men at his disposal, he would take lead command and the Roman would do as he said. 'Yes, Praefectus, it is clear, as it was before and before that. Shall we make ready to depart?'

Gallus looked at the King. He had only told him half of the plan, of course. In the secret meeting with Caesar and the Massaliot, several months back now, they had also discussed the treasure and great statue. He knew that it had gone, in the midst of the battle on the three boats, and that Flavius was in pursuit. Caesar had been clear that his role was to be the wise military head and commander in all that was about to happen. He was to secure the port and the treasure and await further instruction; and, in the meantime, keep control of the King and the Trierarchus. This was an undercover operation away from the glare of scrutiny of Rome and the Senate, but if successful, it would be a stepping stone to Britannia for Caesar and the legions. Not a job for a visible Legate, who was regarded as questionable by the Senate, and established legion, but instead a middle-ranking officer with aspirations to rise and a small force of actual Roman soldiers, supported by a new auxiliary force cultivated for this mission by the Praefectus. Its success and the glory that came with it would all be his and, of course, the Pro-Consul's.

Caesar had heard great things of Marcus Trebius Gallus he had said and, if he were successful here, Caesar would reward him handsomely.

morlain and artur

'There! Do you see them?'

Drustan's boat had pulled alongside and he was pointing back toward Lys Ardh where there were, unmistakably, two sails beyond the distinctive headland.

Around the Ocean side of Oosha they had come and there, as Maedoc had anticipated, the wind had returned and quickly built to a strong breeze. The skill of the coxswain and the men of the Foye, with sail, wind and navigation, carried them forward. They sailed through the night and across the Mor Pretani until, that morning at first light, they reached the coast of Kernovia at the furthest extent of the Dewnan lands. The headland of Lys Ardh appeared off the left-hand wale of the boat. With growing light and the need for stealth and secrecy diminishing, Marrek had quietly sung a lament for all those they had left behind. Many knew the words and joined him in honour of brave comrades and friends, lost under the trample of the aggressor's boot. As Sira Howl appeared on the far horizon, they had raised the Prince's pennant of the great bear with rising sun as a signal of their return. It fluttered boldly in the wind as they headed for home.

Then, as Sira Howl began to climb, crossing the sweep of the bay, the breeze had diminished and their momentum slackened. The pennant flapped more languidly now and the Roman crews had narrowed the distance between them through a combination of skill and desire.

'It is them,' Drustan shouted across. 'Let's draw them to the Foye or to Ictis, get the treasure ashore and then confront them, see how they fare when the numbers are in our favour!'

The Prince jumped on the taffrail and used the arm of the steering oar to balance himself while the Company stood at both right and left wale, looking at the small sails in the distance. He turned to Maedoc.

'Drustan is right, we have to run for port and get the treasure ashore. You and I must fulfil our promise to bring the Venetia Teg to the land of the Dewnan. Then we will face them, but everything must be to our advantage. After all that we have seen, we know what we must do.'

The coxswain looked back over the taffrail.

'Perhaps they know of our treasure and act independently of Caesar and his legions and think that they can take it from us in some way, or perhaps there is something else. You are right; we must get ashore and then decide. I wonder if it might be good to separate here? We head for Ictis and Lord Drustan and Lord Hedrek head for the Foye? They deposit their portion at Dynasdore, we head up Tamara, take Venetia Teg far inland and then reconvene at Menluit, deep within Nanmeur and on our ground, if they want to fight.'

The Prince nodded and strode to the left wale and shouted the plan to Drustan.

His cousin shouted back. 'Very well, I will signal to Hedrek. We will join you at Menluit tomorrow, with all who are able to accompany us.'

Drustan and Hedrek went on, while Artur, Maedoc and the rest of the Company veered in the direction of Ictis. The coxswain called for the oars and all, including the Prince, who now pulled hard for the port. The breeze diminished further and with the stronger pulling power of the galleys, the Romans began to gain more quickly. Maedoc looked back. Neither galley had followed the Foye boats and, instead, both seemed to pursue the single boat.

'Need to keep the pace up, boys. Keep a good distance from them,' he called down the boat.

Artur withdrew his oar and jumped up to join the coxswain for the approach to Ictis.

'What is your plan, Maedoc, to go upriver where the galleys cannot follow?'

They were moving at a good speed now and the coxswain gripped the steering oar, keeping a steady line. He looked back again.

'Yes, they are gaining quickly now and we will not be able to moor, get the Venetia Teg off, and get it away before they arrive. The tide is with us and we need to disappear into the land and let them follow on foot if, of course, that is their intention.'

'I hope that those we've left behind have watched for our approach, for our return, and will support us as we arrive.'

Maedoc looked at him. 'Do not doubt it. There will have been a watch on Penn an Hordh every day since our departure. She will know of our approach, your pennant will have been reported to her, and you know that she has watched over us each day that we have been away.'

Maedoc looked back and for a moment their eyes met, but then his eyes looked beyond Artur. Surprise and urgency transformed his face. 'What is that?'

The Prince spun around. Off the right wale, distant still, but moving towards the mouth of the Sound, was a large number of ships. A quick count said forty, maybe more sails. Others of the Company were on their feet. Maedoc was authoritative.

'Keep rowing, we must make Ictis before they do.' Quickly, the crew resumed their positions and the boat built up momentum again.

'Perhaps that explains why the two galleys have followed us. They intend a rendezvous?'

Maedoc allowed himself a quick further look, before returning his concentration to the rowing and steering of the boat.

'Yes, although most of them look like Curiosolitae boats to me. They know of the demise of the Veneti and may even have been instrumental in some way. Although, I thought they too had had their fight with the Romans. Whoever they are, we need to be in Ictis first. I am sure that whatever their intention, they are not here to support us.'

***

'Nauarchus, Dominus Praefectus Gallus and the Curiosolitae fleet approach. We have had their signal and we believe we are within sight of the Ictis and our agreed rendezvous. The Greek confirms it, and that the other boats have gone to a smaller port. We will continue to pursue the rebel boat a little further, we are gaining on them quickly now, but won't reach them before the port, beyond the headland up ahead. We are prepared for your further instruction, when you are ready.'

Flavius called Gyras to stand alongside him.

'So, this time we have followed the Princeling, bound as we are to rendezvous with the Praefectus. It would be to your

benefit if you could be clearer on which boat the statue is in.'
He paused and then said, 'All of this at least, is familiar to you?'

'Nauarchus, I am familiar with the Port of Ictis. I escaped from there three months and more ago. I had not expected to return. I cannot be certain which boat the statue is in – but the Prince is their leader, surely, he is the route to finding it? Capture him and the statue and the rest of the treasure will follow.'

'Well, Massaliot, as my servant, you will follow orders until we have finished with you and that will not be until the treasure is found.' He turned to face Gyras, and with a dismissive smirk, continued, 'You are a Greek merchant from Massalia; personal gain is your only motive. No doubt you change sides at will to suit your purpose; but let me reiterate, if you wish to see your family and city again, you will work for me in the days to come and only me, until we have the treasure and rebels securely in our possession. Do we understand each other?'

Gyras stared resignedly ahead. 'Yes, Nauarchus, we do.'

'Good.'

He turned and directed an instruction towards the optio. 'Steer away towards the approaching fleet. We are to rendezvous with the Praefectus before we enter the port.'

***

Morlain sat astride Steren Uskis atop Penn an Hordh in the place where he had last seen her, three full moons ago. He stood at the wale and looked up as the boat rowed passed the headland and into the Sound.

'Welcome home, Pryns Artur. You come from great sorrow, but you are here, as I said you would be. You and everyone with you, and some who are not, have shown great bravery in your struggle to survive, in your defence against the aggressor; and it is not over yet. The forces of the enemy mass on Ocean and a great battle approaches. Bring the boat to the jetty at Cuitheyl, wise Maedoc will know. There, carts will be waiting. Move with speed, for others will follow you quickly. Come to me on the hill of the horse where we will plan our next move.'

Steren Uskis turned about, walked, trotted and then broke into a canter away from the summit of the promontory and passed quickly out of sight. For a moment, Artur lingered at the wale, looking at the place where she had been, breathing heavily, controlling his emotion, aware of the magnitude of the events unfolding around him. He turned to Maedoc.

'To Cuitheyl, head to the jetty at Cuitheyl; carts will be waiting to take the treasure and we will stay overnight at Dynas Kazak. From there, we can see Tamara and the Sound and how the enemy moves before we go on to Menluit.'

'Very well, my Lord.'

Then Maedoc looked forward again, his face contorted, as he pulled hard on the oar to steer the boat towards the entrance to the inner Sound. He did not question how the Prince knew about the carts, did not need to; he knew the priestess. Roles were changing. He had played his part as advisor to the Prince while there was distance between Artur and Morlain, but now they were back together in physical proximity, and as long as they remained so, the prophecy held true. As their loyal servant, he would return now to the role of acolyte and gille, prepared to do anything to help them fulfil their destiny. The future of the Dewnan depended on it.

***

'Trierarchus Flavius, welcome aboard.'

The younger man gave a dismissive and mildly scornful look at the Praefectus.

'Of course, you will not have heard,' he smiled superficially, 'I am advanced; my title now is Nauarchus.'

'Advanced by whom?' Gallus looked sceptically at the Trierarchus.

'By the Pro-Consul, naturally, we are very close and it is in recognition of my ability and growing achievements and successful engagements.' He concluded with a further sly and superior smile.

Gallus sighed inwardly. This was not a good start, but perhaps it did not matter what title he used as long as the plan proceeded without hindrance and Flavius and his men performed their part.

'Very well, Nauarchus Flavius, you are welcome; but you come with only two biremes.' *Not much of a flotilla for a*

Nauarchus, Gallus inwardly thought. What has happened to the third bireme that set out with you?

'Alas, Praefectus Gallus, it was lost pursuing one of the rebel boats through a treacherous stretch of water. I had advised against it, but Trierarchus Rufinus disobeyed orders and, unfortunately, he and his complement paid the ultimate price for his folly.'

'And the rebel boat?'

'Of a much shallower draught and, therefore, it did not founder on the rocks. The Pro-Consul and I have discussed the design of the boats of the Veneti and their allies at length over the summer. They confounded us on more than one occasion before we were able to bring the rebel fleet to full action and destroy it. When I have completed this mission on his behalf, I am to lead a programme to develop and take command of a full flotilla of new boats for our navy with shallower draughts, which will increase our capability of engaging the enemy in all situations.'

Gallus contemplated the younger man as he spoke. He had already decided that he did not like him. His arrogance was immediate and distasteful. Arguments with him, he anticipated, would be regular and his optimism for a smooth delivery of the plan was fading.

'That is unfortunate. We have a significant auxiliary force to support our action, but losing a full ship's complement of trained legionaries makes our task a little more difficult than it already is. We need to capture this port and hold it until we have received further instruction from the Pro-Consul. I will need all of the trained legionaries that we have to achieve that.'

'Yes, Praefectus Gallus, but you are an experienced Praefectus Castrorum, I understand, and you will know what to do, I am sure, with the men that you have at your disposal, and will hold the fort, so to speak, for Caesar. My role, given by the Pro-Consul, when we have secured our landing is to recover the fabled treasure for Rome. The loss of the boat will make my task more difficult, but the quality of my men, trained by me and by my officers for this task, will ensure that we are still able to achieve our objective, wherever that may lead us. I will speak to the King. He will be able to spare some of his substantial complement, I am sure, to help us to make up the numbers.'

Against his better judgement, Gallus began to lose his temper. This was not how the Pro-Consul had described the mission to him and it was quickly becoming clear that the 'Nauarchus' clearly did not see him, Gallus, as the commanding officer. He was also, of course, talking nonsense. Only a fool would proceed inland without a force of substance behind him.

'All of your men? The knowledge of the treasure is for officers only until we are ready to act. The Curiosolitae and the King, in particular, must not have knowledge of this.'

'My men are loyal to me and they understand the importance of secrecy, so let me assure Praefectus that we will undertake our mission with skill and integrity, and I can also assure you that I know how to deal discreetly with the King.'

Gallus had heard enough.

'We will discuss this further in the morning. We must move to secure our landing position, and then we will commence full landing at first light.'

***

Majestic Tamara narrowed as they pulled inland, upstream away from the port following her tidal reach. Meandering, she cut through the land and the rowing slowed down as the oarsmen pulled against the strength of her flow. The air of the late summer afternoon held its warmth, giving a false sense of calm and tranquillity, and some brief respite for all in the boat. Birdsong and the gentle rustle of leaves in the bankside trees gave balm to their battered thoughts, and all around swallows and house martins skimmed the water, catching midges and caddis fly on the wing. Ahead, two swans nonchalantly swam amongst the reeds, searching for sedge, beetle and shrimp. On either bank, in the narrow water meadows, cattle grazed and called to each other, while farmers and farmhands occasionally stood and watched them go by as they tended to cattle and other beasts. Nobody had told them, it seemed, of the invading force approaching the shore and, for the moment, the serenity of the great valley and its agrarian rhythm, the endeavour of generations, continued unconcerned and undisturbed.

The boat approached the jetty at Cuitheyl and standing at the end of the track that led down to it were four carts and four suitably strong-looking horses to pull them. The cart hands stood talking to each other and at the front stood Taran, Morlain's gille and manservant, looking anxiously at their approach. As they raised their oars and the boat silently and smoothly glided to the jetty, the conversation of the cart hands drifted across the water.

'Look out, theyze ere; look lively now.'

The carter at the rear seemed keen to continue his point and deliver his conclusion, despite the approaching boat.

'I do ere what Taran says, theyze fort 'em Romins an lived to tell the tale – good fer 'em.' He paused for emphasis. 'But now Romins is in the Zound, threatnin' uz all. Our lady, I've yerd, plots our response. No offence to 'er fineness, but I tell ee, praps shoulda left foriners' wars to the foriners!'

Another jumped down from his cart to await instruction from the gille and could be heard saying, 'Treeve, I tell ee, yer borderin' on disrespectful and no more ov it now. Darn brave warriors all of 'em, I zay. Ad one 'ell of a fight on our behalf and tis an 'onour to assist 'em!'

Another agreed. 'Somat the Dewnan can be proud of and no mistake! Not over yet, tho'; them Romins got it in fer us now. Uzall goter stand together. Do our bit.'

Several gilles stood at the wale and then jumped on to the jetty with the holding ropes, bringing the boat to a stop and tying it off. Instantly, the Company were up and Artur was the first on to the wooden stage. The rest began to remove the hatch that led to the low storage area and prepared to unload.

'Pryns Artur, I am sent with greetings from Dynas Kazak. Welcome home.'

'Taran, it is good to see you and to see the carts here waiting, but we need to move quickly now; it will not be long, I am sure, before we are followed upriver.'

'Yes, the carters and I will help with the unloading. My lady advises, if you had not thought of it already, that once unloaded, your boat is pulled around into the creek and out of sight amongst the reeds.'

'Taran, I had not. Maedoc may have, but we will do that. We must move quickly. One item, in particular, is very heavy, which is your strongest cart and horse?'

'My lady also identified such a need; the larger cart at the rear, which will lead us through the lanes, is for the heavy item. Carter Treeve and I will jointly steer it.'

Quickly, the carts were loaded and the Venetia Teg, manhandled by twelve of them and wrapped in a spare Veniti leather sail, was loaded onto the large cart. They hid the boat and slowly the small convoy began to move forward, away from Tamara, and gradually climbed upwards through narrow, deep lanes. With the Venetia Teg at the front, they needed to move slowly and the carts filled the lane, making it difficult for anyone or anything to pass. Most of the Company, exhausted by their efforts in the boat, trudged wearily along behind, frustration building at the speed at which they moved. Artur and Silyen were at the front, Kea and Gawen at the back. The Prince looked behind as the carts slowed again to a crawl. Kea, Gawen and others around them had their backs turned to him, and he could see, had swords drawn. He did not call out but, instead, made his way through the Company towards them.

'What is it?'

Gawen spoke first.

'We are being followed, I am sure of it. There was something on Tamara as we rowed up, an occasional glimpse. I couldn't be certain, it could have been a local boat, but as I look back now, glimpses again, very brief, and then they are gone.'

'Romans? Curiosolitae?'

Kea joined the conversation.

'It might be, although they have come quickly if it is Romans. Advance Curiosolitae scouts, establishing where we go to report back, would be my guess.'

Artur looked at Kea and raised his eyebrows. 'Silyen can take the rest of the Company on and then we, with Gourgy, Nouran and the gilles, will hide ourselves and see who comes along.'

Artur called to Nouran, Gourgy and Silyen and they walked on a little further. The lane dipped in the land and then, as it began to rise again, wound around a tight bend and a small track opened up on the left. Silyen looked back, with the slightest nod of his head to acknowledge the Prince, and walked on with the rest of the Company.

A large uncut hedge of hawthorn and bramble had grown above the wall that separated the lane from the field and it hid Artur and the others, but with sufficient gaps that allowed them to watch the receding carts and Company, and for anyone who came around the bend.

For a while, nobody did. They were on the verge of walking off to catch up with the others when they heard whispers on the other side of the hedge and then two... six armed warriors were visible through the hedge. Then there were two more, close in with their backs flat to the hedge. For the moment, all of them were looking forward, trying to ensure that no one up ahead saw them. The Prince motioned to the rest to keep still and wait, and they all looked through the hedge. One of the eight Curiosolitae warriors, the leader, stood forward from the rest, and carefully watched the carts and the Company go around the bend ahead and then signalled for the rest to follow him. Artur watched the last of them move stealthily up the lane, drew his sword and signalled for the rest to follow him.

They jumped into the lane and shouted to the scouts who spun around, showing faces mixed with surprise and tension. Their leader, furthest ahead, came back through them, said something that the Dewnans didn't understand, raised his sword and charged.

Artur roared a reply and the Dewnans charged up to meet them. The Prince's sword clanged with the scout leader and the sound of metal on metal reverberated and clanged along the lane. Quickly, it became clear that the Curiosolitae scouts did not intend to stay around for a fight. All of them, including the leader, were through past the Dewnans before they stood back, holding their swords, primed but not coming forward to engage. Four held off several cuts and thrusts from the Dewnans and then, above the noise of the skirmish, all began to distinguish the sound of more carts coming up the lane from the direction of Tamara. The Curiosolitae lead had reached the sharp bend in the road and shouted back to the four engaged in fending off the Dewnans. Again, it was unclear what he had shouted, but the remaining four turned and ran from Artur and the rest, who gave chase. As they came around the bend, two large carts were in front of them, carrying wood for building, each pulled by a pair of large horses. The tree trunks were stacked high.

Once the carts had stopped, the Curiosolitae leader held a knife to the neck of the terrified carter of the first cart. while the four retreating fighters clambered up onto the vehicle. Pressed back into the hedge, but left alone by the fighters, the closest cart loaders looked on alarmed and panicked. The Prince and the Dewnans stopped and waited.

'Cut the ropes!' the leader shouted.

As the ropes cut loose, the side-loading carts spilt their load, further blocking the lane on either side.

All of the Curiosolitae then quickly scrambled over the top of both of the carts and the spilt tree trunks and awaited their leader, who now shouted to the Dewnans. 'Don't try to follow us, Princeling! If you do, there will be more of this and worse!'

He held the carter around the neck now with his left arm, raised his dagger in his right hand and plunged it into the carter's leg, whose face contorted in pain and agony.

'I'm gonna skewer that bastard!' Nouran spoke for them all, but the Prince held him back.'

'Wait… not yet.'

The Curiosolitae leader yanked the knife out, keeping his eye firmly on the Dewnans, and made it look as if he was about to strike again, before letting go of the carter, who fell to his knees. The leader then turned and scrambled over the back of the cart.

Gourgy and Nouran charged forward, clambered onto the cart, past the prone carter and scrambled over it in pursuit, but the Curiosolitae were already clear of the second cart and running down the lane.

'Nouran, Gourgy, come back!' The Prince called to them as Kea and Gawen leant down to try to tend the injured carter.

'We have to stop his blood.'

Artur took his knife and began to cut at the thread that held his sleeve in place. After he had cut half of the threads, he ripped it away from the tunic.

'Use this to stop the blood. Tie it around his leg, over the cut. Gawen, untie the horses, we need to get him to Dynas Kazak as quickly as possible; ride ahead and you will need to carry the carter before you on your horse. He cannot ride himself.'

Nouran and Gourgy were back beside them.

'Are we gonna let em go, after this?' Gourgy looked angrily at the Prince as he gestured to the carter.

'We are, because following them means running in the opposite direction to where we need to be. We need to be up the hill and to do everything we can to try and save this man. The acolytes at Dynas Kazak are the best able to do that. We will fight plenty of Curiosolitae soon. We need to catch up with the rest now, stick together. Come on, Gawen and his gille are going to take the carter, the rest of us will walk.'

***

'Speed is of the essence, noble King Brice. The Massaliot assures me the rebels will head for the former Veneti citadel. My intention is that we surround them there and take the treasure. Your men can consolidate the Curiosolitae's position, as the new masters of river and valley, and I can take the treasure to Caesar and bring great credit to both of us.'

Flavius paused for the translator. He had come alongside and aboard the King's ship in a small boat as the sun sank to the horizon. The King's men had gone ashore to secure a bridgehead. So far, they had encountered no resistance. Earlier, as soon as they had entered the Sound, Brice had sent scouts upriver to try to catch up with and follow the Dewnan boat. He awaited their return.

Flavius continued.

'So, we must move before aid comes to the rebels. This Prince and his company are small in number and there are no Veneti left, or very few. The inertia of his father and his Senate, as the Massaliot describes it, cannot last. We must move quickly. Are you with me?'

The King looked at the Roman. He was young, bold and had a fiery temper, or so he had heard. Could he trust him? Would he finally get what he wanted, a share in the gold and control of the trade of Tamara? He coveted it and now he could feel it; he was in touching distance of it. The plan was for the Curiosolitae to secure the river, but this was more, and a sense of excitement built within him. He was going to say yes.

At the start of the year, he had sent an overture to Mawgan of the Dewnan, offering a strong alternative to the Veneti, but his emissaries were rebuffed amidst talk of kin and the Ocean Peoples. That was old thinking and, anyway, the Curiosolitae shared that blood. They were kin also, but the day of the Ocean People was over and a new reality was quickly emerging. Then, in the early spring, the Belgae Anogin had come to Alet. The Belgae in Pretannia had come to dominate and hold sway over the Durotrages at Hengasts Fort. Anogin had said that he intended to vanquish the Ocean People and their failing ways, claiming that he had significant backing. He had offered his support if the Belgae were able to establish a foothold, but had heard nothing and, as far as he knew, there were no Belgae on Tamara. So this was it; he would never get a better opportunity.

'Nauarchus Flavius, we are ready to support your plan, but what of Praefectus Gallus? He has told me that he does not intend for your men to leave the security of the port and your defendable camp without first receiving word from Pro-Consul Caesar.'

'Yes, caution is his watchword, but fortune favours the brave and the bold! King Brice, I have a very close relationship with the Pro-Consul. I know what he wants and what will impress him. Let the Praefectus build his camp if he wishes. My men will be ashore and ready to move before it is light. The Massaliot will guide us, with your men. Let us go forward together, take the rebels in their supposed stronghold, seize the treasure and withdraw to the port and then, with the battle won and our objective secured, we can discuss consolidation with the Praefectus, if that will make him happy.'

'Agreed...' The King was about to say more, but his eye was caught by the captain of the ship. He looked to the translator.

'Will you ask Nauarchus Flavius to excuse me for a moment?'

He stepped out onto the deck and Flavius listened while a conversation took place, then there seemed to be an agreement and the King stepped back into the cabin.

'Nauarchus Flavius, my scouts have returned. The Dewnan have gone ashore upriver and head for the house of the priestess on the large distinctive hill that you may have noticed earlier as we entered the Sound. They also report that the Dewnan unloaded a very large object from their boat, wrapped in sail hides. The statue I assume. Let us take to our boats just before dawn, we can be up to the quay from where they unloaded and be approaching the house of the priestess at first light. We can transport your men, as well.'

Flavius smiled and breathed in deeply before saying, 'I will brief my men and set our watch for your signal to prepare to depart.'

***

The horse of the lead cart struggled to pull the Venetia Teg as the angle of the incline increased on the climb to the summit of Marghros. The lanes were shallower now, more exposed and up ahead, the beacon of Dynas Kazak glowed, more luminous as day turned into evening. Sira Howl sank to the distant horizon of the Mor Pretani, and when they looked behind them, they saw Tamara and, in the distance, the Sound of Ictis.

Gawen and his gille had managed to get by and ahead with the stricken carter, but the rest, who covered both the front and rear of the small cart convoy, trudged wearily on. In the still, warm evening air, they could hear voices ahead at Dynas Kazak, as they headed very slowly towards them. A sparrowhawk, hunting in the last of the good evening light, dived from height at speed, plunging towards the ground. At the last possible moment, before certain impact, it caught a thrush on the wing and swung up and away, gliding back up the hill on an invisible uplift of warm supportive air emanating from the land, while the wings of the thrush beat in a frantic but futile bid to escape.

Artur and the rest had caught up and walked at the back. The Prince raised his head, looked towards the beacon and then turned around. Walking backwards, he surveyed the lane and the fields to Tamara. There was no immediate danger; instead, it all lay in the ships that he could see in the Sound. Soon they would have to defend themselves, either tomorrow or the next day. It would not take the Romans long to come up the valley and catch up with them. They had to get to Menluit, defend it and, somehow, call for his father's aid. Surely, with the Romans in Ictis, even he would respond.

He turned back just as the rear cart in front of him came to a standstill once again.

'Maedoc, what is it now? Are we never to get up this hill?'

He came to look around the side of the cart. He could see the large white horse but not the rider, who had jumped down. He edged his way to the front, between cart and field wall, and there she stood, talking to the carter and to Silyen. She stopped talking and looked towards him, her slate blue eyes, wide and intense.

He breathed deeply and said, 'Hello, Lady Morlain, we are very pleased to see you.'

'Prince Artur, I am very pleased to see you too.'

Standing in a pair of close-fitting brown linen breeches with light leather boots laced up to just below the knee and a flowing, long-sleeved dark-green tunic, cut open around her neck and lined with a golden trim, she cut a full and luxuriant figure. Her hair, long and dark, but tangled from a day of hard work, riding and organising, cascaded down her back and across her front. For the briefest of moments, despite all that he had seen and what was yet to come, a sense of overwhelming calm and contentment swept across him.

He stood tall and said, 'Unfortunately, we are struggling to get up the hill. The load of the front cart here, in particular, is very heavy.'

'Yes, I see that.' Still her eyes held him. 'I have watched from Dynas Kazak, since you emerged from the deeper lanes over there. In the end, I could watch no more, and so Steren Uskis and I have come to help.'

Extreme tiredness was in danger of overwhelming him. They had to get up the hill.

'Thank you.'

As he spoke, she took in the physical reality of his and the Company's flight. He looked exhausted, covered in sweat and dirt. His long blond hair, matted with a mix of saltwater spray and the mud and grime of battle, was darker than when he had left and a heavy brown-blonde stubble was on his face, that was not quite a beard, like the others. His loose-fitting low-cut tunic, torn in places and with one of the arms missing, billowed slightly in the summit breeze, and his woollen breeches had holes worn at the knee. Despite his tiredness, he looked stronger, less of a boy and more of a man, warrior and leader. It was all that rowing, she thought, and much worse, that had happened since she had last seen him. She smiled, she could not help herself, as his eyes, bright, passionate and appealing were shining through and calling to her, in spite of his dishevelled appearance and undoubted trauma, and it warmed her heart.

They all looked ready to collapse and it was only their sense of support for each other, and no doubt the Romans at their rear, that kept them going.

Morlain spoke to the carter. 'It's Treeve, isn't it?' She looked at him with a penetrating stare. She knew, and he knew she knew. 'Uncouple your horse now and take her to rest in my stables. She has worked hard today. Steren Uskis will pull the cart for the rest of the way.' She looked up for a moment to those around. 'We will need to hold the cart at the back while the horses are changed.'

The eyes of the carter, despite his bold words earlier, lingered while he looked at her and captured a moment with those eyes. She responded warmly and then, with the slightest rise of her eyebrows, he acknowledged her and began to release his horse.

When the mare was free and walking away up the hill, Steren Uskis turned and backed himself in between the shafts without any supervision or cajoling. Morlain stroked his flanks and, with words of encouragement, helped him to get into position. Carefully, she brought the collar over his head and connected the two cart shafts to it. After some final words of affection and support, none of which the surrounding group could follow, the great white stallion took the strain and began to pull the cart up the hill. The cart moved faster than it had all day. Quickly, it caught up with the exhausted mare, who stood in a field entrance with carter Treeve to let it go by.

As the cart pulled away, Morlain walked down to the others that followed and reached into her pocket to draw out some morsels that she fed to each horse. The horses raised their heads with renewed intent, and after further words of affection and encouragement, they pulled with renewed purpose and followed the lead cart up the hill. Morlain stood and watched them go and the Company follow on behind. Artur had waited for her.

'Steren Uskis is a fine horse and strong. We could have done with him further down the hill!'

'He is the Pryns of Horses and the very best of friends, but he pulls strongly within sight of home. He could not sustain this pace from the quay, even he would be struggling now; the mare has given her all to get you here.'

The Prince nodded and they walked on at a little distance now from the rear of the Company. Artur slowed his pace and turned his head to her as they walked.

'I heard your voice, at the crux of the battle and when all seemed lost on Ocean. We all heard it. It has sustained me, reinvigorated me when abandonment of everything might have been my chosen option.'

He stopped and turned to her.

'Morlain, I am so pleased to see you. Although the battle is not yet finished, just the sight of you, the chance to talk to you fills me with desire for life and to live it with you!'

She walked a few paces further and then turned back to him.

'I told you I would watch for you and listen for news on the currents of the air and in the voices of the spirits. If I could help, then I would and I always have, from the very first moment we met, not at Menitriel but many years ago. I waited for you, Artur, prepared myself and developed all the ability I was born with so that I could help you when your moment came, when destiny called; and so I shall, wherever your heart truly lies, but do not play with mine. I have watched while another has taken precedence, and with all the equanimity I could muster, I have tried to be positive and supportive, even if it has pained me deep inside. Who knows what will happen to us in the days to come? How we will be called to defend our friends, our land and ourselves... but one commitment we should make right now is to truth and honesty. Without that, there is no point and our sacrifices, whatever they may be, are meaningless.'

As she spoke, he stepped to her and now took her hands and looked deep into her eyes as she held on to his, searching for an answer she could believe in.

'Morlain, I did not know, I have never felt like this before. Passion, yes, and friendship I have known, but with you I have all of that and much more. When I am with you, when I think of you, I have this overwhelming feeling of rightness, of completeness, and that anything that I… we want to achieve is possible; and you are so clever! I marvel at you and all that you have to tell me. Guide me, take me, and I will be with you and fight for you for as long as the fates allow it. I am madly and passionately in love with you. I stopped myself from saying it before I left, and you were right to caution me and counsel me to be sure, but I find on my return, with you standing before me, that nothing has changed.'

His desire had driven him on, but his tiredness brought him to a halt and he had run out of words for the moment. She gripped his hands and smiled ardently back at him as a light evening breeze blew in from the sea, ruffling her hair and pressing her tunic against her body. She breathed in deeply and looked back up the hill to where the carts were approaching the entrance to Dynas Kazak. She turned back.

'We should catch up with the others. The Romans, of course, are in the Sound and very soon, with their allies, they will approach. We, all of us, should seize the opportunity for some rest and food while we can. We have prepared baths for you all. Not the stuff of warriors, I know, but I think you need it. You look awful!'

'Yes, I would like that! Although, I am not sure Gourgy and Nouran will feel the same.'

'No, perhaps not,' they both laughed. 'It is optional, but I am sure they will be very happy to take part in the feast that we have also prepared.'

They walked slowly up the hill together and talked intently of the battle to come and all that had happened; of Aodren, Lancelin, Ewan, Tinos and Ryol – men of the Valley, not to return in this life, who instead died fighting for an ancient heritage and the freedom to choose.

***

A knock on the cabin door and Gallus looked up from his desk. He was in the midst of writing the early parts of his first dispatch to Caesar, to go with the Curiosolitae supply boat back to Alet in a few days' time.

'Paullus, good evening. How is the anchorage?'

Trierarchus Paullus Barbatius, captain of the Praefectus ship, stood nervously before him.

'Praefectus, good evening. The anchorage is secure. Dominus, I thought you should be aware. I have received word that Trierarchus Flavius has disembarked his biremes, centurions, centuria and all, leaving only a small guard per boat. I understand they intend to proceed upriver with the King and majority of the Curiosolitae, in pursuit of the rebels. They board the Curiosolitae riverboats right now and await first light.'

Gallus looked at the captain and shook his head. 'He is a fool, Paullus, and his vanity and naïve pursuit of glory endangers us all. I should not say these things about a fellow officer, but now he puts us in a difficult position. What of the Curiosolitae? Have the majority of them gone with the King?'

'Yes, Dominus, it seems they all want to be part of the great victory they anticipate. Only a small guard per ship remains.'

'Hmm, well, I wouldn't be so sure about that. As the Pro-Consul often reminds us, they are impulsive and sudden in their decision making, but I would have hoped for better from a Roman officer; and what of our men with the auxiliaries, the supporting officers?'

'It is from them that I receive word. They are powerless to stop the tribesmen, of course; there are many more of them and they follow their King first. It is also difficult to oppose when fellow Romans readily support the attack. They await your instruction prior to boarding.'

'Yes, thank you, Paullus.'

As the captain spoke, Gallus weighed up his options. He was dismissive of Flavius but he had to consider that it might just work, of course. If Flavius and the King could hold themselves together for long enough, without salivating and fawning over the gold and losing all sense of reason and rational action, then sheer numbers alone might prevail, if they were quick.

Gyras the Massaliot had talked in his briefing of the weak defences around the main river valley and of inertia amongst the local ruling elite. Perhaps that was Flavius's intention: a quick expedition upriver, the Massaliot would know where to go and the Curiosolitae scouts would add to this knowledge before surrounding the small rebel group, taking the treasure and returning downriver.

As he thought it through, he began to realise that it might work. So, join them or wait to see if they returned? If it did work, there was one thing that he could be certain of: if the Praefectus and his men were not there, Flavius would ensure that all, and especially the Pro-Consul, knew it. Then, it would be clear to Caesar that Marcus Trebius Gallus had not delivered on his command, nor carried out the very specific personal request asked of him; and that, equally certainly, would be the end of any future special requests from the great man.

'Paullus, how many men do you think are needed to provide an adequate guard for our galleys?'

***

The light of the central fire glowed brightly at Dynas Kazak. The full remaining Company sat along the three tables around it and interspersed between them, the senior acolytes of the house. The feast was nearly over and a sense of anticlimax, the end of a journey, lay across them all and mixed with it, tiredness and great sadness.

They were all hungry and thirsty and had gladly devoured the contents of the sumptuous table provided by the house of the priestess. At the end of the summer, much was available – meats, fruits and freshly made cheese and mead – but they all too easily compared it with the feasts before they had departed for Armoric. Their thoughts of the many who had fallen in the Roman onslaught were never far away.

Morlain spoke quietly to Artur next to her. He nodded his head and she rose to her feet and called the tables to attention.

'Brave friends, you have been through tortuous and difficult days since we last sat around tables such as these, and many who we hold dear are no longer amongst us. You have fought with great courage and enormous strength of will and brought yourselves home to the land of the Dewnan. The fight is not yet over. The enemy at our door intends us great harm and to take what is ours. You are tired and sad at the loss of good friends and comrades but tomorrow we begin again, as all those who fell would have ardently wished. It is what they died fighting for. Take the fight to the aggressor and maybe victory will yet be ours. We will never surrender,' she paused momentarily for emphasis, 'and we will fight until there is nothing left to give or until we have pushed the aggressor back into the sea.'

She had their attention. There was none of the wild and enthusiastic cheering of earlier feasts, but instead grim and determined nods of approval. Several sat up and were about to ask questions, but she stopped them all with a raised hand.

'No questions tonight, no long discussion. Rest now. The bathhouse has been prepared for those who wish it. Bathe, sleep, rest and be ready; tomorrow we stand firm and we say to the enemy, "Come on then, if you want it, come and get it – see how far that gets you!"'

Around the table, nobody stood; but they all looked at each other and muttered encouraging and determined words, before looking back at the Priestesswith eyes of passion, ardour and veneration. Even the older men, battle and skirmish hardened, saw something special in this young woman of fervour, wisdom and eloquence. Something, someone to believe in when all else looked desperate.

Morlain sat down and turned to Artur.

'Brave and inspiring words,' he said smiling, his eyes warm with admiration.

'When you are determined to achieve a different outcome, even when the barriers seem daunting, such words, I find, come easy.'

'Still, you do it very well.'

'Thank you. Artur, forgive me, I must ask you; the ring, you still have it? It has not been lost or misplaced or worse, taken in the heat of battle?'

He touched the hilt of his sword, still attached to the belt around his dishevelled tunic.

'Yes, it is here. If I am honest, I have not really thought of it while I have been away.'

'Would you show it to me?'

He looked at her for a moment, then glanced down to his sword hilt and tugged at the roundel that concealed the ring. He took it out and placed it on the table. At first, it was dull, tarnished perhaps from its extended placement in the hidden compartment, but as they both contemplated it, the discolouring began to clear until it shone brightly back at them. Now that it had been let out, back into the world, the warmth of the combined gold and lapis lazuli grew. It seemed to recognise them both and sparkled in its pleasure at seeing them again.

'The days of its confinement are over,' she said. 'From this moment forward, wear it with confidence. Do not show it off yet, but do not hide it. It is your birthright. Wear it. Wear it on your sword hand. It takes great pleasure in seeing you, and it recognises me, feels my presence, and knows me for who I am and what I wear.'

She lifted her left arm, placed her hand on the table and there, on her middle finger, was another ring of gold and lapis lazuli worked into a reef knot, signifying loyalty and representative of the bond between the wearer and her chosen associates.

'You wear a ring of Ictasus.' He had the sense not to exclaim it loudly, but the surprise in his hushed response was clear.

'I do. It is the ring of Eupheme and there is an intense attachment between these two rings, the rings of Eupheme and Diantha, that spans the ages and brings both strength of purpose and longevity to us. Those who wear them feel their influence and support. Those who follow will recognise that and we are all stronger together.'

Artur slid the ring of Diantha on to the middle finger of his right hand and placed it on the table next to Morlain's hand. The rings, lustrous and buoyant together, back in each other's company after so many years, passed currents of light and sparkle between them.

Artur looked in wonder at the interaction and, if it was possible, the intensity of his feelings for Morlain deepened and he moved his hand across and joined his with hers and held them and the ancient rings tightly together. Then, thinking back to their long breakfast and conversation at the new of Loor Skovarnek, he said, 'There is a third ring that did not return to the land of the Greeks. The ring that Ictasus wore, that was his before the loss of Diantha, where is it? Will it come to our aid, also, when we need it most?'

She let go of his hand and looked at him with resignation before saying, enigmatically, 'I do not know, only the days to come will reveal that.'

She looked away, looked back and changed the subject.

'Artur, I spoke to Winoc. He has gone now to Menluit with difficult tidings to tell.' She paused for a moment and then continued, 'He spoke to me of the Sword of Menluit. We will always owe Aodren and his men a debt. He had the presence of mind and honour to give up the sword when he saw their fate was sealed; and it was a deed of great bravery and purpose, no matter how he may feel now, for Winoc to stay true to his task, when all around failed, and ensure that the sword came home.'

'I said this to him, but he was inconsolable.'

'Artur, the sword is yours, Aodren knew it and its importance before he left, but Winoc has taken it with him to Menluit, which is the place where its new owner must receive this old but important weapon. You must be prepared for that moment, tomorrow or the day after.'

'I will, and what of my father? Have you heard from him or spoken to him? Should I send word to him? He will know, I assume, of the Roman and Curiosolitae fleet?'

'Yes, I am sure he will, and no, I have not spoken to him. He does not favour me. He believes, I hear, that I plot against him in your favour, to make the most of your disgruntlement at your extended exile in Demetae. Nonsense, of course, but in recent years, I reflect, he has listened to and acted upon a lot of nonsense. Even Elowen has not had an audience since Loor Golowan. He has been amongst the Kernovi and the Tin Lords and returns along the coast to Ker Kammel as we speak. Let us hope he sees sense before it really is too late. His brother, your uncle, who I saw five days ago at Dynasdore, is sympathetic and goes to speak to him. We wait to see what effect that might have. Even now with the wolf at his door, his reticence stifles him. How he has changed from the man we both once knew!

She looked around the tables and said nothing for a little while, and then turned back to him and gripped his hand again while the rings renewed their buzz and sparkle.

'Will you join me, away from the Company at least for a little while? I would like to discuss...' she hesitated for a moment, 'to continue our conversation from earlier, if you would like that.'

Morlain's sudden nervousness after her firm and strong delivery while discussing the rings, the sword and his father surprised him. The apprehension that she tried to disguise gave an edge to her voice. There was no need for it and he smiled reassuringly.

'Yes, I would like that very much.'

All around them, the Company were rising from the tables. Some, defying expectation, were heading for the bathhouse, while others went away, quietly, to take the air outside or to one of the several smaller roundhouses where bedding had been prepared and small fires lit to reduce the chill of the cloud-free early autumn night.

The Prince spoke to Maedoc and then to Kea, Gawen and Silyen. They would all meet at first light before the main door. The five of them looked to each other and then he turned and walked away, back to his place at the table.

The roundhouse had emptied quickly and he could not see Morlain. He looked around and there she was, coming out of what he remembered to be her own smaller roundhouse, her bedchamber adjacent. She held out her hand and took his in hers and they walked together through the doorway. Once through, she let go of his hand and secured in three places the thick woollen curtain that provided the door covering.

Artur looked around and remembered the table, the parchments and the large bed, covered with animal furs and, at one end, a number of down-filled linen pillows. A small fire burnt on the hearth and her loom still stood in the corner; but now, in the centre of the room was a large bath, made of tin. This was full of steaming, fire-warmed water with a selection of herbs and plants and floating on top. He looked back towards her with a quizzical expression. She spoke cautiously, still not completely sure of his reaction.

'The bath is mine, made especially for me actually, but you said earlier that a bath would be welcome and so I thought you might like to use this one. I have placed herbs and plants within to provide refreshing aroma for your senses and soothe your limbs and body.'

'Yes, I would like that.'

'Good and, erm, I will look away while you remove your clothes and lower yourself in. There is a step there, you see, to get into it... and then, when you are in, well, perhaps we can continue our conversation, the one on the lane, I mean.'

His smile broadened at her showing, once again, uncharacteristic hesitancy.

'Morlain, please, I am very glad to be here, I have thought of meetings just like this on many occasions while I have been away. I want to be with you and I have nothing to hide, so look away if you wish, but there is no need on my account. The herbs smell good and now I find the anticipation of the heat of the water draws me to it. I have to get in!'

He bent to untie and remove his boots, straightened and removed his tunic to reveal, where mud and grime covered his body exposed to the air, a clean torso and a taut, muscular stomach beneath. His upper arms were firm and full and the muscles in them flexed and rippled slightly as he reached up to run his hands through his hair and straighten it, which had fallen forward as he had bent to take off his boots and lift his tunic over his head.

She had intended to look away, but she did not.

He took off his sword, put it to one side, undid the tie in his breeches and let them fall to the floor to reveal two firm pink and white buttocks. She breathed in deeply and rubbed lip against lip as he half turned to walk across to the bath and reveal, side on, a full and ample manhood. It was not quite what she had anticipated, heard how it would be, when it came to embrace and passion. However, she could not help but notice that the whole thing twitched and became agitated; impatient, perhaps, for the moment to arrive. He put his front foot onto the step and the powerful and defined sinews and muscles of his leg stretched tight as he carefully stepped over and into the water. It was hot! He reached down to the sides of the bath and slowly lowered himself, allowing his body to accommodate the heat and feel the pleasure and contentment rise up and pulse through him. Everything else, all thoughts about yesterday and tomorrow, subsided as the restorative immersion and surge of adrenaline kicked in, allied with the renewed positivity that the heat and surrounding water induced.

She watched and breathed deeply again as his buttocks slowly sank into the water and he came to a rest, sitting on the bottom of the bath. He stretched out his arms along the side and stretched his legs beneath the water, just slightly longer than the length of the bath, and leant back on the raised rear, put there specifically to allow for the comfort and relaxation of a weary head. She sat down on her chair quietly and allowed him to take in all the initial benefit of the bath. He closed his eyes and she sat and watched him for a while as the steam continued to rise and the logs and twigs of the fire, crackled and glowed.

She took a pot of liniment from the table, lifted her chair and brought it to the rear of the bath, dipped one hand into the pot, rubbed both hands together and then gently worked and massaged the liniment into his shoulders, around his neck and down his chest to the water line. He breathed deeply, soothed and aroused as she placed her hands around the back of his ears and carefully but firmly pressed and manipulated his head. Running her fingers gently through his hair, she carefully removed knots and drew it out neatly behind him, over the edge of the bath.

When she had finished, she returned to his shoulders and his chest, worked her way again to the water line and now below. Her arms encompassed him from behind, head down alongside his while her hands gently worked their way down his lower tummy. She turned and kissed him on the cheek and he in response turned his head and caught a second kiss. A passionate, warm and embracing kiss, their lips moist and malleable from the steam of the bath and deep within it, the flicker of her tongue on his as her hands reached the hair above his now fully developed manhood. Gently she manipulated it, felt it in her hand, encouraged it and then gently, slowly withdrew her hands while the kiss continued, then withdrew her lips and stood up behind him. His eyes remained closed, as he took in the aroma of the herbs and continued to breathe deeply.

After a moment, he opened his eyes. She stood behind him and he said, 'Morlain, I am filled with such desire for you; let me see you, let me touch you, kiss you again.'

He was about to stand and turn to her when she said, 'No, don't move. Stay there.'

She walked from behind him. Wearing just her undergarment, she stood before him, unbuttoned it at the front, and as he had done, let it fall to the floor.

Completely naked, she stood for a moment, looking back at him, her confidence restored now, allowing him to take in and enjoy all he saw. She ran her hands through her hair, pushing it back from her face, stretching her body and accentuating all of its parts. Both his anticipation and his pleasure were rising rapidly and then she walked forwards onto the step and got into the bath with him.

For a moment, there was water everywhere as the two of them overflowed the already full bath. She burst out laughing, her wonderful mischievous laugh that he had heard at their first meeting at Menitriel. Artur had been suspicious then, but now he loved it as one of the things that defined her, made her special and made him want her so badly. He burst out laughing too. They fell together in the water and her large firm breasts rubbed against his chest. His slightly raised leg went between her legs and she gently but firmly rubbed against it and his fully erect penis rubbed against her other leg, raising her anticipation and giving him pleasure. Their lips found each other again and dived deeply, embracing and absorbing, and the power of their coming together at multiple touching points sent wave after wave of all-consuming currents of pleasure through them.

Briefly and invigoratingly, their absorption with each other overwhelmed all other thought and feeling. For Morlain and Artur, while they were together, nothing else mattered, and deep within the waters of the bath, two small lights of gold and deep blue shone with a new level of invigorated brightness – happy, content and restored to each other once again.

Suddenly, Artur stopped and rolled around her in the bath.

'Oh Morlain, I cannot wait any longer, but you must sit in your bath! I could kiss you and caress you all day, but now I must have you. You are more beautiful and more desirable than anyone or anything I have ever known, and I believe that I will ever know!'

As they came together, both gasped at the depth and extent of their union and the intensity and climax of their passion.

Then, it was over and both felt the overwhelming resurgence of tiredness as they sat together, squeezed into the end of the bath. She kissed him, stood up and got out of the bath. She dried herself, went over to her bed, got underneath the animal furs and lay snuggled and warm, her head on the pillow, looking across to him.

'Come and lie with me.'

He got out of the bath, dried himself off, came across to the bed and got in beside her.

For a while, he also lay his head on the pillow and looked back at her and then she said, 'That was my first go, with a man. My sisters and I soothe and caress each other on winter's evenings, to keep warm, and in the spring when the smell of new life is in the air. I know what gives me pleasure, or I thought I did, but I did not know that there was such pleasure.' She searched his eyes as he smiled fondly back at her, 'And this was only my first go! How will it be when I am good at it! Let us practise again and then we must sleep.' She held her stern and serious face for a moment, before bursting into laughter again and lifting herself on top of him and engaging in another passionate and consuming kiss.

***

'You join us, Praefectus. What of the camp?'

'I am the senior commander here and my instructions from the Pro-Consul are to command the mission, from landing to securing of the treasure, establishment of camp, to the receipt of further instructions. I asked you not to engage with the King on the matter of the treasure, but you have deliberately defied me and now we have no choice but to follow him upriver and I am, therefore, Nauarchus, compelled to join the attack.'

Gallus, seemingly emotionless, looked at Flavius and then continued.

'I have spoken to the King. I understand there are two likely locations the rebels will retreat to: the large hill, where the beacon burns brightly; or the Veneti fort by a strategic river crossing, several mille beyond. Led by the King's scouts, we will proceed to the large hill and then, if they are not there, proceed overland to the fort. Again, I understand that it is clearly visible from the large hill. Three auxiliary cohorts will come with us, while the fourth will push on to secure the river flank of the fort. If the rebels are at the fort – a more defendable position – we will secure the siege and then decide on how to attack and achieve our objective. Is that clear?'

Flavius's face looked unsure as to whether he should settle on a feigned obsequious smile or a glare of contempt. For the moment, he simply said, 'Yes Praefectus, my men are ready and we await your further instruction.'

'Good, I have left twenty men per galley. I assume that you have done the same and so, with the Curiosolitae, we have a little more than two thousand men; hopefully, enough to do the job quickly and return downriver to establish our winter camp here. You have placed us in a difficult position, Nauarchus Flavius, and I will have to reflect on this in my first dispatch. We only have the Greek's and the Curiosolitae's knowledge of the land to work with and no contact with the ruling senate here. We do not know, beyond the small contingent that fled the Veneti defeat, what opposition we will encounter. If we are to get through this, you will follow my command from here.'

'Praefectus, I will follow your lead as senior officer...' *For as long as it suits my need,* he thought. 'But let me also be clear that I have my instructions and I will have that treasure.' He paused. 'Come, let us not argue. We can both achieve our objective here, and then you will establish your bridgehead and I will sail away to Caesar with the gold.'

Before the Praefectus could say any more or dismiss him, Flavius turned and walked confidently away.

A thin straggle of lightening sky spread across the horizon and there was a distinct chill in the air. The senior centurion called all those that remained on the shore to board the boats. Gallus checked his sword belt, drew his cape around his body armour and walked towards his riverboat.

***

Artur raised his head slowly from the soft pillow and the deepest of sleeps, more comfortable than he had been for many moons, possibly ever. It was a wonderful bed and he had been consumed in the end by overwhelming tiredness.

Morlain was not beside him. He rolled over and there she was, stood on the other side of the room, fixing the belt of her breeches. On it sat her sword that she adjusted to her side. She raised her head and looked straight at him. She had clearly risen quickly and not combed her hair, but Morlain looked more beautiful this morning than she had ever done before.

She looked at him, smiled and said, 'You need to get up and quickly now. I have word from the watch on Tamara. The Romans and Curiosolitae come upriver; boats set out as I speak. We think they intend to come here first and there are a great many of them. We need to hurry now.'

The Prince was out of bed and pulling on his breeches and his boots. For just a moment longer, she lingered, watching his broad back and the strength of his arms as he bent over to fasten his boots, his hair ruffled and unkempt, hanging over his head. Then, as he stood and ran his fingers through his hair to straighten it and remove it from his face, she saw his stomach taut, but with gentle undulations as he breathed steadily.

She allowed herself a contented deep breath, before he said, 'Are the Company aware?'

'Yes, Wenna was here earlier; Taran and the others have been waking them.'

The Prince looked around the room and located his undertunic, before pulling it over his head and leaning down to pick up his belt and sword.

'Artur, we have to evacuate Dynas Kazak; it is not easily defendable. It is a great vantage point but the sweep of the hill is too broad and too flat here at the summit. I had hoped that we would have today to properly leave, but they have surprised me and are coming now; they will quickly surround us and we do not have the numbers to meet them in open battle on the hill of the horse.'

'Yes.' He was dressed and ready now and nodded his head, although sleep still hung around him. 'We will go to Menluit with the Venetia Teg, the inheritance and all from here.'

'Yes, I think that is right, and everyone must go with you, the acolytes, the house servants, nobody should be left behind. Go across land and not by Tamara. Let them think that we are here. We will stoke the beacon and ensure that it keeps burning long after you have left. If they come here, we will delay them and enable you to organise the best defence of Menluit before they arrive. As for the inheritance, the carters rested as soon as they arrived and left earlier on my instruction with fresh and additional horses. I hope that you approve. They will be over halfway there by now. If you had to wait for the carts, it would undermine your evacuation. You will probably arrive when they do.

He was fully awake now, listening and nodding his approval, her words properly registering with him.

'You are coming with us?'

'Not immediately. I have something I have to do first, in pursuit of aid and assistance to our cause, but I will be there.'

Trying to prevent any further conversation, she turned and took her long riding cloak from a peg on the wall, turned back to him and took his hands.

'Artur, you have to hold Menluit. Build your defences quickly and build them well, draw in provisions if you can, and all men and women of fighting age, if they so choose, then prepare for the enemy's arrival. You do not have long, but you must hold Menluit!'

She gripped his hands firmly and her eyes widened as he, in turn, stared back at her. He was going to speak, when she said, 'Know this and remember it always. I love you. It turns out that, in the end, everything was worth waiting for – and now that it has properly arrived, you and I have much left to do and many years ahead of us to do it in. So, no more talking, I will return, two days from now, listen and look for me, but until then, you must hold Menluit!'

She drew him forward and kissed him firmly on the lips, before letting go of his hands, and turning and walking out of the door.

It was still dark outside, but the light of the beacon burnt brightly and lit the yard. A very thin slither of paler sky was just discernible that heralded the imminent arrival of dawn. As the Prince and Maedoc walked out, all of the remaining original Company that survived, with the exception of Drustan, including Silyen, Gawen, Ambros, Marrek, Nouran, Gourgy, Kea, Briec and Tremain, along with their gilles and attendants, stood forward waiting for his arrival.

Quickly, they went around all of the buildings. The Prince, Kea, Briec and Tremaine passed a number of the acolytes and house servants heading to the muster point outside of the main roundhouse. They had covered all of the buildings in their part of the compound and came to the last roundhouse. It was larger than the rest of the supporting buildings and Artur suddenly remembered the parchments, the library of "writings" that Morlain had shown at Loor Skovarnek. As they approached, Bacun the old guard, stepped out from the door and stood tall, waiting for them. The Prince walked ahead of the rest.

'It's Bacun, isn't it? We have to go, are you ready to join the muster at the main hall?'

'Thank ee, yer lordship, 'onoured Pryns, but Oi shant be leavin.'

'Bacun, you have to; a large Roman force is coming up the hill, and we must retreat to Menluit.'

'Tha's right and Oi wish yers all good speed, but Oi shall guard the libry as Oi've allas done.'

'The parchments are still here? Lady Morlain did not have them moved?'

'Them Romins zee, cort us unawares thas the problem, we'd oped to pack it all up today an er ladyship's bin busy drummin' up support in recent days, says weez goin'ter to need all the support we can get.'

Artur turned to Kea.

'Is there a spare cart, anything that we can pack all of this into?'

'Artur, there is nothing, it has all gone. We have to go. They will be here soon and if you are captured or killed, then all is lost before we have started. We have to go.'

'Bacun, please come with us. You know the Lady Morlain, how clever she is, she will replace these parchments, it will take her a while, but she will be able to do it. Come on man, come with us.'

'Most noble of yer, Pryns Artur, and 'onerable of ee young man to be zo concerned about old Bacun, as er ladyship was earlier and indeed said somat similar about replacin' an all that, but these is ages old, an' the work of many ands, zo Oi shall stand my ground, come what may, and don't ee concern yerself.'

'Artur, Kea, everyone come on, we can see lights coming up the river. We have to go.' It was Gawen shouting from the main roundhouse.

'Artur, let's go. If a man has chosen to meet his fate, then he has chosen and we should not deny him that. Come on.' Kea and the others were turning to leave and they could see Maedoc running across to find them.

'Keep out of sight,' said Artur. 'Do not look for a fight unless you have to. I hope they will see that we are not here and move on quickly. Good luck, Bacun.'

'Good luck to you an all, young man. All of uz 'ave ter stand our ground, but the future of all th'Dewnan is in yer ands. Give 'em Romins a good 'idin!'

holð menluıꞇ!

The growing light of dawn caressed the canopy as the Company, acolytes and servants of Dynas Kazak rode and walked. They forded the small gover and climbed steeply as the lane, which was still in dense woodland, rose to the top of the first of the two hills of Menluit, opposite to the hill of the citadel. Many of the Company, including Artur, walked.

Not all of the Veneti had gone with the boats. Aodren had left behind a small garrison to protect his investment and, most importantly, to protect his daughter, who he had determined should stay for not only her own safety, but also for continuity; and because, he had reasoned, Menluit and the valley were all she had ever known.

The Company and people of Dynas Kazak continued and came out onto the edge of the trev fields, clear of the trees between the two hills. People were at work, with picks and spades and dragging what looked like bushes and low carts of soil. On the outer ramparts of the citadel, new battlements were being hoisted and much was going on; and there, towards the top of the citadel hill and approaching the gates, were the four carts carrying the Venetia Teg and other treasures from Artur's boat and the Hill of the Horse.

A man turned and Callard, who had first escorted him and the Company to Menluit, stood before them.

'Pryns Artur, we have been expecting you. You are surprised to see me, I see. I command the garrison that remains. We are small in number, but pleased to have our chance now to contribute to the fight.' He paused for a moment and looked back to Menluit. 'I have been directing defensive works on this side of the fields and my Lady Gwalian asked me to look out for you.'

'Callard, it is very good to see you.' He turned to those behind him. 'Kea, Gawen, will you lead everyone on and across to the citadel? Maedoc and I will follow shortly.'

He turned back to the Venetian.

'Callard, I am so sorry about all that has happened.'

Callard looked solemnly at the Prince, and with the conflicting emotions of great sadness and determination in his voice, said, 'Many of us regret bitterly that we could not have been there, fighting alongside our kin; but you see, we are busy trying to overcome our sorrow through work and application. We will lament them, but first, we must defend ourselves and, perhaps, exact some revenge for all of the wrongs that have been done.'

'Yes, I hope that we can do that. What are all these people doing in the fields?'

'It is my Lady Gwalian's idea, my Lord. We are collapsing some of the shallow mine workings and then covering them with reeds and soil, to try to make them look like normal ground. Mantraps that might hold up a besieging force for a little while, long enough, perhaps, for others to come to our aid.'

Callard raised his eyebrows as he finished speaking. They both knew who he was talking about and the Prince replied as he nodded his head. 'Very clever,' he said and smiled back at the Venetian before his face quickly altered and took on a more concerned look. 'And how is the Lady Gwalian, Callard?'

'Distraught, my Lord, but like us all, she sees that there is a job to be done, a battle to be fought and she puts on a brave face. She is busy coordinating the strengthening of the defences over at the citadel.'

He paused for a moment.

'She will be pleased to see you, Pryns Artur, so I shall let you get on as I must return to my tasks. We have to complete the mantraps as best we can.'

Artur and Maedoc walked on along the broad path to the citadel that dipped between the twin hills and climbed steeply again to the stout oaken gates. As they drew nearer, they could see that extra wooden posts, with their sharpened ends facing outwards, lay positioned along the fence, horizontal to it. These posts had been placed between the sharpened uprights at the top of the fence, creating an additional barrier to the approaching attackers. They walked through the familiar gates to find further intense activity in the large open area immediately within, and then along the fence and amongst the roundhouses of the trev as they ran upwards to Pendre at the top of the hill. Many who were working stopped to look as the Prince entered Menluit, their faces a mix of sorrow and hope, maybe at the sight of him and one more chance to repel the invader.

Up ahead, they could just see the Company at Pendre. Kea and Gawen were directing, taking charge of unloading the treasure. The inner rampart that had surrounded Aodren's hall was missing and there, next to them, was Gwalian, discussing some matter related to the unloading. They ascended the hill and as they approached she turned, smiled briefly and walked down to meet them in the middle of the trev.

'Pryns Artur, it is very good to see you. We have been busy, as you see; what do you think of our preparations?'

Maedoc gave a deep respectful bow and walked on to assist with the unloading and Artur smiled at her as she stood before him.

'They look good.' He looked around him, towards the fence. 'I saw Callard on the way in. Your mantraps are a very good idea, they should halt them at least for a little while and the fence is looking much strengthened.'

She stood before him with a pale brightness in her face, resolute and determined to meet the challenge ahead before giving consideration to all that had gone before. The beauty of her engaging, warm brown eyes still drew him in, and deep within him was a feeling of great affection, in spite of his complete commitment to Morlain. Even in the midst of approaching battle and an uncertain future, it burned strongly.

'Good, we face an immense challenge, I have heard, but hopefully what we have done will hold them back at least for a little while.'

He turned and looked around him at the scene of activity. 'Yes, I am sure it will.'

There was an awkwardness in his voice, a hesitancy that disturbed her. 'Artur, listen, what has gone before and all that we have both lost, let us put it aside for now. We all need to be strong, to fight for our own future and not the one our enemies would impose upon us. You know that and do not need me to tell you. It is about comrades together now and friendship. Whatever has happened, whatever happens in the future, your friendship is so important to me.' She paused for a moment and said softly, holding his eyes with hers, 'You will always have mine.'

The intensity of those eyes held firm for a little longer and then he said, 'And you will always have mine.'

She smiled gently and then said with renewed strength, 'We have looked for your return. It will give great encouragement to the people here that you are back amongst us, and the Company came back to fight this battle and defend our homes; even if the future will not, in this life, include so many that we have held dear. Callard and I, and the garrison, are ready to follow your lead and command.'

She breathed in deeply and continued in an upbeat voice that spoke of her unquenchable inner vibrancy and positivity, no matter what the adversity.

'And there is much yet to do. My father told me of the treasure before he left and your mission to bring it back. The Company and the hall servants unload it now and place it in one of the old food storage pits at the rear of the hall that we uncovered and prepared when we heard you were in the Sound. Wooden planking covers the pit. We will replace the grass turf and place water butts and other items to keep it concealed if we are overwhelmed and forced to abandon Menluit.'

'You have thought of much and much is prepared. I am impressed.'

'Thank you, everyone has worked hard in recent days.

She looked at him and then at the battlements. 'You see also that we strengthen the palisade fence as it faces the trev fields. We are nearly complete on that. We have taken the posts of the inner palisade to do this. I think we only get one chance to defend ourselves, given the numbers that I hear they have. If they are through the outer palisade then it is all over, no matter what fencing we have within.'

'And how many fighters, warriors, do we have? What size is the garrison that remained?'

'One hundred trained warriors to protect our interests, as best they can, at Menluit and on the river.'

He looked at her for a moment and then looked away. She continued, 'I know it is not many, but we have withdrawn all of the river port workers, and also those from Ker Tamara and Dynas Dowr Tewl have temporarily abandoned both forts, and that swells our numbers of fighters also. Now the Company is back amongst us, we number around two hundred, including the other men and women of fighting age here.'

'And yet that still will not be enough to cover the full length of the outer palisade, I am sure.'

He looked towards the fence that faced the fields. 'We will have to concentrate on the fields, I think. It is there, surely, that they will concentrate, and then only a handful to cover the steep climb from Tamara. Let us hope that Drustan, with more men, will arrive before they are here.'

'Yes, and Artur… what of your father? It is his land that is being invaded and threatened. Is there no hope that he will respond?'

'I have come straight from the boat to Dynas Kazak, to be here and I have not been able to speak to him, but Morlain tells me that my uncle has gone to him. We shall see, but for now, we must prepare ourselves. The Romans and Curiosolitae approach and we must prepare to defend and hold Menluit, by whatever means we can and hope that support will arrive.'

Gwalian did not choose to ask about Morlain and her whereabouts and instead said, 'Very well, we are ready. The last of the additional posts are being positioned, and I nearly forgot, we have also added two additional oak gates that will close behind the main gates. They will need a strong battering ram to break both sets down!'

He laughed at her sudden enthusiasm, and as he looked towards the gate, noticed a small group of archers to the right of it practising by shooting at targets pinned on the inside of the palisade fence.

'Pupils of yours, I assume,' he said as he watched their arrows fly.

Her response was an uneasy 'yes'. There was a pause then before she said guardedly, 'Artur, they were my father's slaves.' She looked down and then her eyes rose cautiously to his, 'I gave them all their freedom. Most have left, but some have chosen to remain because they have nothing else. If you will allow it, they will fight with me and we will provide additional cover for all that remains of the warriors of the Veneti and for your Company.'

Briefly, his eyes met hers with no show of emotion, but then they softened and a gentle smile returned. 'Of course; and if they are only half as proficient as you when the battle comes I will be thankful that you fight alongside us.'

A warm, comforted smile returned to her face and two children from the trev ran in front of them. His expression changed and the immediacy of the impending attack, which had been briefly supplanted, now returned fully to his mind. 'We have to get the mothers and children out and those who are too old to fight. It is hard to ignore that this is a desperate situation, so let's get them away while we can, perhaps in the water taxis?'

'Artur, I will organise it. There are others...'

She might have said more but there was a cry from behind. As they turned, members of the Company, the acolytes of Dynas Kazak and others, stood pointing at the door of Pendre. They both ran up the hill and then looked towards Marghros and upon its summit, Dynas Kazak. Flames rose into the morning sky, and it was not simply the beacon. The whole compound had been put to the torch and was burning. The invaders approached. Artur was the quickest to respond. The days that would define him for the rest of his life had arrived and he found that, when he needed it most, both command and authority came naturally to him.

'Gwalian, send all those who need to leave quickly to the riverboats and away. Briec, Tremaine, can you assist? Marrek, Ambros and your gilles, out into the fields, please. Gather everyone in now; the aggressors approach and we need to be ready. Nouran, Gourgy, can you take particular responsibility for defending the gate? We may yet need – I hope we will need – to open and close it quickly, and it is a double gate. That will need strength and determination and the gate will need a stout defence. Gawen, Silyen, can you circulate amongst all who remain when the old, the mothers and the children have left? Gather them here on the steps of Pendre. I will speak to them shortly. Kea, can you and your gille join Maedoc and I? We will look at the defences that face the fields and split the fence into four, and you, Silyen, Gawen, Callard and I will take responsibility for a length of fence each. Marrek, Ambros, Briec, Tremaine, when you have finished your first tasks, I am going to ask you to look after the far and river side.'

***

The ground began to incline steeply as Steren Uskis and Morlain climbed towards Menitriel. As swift as the wind, he and she had galloped behind the advancing Romans to the citadel of Clesek, the supposed warden of the port of Ictis. Morlain had asked him why he had not challenged the invading force to avenge the death of his son. *'We must wait for the call of the King,'* was the unsatisfactory reply she had received.

Why this inertia? Did nobody care about the Dewnan and the Pretan heritage? Did it all end, here? All the greatness of the peoples' past, of the ancestors, did it all fizzle out to nothing under her watch?

Steren Uskis came to an abrupt stop and raised himself onto his two mighty back legs.

No! She and he would explore every option and travel to every corner of the land in pursuit of support for the small fulcrum of defiance that was establishing itself right now in the middle of Tamara's great valley.

Something was called for – a signifier, a spark to confirm the fightback against invasion and inertia, to give hope at their lowest moment and to reignite both passion and belief in the land of the Dewnan. Heulwen would know. As horse and rider approached the door to Casworon's hall, her thoughts briefly turned to other priorities; but she would come back to it, as they travelled across the high ground and would search her memory and all that she had learnt from her mentor. Heulwen would know.

***

Bacun peered through the gap in the door and felt the wind on his face. It had a keener edge here and blew gusts around the empty roundhouses, whistling and moaning through the thatch above him.

There were warriors everywhere. The Curiosolitae, he recognised, he had seen them at Ictis, but the others wore strange clothing – armour of leather and metal. *Romins*, he thought.

Across the compound, a group of men were arguing, it appeared. The Romans checked all the roundhouses and would reach his soon, but he was ready for that; the pit within his roundhouse, hidden by and entered through a large wooden chest, ostensibly full of rugs and furs would conceal him. He and Lady Morlain had moved the most important parchments in to the pit two days ago. They had been careful not to mention it, even to the Prince. Bacun had been moving more until he had heard the first shouts of the Romans approaching. 'Leave the rest,' she had said when she had left at first light; she would find ways to replace them. 'Come away before the Romans arrive,' were her final words to him, but he could not abandon these special things. He wasn't completely sure why they were special, but he had guarded them with such diligence, he would not leave them now.

He took one more look at the activity outside, pulled the old wooden door gently closed and turned back into the house; but as he did so, he heard the latch lift in a flurry of wind. He hadn't closed it firmly enough. The latch slipped and the door swung open with a loud, agonising creak. He scrambled for the chest as fast as his old legs would carry him, but the legionaries were quick and before he could turn and draw his sword, they had him and dragged him out of the roundhouse towards the group of men he had watched arguing. One of them stood ahead of the rest as they approached.

'Who is this?'

'Dominus, we found him in the roundhouse over there, trying to hide.'

Gallus nodded his head as he looked at the aged warrior. 'What is your name?'

Bacun looked up; the Romin could speak the words of the Dewnan. 'Bacun, yer lordship.'

'Well, Bacun. Why is no one here, except you? Where have they all gone?'

Bacun said nothing.

'Come on, I need to know. Quickly, tell me where they have gone.'

'Not certain, yer lordship. Cud be anywhere by now.'

The lead man glared back at Bacun and then, from the group behind him, a younger man stepped forward and drew his sword, stepped forward again and held it to Bacun's neck.

'Tell us, old man. If you value your life, tell us where they have gone.'

As firmly as his weathered face would allow, Bacun stared with disdain at the Roman. He did not know what he had said, but he could guess. He looked down at the sword, back into the eyes of the Roman and simply said, 'Oi dunno.'

'Nauarchus Flavius, stand back, threatening him will almost certainly get us nowhere, and anyway, we all know where they have gone and Gyras here and the scouts will guide us.'

He turned to the officer group behind him.

Pilus Prior Horatius, tie him up and set light to the buildings, let it be clear to all around of our intent and then we move quickly on.

Bacun, only held loosely by his guards, watched in horror as first they lit their torches and then began to set light to the roundhouses. Quickly, the soldiers moved along the line of buildings and approached the house of the parchments. With one last mighty sweep of his arms, Bacun broke free, drew his sword and turned to run towards the roundhouse.

'Ee'll burn that over my dead body, yer bloody fools! Don't yer know was in there!'

They didn't, of course, and even if they had known, they wouldn't have cared. The old warrior said no more. Flavius drew his sword, walked forward, thrust it between Bacun's shoulder blades, twisted hard, and then withdrew it. The old man fell to his knees, blood pouring from his mouth, with his sword arm outstretched as smoke began to billow from the parchment house, and then fell flat on his face in the dirt.

Flavius turned, and without looking towards him, walked back past Gallus and towards the men gathering on the far side of the compound. For a moment, the Praefectus said nothing, as anger again threatened to overwhelm him.

Then he turned and said to the waiting group, 'Let's get the job done. We need to be before the citadel and properly camped by nightfall.'

***

After returning from the lands of the Tin Lords and the Kernovi the previous evening, the King's servants unloaded the carts and wagons of the royal train and required good light to bring items into the hall. Unusually, therefore, the doors to the hall at Ker Kammel were wide open as Morlain and Steren Uskis galloped up from the track that ran alongside Heyl Kammel.

As they approached the door, Elowen rode up similarly on the far side of the hill and crossed the inner ward of the fortress. They dismounted, embraced and strode into the hall. In the midst of the unpacking, nobody stopped them. Or, if they had heard the news, perhaps chose not to stop them. As they crossed the midpoint, they saw Mawgan at the far end, still shrouded in semi-darkness and not at his usual table. He sat, instead, on a low chair on the dais. Around him were several of his close followers. Andras stood behind him and his brother, Idrus of Dynasdore, sat in front of him on a similar low chair. As the priestesses approached, Mawgan looked towards them.

'Ha! I might have known. Your protégé is in danger and so here you are, many moons since your previous visit, no doubt seeking my assistance.'

'King Mawgan, he is not my protégé, he is your son, and yes, I come to seek your help. He is half a day's determined ride from here, yet, it seems, a world away. He faces great peril. The Romans invade the land of the Dewnan, your land, and your son makes a stand of resistance against them. Will you not come to his aid?'

'You are very bold, young lady, to walk into this hall and make demands of me. It is not so long since you were a ward of this court, picked up as a waif and stray by my wife in some distant field and indulged by her, full of goodness that she was. You took advantage of that and now, through your contrivance, you are back to take advantage of me! I see through you.'

She had heard it all before.

'Lord King, if it is boldness I am accused of, let me give you further proof of it and tell you this: already the Roman Caesar has utterly vanquished the Veneti, destroyed their fleet and hung up the Veneti King and Queen and their royal household on a cross to die. Each had the opportunity to contemplate their misfortune as they suffered a long lingering death, pecked at and defiled by the crows and the gulls.'

She looked along the dais.

'Yes, their entire household. If we do not stand and fight now, push them back into Ocean, then more will come as soon as winter has passed. We must stop it now, before it gets much worse and before we are consigned to a similar fate.'

Andras smiled calmly back at her from behind her father's seat and said, 'Priestess, the Veneti's fate is a consequence of their provocation of Caesar. Other nations and tribes across Gaul have reached an agreement with Rome and now live in peace and prosperity. Surely, an accommodation is the sensible approach for our long-term future? The Romans traverse Nanmeur toward a meeting with the great King Mawgan. We stand ready to discuss alliances.'

Morlain stared firmly back at Andras as she put her hand on Mawgan's shoulder and he reached up to hold it.

'Prynces, I am sure you know that as soon as we accommodate them, as you put it, our independence is over. The Pretan heritage we have fought so long to defend will be lost forever. All that is distinct and unique about us will disappear into the great swathe of conformity that is the Roman way. Accommodation for them means that they take control and we do as they say.'

Andras snorted and then constructed a face of fake pity. 'Why must you continue to peddle this Pretan nonsense? Those days are gone, Morlain. They went many years ago and you need to come to terms with that.'

She shook her head and affected a sad and disappointed look.

'It has been difficult to have you at the court of King Mawgan and welcome you as the high priestess, as we should, when you refuse to give up this talk. We need to look forward and an alliance with the Romans, or other potential allies, is the future of the Dewnan!'

The King looked on sternly. Morlain said. 'Do you mean allies such as the Belgae?'

Andras said cautiously, but sternly, 'I might do, if it was an allegiance that was favourable to Mawgan and the Dewnan.'

Mawgan looked to Idrus who raised his eyebrows ever so slightly, while others on the dais looked furtively to one another. Would they really make allegiance with the Belgae?

'And favourable to you, I assume.'

'I only act to serve the King's purpose.'

'Do you? And does that include paying Belgae warriors to invade the land of the Dewnan and threaten its very existence.'

Andras was just about maintaining her stoic appearance. 'I have no notion of what you are talking about.'

'I think you do. King Mawgan, brave and noble King of my childhood, your son remains in great peril, so I will come straight to the point. At the wax of Loor Tevyans, one of the Lady Elowen's acolytes, asked to keep a watch on the movements of the Lady Andras, followed her and the woman Zethar to a remote heath on Tamara's far bank. The acolyte watched while Lady Andras handed over a large amount of gold, given no doubt by you or perhaps by Heulwen, of sacred name, to a large, lone Belgae warrior. Then, on the final day of the moon, this same man led a force of crack Belgae warriors and enslaved Durotrages farmers in an attack against the twin forts at the crossing. I am sure you received word of it. Fortunately, your son and his Company fought bravely and determinedly that day. Artur killed the lead Belgae warrior in single combat, the Company routed the Belgae force and he freed the Durotrages farmers. He and the Company have subsequently gone to the aid of your Veneti kin and again fought bravely against enormous odds, escaped at the end and come home to defend the land of the Dewnan. Will you not come to his aid?'

Morlain paused and Mawgan sat up in his chair and turned to his daughter. 'Is this true?'

'She lies, father, sorceress that she is, and attempts to manipulate us as she tries to manipulate everything. Do not let her. It will be to our ruin.'

Morlain calmly continued, 'Honoured King, there is one other thing that you need to know about the large Belgae warrior. Before Artur went into battle at the twin forts, he confided in me and told me that he recognised him. It was the same man that he had seen through the keyhole of his hiding place, as a boy, and watched helplessly as the brute callously hacked down Heulwen, his mother, your wife, and of sacred and fondest memory to so many of us in this land. King Mawgan, there was a significant size difference between the two of them, a mismatch in normal circumstances, but Artur sought revenge and justice and fought with such resolve. He brought great credit to you and to the Dewnan.'

Mawgan turned again to Andras and, at first, she just shook her head, but the sternness of his look in response to the hesitancy and anguish in her face, and something in the depth of the father-daughter relationship, meant she could not lie, no matter how much she might have wanted to.

Quietly, she said, speaking only to him. 'I did not know. Father, you have to believe me. I swear I did not know.'

And in those simple words, she was condemned. Even if she did not know about his responsibility for her mother's death, she had still associated with the Belgae, paid him to invade the land of the Dewnan and Mawgan could not forgive that.

The spell was broken, she looked like her mother, but she was not her mother and not his beloved wife. How he needed Heulwen now, wished that she were here, with her wisdom and support.

In the dimness of the room, not all could see how his eyes moistened. But, as quickly as the surge of remorse overwhelmed him, he gained control of it again and said, coldly and firmly, 'Go, leave me, and go away from here. Take whatever funds you have remaining and find somewhere different to live, I do not want to see you again.'

'Father, please, I did it for us. We need strong allies and we need to be part of a bigger land, join with the Estrenyons; otherwise, we have no future, can't you see?'

Mawgan called across the hall, 'Guards, yes, you there, will you escort the Lady Andras from the building, please? She is going on a long journey and needs to leave quickly before I am moved to stronger action.'

The guards came forward, up onto the dais. Hesitantly, they urged Andras forward while all on the dais watched on, stupefied by the sudden turn of events; the turn of the tide.

Andras stopped in front of Morlain.

'You were always a usurper and thief,' she spat, 'fawned over by my sainted mother. I hate you.'

The guards urged her forward more strongly now, but she dug her heels in for a moment as Morlain stared plain-faced back at her and said, 'Andras, all I craved was to be your friend, from the first day I came. The big sister I had always wanted.'

'Friends. Don't make me laugh! You wormed your way into my mother's affections and stole all that she had to give me and I have loathed and despised you ever since; but now, you, your children and your children's children will never be free of me. I am resolved. I will breed a line that will wait for its chance, and will not rest until we have our revenge on you, my perfect little brother and all your bastard progeny.'

Now the guards moved her, dragging her across the hall, still making her voice heard.

'Yes, I know about that, ensnaring him in your web of deceit and lies.'

'Please, madam, you have to leave,' said the lead guard.

'Watch your back, Morlain. Never rest easy. I curse you and all who come from you.'

The guards dragged her out of the door and she was gone.

Everyone, even the King, now looked at Morlain, who smiled and said gently, but confidently, 'Do not concern yourselves. She has no power over me and never will have. Heulwen did not just pick up any waif and stray. She chose me for a reason: to help her to realise a destiny that she foresaw, a destiny for Mawgan, Artur, myself and all of the Dewnan, and one that I intend to see fulfilled.' She let that sink in for a moment and then said, 'So, King Mawgan, do you remember the days when you and Queen Heulwen rode out together, wearing the rings of Ictasus and Diantha? I do, they were great days and all the Dewnan looked to you. Well, now the ring of Diantha nestles on Artur's finger and see, here, I have the ring of Eupheme nestling on mine. Will you bring the ring of Ictasus into battle? Will you come to your son's aid? King Mawgan, noble and honoured King, I urge you: quickly now, before it is too late, call the Lords of the Dewnan to battle and raise the Banner of the Rings. Never has your son needed you more.'

∗∗∗

Artur, Maedoc, Kea and Gwalian stood on the walkway that ran around the inside of the perimeter fence of the citadel of Menluit, positioned half a man's height below the top of the sharpened upright posts of the palisade. Additional horizontal posts, which had been positioned, sharpened end outwards at an obtuse angle to the walkway, provided further defence and rested between every third and fourth upright. The intention was that every man or woman who remained should defend a three upright post gap, but they did not have anywhere near enough people to fill all of the gaps. Four hundred defenders were needed to cover the battlements that faced the fields but little more than two hundred remained within the citadel. There was no escaping it, the situation was grave and they all knew it. Artur's optimism about holding Menluit, as Morlain had asked him to, was diminishing. They watched sombrely, therefore, as Callard and the remaining Veneti in the field – Ambros, Marrek and their gilles – walked backwards from the mantraps towards the main gate.

Suddenly, Marrek shouted and pointed, and they all came back quickly. Something glinted on the main path amongst the trees and now they could hear horses' hooves, many of them.

Artur shouted along the fence to the gate. 'Nouran, Gourgy, horses approach. Be ready to close the gate as soon as Callard, Ambros and Marrek are through.'

As they came out of the trees, many of the riders looked backwards. Then, as the front of the column reached the bottom of the dip between the two hills and began the steep rise to the gates, the lead rider looked up towards them on the battlement. It was Hedrek! The Prince ran along the battlement to the gate.

'Hold the gate; riders coming in. Warriors are arriving from Dynasdore!'

Kea pointed. 'Look, in the wood. The Curiosolitae are on their tail. The enemy is trying to cut off the rear. Look, they are coming from the sides, as well – they are only just going to make it. Drustan wields his sword at the back. Come on, Drustan!'

Many of the defenders, on hearing the shouting, rushed to the open space below the fence and around the gate. Artur called down.

'Gawen, it is time for that mighty bow of yours. Others with bows, follow Gawen's lead, we must give them cover as they come in.'

Gwalian beside him, her body as lithe and nimble as the great bowman from beyond RunHoul, swung down from the plank walkway to where she had left her bow. She called to her small group of archers, the former slaves, to join her and was quickly back up again, loading her first arrow. Curiosolitae warriors were breaking out of the wood, coming across the far end of the fields from the right as they watched, closing in on the rear of the retreating column. Hedrek and the front of the column approached the gate, but Drustan was still coming down on the far side, and now Curiosolitae warriors were appearing from the woods on the left of the path, closing on the column's rear.

Gawen and Gwalian stood on either side of Artur. She called, 'Gawen, take the left. I'll take the right.' All of her archers took aim also. 'Wait until they get in range!'

Artur looked to them both and nodded; he knew their ability. Gawen quickly scrambled along the post spaces to the left and positioned himself.

Drustan and several around him looked to the left, and then the right, while the lead Curiosolitae chasers closed in like a v-shaped pincer.

'Nearly there, wait for it!' Gwalian almost seemed to be enjoying herself. She was able now to do her bit, to emulate her beloved father and brother and take the fight to the enemy. 'Are you ready? I will have five of these traitorous vermin before you do, Gawen!'

She was poised, her bow stave contorted to its maximum extent and the hemp string taut. 'Ready, as they rise to the gate. Now we have them – fire!'

Her arrow, swift and true, pierced the lead Curiosolitae in the chest. He stumbled and, in doing so, impeded the two immediately behind him. With lightning speed and accuracy, she fired again and took out a second warrior and then a third; but Gawen was her equal and the left flank of the Curiosolitae began to falter also. Around her, arrows flew as her archers delivered their first shot in anger, and everyone along the fence cheered and shouted encouragement to the galloping riders. Then, from the woods, came a shout. The Curiosolitae warriors slowed and the horses galloped on. Hedrek was through the gate and then Drustan approached at the rear and was through.

'Close both gates – everyone's through. Get them barred!'

Nouran and Gourgy stepped forward and led the shove to close the thick oaken gates. 'Shoulders int'it lads, you erd the man. Les have these buggers shut, quick as we can now.'

Artur jumped down from the fence and ran over to where Drustan was dismounting. 'Cousin, we are very pleased to see you. We had thought that, as the Romans and Curiosolitae closed in, you would not get through.'

Agitated and breathing heavily, Drustan stood before his cousin and said, 'Artur, we set out on this quest together, we have fought hard together and we will finish it together. Although, yes, it was a bit touch and go there! At least, we have some able bowmen on our side.'

'Bowmen and bowwomen. Gwalian led the firing, brought the first Curiosolitae down and several more with rapid firing. Gawen, of course, matched her.'

Drustan smiled at his cousin. 'Really? Then I am glad that she is here also. That was some very accurate shooting. She must have been practising.'

Artur smiled back, 'Yes, I believe she has!' Then, looking around at the horses and the dismounted riders, he asked, 'Drustan, how many do you bring?'

'Eighty-five of us left Dynasdore at first light and all, as far as I am aware, have come through. I brought up the rear, as you saw. Artur, my father was not at home when we arrived yesterday, and instead had set off to talk with your father at Ker Kammel. The Lady Morlain, it seems, has been at Dynasdore in recent days. He has gone to try and persuade the King to action. As we rested and ate before sleeping, word reached us of the Roman and Curiosolitae force, in addition to the Romans that pursued us. So, we asked for volunteers at Dynasdore and in the immediate surrounding farms and rounds to join us in the defence. Some of the men of the boats re-enlisted, but many were exhausted and wished to see their families again, and so the men that we bring are a mix of old comrades and fresh fighters.'

'Cousin, it is good to have all of you with us. We still cannot cover every post gap, I think, but we are much strengthened and much heartened by your arrival.'

The man of Dynasdore handed his reins to his gille and looked around as the gilles led the horses from the gate. He looked back to his cousin and said quietly but with urgency, 'Artur, it is a considerable force. We came along the old track from Menitriel that leads down to the ford. We saw them and there were many, coming around the hill over there as we galloped along the line of the gover. They must be on Tamara as well, and at least some scaled the cliffs, I assume, to close in on our right flank as we galloped to the main gate. They will surround us soon, I am sure.'

'Yes, I know. Cousin, we must gather and inspire our people; the odds are heavily against us still, but you and the men of Dynasdore rekindle a small flame of optimism. We can do this!'

'Artur, you need to come and see!' It was Kea, still up on the battlement.

Artur, Drustan and others scrambled up. To their right, as they looked, the land dipped away in a gentle sweep around the hill of Menluit until it came to the small conical hill on which sat Cantassa's sanctum. It was quiet now, with no obvious sign of occupation. Within this quadrant of view, this arc of a quarter circle, the land descended from Menluit, flattened for a short distance and then rose again, providing a bowl-like shape or portion of an amphitheatre that the Romans would recognise. Several dips were cut into the higher ground on the far side as they looked. These folds in the land were entrances to the natural theatre where a spring-fed watercourse fed the gover and moved on to Tamara. Through these entrances, the Roman and Curiosolitae force came, directed by their commanders, forming lines on the far side of the bowl and spreading out and around Menluit. Quickly, a line formed around the edge of their arc of vision and then away beyond Cantassa's hill, out of their vision.

A division of the Curiosolitae began to fill the land that led immediately away from the path to the gate. Then, a division of Romans appeared in the land that led around to the hill of the sanctum. Finally, coming in behind them, on and around Menluit, was another division of Curiosolitae.

Artur turned to Drustan and looked across to Maedoc, Kea, Gawen, Silyen, Callard and Gwalian. 'We are going to have to try to cover the far side as well, it seems. Can you gather everyone, before they are all in position and ready to move, or whatever they intend to do next. Callard, while we are talking to everyone, could you position a few of the garrison around the full circle of the battlements? Just enough so that we can see everything they are doing.'

Tremaine came rushing from between the roundhouses and across the open space between them and the battlement. Artur looked to him as he approached, his face full of urgency and agitation.

'Pryns Artur, Tamara carries many Curiosolitae, thirty boats at least. Men have disembarked from a small number of them on this side of the river, and they move around the base of the hill to the far side of the citadel. Most, though, wait on the opposite bank. It looks like they mean to cover our escape rather than scale the bank in any number. For now, at least.'

'Thank you, Tremaine. Leave a few men to watch their movements and then tell everyone else to gather here as quickly as possible now.'

He jumped down from the walkway and walked towards the centre of the open space. The defenders began to gather and soon all, bar the essential watch, stood around him as he clambered onto one of the empty carts that had been brought back down the hill from Pendre.

'Our task is to hold Menluit. The men of Dynasdore have arrived and we can maintain the defence with their help. For now, there are many more enemy forces, so we must not lose concentration and be ever vigilant, night and day. We have sufficient provisions. We must look to each other, support each other, and then hope that others will come to our aid. Even now, the Lady Morlain and others have gone to rally support, but we must hold out for at least the next three days. We can do this. They want to take all that is ours and then they want to control us. We have to hold Menluit!'

He paused and looked around him. Grim and sombre faces looked back at him.

'In daylight, we can see further and watch more with fewer people, so we will take watches, half of us watching, half of us resting. During the night, however, we must all cover the perimeter, there are only just enough of us and we cannot allow any unseen approaches. Callard, Drustan, Hedrek, the rest of the Company and I will take responsibility for sections, not just the trev fields, as I've said previously. In a moment, we will split all of you amongst these leads.'

He paused again. Gwalian and Maedoc were coming through the assembled defenders, dragging something. Drustan and Callard helped to clear the way. Gwalian stood before the cart and those around her stood back to allow her some space.

'Pryns Artur, this is the Sword of Menluit, you know it and all those who are here know it. My father ensured it came back to you from Armorica, before he died fighting valiantly against the Roman aggressor. For many years, only my father has drawn this sword. No others would dare to try, for only the Lord of the Crossing, protector of Nanmeur and Tamara's chosen defender can wield it.'

Artur jumped down from the cart and stood before her. Gwalian continued, 'The sword is the gift of Tamara, the goddess and spirit of the Great Valley, a power of the ancient days. Many have given their swords to her, by casting them into her watery depths, but this sword is presented by her to the Lord of the Crossing, Orsa's heir, to protect and fight for the Valley and all that we hold dear, and it is always sharp for this purpose.'

She paused, looked about her and then said quickly, 'Even with the Romans at the gates, we must do this properly. Three at least must try to unsheathe the sword before the rightful heir; it has always been so, leaving no doubt about the chosen one. Drustan, Kea and Gawen must try to do this with as much strength as they can muster, and in doing so, represent men from all the Dewnan lands. As the heir of Aodren, last Lord of the Crossing, I will also try.'

Drustan, Kea and Gawen each came forward, gripped the scabbard and hilt and tried to remove the sword, but they could not. It was heavy; you could see that in their faces. All three were muscular and capable of lifting and pulling with great strength, but they could not draw the sword. Gwalian could not lift the scabbard off the ground and so, instead, gripped it, resting it upright on the ground and then pulled hard. She could not remove the sword either.

She continued to hold the scabbard upright as Artur stepped forward. All around him held their breath, while he guardedly gripped the scabbard and lifted it. It weighed nothing and he lifted it with ease. The gathered defenders smiled, in partial relief, but also at his genuine look of surprise. He breathed in deeply, gripped the scabbard, pulled on the hilt and the sword slid smoothly and silently out.

He jumped back on the cart and held the sword aloft. As he turned the hilt in his hand, it caught the rays of Sira Howl and reflected them down onto the massed defenders.

'Hope is alive! I am Lord of the Crossing and will lead the defence of this Valley and all the lands of the Dewnan, continuing the fight that so many have bravely fought before.'

As he spoke, the ring of Diantha, determined to be as bold as any sparkling sword, twinkled and winked on his hand. Many of those watching noticed and whispered comments passed amongst the assembled group.

Artur continued, 'Comrades, friends, to the battlements, let us prepare for our vigil. Our ancestors are with us. The ring of Diantha is on my finger. Tamara gives us her blessing with this sword. We must be strong and concentrate, we will prevail!'

The Company, Callard and several other senior members of the Veneti garrison, quickly went amongst them and split the defenders. As Sira Howl reached his midday peak and began his gradual decent, they took up their posts, positioned their weapons, agreed day watches and looked on as the Romans and Curiosolitae laid their siege.

***

Marcus Trebius Gallus, accompanied by the senior centurion Pilus Prior Horatius, inspected the front lines of the siege. They had reached the Curiosolitae who were lined up adjacent to the path to the gate.

'Send word along the line for the Massaliot.'

After a while, the grim-faced Greek came up the hill with Flavius and one of his centurions.

'Nauarchus Flavius, thank you for joining us, but it was the Massaliot I wished to talk to. I would not take you away from your siege deployments.'

'Praefectus Gallus, our siege preparations are complete and I am ready to lead my men in an assault on this disappointingly inconsequential citadel in the morning. I have spoken to the King and we will be ready at first light. We will have dealt with the rebels, captured what we seek and be on our way back to the port by tomorrow afternoon. I am optimistic of an audience with Caesar by Nonae September or Idus at very latest. Are you prepared and ready to join us?'

Gallus fought the urge to strike Flavius and, instead, told him, 'Nauarchus, you will not attack at dawn, unless on my command. There has been no resistance to our approach, no response to our burning of their temple. It is as if they want us to move to this point, to draw us in. It makes me uneasy; something is not right and I wish to consult with the Massaliot further.'

After listening to them both with increasing frustration, Gyras said, 'I will tell you again what I think. There will have been a depletion of warriors in the citadel, we have to imagine, with so many Veneti having gone to the fight in Armorica. The King of the Dewnan is weak and does not defend his land as he should. His son is young but has the potential to be a much stronger leader. He led the boats that brought the treasure here and no doubt organises the defence of the citadel as we speak. In fact, I think I glimpsed him on the battlement, although it is hard to be sure, my sight over distance is not as it was. Then there is a young high priestess. You burnt her temple earlier. She is the dangerous one, who probably directs the response of the countryside around us, and maybe in the citadel or, more worryingly, I would suggest, might be out raising support. She is clever, determined and not given to rash and impetuous actions, as so many of them are. You need to be prepared to deal with her.'

Flavius snorted as the Greek paused to consider what he would say next.

'You are asking the legionaries of Rome to quake in their boots at the prospect of a boy, a handful of defenders and a woman, please! Praefectus Gallus, surely, we must storm the battlements, take the treasure and withdraw to the port. You establish your winter base and I cross the sea to the Pro-Consul. Let us not delay any longer than we have to!'

Horatius, standing dutifully aside and looking back into the woods, raised his head. Something was happening at the furthest extent he could see. He walked away quickly to find out more. There were shouts in the wood, a clash of sword on sword and, all around them, men turned towards the sound. Gallus and Flavius drew their swords. Horatius ran back.

'Dominus, they are coming up from the stream very quickly, quite a few of them. Mainly swords and several supporting bowmen, or possibly women. Hard to tell, they dress alike.'

He ducked as an arrow whistled through the air past him, and another struck his helmet. Gallus quickly took charge, with both Latin and Curiosolitae words.

'Prepare to engage, take cover!'

'Nauarchus Flavius, take the Greek back to your position. We will deal with this and do not do anything further without my command.'

***

Maedoc, his knees bent and head just above the line of sharpened upright posts, studied the Curiosolitae and Roman line intently. He made a quiet noise of affirmation and then stood back from the fence and moved along to where the Prince crouched in the adjacent space talking to Gawen.

'Artur, look over the fence and along the path and a bit to the right of it, as it enters the trees. Just behind the line, there are several Romans talking to each other and beside them is that Greek trader, Gyras. I thought I had seen him on one of the boats that pursued us.

Artur cautiously lifted his head above the top of the fence.

'Yes, I think it is.'

'So, he has led them to us. He was assessing the land and us and he's given them the confidence to pursue this because of what he has told them. I knew he was up to something! Just wait till he comes into the range of my sword arm!'

All three of them now looked again to the besieging line where crows, disturbed by something, took flight from the trees above and the Curiosolitae warriors began to turn. The sound of metal clattering against metal grew louder, and they saw the occasional glint of reflected light deeper in the trees.

'They are being attacked from the rear!' Maedoc spoke first.

Along the perimeter fence, others stood to watch as the Curiosolitae by the path, and the small number of Romans amongst them, turned to face whoever came at them from within the woods. One of the Romans, who was tall, helmetless and distinctive from the rest, had taken command and was directing both Roman and Curiosolitae.

Then, a sword was raised, a face appeared and then several more, not yet distinguishable, and they began to fight on the path. Still, the Curiosolitae had their backs to them. Suddenly, a blade pierced through the back of one of the Curiosolitae warriors and the deep red blood spurting out from him was clearly visible. The blade withdrew and the warrior fell to reveal the first of the advancing attackers. He was short and stocky, with long grey hair and a matching beard. Even at this distance, many on the palisade recognised the diminutive but determined figure of Lord Casworon.

Others began to appear and more Curiosolitae and several of the attackers fell as the fight continued. Casworon and his force were fighting in a square, pushing their way along the path. Several carried bows, slung across their backs, but all now fought with a sword as they sought to break their way through.

The Prince turned away from Maedoc and Gwalian and shouted to the gate, 'Nouran, Gourgy, open the gates.' He turned back to Gwalian and Maedoc. 'We are going out to give them cover as they come along the path. Gawen – cover us from the battlements!'

The Prince's section stood ready, others joined them and he led them out through the open gate. Slowly, Casworon's force extricated itself and the rear of the fighters, with Casworon now back in their midst, began to emerge. Artur drew the Sword of Menluit as arrows continued to fly, some striking home, some missing their mark. The Roman leader and several other Romans alongside the Curiosolitae fought hard and were beginning to gain the advantage. The rear of Casworon's Dewnan still engaged. The old warrior seemed to be tiring, but none of those who remained would leave his side. The

Prince stepped forward to assist and, as he did, Maedoc came alongside him and the men of the Prince's section, along with Gwalian and her archers. They charged forward and swung into the flanks of the Romans and Curiosolitae on both sides of Casworon and his people, preventing those further down the line from surrounding them.

'Pull back!' The Prince shouted across to Casworon. 'Pull back; we are fresher, we can cover you. Pull back to the citadel!'

The older man nodded his head, red-faced and panting, and he, and those around him, slowly moved backwards away from the clash.

Nouran and Gourgy, unable to resist, had left their position as guards of the gate to join the fight. 'Gettin' bored with gate duty – openin', shuttin'. Feel the urge, brother, to stick it in a few of these Curiosities!'

Maedoc stood beside the Prince at the front of the sword-swinging Dewnans as they hacked at the Curiosilitae line and made eye contact with the trader from Massalia as he looked beyond the front line. Gyras tried to look away but knew that he could not. He was to blame, partially, but how could he tell them that he had no choice. Would they care? Whatever they thought, if they broke through, he would stand and face the charge against him.

Gwalian was the most effective of all in the attack. A little way to the rear of the line, she led her small group of archers. They moved left to right and back again, looking for gaps in the Dewnan line, before firing through them with deadly accuracy and keeping the siege line beyond at bay. At least, for the moment.

The lead Roman ahead had withdrawn a little and was shouting instructions. To Artur's surprise, he understood what he said, 'Take down the woman with the bow and those supporting her! Where are the sagittarii?'

Three Curiosolitae ran forward and positioned themselves, waiting for their moment. Artur looked behind him and saw Gwalian, who was firing on and looking along the line.

Desperately, he shouted, 'Gwalian, bows on your right!' as loud as he could as he parried another sword thrust and Maedoc cut deeply into a belly in front of him.

Now the former slaves were exposed; they could not fire as quickly as the woman of the Veneti and the arrows flew towards them faster than they could respond. She saw one and pulled a comrade down as it flew over their heads. But then an arrow struck a shoulder of another on her opposite side and he staggered back.

She rose with determination, responsible for those around her, and moved so fast that the enemy bowmen were not able to react. Instantly, she loaded and fired twice, taking down two of the Curiosolitae, with arrows that pierced an eye and the heart respectively.

Following her lead, the archer she had pulled down, stood, flexed his bow and fired straight into the third Curiosilitae's belly.

'Good shooting!' cried Gwalian.

That was close enough for the Prince and he called back to her, 'Move back; take the archers back and get ready to cover us. Nouran, Gourgy, got to go – not going to win the fight here. They will find a way around us soon.'

Maedoc swung his sword in front of him, slicing two legs and continuing to swing it wildly. Artur grabbed his arm, pulled him back and shouted, 'Back to the gates! Gwalian, Maedoc and I will pick up the wounded archer on the way back.'

They backed away, turned and ran along the path as the arrows flew between them towards the Curiosolitae line. A number of the Curiosolitae tried to give chase, but Gwalian and her remaining archers brought them down and once Artur, Maedoc and the rest had passed, backed away swiftly and then, out of range of any Curiosolitae or Roman archer, turned and ran back up the path. Artur and Maedoc waited, watched them through the gate before following them as the guard, in high spirits now, heaved both sets of gates shut behind them.

***

Gallus watched as they retreated into the citadel. It was a setback. There could be no denying it. At least, he had sent Flavius away, but word would spread down the line. The lack of any attack during their approach to the citadel had lulled them into a false sense of security and the frailty of their position was exposed. He could not rely on the efficiency of the Curiosolitae auxiliaries to maintain an effective defence of their rear and his thoughts turned to a redistribution of the siege line.

Bodies lay all around him, mainly Curiosolitae, but several Romans had also fallen, including his senior centurion, Horatius, which caused him a pang of regret. He was a promising young commander who had risen quickly and had been with him for several years. Horatius had been taken down by one of the two fat Dewnan warriors, who, he had to acknowledge, swung their swords with great efficiency despite their girth.

He turned and a little way into the trees, away from the fight, he was surprised to see that Gyras the Massaliot still stood with his legionary minder. Gallus walked across to him.

'I take it the young man was the King's son you talk of?'

'Yes, Pryns Artur of the Dewnan. His bravery has increased through the battles he has fought and, I am sure, through the things he has seen.'

'Who were the warriors that fought their way through?'

'I do not know. I have not seen them before, although I think the old man would not have lasted much longer, before collapsing, if the Prince had not intervened.'

'Hmm and the woman with the bow... the Priestess you speak of?'

'No, the daughter of the Veneti lord of this place. He has not returned, because if he had, she would not be out here. She is very skilled with the bow.'

'She is indeed; she made the difference, I would say, despite the tenacity of their fighters.'

Gallus turned away and looked towards the battlements of the citadel. He had tried to have her killed, he had to, he knew that, but she had quickly dealt with that. Her eyes, supremely alert, had scanned the line and reacted with great swiftness and dexterity to what they saw. Once, twice maybe, they had met his and for the tiniest moment had registered him and then moved on. Now, he could not get those eyes out of his head.

***

Casworon and his comrades sat exhausted on an area of grass in the open ground between the roundhouses and the battlements. The Prince was the last through the gates and after helping to close them, walked across and sat down next to the old warrior.

'Lord Casworon, you bring us great hope, although I am not sure I would have attempted it. We are honoured to have you here.'

The old man's long, white-flecked hair hung loosely in a mixture of straight and curled strands across his face. His beard had specks of blood and mud interspersed with the damp of sweat and the grey and black stray whiskers. Slowly, he raised his head, his face red and blotched with exertion and exhaustion. His eyes were bloodshot and his simple tunic and leggings stained with the marks of sweat, piss and blood. He raised his gnarled, bruised sword hand and pushed his hair back from his face.

'Thank ee, Lord Prince. We thought of the poor brave souls 'ere in our actions and a desire to come to support ee. T'would be a falsehood tho' not ter acknowledge that 'er ladyship came by Casworon's erly and said ee needed help, sort of 'elp such as only warriors of experience can provide; although I zuzpect experience is somat yu've ad lots of recently. Go elp 'em Casworon, she said, if yer can; take others. So 'ere we are, Casworon, missus Casworon and forty brave souls, although some wuz lost in yonder trees, ready ter fight the ole bloody Romin army if needs be!'

His tired face broke out in a grin and what remained of his teeth were revealed, distributed randomly in the gap that had emerged between his dry, chapped lips; and then he said, 'Albeit, an only if yer feel able ter oblige, I should be grateful for a short bit o'rest first.'

Artur laughed. 'I think we could all do with a bit of rest while Sira Howl is above. We must all keep watch from the battlements, however, after dark. With your arrival, I think we have just enough now to cover the full perimeter.'

'Right yer are, direct and uz'll do as ee asks. I 'ave no doubt er ladyship went to yer father. She'll be back with 'em afore much longer. If any'un can persuade em, she can, special lady an defender o'the Dewnan. Then, we can all go stickin' Romins and Curiosities together!'

The grin again and then, as he raised himself aching and weary to his feet, he said, 'Now, if I might scuze myself for a wile, Oim gona ask missus Casworon ter soothe my sore ed an shoulders with er wondrous ands afore our night duties begin.'

Artur smiled and nodded his agreement. The old warrior walked slowly to a woman sat cross-legged and talking to others around her. She looked younger than Casworon, although his battered, aged looks might well be a consequence of his many battles. Her hair hung long, down and across her chest; black with grey flecks. Her eyes had an alertness as she engaged in conversation with those around; and, of course, he now realised that she was one of the small group of warriors, along with Casworon, fighting until all of their people were through. The old warrior sat down in front of her, leant back and rested his head in her lap. She looked at those around her with her eyebrows raised and then down at him. He said something that made her laugh, in spite of their exertion and their losses, and slowly she began to run her fingers through his hair before gently gripping and manipulating his shoulders.

Artur smiled as he watched and thought of Morlain – where was she right now? With a further smile, he thought of the previous evening, then jumped to his feet and walked away to look for Gwalian, to congratulate her on her excellent shooting.

***

Darkness fell quickly, clouds built, the wind freshened from Ocean and rain began to fall. Simple campfires burned and flames flickered in the wind all along the siege line, warming evening rations. The Roman section of the siege had erected small tents behind the line and the wind tugged gently at the bases and the flaps of the entrances. The narrowness of the valley did not allow their usual camp arrangement, but still, through habit and training, the tents had a recognisably rectangular and defendable shape. They had dug a ditch around them and set a guard; but it was a cursory arrangement. They did not expect to remain long.

Spread away from the camp in both directions, in a line that undulated like a length of rope slung casually around the base of the hill, was the Curiosolitae line. Spears and shields were stacked ready for use, while the warriors sat talking quietly, wrapped in heavy cloaks against the increasing dampness. After the breach, Gallus had ordered the line to be tightened and moved forward, so it was still out of range of the defenders' now proven sagittarii, but tight enough to provide an increased pressure of men from the besiegers. Behind the line and on all of the high points around them, the Praefectus had also positioned small watch detachments to ensure a better warning of any further attack from the rear.

In one of the tents, Flavius and King Brice discussed their situation in quiet voices and without Gallus, against his express command. In his best Latin, the King spoke purposefully to the Roman.

'My men are all in position. We have all sides of the citadel covered. Others wait on the opposite bank of the river for any who try to escape. We must attack at first light, but the Praefectus seems hesitant?'

'After the earlier debacle, he no doubt licks his wounds, but we must reassert our position and take control. My men are ready. The Praefectus is used to the siege tactics of Gaul against large oppidums, not small fortlets such as this, and is unsure, I fear, of what to do next. I, however, come from a different bloodline. What do you propose?'

'Ladders positioned against the battlement on this side, away from the main gate. We place them during the night. My men have been constructing them...'

He stopped mid-sentence as the sentry outside the tent said, 'Praefectus Gallus, Dominus.' This was partly to acknowledge Gallus's approach, but also to warn those within.

The King and Flavius stood up as Gallus strode into the tent and, for a moment, looked testily at both of them before saying, 'King Brice, Nauarchus, prepare your men; we will attack in the final hour before dawn. King Brice, I will look to you to scale the battlements here and around to the far side of the citadel with those ladders I know your men have been constructing. Nauarchus, you will lead the main thrust of our forces here, utilising the King's ladders. I, meanwhile, will lead the rest of our men, with the Curiosolitae division positioned before the main gate.'

For a moment, he looked back at them, full of irritation, expecting them to say something, but they did not, perhaps still surprised by his sudden entrance, and so he continued, 'Realise this, both of you. We should not be here. It is against my better judgement that we are, treasure or no treasure, and the breakthrough earlier underlined the frailty of our position. This camp will be very difficult to defend if they come at us in any sort of numbers. We should have stayed in the port but we are here and so we quickly need to try to overwhelm the citadel. If we are not able to do that, we will withdraw back to the port and a defendable position tomorrow afternoon.'

'Praefectus, you seek to apportion blame for the failure earlier, that is clear, and now you agree with what we have been saying all along. We need to attack.'

Flavius turned and smiled slyly at the King.

Gallus had had enough. Regardless of the King's presence, he stepped forward, grabbed Flavius by the collar of his tunic and pulled him towards him. 'Take care, Nauarchus. No, let us be clear, Trierarchus. If you continue in this vein, I shall have you arrested for insubordination and shipped back to the Pro-Consul in chains, with a full explanation for him as to why I have done so, do I make myself clear? Your position of authority is purely an illusion on your part and the King should know that. You are under my command and you will do as I say. Now, prepare your men and await my instruction.'

***

The three priestesses, comrades and old friends, stood together under the partial shelter of a densely leafed tree. Steren Uskis and the other two horses stood beyond the tree, impervious to the rain, quietly eating where the grass was more abundant.

'I am anxious, I will confess. I have never done it properly, never had cause to. It was hard. I remember that. Heulwen cautioned me to use it sparingly, only when it was really needed. She began my training but did not finish it and there is a nervousness against visible magic, as they perceive it, something they do not understand, amongst the Lords of the Dewnan.'

'Morlain, dearest,' Cantassa said, holding her eyes with hers, warmly and determinedly. 'No rule or misguided principle of the Dewnan lords matters now. Our interventions will define our lives and, we hope, many lives to come. None of us can be sure that we will deliver when we are called upon to do so, but we are determined to try our very hardest! And I, and all who stand with us, have every faith in you. It is time to reignite and give fire to the Dewnan, and all that we stand for, and to send the invader to the place that they belong.

Elowen smiled resolutely at both of them, and also at the exchange between her two friends.

'We are ready then. First, we will support a brave and determined stand; distraction and a sapping of confidence is our objective. Then, Morlain, High Priestess of the Dewnan will ride forward to battle!

***

Rain was falling heavily and the night wore on, dawn was not far away and they were all wet through, despite their heavy cloaks. Each defender held to their post space and watched for any sign of movement towards them. Fires still burned around the base of the hill and among the trees. Occasionally, they caught a glimpse of movement, but despite this, it appeared that the both Romans and Curiosolitae stayed in camp for the night.

The watch had commenced at dusk. Casworon and his people were allocated post spaces on the sparsely covered far side of the battlement where Marrek, Ambros and their sections covered two post spaces each. Artur had gone with Casworon to his deployment and then slowly made his way back along the barricade as it faced Cantassa's hill, passing Silyen, Hedrek, Kea, Callard, Drustan, Gawen and their sections. He had spoken to them all, taken their opinions and views on possible actions, and the potential turn of events.

As he crossed the abandoned trev to the battlements above Tamara, rivulets of water ran down the hill and between the buildings. The roofs of the houses dripped consistently and heavily onto the ground, creating gullies along the pathways that wound down the hill. Large puddles of muddy brown water were forming now by the gate and against the perimeter bank on which the fence and battlement stood.

With Tremaine and Briec, he peered down the steep fall to Tamara, which was all rustle and swirl. The joyful, confident, chattering and bubbling river cascaded forward and gathered fresh supplies of water to her cause. They could not, however, see any of the Curiosolitae; and so he picked his way back through the trev, past the worst of the mud and walked on. Here, he acknowledged the gate sections, where he could see Gwalian, Maedoc and the others of his section as they crouched against the battlement, watching for movement.

***

Gallus stood behind the section of the line under his direct command, just out of range of the sagittarii and the female sagittarii who had done so much damage earlier. He felt agitated, by her, and by the King and Flavius. He was not in control, even if he had been clear and authoritative with the Trierarchus, it did not feel right. He was uneasy and could not be certain they would do as he said, even if his reports told him they lined up in their positions, waiting for his command. This rain did not help. The ground was sodden underfoot. It would not be easy to move swiftly up the hill, and yet their attack depended on speed and surprise. He had been awake all night and now, when he needed to be alert, he suddenly felt very tired.

He looked for the first sign of light, a paler sky, an indication, even in the rain above the trees that ran along the far side of the path. Bearers, carrying ladders, stood ready to advance. To their rear stood pilum throwers who would keep the defenders occupied while the bearers positioned and secured the ladders. All waited doggedly for his direction, while the rain ran down their faces and seeped through their armour and clothes. On the path, the ram bearers, twenty of the stoutest Curiosolitae carrying the largest tree trunk they could find, with a sharpened metal end they had brought from the ships, stood ready to assault the gate, covered by pilum throwers and sagittarii. He had been at several successful sieges in Gaul but this was different. There was nothing sophisticated, no ballista or engineer support; instead, if they were to be successful, grit and determination with basic implements would be their route to capturing the citadel.

He turned to his new senior Centurion and said, 'Pilus Prior Arvina, send runners to Nauarchus Flavius.' He would not undermine the Trierarchus directly to the men. 'And to the King, and tell them this: listen for our battle cry and watch for our movement. As soon as we advance, they should do the same. Speed, of course, is essential if we are to succeed. Wish them good luck from me and if all goes well, we will come together, as agreed, at the large hall that the Massaliot has described at the top of the hill. That is all.'

***

Flavius saw the runner approach. Darkness was lifting. He listened to the runner's message, nodded his head grimly and stood forward, ready to react to the anticipated sound of attack. He would follow the Praefectus for now, but he would have that gold and it would be the foundation of his future career. All of the successful military men had built their fortunes from the profits of their campaigning and he would do the same. Then, when they returned to his father, he would make sure that Marcus Trebius Gallus, jumped up nobody that he was, got what he deserved; and that would not include any of the gold.

As he dwelt on these thoughts of revenge, the light around him grew. Consumed by his self-serving bitterness, he did not at first realise the light grew more rapidly than it should have done. Not the returning sun, but instead a sudden manufactured and growing luminescence, wrapping around and swallowing him and his men from the rear. There were shouts and cries behind. He spun around with his men and looked to the crown of the small but distinctively conical hill behind them. Green and blue, the light fizzed and crackled, a beacon burning increasingly brightly, lighting the whole slope of the hill. At the very centre were two women, unnaturally tall, their faces and their exposed arms painted red and blue, eyes wide with anger and vitriol, consuming and spitting scorn and venom on his men who increasingly cowered before them.

Astride the hill they stood, their hair stood on end, maliciously resplendent, looming over and drawing them in. They held a large staff in one hand, while the other rose over them, its intention unclear, intimidating and threatening them. Words came from their mouths that none of the Romans understood; incantations and curses, piercing the ears of all who stood before them. Then, with a forward flick of their staffs, came bolts of fire like a serpent's roar that laughed at them and played with them as they scorched just above their heads. Many of the men involuntarily ducked and began to back away, stumbling, and the discipline of the lines began to break. Flavius and the others around him stood transfixed. Instead of rallying his men to respond and make a defensive position, he too started to back away. To his left, the Praefectus had begun his attack, but Flavius was now ensnared within the malevolent gaze, meant only for him and those around him. Spellbound, he did not hear the very thing he was supposed to listen for. With his men in disarray, their leader haunted and held by those cruel eyes, boring into him, questioning him, hurting him, he could not follow and he and all around him recoiled before them.

**

A thin line of lighter grey grew above the trees.

'Arvina, get the men ready. Remember, get those ladders up and secured as quickly as we can. Pilum throwers we are relying on you. All of us, keep close together.'

Some of the men looked toward Flavius's position and above to where a low green and blue light flickered on the conical hill that faced the citadel. Around it, within the light, there looked to be two figures, dancing and gesticulating. It was hard to tell from this distance. Gallus briefly turned his head and looked. He had seen it before at several oppidum sieges. It could be quite intimidating. You had to look them straight in the eye with genuine defiance or ignore them. The intention was to distract as the far more frightening contingent of warriors came at you while your guard was down. He hoped Flavius was up to it.

'It's nothing, just posturing, prepare to attack.'

He took a final look to his left and then right.
'Charge!'

***

'That's it, you charge straight at us, bring your ladders if you want to, and come on, just a little bit further.'

Gwalian was side on, with her head just above the top of the perimeter fence and her bow and a loaded arrow poised ready to fire. She watched as the tall Roman led the mixed line of Roman soldiers and Curiosolitae warriors towards them. The ladders made clear their intent and the presence of the spear throwers revealed how they intended to cover the carriers when the Dewnan defenders chose to launch a response.

Gwalian glanced at Artur and Maedoc and raised her eyebrows slightly. All three turned again and watched as the Romans drew nearer.

***

Callard shouted to Drustan.

'It is Cantassa, look and Elowen!'

Drustan shouted back. 'It is Elowen.'

Others were shouting along the fence: 'Lady Elowen!' 'Elowen!' 'We do not stand alone!' or 'Surely, now the King will come!'

'They invoke the spirits of water, wood and stone; the land of the Dewnan rising to face the aggressor!'

Callard ran along the fence to Drustan.

'It is having quite an effect on those Romans. Should we go to the Prince? Do you think we should attack? They are in some disarray down there.'

'No, we will watch their discomfort. I can hear the charge of attack on the Prince's side. He may yet need us, but for now, we should maintain our position.'

He looked over the battlement again and said, 'The priestesses command powers, I have heard my father speak of them. Special powers, handed down from the ancestors and the ancient days; magic some call it, or perhaps to those who enjoy more straightforward thinking, the clever use of illusion. It is part of the step from acolyte to priestess or priest. Only those who master it can progress. For a short period, perhaps longer with two of them, they can hold a set group in their power, appear far more than they are and strike terror into the uninitiated. They will not be able to keep it up for long, though, even if there are two of them. It takes great concentration, focus and strength of the mind, and it is very draining. The paint and the hair, of course, are just for effect. What they do with their minds and eyes does the damage. If it is used, and it is only used in the most difficult of circumstances, it is often to provide a diversion while something more tangible and genuinely painful is brought to bear.'

He turned and grinned at Callard.

'So, perhaps we should be looking behind them really, for what is going to come next.'

***

They were running quickly up the hill now, on drier ground. Gallus breathed heavily. There was still no response from the battlements, and alongside him on either side, the ladder bearers were keeping up. He was a pace or two in front, as befitted the leader, but they would all reach the bank and fence at the same time, which would ensure that they could get the ladders up. The defenders would not be able to fire at all of them at the same time.

He He looked quickly surveyed the line on both sides of him to ensure that all went well with the section. Then, as he looked forward again, his right foot sank. He could find no firmness beneath it and was going too fast to stop. All of the front line was going too fast to stop, and as their legs continued the act of running, they all fell forward into a large, cavernous hole that opened up before them.

As he fell, Gallus frantically grasped for anything to hold on to. Flailing forlornly in the air, he twisted sideways and saw that an extended hole or deep ditch had opened all the way up the line. As the hole revealed itself, his men fell headlong into it. Ladders flew through the air, thrown up by the men in a futile attempt to bridge the gap and the chasm that was opening beneath them. All had kept close as he had instructed and those behind fell on top of those in front.

Screaming and cries of pain began almost immediately as hidden teeth bit into these prone and falling bodies. His last conscious sight was of upturned spears, which had been planted deliberately to catch them and were now impaling many of his legionaries. Those who had bravely charged up the hill alongside him, were gorged and devoured by the vengeful land as it joined in the defence of the embattled citadel.

A sudden searing and intense pain shot through his head and he heard and saw no more.

***

'Got him!'

Gwalian could not help but show her pleasure at how well the mantraps had worked, but then, as the screams and cries for help continued, her smile subsided. She looked grimly back at Artur and Maedoc and again over the parapet as the light of the early morning revealed the full destruction that the mantraps had wrought. The middle of the Roman and Curiosolitae section had taken the brunt, but now, with their leader gone, the whole of the line retreated to their original position in a state of some confusion.

***

As the green and blue light receded, a small group of mounted warriors appeared on the summit of Cantassa's hill, lined themselves up, briefly held the line stationary, and took stock.

'Look, it is as I told you!'

Drustan, with Callard and Kea beside him, pointed as the mounted warriors began to walk their horses forward together, slowly building momentum.

The Dewnan did not, as a rule, fight on horseback, preferring to stand on Mamm Norves with sword and shield. The concession here was to allow the leader of the warrior group to play his part. Unable to stand and run as he once did, he could still swing his sword arm at a passing foe, as long as his legs did not bear his weight. Elowen and Cantassa's dual purpose was then revealed – to prevent a unified and concerted assault on the battlements, but also provide the best opportunity for him to succeed in the ensuing chaos.

'The Lord of Killas leads the line! I did not think him capable. I hope this will not end badly.' Callard spoke frankly, as the horses moved faster and each of their warriors leant forward with their swords drawn, pointed towards the enemy.

'Look, the Romans are regrouping; the spell is broken. The men of Dynas Killas need to arrive quickly now, there are many more Romans. What is their objective?' Kea looked on and voiced the growing concern of all three of them.

All stood, agitated as they watched, and Drustan said, 'They are too far away for our archers. Is there a way through the fence? Can we pass through and go to their aid and get the archers closer?'

Callard turned to him. 'There is a small gate, further along the battlement from here, a door really, hidden in the bushes and the undergrowth on the outside. I do not know when it opened last; we will need to hack our way through.'

He looked down to the sea of swords that began to overwhelm the men of Dynas Killas. His face was full of anguish and dilemma when he looked back.

'Lord Drustan, is it wise to break our defence with attack now?'

'We cannot abandon them. We went to the aid of Casworon; we cannot abandon Killas now. It would not be right!'

Kea was already moving and called to his section, giving directions and leaving only a handful of defenders to watch from the battlement.

'If we are going to act, we must do it quickly, and do it now.'

Callard and Drustan did the same and Hedrek, watching the unfolding scene, called that he would join them. The whole of this side of the defence, therefore, prepared to go to the support of the men of Dynas Killas, leaving a small group to watch from the battlements.

Callard took them to the gate, which had not been used, as he had said, in recent memory. It was, in origin, the opposite door to the one that led down the steep path to Menluit Quay.

It took four men, pulling hard, to get it open. Then, once it was open, thick bushes and tall grass, which hid it from external eyes, blocked their way. They hacked at it now and cut a way through with sharp swords and rapid, repeated blows.

In single file, they all made to rush out, but a number caught and snagged their tunics on the bushes in the narrow gap they had created. It impeded them, created a tumbling feel to their intended charge. When they all finally lined up alongside the four leaders, the men of Dynas Killas were already in the midst of the Roman section, hacking and stabbing at the legionaries, who had begun to drag them from their horses. They disappeared under sword and strong arm, never to rise again.

At first, the defenders of Menluit briefly stood and watched, morbidly entranced by what they saw. Then, Kea shouted a cry to action. This was swiftly echoed by Drustan, Callard and Hedrek, and the Dewnan line, driven to emotional, impetuous and rash action, without any form of organisation, as Caesar had observed, charged down to the fight below them.

***

Flavius, back in the midst of his men, lifted his right arm, swung and jabbed with his gladius and then, raising his left arm and holding his scutum across his upper body, deflected a blow from one of the enemy cavalry above. He was angry and felt a fool; he had been overawed and all of them nearly overwhelmed by the sorcery of the two women. What sort of trickery had caused him and those around him to see something very different from reality? What sort of devilment did they face? Whatever it was, now that it had passed and been revealed for what it really was, he was determined to recover their position quickly, starting with this futile attempt to overrun them, led by an old man who somehow retained his seat, even though it looked like he would surely fall out of it at any moment.

He could not look away from the fight, but was the Praefectus already scaling the walls? Was the King already in the citadel? He could not tell, but he and his men had to get back to the main assault as soon as possible. HeHis men took more of the riders down. Their cavalry lacked any form of real competency and so it would not be long now; they would have them all, including the old man. He jabbed and swung again and cut into the leg of the nearest rider, causing a cry of anguish from above. Holding his scutum above him to shield against any retaliation, he stabbed home his advantage with his gladius into the upper leg of the lurching rider. On the other side of the horse, his men grabbed the rider as he reeled backwards and pulled him down before he could strike any more. They kicked, hacked and stabbed at the man as he tried in vain to lift his sword arm in defence.

Flavius retreated from the fight to take stock. Breathing heavily, he reached into the front of his helmet to wipe the sweat from his brow. To his right, there were shouts and then another group of tribesmen charged down the hill of the citadel towards them. Again, it was a small group. More of them than the riders, but they would still be no match for his men. Had they come from the citadel? Yes, they had, but not by the main gate, so there must be another way in. This was his chance to recover his position. He called across to the nearest centurion to him.

'Centurion Pontius, I will leave these horsemen to you and your centuria now. I and the rest of the men will resume the approach to the citadel. When you have dealt with the horsemen, take your men to the top of the conicle-shaped hill, secure it and tie up those sorceresses if you find them and bring them to me, alive and undefiled.'

***

The attackers of the main gate stood back at their original position. The attack and their leader had foundered on the mantraps and their sense of purpose and organisation had, for the moment gone, while the leaders that remained attempted to rally them.

Shouts and the sounds of weapons clashing were now coming from further around the battlement. Gawen, Nouran and Gourgy ran across to Artur's position and he spoke to them hurriedly, along with Gwalian.

'They will not attack again while they try to retrieve their comrades. Do not fire on them until they have done so, or unless they attack. I am going to Drustan. I hear fighting. Hold your positions here; I will be back soon.'

The number of defenders around the battlement quickly reduced as Artur and Maedoc ran to find out more. In growing disbelief, the Prince shouted up to one of Drustan's men that he recognised.

'Where is everyone?'

The guard turned and looked frantically down to them. 'Pryns Artur, is good to see ee! Em gone to the aid of Lord Killas, although, looks quite 'opeless from 'ere!'

Artur and Maedoc clambered onto the battlement and there, at the foot of the slope, they could see ten men on horseback, surrounded by many more Roman soldiers. Two were dragged down as they watched, daggers and swords raised and thrust into them as they fell to the ground. In the midst of it all was the unmistakable flowing grey hair of Lord Killas, tottering precariously as he struck his blows, fighting on.

'How many men did Lord Killas attack with?'

'Oi couldn say for definite my lord, thirty prhaps. They'm taken a few of em Romins down, but mostly they just fort 'ard to survive.'

Artur shook his head, looked down the slope and saw Drustan, Kea, Hedrek and Callard launch a charge against the Roman force. The Romans focused on the remaining riders, but then a large section at the rear began to turn while a small but very vocal individual shouted instructions. The ease with which they turned, positioned themselves and prepared to advance in cohesion towards the roaring, brave, but disorderly charge of the Dewnans was striking.

Artur and Maedoc looked on dismayed.

'How have they got out? They should have stayed here!'

'Therze an old gate, bit further up. 'Em saw the bravery of Lord Killas and wanted to 'elp im an is men. Trouble is there's too many of 'em Romins.'

Maedoc said, 'My Lord, if we had been here, we may have felt the same, as with Lord Casworon?'

'Maybe, but with Casworon we acted when it was clear there was a good chance of them getting through.'

A front line of Roman shields met the Dewnan charge and stood firm against the onrush and the strike of swinging swords.

There was no hope of them breaking through to the men of Dynas Killas; instead, shouts along the siege line alerted more Romans and Curiosolitae to the foray from the battlements and slowly the line began to bend around and cut off the potential for retreat.

'They have to come back now or they will be cut off and surrounded.' The Prince looked on in exasperation and then turned to the sentry. 'Show me where the gate is. I am going out.' And to Maedoc. 'Go back to the main gate, call Gawen and Gwalian and any other archers available. Again, we need their cover if we are to stand any chance of getting back.'

'Is that wise, Artur? If you are lost, all is lost.'

'If they do not retreat now, they will be overwhelmed and the Romans will scale the ramparts by this evening. I have no choice, and they will not hear me from here. Maedoc, please go quickly.'

Maedoc jumped down from the battlement and ran back in the direction of the main gate, while the sentry led Artur to the door.

He stepped his way through, drew his sword and charged down the hill. Quickly, he was at the back of the Dewnan, all of them roaring, cursing and shouting, while in front of them the Roman line taunted them from behind their shields. He pushed between Drustan and Hedrek and, with them, thrust at the Roman line.

'We have to go back!' he shouted above the din. 'They are holding you here, keeping you engaged while they surround you. We must go now! Or we are surely lost. Back to Menluit!'

Sweating heavily and with grime smeared across their faces, the brothers looked at him. Drustan said nothing, but nodded as he continued to strike blows.

Hedrek responded, 'You are right. We will hold the line. Can we get back?'

Artur parried a counterthrust from the Roman line and shouted to Callard, 'Callard, lead us back. Take your men back; we must get behind the battlements. Everyone, Kea lead your men back.'

The Roman line, sensing an advantage, began to move forward, pressing at their attackers. Artur looked to his right,

Curiosolitae warriors were running along the line of the hill. They had to go and they had to go now.

'Back up the slope, back to the gate, retreat!'

He had taken full command and all those around him recognised his voice. Warriors turned and ran back up the hill, while those immediately around the Prince, including Drustan and Hedrek, moved backwards quickly, deflecting blows and thrusting back where they could. The Roman line began to swing round to encompass them and cut off their escape. Above them, spears were now coming down, taking out individuals as they ran up the hill. Artur looked about him and could see Kea and his men fighting on the right-hand side while Callard, it seemed, just held the left. They were close to the battlements now, but the gate was too small. If the advancing Romans continued to approach like this, they would not all get through and close the gate before the Roman force streamed into Menluit after them. Artur and those around him lunged forward again, swiped and thrust at the Romans. Then the sound of rushing air came from above and he looked up.

'Spears coming in. Drustan, stand aside!'

A spear struck the ground in the midst of where they had both just stood. More rained down, causing confusion and disorder around him as their descent met their targets with increasing, murderous regularity, but still Artur, Drustan, Hedrek, Kea Callard and a committed group of warriors around them held the attackers at bay. Another rush of air, but now arrows, flying to their support. Artur looked behind to see Gawen, Gwalian and a line of archers on the battlement. He turned back, parried a blow and breathed deeply. It was now or never.

'Back to the gate. Everybody back through the gate. Kea, Callard, lead your men in!'

Kea and Callard were at the gate and their men were filing through as quickly as they could, but it was tight and a queue was building, causing many to push, shove and shout whilst Kea and Callard tried to keep some form of order. Artur and the men of the Foye stood with their backs to the gate, swords drawn, tense and breathing heavily, watching the force before them and listening for the sound of spears above. The Romans, who were now perhaps fifty strides away, stopped to reorganise.

They all knew that, when it came, it would be a frantic rush to the gate and so stood apprehensively waiting for the signal. Arrows still sought the Curiosolitae but had ceased against the Romans, who had reorganised their shields against them. Kea called to them.

'Artur, Drustan, Hedrek, we are all through, come on!'

As they turned and ran, it was quickly clear that the Romans had been waiting for them to do so. There was a cry from behind the Roman line and they surged forward in pursuit of the Dewnan, quickly gaining on them and closing down the fifty paces, in spite of the gradient up which they ran.

Kea, who remained on the outside of the gate, shouted to them desperately, 'Form a line, form a line, one after the other. It is the only way to get through.'

Not looking back, just running, arrows flying above them, they did as he said, in a single line. The first of the men of the Foye forced their way through the gate, as Kea stood beside it.

In the scramble to turn and run, Hedrek and several of the others had forced his younger brother and the Prince forward, while they brought up the rear. Artur and Drustan ran as hard as they could. As they approached the gate, they heard a thud behind them, but continued running. When they got to the gate, they turned and there was Hedrek, on his knees, felled by a spear launched from the front line. He was not dead yet and two of his comrades were trying to lift him and drag him forward.

'Brother!'

Drustan raised his sword to run back down the slope, but Kea was ready for him and held him back. Artur grabbed Drustan's other arm and they shoved him through the gate as Hedrek took one last look at his brother, before the Roman line ran over him and his helpers, dispatching them swiftly and trampling them into the mud.

'All through!' shouted Kea after he had grabbed and pushed Artur through, and then swiftly followed behind him.

The gate was heaved shut and the old iron bars that had kept it shut and locked for years were forced back into place. Maedoc, always resourceful and thinking ahead, even in the face of great calamity, had prepared a way of blocking the gate as the desperate retreat had unfolded. He now gathered others around him and they wheeled wooden carts as fast as they could in front of the gate. These were loaded with as many heavy items as they could quickly find, which wedged the gate further against the approaching attempt by the Romans to break it down. There was a loud thump against the gate and it flexed on its hinges as those outside tried to heave it open, but it held. The archers above them on the battlements still did their work, while they waited for the next attempt on the gate, but it did not come. Artur went across to Drustan, who was now sat on the ground beyond the carts.

'Drustan, I am so sorry. He fought bravely for us all.'

Drustan raised his head, his eyes full of tears, and shook his head wretchedly. 'It is my fault. He came out to support me, to support us. We should not have gone out, rashness came and took us, cousin forgive me,' he sniffed loudly and looked away and then said more quietly, 'Hedrek, forgive me; we should not have gone out.'

'You went bravely to the assistance of others. Hedrek would have followed you as you would have followed him. He died with honour fighting this battle, we will always remember him.'

He touched his cousin's shoulder, but Drustan just sat looking down at the ground, shaking his head.

'Artur, you need to come and see this.' It was Gawen up on the battlement.

Before he went to Gawen, Artur spoke to Maedoc. 'Good friend and wise ally, you had thought of how we would block the gate. Thank you. How stands it at the main gate?'

'The Romans and the Curiosolitae still lick their wounds and recover their dead. They will recover soon, I am sure, but Nouran and Gourgy watch the gate and their movements. If anything changes, they will send word to us.'

'Thank you, Maedoc.'

Quickly, he was up and alongside Gawen.

'Why do they not try harder with the gate?'

'I suppose they have seen how hard it was for our people to get through. Frankly, given the accuracy of Gwalian's shooting, she could probably hold the gate on her own – and those that she has trained give her strong support.'

Artur smiled grimly as they both looked across to where Gwalian crouched with head just above the top of the fence, bow poised behind her.

'Yes, we have much to thank her for, and you, of course. There is something in your build, both of you, male and female, that suggests you were born to do this, to work your bows with great skill. Twice now you have got us out of a difficult situation.'

'It is what I and, from what I hear, Gwalian have trained ourselves to do, but look, come and see what they do now. They have many ladders; look, one is carried by every third or fourth man. They mean to come over the battlement, not through the gate.'

'Yes, we must prepare.'

He looked sadly to the bodies of Hedrek and his two companions, face down, half-buried in the mud, necks and heads bent crooked from the trampling of many feet, bloody gouges in their backs from the incision of many swords; and beyond, to bodies across the open ground, spears protruding from their shoulders, backs and pierced skulls. The foray had ended in a mix of defiance and chaos, and they had lost at least a third of those that had gone out.

'How did it end with Lord Killas?'

'He battled until his death and was the last to fall.'

He could see the irritation in the Prince's face. 'Artur, I believe his intentions were good. He distracted the attackers here. If those who came against us at the main gate had not foundered in the mantraps, well, I am not sure we could have withstood a full assault. Small interventions by our friends have prevented the full force of their attack and that, I think, can only be good.'

'Yes, Gawen, perhaps you're right, but I think that their best attempt at full attack is coming. We are not, by any means, out of this yet.'

***

Flavius had watched as his men had closed in on the retreating rebels. It had not been clear where the gate was exactly, and then he'd seen it. It was no more than a door really. Only the excellence of their sagittarii had enabled their escape.

He and his men couldn't go in through that gate, that was clear. It would be impossible to get through and establish a defendable position. Back to the original plan then. Despite his rush to get into the citadel, he knew his men needed a pause to gather their equipment and re-establish their order for the assault over the battlement. He also needed to agree with his centurions about how to deal with the sagittarii and get the ladders up securely, and so he had temporarily withdrawn the assault to do this. As the men withdrew to their position and the order was given to relax, Flavius turned from the fight and took his helmet off, wiping his brow with his arm.

One of the optios came forward. 'Dominus, there are messengers from Praefectus Gallus's section and from King Brice.'

The messenger from Gallus's section stood forward first.

'Nauarchus, Dominus, I am very sorry to inform you that the Praefectus was killed in our assault on the rebel fortress earlier. He lies at the bottom of a disguised pit dug by the rebels. Our men that fell with him cover him, many impaled on sharpened wooden stakes especially laid to capture and impede. We have retrieved the bodies of those who were not killed outright, but a number were immovable in the time that we dared to spend within range of their sagittarii. His body is below theirs and we cannot get at it.'

Flavius asked quickly, 'And the assault foundered with the Praefectus?'

'Yes, Dominus. We have lost around fifty men alongside the Praefectus. Some still linger in great pain, skewered by the stakes. We listen miserably to their awful screams. They are beyond retrieval and we can do nothing for them.'

The messenger looked forlornly at Flavius, and then seemed to collect himself and said, 'I am charged to say that Pilus Prior Arvina and the other centurions await your command, as Nauarchus and now the commander of senior rank. They are regrouping the men and identifying a new line of approach around the pit, but await your further instruction.'

Briefly, it crossed his mind that if the Pilus Prior had known the full extent of Flavius's actual seniority, he might not have conceded the command. Gallus had clearly said nothing to his men on this, despite his outburst in the tent. Quickly, he dismissed this thought and said, 'Very well.' He then turned to the Curiosolitae man who, along with the King, was one of the few tribal Latin speakers and said, 'And what of King Brice?'

'Noble Lord, we waited for the signal of attack, which did not come. We have held our position, as agreed, around and on the far side of the citadel hill, along the river. The King, however, respectfully adds that if you are not going to attack, he will. Although, as I left him, word had arrived of the attack on you here.'

Flavius felt a strong swelling of adrenaline. His mind was racing at this unexpected turn of events. Complete command. Now he would certainly have the gold and send a victory back to his father, before leading the conquest of Britannia alongside Caesar, and establish a new province for Rome and benefit from all of the riches which that would bring. His moment had arrived!

First, he spoke to the King's messenger. 'We will be ready to renew the assault. It will be done with ladders and we will go up over the battlement when the sun is at the sixth hour, at meridies. Tell the King that he and I will lead the attack on this and the far sides, respectively.'

Then he spoke to the Roman messenger.

'Go back to the Primus Pilus. He is to ensure that the main gate is covered, but he is to feign dejection and difficulty. If they are taken in, many of the main gate defenders will respond to our attack on this side. He must wait for my word, but on receiving it, he should storm the main gate.'

He looked across to the small hill on which the sorceresses had stood, and from where the old man and his futile foray had come, and recognised that it would probably afford a view of the whole battlefield. There was probably an hour before meridies and he resolved, immediately, to join the centurion and his men who had been detailed to take command of the hill earlier and to take stock. Taking one of the optios and two men to act as runners and deliver further instructions to the King and Arvina, he set off across the road that ran along the low point of the valley and walked up the steep rise to the hill. As he scrambled to the top, the centurion came to meet him.

'Nauarchus, we have secured the hill and the building here; some form of temple or shrine, it seems. Perhaps it is the house of the sorceresses we saw earlier.'

'I am assuming you have not managed to locate either sorceress?'

'No, Dominus, they have retreated to a secure place in the land around here, I am sure.'

'Yes, no doubt.'

Flavius gave the centurion a dismissive glare and looked beyond him at the deployment of the centuria.

Eager to change the subject, Pontius continued, 'Dominus, the hill gives a good view of the citadel and the land before it. We can see the position of Praefectus Gallus, although he has not advanced as much as I would have expected... then here, before and below us, your own strong position, while away over there and around the hill and out of sight is King Brice's line.'

Flavius took in the view of the land before him. After he had noted the various positions, the centuria, the auxiliaries and the overall state of the siege line, he turned and said, 'Centurion, you should know that Praefectus Gallus has been killed during his section's assault on the main gate of the citadel. I have assumed overall command of this action, and you will follow and obey my orders, is that clear?'

Pontius could not help but look surprised, 'Dominus, I am sorry to hear of the Praefectus's death. He was a good man, but I am, of course, very ready to follow your command.'

'Good, you will maintain our hold of this hill. It is a good vantage point for the battle to come, as you have pointed out, and for spotting the approach of any relief force. Pontius, I am giving you the responsibility of keeping watch and defending our rear. I expect to be in the citadel and to have our position secured by sundown. We will depart tomorrow morning and you will hold this position...'

He stopped talking mid-sentence and looked to Pontius's optio who stood beside them both, agitated, but not wanting to interrupt.

'Yes, what is it?'

'The King's line, Dominus, it is being attacked from around the citadel hill, probably from the river. There seems to be quite a lot of them.'

Pontius ran to the other side of the hill, where a number of the centuria stood, looking and pointing. Flavius joined him quickly to see a sizeable force of attackers, perhaps even a full cohort; although, as more were still coming around the hill, it was hard to tell. They pushed the King's men back and presumably had done all of the way from the river.

Flavius looked on dismayed.

'He is supposed to hold the river! Centurion, defend this hill against any that come against it. I am going to divert our men to support the King's position. Await my further command and send word immediately if any other forces attempt to relieve the citadel.'

'Yes, Nauarchus.'

'You,' Flavius called to one of his runners. 'Go to Pilus Prior Arvina. He and the auxiliary commanders must secure the position on the riverbank on his side of the hill. I do not want any other force crossing the river and they must secure our access to the road. Is that clear?'

'Yes, Nauarchus.'

The runner set off to Arvina and then Flavius turned to both his optio and the other runner and said, 'Come, back down the hill, as quickly as we can now.'

***

'It is the men of RunHoul!'

Artur worked his way along the battlement to where he could see Marrek ahead.

'Pryns Artur, the men of RunHoul are here. Look, my uncle, Kenver, leads the charge down in the field. He brings five hundred or maybe more. They have responded to the call!'

Artur looked over the battlement and surveyed the unfolding fight. To his right, he could just see Tamara, preparing to skirt the flank of the hill of Menluit, sparkling in the renewed light of Sira Howl, high in his zenith and watching over the land. Before him, a thick line of warriors fought ferociously, piercing the defence of the Curiosolitae besiegers. Already, they had pushed them back and, at least for now, the circle of the siege was not complete.

'We both know who has instigated this and, hopefully, she and more will join us soon. Casworon, Killas and now your kinsmen. Marrek it is a good sight to see!'

Briec joined them.

'Pryns Artur, they crossed Tamara upstream and have fought hard to get to here.'

'They fight hard now, Briec, but the bulk of the Roman force is on this side of the hill. They will need to maintain a strong attack if they are to work their way around much further.'

'Can we not give support?' Marrek said. 'I should very much like to fight with my kinsmen.'

Artur was clear: 'No one is to leave the trev and go beyond the battlements. We have only just managed to avert near disaster, our resources are depleted as a result and good men lost. We will not abandon the battlements again while the bulk of their force remains.'

Marrek said nothing and looked grimly at the fight below.

Artur continued, 'We will deploy all the archers, while the focus of the fight is here, but will only fire if the Curiosolitae are properly within range.'

Briec spoke now. 'Artur, the men of RunHoul and others with them, also fight on the opposite bank of the river, where a smaller group and the Curiosolitae maintain a strong defence. We cannot reach them with our arrows, but we watch them and cheer them.'

'Thank you, Briec. Find me or send word if they make progress or if the Curiosolitae prevail.'

the banner of the rings

Centurion Pontius had placed a watch around the boundary of the abandoned house and outbuildings at the summit of the small distinctive hill. The centuria watched the land, for movement and new arrivals, while the main Roman force below reasserted their position.

The Nauarchus led a strong counterattack against the newly arrived rebel force. He had not swept them away, but slowly pushed them back. They, in turn, had fought with spirit and others had arrived in the mid-afternoon, re-energising them; and why not fight well in defence of their land and homes? Over several hours, men had been lost, but through weight of numbers, the Roman force had slowly forced the rebels to a high point in the land. It was not a distinctive hill, but defendable, away from the wall of the citadel. Here, they held firm, and as dusk crept up from the valley floor, the two sides reached stalemate, at least for the evening and night ahead. Campfires began to emerge and fighting was suspended. The Roman force, with its Curiosolitae auxiliaries, once again surrounded the citadel as far as Pontius could see, while on the far side, they kept a dual watch against the rebel attackers, front and back. He wrapped his cloak around him and held his arms to his chest against the mizzle and the damp that remained in the air. The sodden ground added to the chill, despite the thick and glowering cloud cover. It would be a dark and difficult night.

Earlier, he had noted a stream running around the base of this hill. In daylight, he could see a reasonable distance upstream, but as the light faded, he looked to where the stream ran, shrouded in semi-darkness in its steep valley, and noticed a small white light moving quickly. It was coming towards them along its course. A rider perhaps, it was hard to tell. Whatever it was, whoever it was, it was coming quickly. He listened hard for collective horses' hooves, but there was no sound, so not another attacking force then. Several of his men had seen the light also. It bent to the left from their view, following the line of the stream, but then sharply to the right, maintaining its speed, and then came up the hill towards them.

The intensity of the approaching light held the centurion's eyes, mesmerising him and then, collecting himself, Pontius shouted, 'Draw gladius, prepare to engage, get ready!'

His call drew the light to him. He could not see beyond its brightness. Only at the last moment did he perceive the chest, shoulder, knee and fetlock of a large white horse, rising majestically above him. Instinctively, Pontius ducked, but not enough to avoid the strike of its hoof, kicking his head hard and sending him sprawling to the ground.

The light dimmed and all now could see the horse and its rider, cloaked and hooded, holding a simple rein of soft leather in one hand and in the other a large wooden staff. While their centurion sprawled and spluttered on the ground, the men hesitated to respond, but with their gladius drawn, they slowly edged closer. Several looked to the hood and a pair of slate blue eyes within, wrathful and piercing, stared back at them. All who saw those eyes bridled and faltered in their step. She flung back her hood, raised her staff to the evening sky, its luminescence growing again and giving light to the whole summit of the hill, and spoke with a voice that fully conveyed her disdain, scorn and contempt for them.

'Why are you here, in this sanctum, blessed place of this sacred land? Defilers! Your fate will be miserable, torrid and painful; an end that befits mean, contemptible bullies and aggressors. This is Dewnan land, land of Pretan fame, and we will not yield!'

She swung her arm and a giant phosphoric spark from the end of her staff caught on the thatch of Cantassa's abandoned building. Despite the dampness around, the roof and main body of the building beneath it were alight in moments. The horse reared on his back legs, swung around, and as he did, she wielded the staff about her, scattering any who tried to come near. The horse pressed hard on his immensely strong back legs and, before the centuria could recover, she had gone, away down the hill and towards the main Roman force.

Pontius, mildly concussed and confused, raised himself onto his arms, turned and sat on the ground, his helmet skewwhiff; mud was smeared across his face and he looked on as the abandoned building burned. Many of the centuria ran to the boundary wall to watch the horse and rider's charge down the hill, which was lit by the renewed light of the staff held out before her and Steren Uskis. Morlain's long dark hair, free from its hood, was now flowing abundantly down her back, resplendent in the continued wind of their movement.

'What was that?' was all the centurion could say, rather stupidly, as he looked to those that stood around him. Then, with a slight movement of his head and his eyes, he said, 'We should warn the Nauarchus.'

But it was a little late for that.

***

'Look! Look!, Cantassa's house is ablaze!'

Many stood on the battlement and watched as the flame sprung into the evening sky and then, bustled, pointed, talked excitedly as the white light, the source of the fire, charged down the hill toward the Roman ranks.

'Artur, it is Morlain. It can be no one else.'

Maedoc stood close to the Prince and spoke urgently.

'Yes, yes, of course, it is.'

Artur made his way rapidly along the battlement towards the main gate. 'Gourgy, Nouran, open the gates, I am coming down.'

All the defenders watched as the light approached the now illuminated Roman line. Turned spears pointed, making ready to repel. Casworon, who had not been able to resist working his way along the battlement to watch, spoke for many.

''Tis a noble gesture, but t'will surely founder, futile against those Romin spears!'

No sooner was it said than gasps rippled along the line of watchers. Sparks fizzled and crackled within the source of the white light and flames leapt forward, licking and probing the Roman front line. Wooden shafts, turning hot and black, disintegrated in the hands of all who stood in the way of the white light, scorching and blistering skin and bone amidst sudden and startled screams of pain and anguish. The horsehair plumes on helmets or cassis caught fire and metal heated, burning human hair and searing skulls, to cries of agony from contorted faces as men frantically grappled with the leather ties that held the cassis firmly in place, trying to remove them from their heads.

The ranks recoiled and parted before her and the Prince of Horses, the largest and strongest of his kind, thundered through the besieging line. Into the gap between the siege and battlement she rode, and then turned when she reached the earthen bank with its palisade atop, and with a final gesture of defiance, cast sparks and flames into the evening sky, before riding along the battlement towards the main gate.

Artur was outside, watching the path and the Roman and Curiosolitae forces opposite when Morlain and Steren Uskis came along the battlement. Nouran, Gourgy and some of the men of the gate stood with him.

'Sh'em a dab and with that ole fire stick!' Gourgy could not help but observe.

Artur smiled as horse and rider approached and rode quickly in through the gate. Swiftly, the Prince and guard of the gate followed, while those within hauled both sets of gates shut.

She swung down and spoke quietly in the ear of Steren Uskis before turning, with the staff in her right hand, and walking decisively towards Artur. Her face, spattered with black fleck traces from her pyrotechnic scything of the Roman line, shone with the sweat of determined effort. Her hair, tangled from exertion and swiftness of gallop, tumbled across her mud-splattered cloak.

He strode towards her, confident and walking tall with his sword still in hand. His face, etched and worn by the weather and all that he had seen, unexpectedly spoke of authority and command, rugged perhaps and certainly matching her determination. He was very pleased to see her, she knew it instantly, and all that had gone between them since his return, despite her absence of two days and the presence and influence of others, still burned brightly and reached from him towards her. She returned it in full measure, and as each smiled warmly, in spite of their dire position, they dropped the sword and staff to their side and embraced each other with great pleasure.

Many around looked on, with eyes brightened and smiles heartened, but Gwalian looked away. Her bow poised, she peered out over the top of the battlement, ready to deal with any attempted attack.

***

Flavius strode angrily into the small tent where he had been conversing with King Brice before the appearance of the white light.

'Women and sorcery, noble King! Their devious and manipulative ways undermine the very fabric of humanity! No civilised Roman woman would act in this way and, if they did, let me tell you, their husbands, fathers and brothers would rapidly bring them under control. All this trickery and their stunts will get them nowhere in the end and soon, if we do not kill them first, they will find themselves sat in the slave market, ready to serve and provide for the needs of their masters!'

'Do not underestimate her, Nauarchus. There are few brave enough to charge headlong at a fully armed detachment of Roman soldiers, white light or no white light. She came through your watch on the hill and then through your soldiers here. Why has she only arrived now? What does she herald?'

A cynical sneer spread over Flavius's face. It was one usually reserved for his dealings with Gallus, and which he thought gave him an edge over those who said things he did not like.

'Are you an apologist for these people? Have a care, King Brice, Rome does not look favourably upon rebel sympathisers.'

The King snorted and with a withering stare, replied, 'I mean nothing of the sort, only this: we need, to act decisively now or leave. We are not in the fort by nightfall as you had hoped and instead, they slowly chip away at us. The arrival of the priestess, for I am sure that is who the rider was, means something and so we must act while we have the advantage of numbers. I have a plan to overcome the surge of attackers on the far side of the fort, and then for us all to come together and make one final, sustained assault on the main gate.'

Flavius stared back at the King. If there was any chance left of achieving his objective, he needed him and his Curiosolitae warriors. His irritation softened and the conspiratorial face of previous conversations returned as he gently nodded his head.

'Good,' said the King. 'Then come and share some of your wine with me, and I will tell you what I propose.'

***

There were many gaps in the positions along the battlement where the defenders had once stood, around Kea, Drustan and Callard, where Hedrek had led his section. Artur led Morlain on a review of the defensive position and stood talking quietly to her, a little way back from the battlement, explaining what had happened.

'I do know that he meant well, but Lord Killas's attack has undermined us. There were no more than thirty of them. What chance did he think he had? I do wonder if age dimmed his senses.'

Morlain surveyed the sparse battlements. It was worse than she had thought. They had done well to hold out for this long, but she could not let Artur's comments go by without response.

'Artur, Lords Killas and Casworon came to your aid with all they could muster. Brave and fearless, they fought determinedly, giving the Romans plenty to think about, instead of thinking about scaling the battlements. Both are men of the valley, Artur, from the old families, and their distant ancestors were here, before the Lords of Achaea, before the Pretan. This sacred land courses through all of us. It is part of us and we are part of it, and none more so than Casworon and Killas. In their words and actions, rock, earth and water speak, as well as the voices of countless souls who have gone before, lived and breathed this valley and this land. They are the original Ocean People, of uncertain beginnings, who were here from the early days. The temples and barrows of their ancestors still stand watch on the hilltops and they will never allow it to be said that the descendants of all who lie in those barrows stood by when the men and women of Nanmeur were in need.'

Artur turned to her, smiled lightly and shook his head, 'You bring such sense and insight, but the unavoidable fact remains that we lost good men in both actions. It has diverted the enemy from an all-out attack. If they attack in the morning and there is no further relief, we will not, in the end, be able to repel it.'

He looked at her and then said, 'We are in a perilous position. You must see that. Tell me again about my father.'

'I have done all I can, Artur. Your sister, banished, will not influence him again. I left him to his plans. Your uncle, I hope, goes to raise all the men of his lands, not just those adjacent to the Foye. I have been to the Kernovi, spreading the call for assistance. On the opposite bank of Tamara, I have sent word to the kin of Marrek and Ambros, when I saw your return to Ictis. I have seen them recently and asked them to try to rally the men of the Durotrages that you helped. I have also been to the families of Lancelin, Tinos and Ryol. I understand their grief at the loss of their sons, but they have allowed an army to march up the valley and now they must make amends and avenge their sons! At least that is what I have argued. Soon, we will be able to tell if I have made any difference.

'So you see, Artur, I have worked very hard to raise the heirs of Achaea and I am still not assured of success. Perhaps then, the support of the old families seen in this light, small as it may be and wildly reckless as it may have been, should be welcomed as it was freely given and needed no more prompting than being told that the enemy was at the door.'

'Yes, you are right, of course, and I was not ungrateful to Casworon. He fought bravely, as did all those around him, including Missus Casworon, who I was introduced to.'

He took her hand and looked at her with a sly smile, but then as quickly as it had arisen the smile faded, replaced by a face full of appeal, 'I wish we could have got to Lord Killas. Morlain, it was I who went out to get them back, urged them to abandon the men of Dynas Killas. Half of them were lost already. There were too many Romans. It would have been folly to lose all of the men on this side and lay open the doors of Menluit.'

She looked solemnly back and gently squeezed his hand. 'All great leaders must choose between immediate need and the overall objective. You did not want to decide in this way, but you had to. If Lord Killas was here, he would say the same thing. The brave sacrifice and determined charge of the men of Dynas Killas will be remembered in song and story, for many lives to come.'

It was dark now and only the closest positions were visible in the gloom. Behind them, close to the hall at Pendre, a fire burned. Food was being prepared, to pass along the battlement.

'What do you propose to do now?'

'We will watch from the battlements and prepare for the assault, which is surely coming.'

'Do you think they will attack tonight?'

'I don't know, but we cannot be certain they will not.'

She looked back at him and then said, 'I think they will not attack, not until early morning. They are resting, having fought all day to re-establish their position. The attack will not come yet.'

He looked back at her, considering what she had said. She continued, 'Gather everyone, Artur. Leave a token watch if you wish, but gather everyone around the fire, let us eat and talk together. They need to hear from you, and perhaps from me, and they need to see each other, before, together, we swing our sword arms and flex our bows in the morning. It is important, I think.'

He looked around. Grim and sombre faces caught his eye. He breathed deeply and looked back at her.

'Yes, we need to motivate each other, for this thing that we must do. We will meet for food as soon as all can be gathered, but we will leave one on watch per section, a volunteer.'

He called to Maedoc who sat close, sharpening his sword, and word went out for all to gather.

***

'So, listen to me Greek, you will stay close by me. Just before first light, we will attack the citadel and break our way in. My men will deal with any remaining resistance and, once the gates are open, we must move quickly. You will show me all that you know and take me to where they are likely to have hidden the treasure. Do not fail me, because if you do, you will regret it. We are here because of your advice. For your sake, I hope that you have given the right advice.'

Gyras looked coldly back at the Nauarchus and sullenly nodded in acknowledgement. He was bedraggled and his clothes were wet through. No tent and cover for Gyras, it seemed. He did not know where the treasure was, but hoped against hope that it was in the large hall at the top of the citadel. If not, well, then his fate was set. Unless he could escape, but his guards so far were very attentive; no doubt as frightened by Flavius as he was. Miserably, he watched as the Nauarchus walked away to give instructions elsewhere.

Mercifully, his pouch remained against his chest and none had searched him to take it from him. What use were coins though in a wet and muddy field in Pretanike? If he revealed them to his guards, they would just take them from him. No, he had to wait for his chance, but as the midnight hour approached, his natural optimism, his belief, based on his experience that he could get himself out of any situation, was beginning to fade. He hung his head dejectedly and thought of home and warmth. At this time of the evening, they would be midway through the evening meal. Inwardly, he smiled. In the months to come, they would wonder where he was and why he was away even longer than usual, he hoped. Then, as time passed, they would come to conclude that some unfortunate event had befallen him and gradually get used to his not returning, and life would go on.

***

Slowly, they came out of the darkness, up through the trev from all corners of Menluit and the full circuit of the battlement, to Pendre, the house at the top of the trev.

Tiredness was on their faces and despite the occasional comradely laugh, most of them were subdued and wistful. In front of the steps was a fire with a large cauldron above it, full of a hearty stew of meats and vegetables from the store. From it, the aroma of summer herbs mixed with the smell of smoke and fire in the air.

Missus Casworon had taken charge of the cooking, supported by several of the women of Casworon's hall – fighters and feeders. Gwalian and several of the gilles came down the steps, carrying a tall stack of wooden bowls and handfuls of wooden flagons. Behind them, Maedoc rolled a large barrel of mead. It was an impromptu and basic feast, but pale smiles spread in the firelight, as faces that had not seen for several days were recognised, and a bowl of stew and a flagon of mead began to be handed to all.

Morlain stood amongst them and spoke to the acolytes and servants of Dynas Kazak. Artur watched her from the steps, as Gwalian came back up for more bowls and caught his eye. She smiled a soft, sad smile and his eyes followed hers as he tried to return a warmer smile as she walked on by. He looked back to Morlain and found her looking straight at him. Instantly, she looked away and said something to the acolyte next to her. Then, she looked back at him calmly, without expression, turned away from the acolyte, and walked towards him.

'Are all here?'

'Yes, I think so. I see all of the battlement section leaders. Only Marrek is missing and he volunteered to keep watch where his kinsmen are camped.'

'Ah, that is a shame. A song would have been well received by all tonight, I think.'

She took in everyone that sat on and around the steps and said, 'It is a small group, what should be our tactics come first light?'

'We have lost about one hundred, I think. Some in support of Casworon, but most before the battlement door and under their spears. They have had casualties, but even so, they still outnumber us by at least five to one. It is difficult and we must wait to see what first light brings. If they continue to line up around the full perimeter, I do not know what we will do, except to fight bravely and repel what we can and perhaps make a stand here, at Pendre, if they breach the battlement. All of the boats have gone from Menluit Quay with the mothers and children, maybe there are a few of the older boats left, but they will not hold three hundred or anywhere near that number. A few of us can swim, but for most, there is no escape that way.' He lowered his voiced. 'It is a fight to the death, Morlain, and if the relief does not come tomorrow, we face an uncertain future.'

Both watched as filled bowls were passed around and others were carried to those who remained on the battlements. Morlain responded, 'Yes, that is important, but while there is a chance, let us still believe and go to our task believing that we might yet prevail. Come, eat with us, with me. Where is Gwalian?'

'She went to get more bowls, I think. I will go and find her.'

'No, I will go and find her, help with the bowls. You must talk to the Company and to the others. There is still hope and you must convey that individually and collectively if we are to have any chance of success with our defence.'

Morlain walked up the steps and in through the great door of the hall. At first, she could not see anything or anyone. She walked a little further and then, as her eyes adjusted to the darkness of the room, there was Gwalian, sat at the round table with her back to the door. Her head rested on the back of one of the tall chairs and her hands clasped together in front of her on the table. She was weeping. As Morlain drew nearer, still unperceived by Gwalian, the woman and warrior of the Veneti, one of the few left of her kind, sniffed, looked up to the rafters, shook her head and then sobbed again.

'Gwalian, it is Morlain. I have come to look for you.'

Gwalian swung around in her chair, wiping the tears from her eyes with her tunic sleeve and sniffed again.

'Oh, it is you. Forgive me.' She wiped her face again. 'You are all waiting for the bowls.'

'The bowls can wait. Gwalian, I am so sorry for your loss, I…' For once, she did not know how to say what she wanted to say.

'Are you?'

'Yes, I am. Your father was an excellent man and served this land well, as did the bravery of Ewan and Lancelin. We all wish they had returned. That the fight had gone differently.'

Gwalian looked coolly back at Morlain in the half-light. 'Well, it did not, but I suppose it is for us who stay behind to pick up the pieces and make the best of it when they, who can, return. Although, no doubt you already have a clear view of how it will all turn out; if, of course, we get out of this siege.'

Morlain said nothing and the two women stared at each other. Then she said, with firmness but warmth in her voice, 'Do you know, I think we, you and I and many of those who sit on the steps of Pendre, will get out of this siege. And when we do, and when we have vanquished the aggressor, there is a brighter future waiting for us all.'

Again, there was a pause as Gwalian continued to look coolly at her before she turned away and stared across the table to where Aodren would have sat, and where she and Artur had sat before. Morlain spoke again, quietly, 'I do not plan nor control everything, Gwalian, and I would have fought for you both, today and always, if your connection with Artur had continued.'

A resigned smile rose across Gwalian's face as she turned back to Morlain and guffawed. 'Yes, I am sure you would, you being so wise and good. I am not surprised, really, that he has chosen you.'

She paused and looked to the ground and then, with another sob mixed into her voice, she lifted her head and said with sudden animation. 'Oh Morlain, how has it turned out like this? I have always tried to be positive in everything that I do, be optimistic, engaging and see my life on Mamm Norves as a gift to be grasped and made the most of – but I have never felt as low and desperate as I do right now!'

The tears flowed freely and her whole body convulsed in her grief. Morlain walked forward, took the woman of the Veneti into her arms and held her tight while she cried uncontrollably and tears rose in Morlain's eyes.

Morlain let go of her embrace and stepped back, but still gripped Gwalian's arms and said, 'Listen, your optimism and your determination are two of your best qualities and we, all of us, your friends, need them now. Please, do not desert us, when we need you most – and from what I hear, you are pretty good with a bow and arrow as well! You are vital to the defence of Menluit. We cannot do it without you – and you know that I do not say that just to bolster you, it is true!'

Gwalian smiled palely and nodded her head between the subsiding tears, before Morlain continued, 'And know this, we will get out of this siege if I have anything to do with it – and you and I have a big part to play in what happens next. I am not sure how, exactly, yet, but I know it, I feel it. Our future is entwined and we have much to do, today, tomorrow and in our lives to come. So, where are those bowls? We need to get back.'

On the steps, Artur spoke quietly to the Company and those around, occasionally clasping shoulders while engaging his warriors with firm and engaging eyes to indicate his determination and continuing resolve; but they all knew their peril and resignation filled the eyes of many, despite the restorative and comforting benefits of the stew. As Morlain and Gwalian returned, he watched as they came down the steps to the cauldron and then said to the assembled group, 'More bowls, for those who do not have food.'

Finally, everyone had their stew, with Artur the last to take his, before the Lady of Casworon's hall served herself and walked down to join the other Casworons. Subdued conversation and the togetherness of a shared fate coursed through the assembled defenders; many spoke to their companions, but it was the crackle and spit of the still well-fed cauldron fire that was the loudest sound of all.

After a while, Silyen, sitting midway down the steps and watching the progress of those eating their food, particularly Morlain, got to his feet. He turned towards Artur, who now sat at the bottom of the steps, and said more loudly, so that most could hear him, 'Pryns Artur, with your leave, you have come around and spoken to us all, positively, encouragingly, and we are ready for whatever is to come; but a story would also serve us well now and give us additional inspiration. A tale of the ancestors perhaps, and how our heritage has brought us here on this evening, all of us together, fighting a mighty foe. Look, there is a break in the cloud cover. The Mother Bear and her son look down on us again, seeking to reassure us. The heir of Orsa is amongst us and undiminished, is it not propitious? Does she not force back the darkness, however briefly to encourage us on this of all nights?'

Artur tipped the last of his food onto his mouth, wiped his lips with his sleeve and smiled back at the man of the Far Island, 'Yes, Silyen, I am sure she does. Perhaps the Lady Morlain would favour us with a story?'

Morlain, who sat towards the top of the steps, amongst her acolytes, rose to her feet and looked around at the many faces that turned towards her, bright and clear in the glow of the fire.

Morlain smiled at them all and looked down to Artur. 'Pryns Artur, I will tell a tale of stones and rings and defiance in the face of unwarranted aggression. A story that spans many generations, made necessarily brief by the approach of midnight, the need for sleep and the swift approach of the new day. It will tell of the dividing of this land, of treachery and greed and the diminishing of the mighty Pretan. An honest story and one, you might think, of decline, sorrow and defeat; and so it was for many who lived through it, but it is also a story about standing our ground and the importance of those chosen to fight the definitive fight and take charge of our destiny.'

The Stealing of the Stones

Umgras brought the Stones of Cylchau y Seren to the central plain of the Sacred Land, and when the dhreic lay slain, the stonemasons of Mata rebuilt it there.

From all parts of ancient Albion, many came to marvel and wonder. The priests of the land, in response, conceived and built an ever-more intricate place of avenues and circles, mixing all that they knew, all that had gone before with the new ways of the Pretan pioneers and the skill of the Mata. But these custodians of the Sacred Land, long used to being the leaders, soon began to resent the awe with which the Kings and people of Albion held the newly arrived Pretan and their allies, the Mata, or "these dubious Ocean People" as the priests began to call them.

Believing it an impossible task without the vanquished Umgras, the priests now called for more I Main Brith, the glistening stones of the Cylchau y Seren, and the challenge went out to the temporal lords of the Pretan and the Mata.

"Bring more of the I Main Brith from the land of the Mata! Prove that your greatness, fame and prowess go beyond the slaying of a dhreic. Bring more I Main Brith to the Sacred Land; show the people of Albion that your greatness is not an illusion, honour the holy ancestors and truly demonstrate your reverence for the Sun Father and Earth Mother."

Piran of the Pretan had a son called Talan and a daughter called Meraud. Cadan of the Mata, the dhreic slayer, had a daughter called Arianwen. Talan and Arianwen came together and through them, the union of the two peoples was stronger still and Talan, forthright and brave like his father, took up the challenge of the priests. He and Arianwen travelled to her homeland and went to the quarry of the pillared stones, given by

Mamm Norves to her chosen people and in honour of all who had gone before.

At first, the task seemed impossible. The Mata, using ropes and many willing and devotional volunteers, had dragged the quarried stone the short distance to the original site of Cylchau y Seren. How could they drag the stone to the Sacred Heart of Albion over hill and mountain and across broad and flowing rivers?

Sira Howl shone warmly upon them and all day they sat with good food and mead and contemplated the stones, fresh in their quarry, sparkling in His light, until Meraud, wise beyond her youth, who had accompanied her brother on his journey, rose to speak.

"Brother, we are Ocean's people, the children of Thurien! No talk of dragging over hill and high mountain is required here. Instead, move the stone to the broad and embracing Ocean, ever our stimulus and opportunity, along full stream and river course on boat and craft, down and not up the hills and transport around the land of the Mata, along the great rivers of Albion until we are as close as we are able to be to the Sacred Land. Then, we can drag them!"

Talan was enthused by his sister's words and she continued, "In this, we will prove our eminence and found a great land. Let yours be the first of many voyages to come where great sailors, heroes and the lords of the Pretan and the Mata, and all who join them, travel to explore and bring back new riches and treasure. Show what is possible brother! Many will follow and seek to emulate you in Ocean's great land on ancient Albion's shores and the fame and influence of the Pretani will spread to many lands near and far. Show the way, and with Arianwen, noble Prynces of the Mata, begin a great dynasty that will lead and inspire our people."

The first of the great Pretan tasks, the challenge of the priests, had its response. The great temple of the Sun Father, the house of the ancestors in the Sacred Land, became even stronger and more I Main Brith came to the sacred lands that surrounded it. The Pretan lords were in the ascendancy and the masons of the Mata were revered throughout the land. Talan and Arianwen founded a long line of Pretan Kings and Queens; and Albion sparkled like a great jewel in the silver ocean. Many voyages followed as the lords of the Pretan sought to emulate those early voyages, of Venetia, Thurien and Talan, sailing on Ocean, searching for metals, minerals and resource, and bringing back stories of strange and distant lands.

Then, when all thought of them was nearly lost, the children of Aleman began to arrive on the shores of Albion. The words that they used, said with a different emphasis after many years apart, were still familiar to the children of Thurien and this, along with their proficiency with the bow and arrow, and the beakers and jewellery that they carried, confirmed the new arrivals as being descendants of the great Pretani mother. There was great celebration. The new arrivals brought new skills, new impetus and further enhancement to the great temple and land around. All across ancient Albion, which many now called Pretannia, and across the Mor Pretani in the lands that we now know as Celtica and Armorica, a great Pretan hegemony was established and the land and its peoples lived happily together for many lives and many generations.

The children of Aleman had done as Olian had asked in the beginning. They had pushed across high mountain, through steep valley and mighty rivers towards Sira Howl and His returning light, taking the message and the words of the Pretan with them. In the end, however, they went too far, delved too deep, into the vast flatlands beyond the great forest and awoke the people there, banished by Mamm Norves many, many lives before, to a barren and oceanless life. The forest had held them back and created a divide that had gradually dulled their memory of the great flood; but now the Pretan rekindled their memories, helped them to recall what, in their minds, they had lost. Stealthily, deviously, they infiltrated the children of Aleman, converting them and imbuing them with their avarice and destructive ways; and in this way edged ever back towards the ocean and the sacred land of Pretannia. Revenge and domination they sought, and to take control and call their own all that was not theirs.

Once established, they fought aggressively for change. Men, they said, must lead and rule the land and women should serve the men. Some, who had distant relations and kinship with these "Estrenyons", long before the Pretan had come to Albion, began to agree with them. Priests, descendants of those humbled by the intelligence of Meraud and the bravery of Talan, saw their chance to reassert their dominance and so, gradually, disguised as the children of Aleman, they spread their control across Pretannia, overrunning the Sacred Land and Temple of the Sun Father. They tried to rebuild and reshape the Temple as a mark of their triumph, but the skill had gone and the stones collapsed or sank into the ground. Eventually, they lost interest, walked away from the all-seeing Sira Howl and returned to the many gods of the Estrenyons. The great Temple fell into disuse and the grass grew all around.

Battle followed battle and the Pretan, the Ocean People, too often the defeated, retreated back towards Ocean' from whence Ronan had come all those years before.

Now the Estrenyons said that they were the true Pretan! They would apportion all of the land and someone, a man, would own every piece of it. These men would dictate who could enter the land and what could happen on it. They dismissed the great voyages and said that this was the lot of traders and not the "great lords of the Pretan". Instead, farming their land and growing fat on the wealth of its produce was what mattered. Pretannia was theirs and the Ocean People, they said, belonged in the ocean and they would not rest until they had removed all traces of them from the land.

All seemed lost, but then, from an unexpected place, hope rekindled. A small flotilla of boats came, after a long and perilous journey, from Achaea, a great land by the shores of the Middle Sea and a place where heroic voyages were still revered. They came for kassiteros to make their bronze, led by Ictasus and his daughters, wearing golden rings inlaid with deep blue and sent by the King of the Achaeans to secure the supply.

Distraught was the land of the Dewnan, laid low by the constant war of the Estrenyons. Ictasus and the Acheans built a colony and a port at Ictis with warriors and traders, and slowly spread out from their colony to influence the land of the Dewnan. The banner of the rings, symbolising those first Achean arrivals became a symbol and a familiar sight across the land, a symbol of triumph against adversity, a symbol of hope.

The Achaeans were not aggressive and traded their expertise and their support in return for the kassiteros that they sent to Achaea. They worked alongside the Ocean People, recognising and admiring what remained of the Pretan influence; and more fighters joined the colony and gradually, with the Dewnan, rebuilt their fighting ability, their confidence and belief. Then, when they were ready and with a great army, the size of which had not gone forth for many years, took the fight to the aggressors. One summer's day, in what is now the land of the Durotrages, they called the High King of the Estrenyons to battle.

The Estrenyon horde fought with sword and shield. They had repudiated the bow and arrow, and knowing that the men of the Dewnan retained their Pretan prowess with the bow, claimed it was the weapon of cowards; but the Achaean and Dewnan lords laughed at such nonsense and said that each should fight with his own weapon. The Lords of the Dewnan marched with new confidence into the land occupied by the Estrenyons and took up their position on a distinctive and prominent hill by the ancient Path of Ronan, only a day's march from the old temple of the Sun Father.

Angered by their temerity, the High King of the Estrenyons marched out from his hilltop fort, past the ancient temple and along the Path of Ronan. As he approached, the many banners of the Dewnan and the Achaeans fluttered in the afternoon breeze and there, prominent amongst them, was the banner of the rings, invigorating the warriors of the Dewnan.

Complacent from the long series of victories that he and his predecessors had achieved, the King ordered an immediate attack, but now it was different, the tide had turned. From their elevated position, the Dewnan rained arrows down on the Estrenyon horde. Where previously they would have charged hastily, they now held their ground and let the arrows fly. As the aggressors reeled before the murderous and devastating volley from above, they came forth with sword and shield and met the Estrenyons in open battle. Weakened by the arrow storm, and with the Dewnan and Achaeans bearing down on them, the horde collapsed. They tried to flee, but their fate was sealed. The brutality of the Estrenyons and the loss of good friends and innocent souls filled the mind of the Dewnan and the rout turned to slaughter.

The Dewnan and the Achaeans won a great victory that day and the future of their land was secure for many lives to come. Together, now, they built a series of great defences against the Estrenyons. The ancestors of the Durotrages, freed from their oppression, joined with them...

Morlain stopped and looked down at Artur, who was listening to a runner from the far side battlement. He looked to Morlain and shook his head, then said to all with urgency, 'Everyone to your sections, and your positions, and be ready.'

He looked again to Morlain and then ran in the direction of the far side battlement. Maedoc went with him and Ambros alongside, returning to his station, while Morlain quickly made her way down the steps.

As they approached the battlement, shouts, swords clashing and cries of anguish grew louder. All of the watch looked anxiously over the battlement and a yellow-red tinge grew in the darkness with smoke rising, discernible at its limit.

Artur, Ambros, Ambros's gille and Maedoc clambered onto the battlement, and the guards stood aside as they looked over. Flames rose into the night sky. Arrows, some carrying fire, rained into the makeshift camp of the men of RunHoul, and a press of Roman soldiers and Curiosolitae warriors surrounded them, out of range of any response from the battlement. As they watched, fighters fell before the concerted, determined onslaught and it looked irredeemable as the enclosing forces swallowed up more of the RunHoul Dewnan. In their midst, a series of fires burnt. Baggage and several of the defenders were set alight by the burning arrows. Screams of pain and anguish filled the night, unnerving and weakening the resolve of those on the battlement. Artur looked on horrified and Ambros roared in anger. Even after Gwened, this was gruesome and they watched helplessly as the men of RunHoul met a terrible end.

Morlain clambered up on the battlement and stood by their side. All of them now stood tall and did not turn away while their compatriots, who had quickly dwindled in number, fought valiantly on. Then, a warrior came into view, running towards the rear of the Roman line. Artur stood forward, grabbed the top of the battlement and peered over. The back of the head was familiar. Consumed by what they saw, they had not thought to ask why Marrek was not here. The Prince turned back to the guards.

'Romins surprized en in the dark.'

Then another.

'Surrounded 'em afore they could do anythin', rainin' fire arras down. Lord Marrek said ee could not stand an watch is kinsmen die and do nothin'. Told uz to wait ere and tell ee. Sorry, but one less won't make a difference.'

The Prince looked at the man and then out beyond the battlement again. Marrek was fighting determinedly and a last song of defiance could be heard as he went about his task. One of his opponents lay flat in front of him but four more had detached from the back of the Roman line. Artur clambered up onto the fence of the battlement. Ambros was quickly alongside him.

They were going to jump down onto the field when a firm but familiar voice behind them said, 'No. Artur, Ambros jump down, there is nothing now that any of us can do.' Morlain paused and then said. 'Will you save one man and put three hundred in jeopardy instead? Marrek has made his choice and we must honour it, but we do not, necessarily, have to follow it.'

Artur and Ambros, stood astride the fence, unwavering, but remaining where they were as the man of RunHoul fought doggedly on. They knew his song and now their voices and those of many around them rang out in support of their friend and comrade.

Forth the Dewnan brave and true
We shall not submit to you!
Stand with us for freedom's voice
Sing with us our song of choice!

Then, as Marrek deflected and lifted a thrust, another came swiftly in, too quickly for him to react and the sword pierced deep within his ribcage. The song faded and all watched, desolate as he bent, doubling over the penetrating sword, pushed backwards and swung his sword again, but his swing was loose, erratic and another thrust entered his side. He staggered, tried to lift his sword and fell backwards onto the ground. His head and arm seemed to lift slightly, but as they did, one of the Romans stood forward and stabbed his sword into Marrek's heart. Then, without a second thought, he and those who had responded to Marrek's charge, turned back to the main fight, which had now extinguished all that remained of the men of RunHoul.

Artur and Ambros turned and jumped down on to the battlement. Artur said to Morlain and anyone else who cared to hear, 'I am going to prepare the sections and will work my way around to the main gate. I am sure they will consolidate before they move again.'

Morlain stayed with Ambros to comfort him and all around as best she could, but also to watch the movement of the Romans. The attack on the men of RunHoul did not herald a more substantial approach to the battlements, so what did they intend? Was it consolidation? Certainly, they were meticulous in ensuring that none of the men of RunHoul survived.

As she watched, all of the Romans began to move back around Menluit, away from Tamara and towards the small battlement door. They were moving quickly now. With Ambros back on his feet and talking to those around him, she followed along the battlement, past Silyen and Kea, both looking over the battlement. When Morlain got to Drustan, over the door, she stopped. Those coming down now joined with the rest of the force, doubling their size and all of them began to move.

Drustan watched with her. 'Either they are leaving or they are all heading for the main gate,' he concluded.

Morlain nodded as she watched. 'I think you are right, but I don't think they are leaving.'

Morlain negotiated the watchers as she continued around the battlement. Ahead, she could see Artur. Despite the developing crisis, he looked up and smiled as she appeared before him a little breathless, sword by her side and staff in her hand.

'They all come to the main gate. I think they mean an assault at first light, all their forces are concentrated here.'

'Yes, Gourgy has sent word, the battering ram is prepared and they mark the mantrap to ensure they do not fall prey to it again. They clearly intend to come quickly from that direction. Tremaine reports that the Curiosolitae have repelled the men of RunHoul by Tamara also and prepare the boats on this and her far bank for a quick departure if they can get what they want and, perhaps, even if they cannot; but they are not just going to leave, that seems clear. There are many of them, Morlain.'

She breathed in deeply as their eyes met, 'So what will be our response?'

'We set a small watch around the rest of the battlement in sight of each other as the light grows, but everyone else will go to the sections around the gate. Gwalian and Gawen are preparing the archers as they come in from around the battlement. The rest of us need to prepare now with our swords drawn and our shields, if we chose to use them, ready to withstand the attack. We will not stop them from putting their ladders up, no matter how fast the archers fire, so we must prepare to fight on the battlement, and to try and hold the gate.'

Kea and Silyen joined them and the man of the Kernovi spoke first.

'We are here with Casworon, Marrek and Hedrek's section. The Romans are not before our part of the battlement, we are sure of it. Ambros holds a small watch across the far side of the citadel. He has several of the younger runners, who will come quickly if there is any sign of threat. Drustan covers the door and battlement towards here.'

'Silyen, can you take yours and Marrek's section to bolster the gate, join Nouran and Gourgy there. I think they are going to make quite an effort to break the gate down. Briec and Tremaine are already there; and Kea, can you try to space the archers and warriors alongside those who are less strong, less experienced and more frightened? Can yours and Hedrek's section cover that?'

Both nodded their acknowledgement and went away.

With Morlain beside him and the defenders organising around him, he surveyed the Roman lines, breathed deeply, preparing for the imminent and defining encounter.

She said, 'You are the Lord of the Crossing and you wield the Sword of Menluit. Right is on our side. They are bounty hunters and aggressors made up of conflicting interests, only brought together by their desire to take and control. We stand with you, our people, and our land; that is what we defend today.'

He continued to look ahead, then turned and looked at her with a brief smile and said, 'I know.'

He jumped down from the battlement and walked away to the defenders at the gate. Morlain looked across the land as the light grew. Torches were extinguishing and she could see neat lines of soldiers arranged into four divisions, large rectangles, lined up out of range of the Dewnan arrows. The Romans formed the middle two divisions. The division to her right, mainly Curiosolitae, stood forward of the middle two. In front of this division, stood a more distinctive man, or at least he clearly thought that he was as he strutted in front of his men, a tribal leader perhaps or maybe even the King. Amongst this group, towards the rear, she could also see archers, and to the side of the division, a fire burned. The division on her left, also Curiosolitae, stood as an end in a rectangle. They were not as neat as the Roman lines and straddled the path that led to the main gate. In their midst was the great battering ram, fashioned from a wide-girthed tree of the woods. Fixed firmly to its front was a sharpened iron end that was intended to pierce and cut through anything standing in its way.

In front of each division were individual warriors, wearing the skin of an animal that she did not recognise and holding what looked like the Carnyx, a horn-like instrument. She had seen an example of it from Gaul and its sound came from the shaped representation of an animal's head, but here the opening was circular, plate-like, with a large hole in the middle that led back into the tube of the instrument. A low hum of sound came from the fields, of soldier talking to soldier, warrior-to-warrior. They were all paused and waiting for the direction to begin. As she watched, either a Roman with his distinctive plume topped helmet or a long, bushy-haired, bearded Curiosolitae warrior, barked instructions and gave encouragement. It was unclear what the Roman leaders were saying, but she strained to hear the words of the Curiosolitae. "Spare none," was clearly audible and so their intention was clear. She looked along the battlements. Many of the defenders surveyed the scene as well and heard the Curiosolitae words. They all, no matter what their previous experience was, or their capacity for bravery, looked on with great unease.

Suddenly, the horns sounded loud and in unison; the signal of impending attack. Each of the divisions stood to attention. Poised and ready. One blast and a lingering note, then a second. As the second note faded, men carrying spears came running through the front ranks, formed a straight line. They then ran about twenty paces, placed their feet, bent their backs and launched their spears. The suddenness of the manoeuvre, not the charge perhaps they had expected, caused the defenders on the battlement to watch in terrified awe as the spears, with an increasing rush of air, descended towards them.

Morlain drew her sword and shouted along the battlement. 'Take cover. Get down, in against the battlement!'

Further along the defence, Kea and Drustan were also shouting. Many bent down, and did as directed, but not all. Some looked up, suddenly conscious of the rushing air and the hard metal, pyramidal tips of the spears entered their surprise-induced open mouths and split their skulls asunder. Others stepped backwards and the spears buried deep into their chests, causing them to stagger, dumbstruck and amazed at the bent soft-iron shank, sticking out of them. The power of its impact and their shock forced them back and off the battlement, and their blood showered all who stood close by. Several of the spears cleared the battlement and struck or glanced several who scurried below. Their cries of pain and anguish filled the ground behind the battlement while others around, wide-eyed with fear, rushed to help them.

As she crouched below the battlement, and as the cries of pain continued below, Morlain looked along the line again. The post spaces on either side of her were empty and Gwalian and her small group of archers clambered into them. The woman of the Veneti gave a cursory nod to Morlain, holding her bow in one hand and with a large quiver of arrows on her back.

Cautiously, they raised themselves and, as they did, the horns sounded again, booming menace across the hill. Now a great roar went up from the Roman lines. All of the defenders quickly raised their heads above the fence to see three of the divisions running towards the battlement, bellowing, calling, with faces of anger and threat, and their swords drawn. Some carried ladders and those that did not, in the middle two divisions, beat on the inside of their shields with a practised crescendo of noise. Then, as they came within range of the Dewnan arrows, they raised and carried their shields above their heads, protecting themselves and a close by ladder carrier. The spear throwers had retreated to a further pile of spears and were rearming themselves, while the ladder shields and ladder carriers approached the battlements.

'Gwalian, take out the ladder carriers. Gawen, the ladders – take out the ladders!' Morlain shouted down the battlement.

Gwalian had fired her first two arrows and was about to let go of the third when she staggered, all of them staggered, hanging on to the fence as the battlement rocked. The great battering ram struck the gate with force and sent the shock of its impact reverberating all the way along the structure. Quickly, Morlain stood back and looked along the battlement. She could see Artur and Gourgy above the gate and Nouran on the far side, with archers around them, firing down on the ram carriers, and Silyen and Maedoc helping and directing others on the ground, pushing and pulling heavy items in front of the gate. Again, the battlement shuddered as a second thrust of the ram struck and she saw that the inner gate buckle slightly inwards.

Gwalian shouted and, as she turned back, the ladders were up with their tops protruding above the fence. She and those around her fired down. Several of the attackers lay on the ground around the ladders, struck by the arrows of the defenders; but now the shields deployed above their heads protected far more than in the early skirmishes, as they forced their way forward onto the lower rungs.

Morlain drew her sword. 'Get ready to repel! They are coming up. Push the ladders back if you can,' she called along the line.

Maedoc and Gawen, directed by Artur, came running back from the gate. Gwalian was still trying to pick out targets, taking cover, then leaning over again and finding another, as she and now Gawen held off a mass surge for the moment. Despite this, there was a man on the ladder before them and, with his shield above him, he slowly and purposefully made his way up.

'Maedoc, help me push the ladder back!' Morlain cried.

They got hold of either side of the ladder as it lent on the fence and then, with a determined heave, pushed the ladder away from the fence. Others along the battlement followed their lead and ladders started to move outwards. Held determinedly by those below, the ladders proved hard to move. Morlain swung her staff around and placed its bulbous top against one of the rungs, while her hands gripped tightly on the shaft. She then shoved hard, trying to concentrate her mind, to wield the staff and show her ability. Maedoc, who understood her likely purpose, knew better than to touch the staff and, instead, jumped down to find another post to shove against the ladder.

Further along the battlement, Drustan and Kea had also seen the need to follow suit and were using larger posts to shove the ladders back. Some went back and, if they did not, the defenders hurled the large posts down to knock the climbers off the ladders. Morlain pushed hard, trying to focus her mind, but a spark of fire from the staff was all she could manage. It cut through several of the rungs, enough to create a gap that the climber would not be able to clamber over without lifting his shield, but her strength failed her and she could do no more as the ladder crashed back against the wall. It was a temporary and exhausting reprieve.

The battlement juddered as the ram struck into the gate. Morlain staggered back, shattered by the effort and mental concentration needed to bring power and flame to the staff, and collapsed onto the battlement walkway, still holding her sword. Maedoc caught her and stopped her from falling off, but she had to put her staff down as its vibration and friction had burnt her hand painfully. Maedoc stooped to appeal to her.

'Madam, do not try to do too much too quickly, you must rest, if only briefly. Step down from the battlement.'

Then, he had to respond to another surge up the ladder. Others looked along the line, seeing she had fallen and, for a moment, the fight in them faded. Drustan, Kea and Gawen, trying to hide their anxiety, sought to rally them.

It was not as she had intended. She had learnt that the foundation of her ability was in her faith, that she could overcome all that she faced, but even she had doubts now. In the exhaustion of her mind, everything around her slowed down. Unintentionally, but rapidly now, the possibility grew in her mind that, even after all her efforts, the King might not come and the Lords of the Dewnan would accept their fate and not repel the incursion and domination of the Roman aggressor. Without them, and faced with the huge force that had now been revealed to her by the established daylight, an uncontrollable, uncharacteristic bitterness surged through her. Suddenly, she was conscious of shouting and the fence shoved and rocked from the outside. A great press of men pushed against it, intent on killing them all. Had it then, actually all been for nothing? Was this the end of the Dewnan, a brave but futile last stand?

She raised her head and looked along the battlement again. Ladders poked up above the fence line and defenders fought doggedly on, dragging more heavy objects from within the trev and hurling them down on those who tried to climb. The archers, in between, picked off as many attackers as they could, as falling items caused temporary confusion below. As she looked, Morlain felt the battlement shake again as the ram struck its target. She then caught a glance of the grim determination of Gwalian. Sweat and dirt were smeared across her face and her tunic was torn from catching it on the fence as she reached up and lent over the battlement again to fire another arrow. She was saying something, only just discernible in the din of the assault.

'Morlain, can you hear me, are you all right?' The question was followed by a sudden look of anguish in the midst of her determination. 'We need you, Morlain. Don't give in now!' Then she leant over and fired again.

Near to Drustan, two of the attackers were over and their swords were out. One of the defenders – she could not see who – fell backwards, leg spurting blood. Drustan and Kea were there quickly, their swords clashing, Kea's sword cut through one of the Romans and he was shoved back over the battlement, falling onto others as they climbed the ladder, scattering them. Drustan took the other, sliced his leg and then manhandled him back over the battlement. Gawen fired with great rapidity and just, only just, stopped the climbers from scaling the fence. It could not last.

Now another was up at face level, several post spaces away from Gwalian. There was a shout and she spun around and fired her arrow straight into his eye. He yowled in pain and Maedoc leapt along the battlement and shoved his sword through the Roman's throat. Again, blood sprayed everywhere, across many of the defenders, as the Roman briefly rocked and then fell on all of those coming up behind him. Gwalian leaned over and fired four rapid arrows, each of them burying deep into a prone body below. Morlain got up grimly and unsteadily to her feet raised her sword and prepared to join the others in holding back the climbers for as long as they could.

The horn blew again and the shield-covered climbers briefly stopped trying to scale the battlement. The spear throwers came forward and threw another volley.

'Take cover, spears coming in!'

Most did take cover now, but still the spears managed to pierce several on the battlement and the sight of them falling sapped the morale of those around them as the climbers began again.

Then, Artur was by her side, breathing heavily.

'It is much worse than we might have imagined, even when we spoke before. By concentrating their force here, they fully emphasise the difference in the size of our defences. This is also the definitive moment for them, of course. It works now or not at all; and for us, unless things change very quickly, well, there are just too many of them and they will overwhelm us very soon. The gate will not hold for much longer and I do not think we can hold their ladders and climbers back for much longer either. Do you agree?'

Her words to him, spoken only a short while before, now seemed hollow and foolish. She had directed him here to make his stand and then gone away to look for support, but unless that support turned up very soon, they were all doomed.

'Yes,' she said, 'I think you are right.'

He saw the look in her eyes and brightened determinedly before her. Behind them, the ram crashed into the gate, the sharpened metal end pierced through both sets of gates amidst shouts from inside and outside, and the battlement trembled.

Silyen came running.

'Artur, they are cutting away at the outer gate. You must come.'

The Prince looked to him, nodded and turned back to Morlain, pressing her free hand in his. 'Morlain, it is not over until it is over, that is what you would say and I say if we are to go down, we may as well go down fighting. Take the fight to them! Far better than waiting for them to overwhelm the walls or break down the gate. Let's go out to meet them, you and I and anyone else who wants to join us. We can create a diversion so that those who want to get away, whose fight this never was, can do so through the battlement door.'

She looked at him and her face sharpened as he spoke; she needed him as much as he needed her and now, at this crucial moment, it was his turn to be the inspirer, the believer and with his words, he resparked her mind, broke her melancholy and brought her back.

'Yes.' She squeezed his hand quickly and slowly got to her feet. 'Forgive me, I was knocked back earlier, but now I have returned. Let us rally our comrades and then come together and ride out to meet them.'

***

'Dominus, a report from Centurion Habitus at the gate with the Curiosolitae. He says that he thinks maybe three more batterings with the ram and they will be through, they are changing ram carriers now, and they have chopped away a large part of the outer gate. A number of the Curiosolitae have fallen to their sagittarii, but there are still plenty of men capable of swinging the ram. He sends word that soon they will be ready for you to enter the citadel.

Flavius, stern-faced, watched the assault on the walls and the gate, surrounded by several junior officers. Somehow, the defenders still prevented his men from scaling the walls and his frustration grew. They should have been in by now. He had read his father's descriptions of his battles in Gaul. In those accounts – stories and reports that caught the Roman imagination – the ingenuity, determination and bravery of the Roman soldiers nearly always overwhelmed the enemy and often a large enemy force. There could not be more than a few hundred within this citadel and yet they held them at bay, throwing everything that they had – literally, it seemed – from the citadel walls.

The news from the gate, at least, was better, but they had to control the walls if they were to enter the citadel, quickly find what they sought and then withdraw.

'Optio, thank you. I will be with you shortly.'

He looked behind him to where Gyras stood tethered to a tree.

'Prepare the Greek, do not untie his arms, but prepare to bring him with us.'

Then, he gave his instructions to another optio.

'Send word to Centurion Dexipus and the King. It is time to deploy the fire arrows; we must get over that wall.'

The optio turned and left and Flavius looked back to the attack. He felt the hilt of his gladius, straightened his sword belt, lifted his helmet and placed it on his head. Then, after adjusting his head within it, he began to tie the leather strap that held it in place. As he did so, twigs snapped, the undergrowth rustled and a legionary appeared behind him, out of breath and waiting for permission to speak.

Flavius turned irritated towards him. 'Yes, what is it?'

'Nauarchus, the boats are being attacked. A large force approaches on boats up the river and there are men coming along the steep cliffs through the woods. Centurion Telesinus sends word. He is not sure how long he can hold them!'

Those who stood around Flavius looked across to him and then to each other, but for a moment, the Nauarchus said nothing and stared coldly at the messenger. Then he turned back to the battle before him with a manic look in his eye, before bellowing, 'We have to take the citadel now!'

***

'Sister, sister, can you hear us? We are coming. Prepare now, prepare to ride forth and bring your Pryns with you. We are coming!'

Steren Uskis whinnied and took short steps from one side to the other, anticipating and unable to stand still. Morlain's eyes narrowed, the words were clear. They were close.

Within the walls of Menluit, most still fought on the battlement, holding the ladder climbers, but they were running out of things to throw. The ram, stuck in the inner gate, had not quite broken through. One more swing would do it and now the attackers worked to get it out. The defenders fired arrows through the hole that it had created, while others fired down on the ram carriers from the battlement above the gate, but a wall of protective shields, on the top and to the side, limited the damage.

None had left by the battlement door; instead, all chose to follow Artur and Morlain out of the gate. Now they fought and waited for Morlain to be ready and for the signal to jump down, run for the open gate, and follow their leaders into battle. Artur, at the gate, looked back to her and raised his eyebrows as if to say, *are you ready*? She looked at him, deep in thought and then, breathing deeply and with a look that said she had come to a decision, swung her leg over Steren Uskis's back and jumped down. The horse bowed his head, she spoke in his ear and he turned and cantered away, up toward Pendre and the top of the hill. With her staff in one hand, she drew her sword, walked purposefully towards Artur and he walked towards her.

'I am ready, but we shall fight together on foot, you and I and all our friends, and we will take our fate as it comes.'

The roar and clamour continued around them, but he stood and looked into her eyes. 'Yes.' The briefest of pauses and then he said, 'Morlain, you and I were meant to be together, to live life together, and whatever happens today, you will always be part of me. You are beautiful and wonderful and clever and I am so grateful that I have known you!'

She smiled, speed was vital now. Feeling back to her indefatigable, tenacious self, she said, 'Artur, death is not a conclusion, even if that is to be our fate today. Our future is together, in this life, the next and many lives to come.' She opened her eyes wide and smiled wryly. 'You will never be free of me now. Let us take the fight to the Romans and show them what it means to invade and abuse our land. I am ready if you are.'

Their eyes held each other's for a moment longer and then Artur looked away towards the battlement. From the far end, there was shouting and pointing; he could not hear what they said and so ran towards them. Drustan ran along the battlement pointing back to where he had come from.

'The Banner of the Rings. They are here. They come along the old path, along the gover and to the old door, clearly visible now after the rain and the trample of battle. They are here cousin, and they have taken Cantassa's hill!'

Artur jumped up on to the battlement. On the high ground to the left of Cantassa's hill, he could see men, warriors approaching. They would arrive at the battle around the hill opposite and so the Romans would not see them until they were on top of them. No doubt, their scouts would pick them up before then, but on the hill where Cantassa's sanctum had stood there was now a great banner with three rings being held aloft by a warrior of the Dewnan. The grim, grey cloud cover still dominated the sky, but the mizzle had stopped and a fresh breeze blew across the land.

Artur gripped the hilt of the Sword of Menluit. The ring of Diantha glowed on his sword hand and many along the battlement saw it and took fresh heart.

The small group of Romans on the hill, it seemed, were quickly despatched, save three who now ran down the hill in an attempt to get away and raise the alarm. Two of the newly arrived Dewnan stepped forward, raised their bows and fired. Two of the runners fell as they ran, their bodies crumpling and distorting as their heads struck the ground, but the momentum of their movement carried them forward. The third ran on and they let him go, as a herald of doom to all who now fought before the battlement of Menluit.

Arrows dowsed in fire began to fly over Artur's head as he watched, and still the climbers came. As those around him hesitated and took cover in the face of this deadly rain of fire, more got onto the ladders and began to climb. Behind him, carts and the thatch of the nearest roundhouses were now alight and parts of the battlements burned. Along the walkway where post spaces were no longer filled, there were small but unchecked fires and soon it would all be alight. Artur shouted to Drustan, Kea and Gawen. 'Pass the word, be ready.'

'Gwalian,' he shouted as he ran past her, 'be ready!'

She turned and looked back at him, grave, tired and nodded, before reaching over again and firing another arrow.

He ran to the gates where Nouran and Gourgy stood ready to open them, with two each of their section. The ram had now gone, withdrawn for its final battering. Morlain stood ten good paces back, while all the others who had stood above it, and most of those who had stood behind it, were down and behind her. Maedoc, Silyen, Tremaine and Briec were there, their swords drawn, arms trembling, their bodies resonating in anticipation of what was about to happen.

Morlain stood, her sword raised in her right hand and her staff in her left, her face taut in a deep frown of concentration. On her left hand, and integral to the intensity that she had built up, was the sparkling ring of Eupheme.

As Artur came up to them, she turned her head carefully to him and said, 'We are ready.'

He looked at her, at his comrades, and then along the battlement, parts of which were now fully alight, and to the faces

– the rest of the Company, Gwalian and her archers, Callard and the Casworon's – all looking to him, waiting for the signal.

'Then let's do it!'

'Yes, let's do it!' they roared back and Nouran and Gourgy gripped the gates to open them.

Artur turned to the battlement and swung the Sword of Menluit high and as he did the rings of Diantha and Eupheme spoke to each other, glowing brightly with purpose on the hands of Artur and Morlain, as she gripped her staff with intent. An arc of light seemed to form between them, symbolising their ancestors, family and all that had gone before – all that was right and worth fighting for, all that they believed in and made them distinctive, embodied in these two young people; the hope of their nation as they prepared to venture forth. From the battlement, all came running across the ground to the gate.

Morlain raised herself to her fullest height and it was noticeable how, as her stature grew, so did the stature of her staff, and a developing, dazzling light and a growing spark of fire cascaded from it. The gates opened quickly on the attackers. The ram with its carriers, which was moving swiftly to its anticipated final battering, approached the open gap. The carriers were blinded by the light, and before they had the chance to cross the threshold, Morlain flicked her staff and a bolt of energy scythed through the metal end and cracked the tree trunk asunder. Sharp splinters scattered amongst all who stood before the gate, cutting and sticking into faces and bare flesh, while those who carried the ram cried horribly as they felt their hands and arms burning, their clothes alight, and the raging fire consumed their bodies within the spreading combustion of the energy bolt.

Sira Howl shone brightly above the treetops, but for those before the gate, Morlain's light was all-consuming, blinding them to everything else. She steadily turned her head, her face full of anger and intent, and said to Artur, 'Follow me, surround me, but do not go beyond the forward reach of the light. We will consume them and engage them only under the light.'

Artur nodded and looked to all around them. They had all heard her.

Again, she flicked her staff and a bolt of energy, now with increased fire, sprang from it, scattering, scorching and burning all those who stood in her way. Faces and hair were alight, crackling and melting before them. She moved forward, firmly gripping the staff with her left hand and her sword with her right, her face, red and contorted with effort and application. The Dewnans who stood around her, protecting her while she did her work, could see all before them. Artur and the others despatched many who escaped the burning, but could not escape the light, and Gawen, Gwalian and the archers fired from within its protection, picking off target after target. The battlements burned behind them, but none of the attackers got through. They could not see into the light, could not see what it was that attacked them and recoiled in fear. Their attention diverted, they were uncertain whether to run or hide from the consuming, destructive and devouring luminosity.

***

Gyras's guards had loosened him from the tree, although not completely untied him, as instructed by Flavius. His hands remained tied, but now he watched with the rest in amazement as the blinding ball of light came out from the gate of the citadel and cut a swath through the massed lines of the Romans and Curiosolitae. Flavius was incandescent and in his rage, appeared to forgot that he was supposed to be joining the fight. It quickly got worse. The light, and the fighters that shielded beneath it, started to make strong progress across the hill before them. Gyras stared, fascinated. For a moment, he forgot his predicament as the ball of light, with two distinct, smaller but vibrant points of light within it, one fixed at its centre, the other moving, flitting about at its leading edge and moved forward from the gate. Flavius turned back and began to walk quickly towards him, his face a strange shade of purple. His eyes were red, his mouth growling with aggression and his whole body was shaking with anger.

'You have not told us that they could do this! What is this sorcery and magic that they deploy? What else are you hiding, you miserable piece of Greek shit?' In his rage, he fumbled for his dagger. 'I am going to make you pay for this! Death is all that is appropriate for a double-dealing bastard like you.'

He drew his sword and ran at the Massaliot.

'Nauarchus, please, I beg you. I knew nothing of this.'

Flavius, his face twisted with fury and desire for what he perceived as appropriate justice, or vengeance, raised his sword, ready to thrust into the Greek. 'You lie arseho…'

He said no more. In the act of opening his mouth to say the word, an arrow entered it and pierced all the way through and out the other side of his skull, followed swiftly by another in his cheek and one in his belly. For a moment, he stood before Gyras, rocking, with a cynical leer, his lip dragged upwards by the shaft of the arrow protruding from it, before his body fell forward and what remained of his face fell with a thud into the grass and the mud at Gyras's feet.

Men were running through the trees now, warriors, but not Curiosolitae, and the sound of the clash of sword on sword and sword on shield built. Then, there was a roar and a charge from further along in the woods. All of the Romans were engaging, including his guards, and some had already fallen. One of the warriors ran up to Gyras, a bow in his hand. Had he brought down Flavius? He wasn't sure. The warrior produced a knife and Gyras flinched.

He could speak the language of the Ocean People, of course, and he said with urgency. 'I am a friend!'

The warrior glared at him for a moment and then cut the ropes that bound him to the tree and the ropes that tied his hand. 'You are free, go!'

Gyras could have hugged him but, instead, simply said, 'Thank you.'

Then, walking carefully at first, he went from tree to tree, back through the ongoing fight. When he thought he was clear, he started running, running as fast as he could and for as long as he could, back along the road to Ictis.

***

Morlain's body convulsed and she stumbled. Staggering backwards, she breathed out in exhaustion and said, 'That is it. I am spent, I can do no more.'

The light had gone, but now they had space to fight amidst the bodies of burnt, stricken and arrow-pierced Romans and

Curiosolitae that littered the ground, while the roar, shouts of abuse, cries of pain and clash of metal increased in volume around them.

'Maedoc, Gwalian, help her,' Artur shouted. 'Get her to safer ground; she needs to rest before she comes back.'

A gap had opened before them in a semicircle as the attackers had learnt to recoil from the light, which allowed Artur and the defenders of Menluit brief pause to look around them. On the far side of the hill, and across the path, the Romans and Curiosolitae responded as a large body of Dewnans came down from the woods; the followers and retainers of Clesek, Lancelin's father. They were pushing them towards Artur and the Menluits. Around the hill, other warriors came.

'My father and the men of the Foye!' Drustan cheered at the glinting weapons of earlier. Attacked from all sides, and surrounded the Roman and Curiosolitae divisions, they fought doggedly on.

Only the Curiosolitae division on their right, led by their King, had space to manoeuvre and turn, as they did now. The Banner of the Rings came forth, accompanied by a great rumble and collective shout and roar that came down from Cantassa's hill towards them; and there, alongside the banner bearer, leading the charge, came Mawgan, King of the Dewnan.

All of the Menluits cheered, yelled their support and rejoined the battle, but the fight was far from over and the Romans and Curiosolitae that remained realised that their only hope was to fight their way out. It was an almost impossible task and now they had to face the repercussions of their actions.

The battle raged on into the middle of the afternoon; trained battle-hardened soldiers fighting with the defenders of the Sacred Land. Slowly but surely, the Romans and Curiosolitae were overwhelmed, stabbed, trampled, slashed and pierced with sword, arrow and recovered spear. All with a mind to avenge the horrors that the Dewnans and the few remaining Veneti had either seen or heard about – the slaughter of the men of RunHoul and the horrific treatment meted out to their Veneti kin in Armorica, fellow peoples of the Ocean, by the controlling, abominable and uncaring Roman aggression.

Eventually, any distinction of division was gone and the last of the Romans and Curiosolitae fought all who came against them. As he defended and dispatched his foes, Artur, with the Company around him, looked up and saw before him the Banner of the Rings and his father and the warriors of his house. They fought their way towards King Brice and his men, who were a short distance beyond him near an unburnt section of the battlement wall. Then, Mawgan also became conscious of his son close by. Another stab and dispatch by them both and they came together, fighting alongside each other; and for Artur, the din of the battle subsided as his father wielded his sword and shouted to him, 'You have been brave, Artur, led your Company and fought well.'

He breathed deeply and thrust at the Curiosolitae before him and they could both now see the Curiosolitae King and his bodyguard ahead of them. Aware of Mawgan's approach, the King looked towards them.

'Brice has tried to take my kingdom and he must pay!' Another thrust and another defence and then Mawgan spoke again. 'When this is done you will come to Ker Kammel or to Porthmetern and we will talk about what part, as my son, you will play in my kingdom.'

As he withdrew his sword, their eyes met. Mawgan's face was stern and determined but his eyes wider than in their previous meetings, as he looked on his son. Another warrior charged towards him from the pack. The King gripped his sword with both hands, ready to defend himself and chopped at the attacker. As he did so, a ring of gold and lapis lazuli shaped in the form of a shield revealed itself on the middle finger of his sword hand. It was the shield ring of Ictasus.

Artur saw it and clasped his right hand around his left as he swung the Sword of Menluit alongside his father. The glow of the rings intensified in pleasure at their proximity after so many years apart and an arc of light sprang between them, in spite of the carnage.

Mawgan looked to his hand and looked back at his son. 'You wear your mother's ring. I had thought it lost, taken in the raid that killed her, but here it is, restored.'

He stopped and turned fully toward Artur, looking intently at him, as it seemed a sudden thought took hold of him; and across his face spread a simple and genuine smile.

A Curiosolitae warrior rushed towards him, but one of the warriors of the King's house thrust his sword into the attacker's chest. Other warriors engaged, forcing an undefended gap to the King for a moment, and through it, Brice pushed, slashing at the house warriors who tried to lunge towards him, and thrust his sword into Mawgan's back.

'You should have made a deal old fool, and now we are both going to die!'

The shock of the incision extinguished his smile and as Mawgan's body arched forward the glow of his ring faded as he crumpled to the ground. The warriors surged around him and the Curiosolitae and their King moved backwards, ready to engage them.

Artur knelt beside his father, who still breathed, fitfully.

'Hold my hand, Artur, my ring hand with yours.'

His body shook and he shivered violently.

'I thought I saw your mother, after all these years!'

He tried to breathe.

'I will see her again soon.'

His throat convulsed and blood seeped from the corners of his mouth. Artur frantically looked around and then looked back.

'Father, Morlain will come, she is good, she can heal your wound. I know she can.'

Mawgan's eyes softened as he looked at his son. 'No, I don't think so, not now.' He gulped as his throat convulsed again and he took a rapid intake of breath, still shivering. 'Look to her Artur; she is a good woman, you and she will do well. I know it.'

He coughed and retched suddenly and blood spewed out of his mouth. He swallowed as best he could and then, with his whole body shaking, he said, 'Take my ring, look after it.' He swallowed and prepared to speak again, 'Artur, your mother loved you so and I…'

His voice was lost as his body convulsed into a violent seizure, rose from the ground and his eyes, filled with pain, looked finally at his son. Then, rigid, he collapsed on the ground. He was dead.

Artur looked into his father's staring lifeless eyes, gripped his hand, leant forward and kissed his sweat and blood splattered forehead. Above the battlefield, the clouds parted and blue sky and the rays of Sira Howl at the height of his daily climb shone down upon them.

Then the roar of battle came back into his head. Maedoc was behind him now and Kea and Gawen fighting close by came across. He took the ring of Ictasus from Mawgan's finger, put it on the middle finger of his left hand, stood and looked to them all and said, 'Now we will end this.'

***

Morlain sat in the field before the burnt and battered palisade fence of Menluit. The battle was before her now. Here, all that remained were bodies and the rear of the combined Dewnan force, ready to engage if the need arose. The end would not be long.

Maedoc and Gwalian had brought her back, exhausted from her exertions. Maedoc had quickly returned to the battle to support the Prince, but Gwalian had stayed with her, tired too after her continuous arrow shooting from the battlement. Then, Elowen and Cantassa had arrived on horseback with herbs in their saddlebags, and Elowen had administered them. Now, Morlain felt her strength returning and all four looked on at the battle, anxious for signs of a conclusion and an ending.

Morlain touched her hand and raised it to look at the ring of Eupheme on her middle finger. All could see that its glow grew in intensity.

'He needs us. They need us,' she said. 'Come on, one last push.'

***

Artur charged at the Curiosolitae line, the Sword of Menluit held with both hands above his head, swinging and slashing. Maedoc, Kea and Gawen were alongside him, all now fighting with swords at close quarters. The King of the Curiosolitae's men, the last of the aggressors, were backed up against the outside of the battlement. The King was in the centre and around him were perhaps one hundred men, no more. They deflected and held back blows, but now Artur, utterly incensed, scythed and stabbed into their midst. The rest of the Company were arriving, Nouran, Gourgy, Briec, Ambros, Tremaine, and at the last, Drustan and Silyan with their swords drawn, having finished fighting alongside the men of the Foye, on the far side of the hill where the Romans were utterly vanquished and destroyed.

Artur slashed with determination, forcing his way towards the Curiosolitae king. Maedoc tried to stay with him, and Kea and Gawen also tried to support him, but Artur only had one desire. He took out the man in front of him and surged forward, then the next and surged forward again; he was grim-faced, enraged and intent on revenge, looking the King in the eye as he got nearer.

Brice, who was around twenty summers older than Artur, and smaller and stockier, held his sword and his shield, ready to engage.

'What, little Prynsling, come to die with me also? Who will rule in your place if you throw away your kingship in the foolish pursuit of me? I have heard the Belgae are keen to take over!'

Artur lunged forward and swung his sword with such force against the King's shield that he staggered and moved around to his side. Artur went around with him and Brice continued his half circle, and then stopped and looked mockingly at the Prince.

'Not bad. You hit with force; but now you see that I have you with your back against the wall and my men all around me. If we cannot have this land and its trade for our own, then we will leave as much chaos as we can and killing you will give us all great pleasure.'

He thrust forward and Artur parried the blade, but now the warriors around the King turned also and thrust their blades. Artur rapidly parried them all but then they came again. One nicked his right leg and he gritted his teeth at the pain, breathing and panting heavily. Then, with a mighty effort, he parried their thrusts and slashes again. He was weakening and couldn't keep it up for much longer. He swung his sword again, and as he did, there was a sudden rush of air and the two warriors next to the King collapsed, each with two arrows in their back. He lunged forward and stabbed the King deep into his leg. Brice dropped his shield in pain, and instantly, as he did, Artur ran his sword through his chest. The Prince pushed him back off the blade with a grim face of satisfaction and watched him fall. Now, he surged against the remainder of Brice's warriors, while the rest of his Company came towards him from the edge of the fight, led by Morlain and Gwalian. One was scything and cutting her way through the remaining Curiosolitae with her sword, and the other had her bow poised, ready to use it and bring aid to any of her comrades who needed it.

Finally, there were no more Curiosolitae standing – all of them were slashed, stabbed and dead, apart from the King who lingered on, prone on the ground and unable to move. Artur stood over him, exhausted and breathing heavily.

'No chaos here, Brice; instead, order and right are restored. You have utterly failed in your miserable plan, death is almost too good for you, but to your end, you must now go.'

He raised his sword and plunged it into the King's heart. The battle was over.

***

Slowly, they came together, the Company and defenders of Menluit. There was no wild jubilation at victory, but instead a grim, tired satisfaction. The bodies of their comrades lay all around and in the morning they would all work together to ensure the best burial for them all. Not individually in stone-lined tombs, as was the normal way – there were far too many for that – but buried in Menluit hill. The Company would dig deep into the ground where they had fallen, to ease their passage to the Underworld, with their weapons and the items they carried. Then, when they had finished, they would burn the hundreds of bodies of their enemies that littered the field, pile them high and set fire to them.

Idrus and Clesek came to Artur, as he stood flanked by Morlain, Gwalian, the Company and the defenders of Menluit. Idrus spoke first.

'Nephew, I have lost a dear son and brother and we must first grieve, but in the days to come, with your leave, we will talk of kingship and how you will succeed your father. Before then,

Glonek here and his men will carry your father's body back to Ker Kammel and there we will bury it in the cemetery by the sea, five days from now.'

He looked at both Artur and Morlain, conscious of all that had happened.

'Will you come for the burial?'

Artur said, 'Yes, of course.'

Morlain nodded and added, 'Elowen will join him on his final journey in this world and prepare him for his journey to the next.'

'Very well,' said Idrus, 'My men and I will return to Dynasdore and the Foye and I will see you there, five days from now.'

Clesek stood forward.

'Prince Artur, my son and our Veneti friends have been avenged today and I stand in honour of your victory. Soon we must talk about Tamara and all that we can do to benefit from the wealth that she bestows, but tonight we will return to our homes. Tomorrow, some of my men will return to help with the burials and the burning. I, with the rest of my men, will deal with their boats at Ictis. If, that is, they have not left by morning.'

'Lord Glesek, thank you, your help will be most welcome and your intervention, and that of uncle Idrus, has turned the day here. I will always be grateful.'

And so, all those who came to the defenders' aid went away from the battlefield, at least for the night, and soon the field, bloody, muddy and strewn with bodies, was eerily quiet. Others, if they had homes to go to, drifted away as well. As the defenders walked up the hill towards the destroyed battlement, Casworon walked alongside the Prince.

'Actually, if ee don't mind, Pryns Artur, me an' the Missus an th'Casworons'll get off fer th'night also, put our feet up an all that; think of comrades lost, get some shut-eye and come back in the mornin'. It's all been a bit exaustin' for ol'Casworon.' He paused and then said, 'Glad we came through though and an 'onour to fight with ee!'

Artur turned to him and smiled. 'And with you, your fighting reputation is deserved, I see, and you brought us hope in the beginning. We could not have done it without you.'

'Oi wouldna missed it for anything,' he said and then, with his followers, turned and walked away, back down the hill.

They ascended, saying little, but looked at each other and smiled palely and tiredly, and then Silyen said, 'Who's that?'

Up the hill, close to the mantrap, a man wandered erratically around the battlefield, weaponless. His clothes were torn and he looked battered, dishevelled and uncertain of where he was.

'It's a Romin,' Gourgy growled coldly. 'Looks like we missed one.'

He and Nouran drew their swords and began to walk at a stronger pace up the hill. Morlain quickly joined the Prince and said quietly, 'No more killing today, Artur. We have done enough for many days. He is no threat to us now and something tells me that he is a sign, and that he may be of use to us.'

Artur frowned and looked back at her. 'How can he help us?'

'I am not sure yet. It is just a feeling that I have.'

Artur nodded as he looked forward again and carried on walking and then called, 'Gourgy, Nouran, hold on. We will find out who he is first. Wait for us.'

the birth of a legend

Julius Caesar pushed his chair back from his campaign desk and rubbed his eyes. The wick of his desk oil lamp flickered as the oil ran low. He was tired and it was time to sleep before he began the long journey back to Ravenna.

It had been a long campaign season. His decision to march against the Morini and the Menapii prolonged matters further, but it was necessary. Despite not joining the Veneti fleet, as threatened, they still made belligerent noises and their ships, as with the rebellious Veneti, could impede his intended crossing to Britannia. He had, therefore, followed up his – and his legate's – defeat and punishment of both the Veneti and the Venelli-led rebels by marching across all of Gaul, facing Britannia. This would emphasise his control and rule over all the tribes and show the tribes of Britannia, whose spies he knew were watching, what he was capable of. Then he had attacked the Morini and the Menapii. Unfortunately, it had not quite gone as he had planned. The wretched and insistent rain had been their undoing and so he would revisit the problem in the next campaign season. The foray had, however, shown him that the best route to Britannia was almost certainly from the Morini lands; indeed, you could even see Britannia from there, although the locals claimed little knowledge of it.

Now back with the army at their winter quarters, amongst the Aulerci and Lexovii, he tidied his affairs. He had spent time with his writer this evening, helping to draught the next of his commentaries on the wars in Gaul. The keeper of the battle record had joined them for supper. He was the recorder of who went where and who did what, of deaths and of valour and award, who helped him to recall and record particular details. Then, when they had gone, his attendants had come in and packed most of the tent. They would leave early the following morning and, now as winter set in across Gaul, he looked forward to a return to Ravenna and his next move in the politics of Rome. While the work had gone on around him, he had looked through some outstanding parchments that he would carry in his saddlebag. Then, when they had left him, he had spent some time concluding them and packing them tidily into his bag.

As he looked to his bed and considered sleep, there was a functional cough outside the tent and the centurion of the Pro-Consul's guard lifted the tent flap and stepped inside.

'Centurion, what is it?'

'Pro-Consul, Dominus, Marcus Trebius Gallus is outside and asks if he might have an audience with you.'

For a moment, Caesar stared expressionlessly at the Centurion, wondering if his tiredness had deceived him.

'Marcus, Trebius Gallus?'

'Yes, Dominus.'

'Is he alone?'

'He is, Dominus.'

Caesar stood, eyes narrowing as his mind worked on the possibilities and he said, 'Alright, show him in and, Centurion, do not go far from the tent, I may need you.'

'Dominus.'

After a short pause; Gallus stepped into the tent. He looked different from when Caesar had last seen him. His hair, although well-kempt, was thicker and bushier than normal for a Roman, certainly for an officer. He had a pronounced, and by the look of it, recently received scar running down from his forehead and along the line of his ear to his jaw – a scar of battle, surely. His clothes, however, were neat and pressed in the Roman way, and he had clearly shaved this morning. For the most part then, he looked like an officer of the Roman army, the officer that he had given his secret instructions to, back in the summer; but something was different and he could not quite see what it was. Caesar spoke slowly and quietly, preparing for news he did not want to hear.

'Praefectus Gallus, what brings you to my tent at this hour? Have you left your cohorts in capable hands in Britannia? I received your departure report, what? Nearly two months ago now, but have heard nothing from you since. We agreed that your mission was secret and not to be reported on until you had established your position. Is that what you have come to tell me? That you have secured the port of Ictis? If it is, you could have sent one of your men. Then we can correspond over the winter and agree our plan of approach for the new campaign season.'

He stopped and looked at Gallus and said, 'Tell me, Praefectus, why do I have the feeling that you have not come to tell me that and, instead, something that I do not want to hear?'

Gallus breathed purposefully for a moment, preparing himself, and then he said, hurriedly, nervously, 'All dead, Pro-Consul. Only I am left alive.'

Caesar stared clinically at the man before him and said calmly, but with a hint of menace, 'All dead, what do you mean? They cannot all be dead. You took virtually a full legion, if you include the auxiliaries. What of them and of Trierarchus Flavius?'

'The Trierarchus is dead, an arrow through his head. He insisted on pursuing the treasure before we had established a proper base at the port, left against my express orders and took the Curiosolitae with him. The local tribe surrounded them. My men and I tried to rescue them, but we got embroiled, weighed down in the mud, and they overwhelmed us. Then they took our galleys and burnt them. They are strong fighters, the Dewnan, on land and sea, their priestesses command a terrible power and they use their land of rivers and deep valleys to entrap any who are not familiar. It is not the way to enter Britannia, Pro-Consul. I have come to tell you that and to stop you from wasting any more good men.'

Caesar's face was stern with a building expression of contempt. He had misjudged the man before him. Crassus had recommended him, but it was obvious now. He would soon deal with him, but first some more questions, because none of it rang true. Any capable Roman officer should be able to deal with a range of terrains and enemy tactics and "priestesses with terrible powers". Presumably, some warped and lesser barbarian version of the Vestal Virgins, and anyway, what sort of powers? It sounded like nonsense.

'Praefectus, it seems to me that you have actually come to tell me that you have failed and to such an extent that you have managed to lose over four thousand men in doing so and, within that, if I recall, over one thousand well-trained legionaries. I told you that the Trierarchus was hot-headed. That was why I sent you; to make sure he did not do anything foolish and because you told me that the auxiliaries had a command of the sea and a detailed knowledge of the land and were prepared to provide a bridgehead to Britannia. They deceived you, used you and led good Roman soldiers to their death as a result.'

The Pro-Consul was being careful not to shout, but his face portrayed his building fury as he spoke. There was a further question.

'Where is the Greek, Gyras the Massaliot? Dead as well? If the territory was so dangerous, why did he not tell us this and instead give us such a positive report? Did he not say that the country was wide open with an impotent King and the Veneti gone? How then have you still managed to lose four thousand men?'

Gallus looked bleakly back at him. He was very sorry for the loss of all of his men. Although, while he lay half-dead in the pit of sharpened stakes, he had no control over that; and he had come to see in recent weeks that the Roman and Curiosolitae force should never have crossed the Mor Pretani in the first place. That was his real mistake. Still, he regretted the loss of so many lives, men just doing their job, directed by others who should have known better.

'I do not know where Gyras is, Pro-Consul, but a new and powerful group have taken control in Britannia and it is they that we came up against. The old King is dead. A new young King, brave and determined, leads the Dewnan now, alongside his wise and powerful queen...'

'Stop – that is enough!'

Caesar strode forward quickly, grabbed Gallus by his collar and spitting words, but still not raising his voice, said, 'You dare to come in the tent of the Pro-Consul of Rome, the greatest power on Earth, and apologise for these people? These barbarians have seen your gullibility, lured you into a trap and butchered good men for their own twisted notion of defending their nation at the end of the world. I will tell you this, Praefectus...' He spat the words out, 'I am going to Britannia and no trumped up young tribal leader in sop to the women of his tribe (who ever heard of it?) is going to stop me!'

His eyes hard, aggressive and angry bore into Gallus as he held him tight. Gallus tensed himself, waiting to respond to anything worse that the Pro-Consul might do, but instead, Caesar, still holding firmly to his collar, shouted, 'Centurion!'

The Centurion stepped in at the call.

'Take this man away and tie him up in the isolation tent, nobody must speak to him, and when you have finished, tell the Primus Pilus that I wish to see him.'

The Centurion called for assistance and took Gallus from the tent. The man went easily, resigned to his fate it seemed, almost as if he expected it – or as Caesar reflected – he wanted it.

When they had gone, Caesar paced angrily backwards and forwards. He was furious with Gallus, but he was also furious with himself. He had made a mistake. Fortunately, he had had the sense to keep the attempt to land and establish a forward camp secret. He knew it was risky, but even then, surely, he reasoned with himself, he could not have expected such a dereliction of duty. Establish the camp and secure a base you can hold while assistance comes to you, if needs be, and then foray out to meet the locals. *It was basic military practice. How could it have gone so wrong?*

He stopped and shook his head, his mind was whirring, calculating how he would respond.

Removing any damage to Caesar and his reputation was his only concern. In a basic, primal way, he was sorry for the death of his son, but it did at least remove him as a threat to his standing, and where better to lose a secret son than on a secret mission? There was no problem, in his mind, with having an illegitimate child, but the boy was impetuous and hot-headed. He probably had some key part in the fiasco, and if he had lived and come back with success, he would have demanded too much in reward. He was too dangerous and his death, at least, was a relief to Caesar.

Gallus, of course, had to be eliminated; the only person, as far as he knew, who could cause damage in Rome; and anyway, such a huge and disastrous failure, even if it was secret, demanded a summary and terminal punishment. As for those who had gone to their deaths, Roman deaths... when he had finished giving his instructions to the Primus Pilus, he would get the keeper of the records and his writer back. Some altering of the lists of those lost in battle in Gaul would be required. Of course, the records never accounted for more than half of those lost in battle, but it would be good to see some of the names of those lost on the mission appear on the lists; it would help to divert any suspicion. Then, perhaps they would review the Commentary for the year so that he could ensure that no reference that might cause damage was included. He had made no reference to the mission and only one reference to Gallus that would almost certainly cause no harm and was important anyway to his justification for attacking the Armorican tribes.

Perhaps he could make more of the Curiosolitae's part in the rebellion. He would look at that. He would also need to take the keeper into his confidence at least, but the keeper's future prosperity and indeed, his well-being, were in Caesar's keeping. It would not be a problem. And the Curiosolitae, well, nobody in Rome cared about them, of course. Few in Rome knew anything about Gaul unless he wrote about it; but it would not pay to be complacent. He would quietly offer their new leaders inducements and ensure that other benefits went their way. It would keep them quiet for a while, for as long as you could ever rely on a Gallic promise, but long enough for him to move on to new triumphs and beyond any negative impact from this sorry episode.

There was another cough at the tent flap and the Primus Pilus stepped into the tent. 'Secundus, good evening. I have an important job for you, one which I would like you to undertake personally.'

***

Gallus sat tied to a post in the isolation tent, just outside the camp defences. He knew all about the punishment tent, which was, in effect, the prison unit for wrongdoers for the army on campaign. As Praefectus Castrorum, he had overall responsibility for this unit and now here he was sitting in one. Normally, the tent or the unit held soldiers accused of dereliction of duty. Fustuarium, stoning or clubbing to death was their fate, and might yet be his, he thought morosely, if they did not come for him. Something had to happen soon, an hour must have passed since the guard had placed him here and the midnight hour approached. He needed conclusion; he had done as he had said, as she had asked and now, more than anything, he needed to know what would happen next. He would do anything for her. Would she do the same for him?

The flap lifted and a man stepped into the tent. It was darker by the door and, at first, he could not make out the man's face. Then, as he drew nearer, recognition spread across Marcus's face. It was his old colleague and friend from the VIIth, Secundus Avilius.

'Secundus, it is good to see you.'

The Primus Pilus spoke quietly and hurriedly. 'Marcus, don't… don't be pleasant with me. What have you done? And where have you been?'

Gallus looked back at his old friend. He was agitated, unhappy about something. Uncharacteristically, he seemed nervous; his hand hovered over his dagger hilt and then, he realised why.

'Oh, I see, you are to be my executioner. At least, it is not Fustuarium.'

'Marcus, I am sorry. If there was any other way… but the Pro-Consul… I have a family at home in Lucca. My fate is their fate, you must see.'

Thinking quickly, Marcus said to him, 'Secundus, there is another way. Has the Pro-Consul asked for proof of my death?'

'No. Only that I ensure that it is done and that your body is buried away from the camp. Marcus, he will know if you live. He has men, spies everywhere.'

As the Primus Pilus spoke, the tent flap gently lifted again, although he did not seem to hear it, and another figure slipped into the tent. He raised his dagger.

'I am so, so sorry.'

'Put the dagger down, if you value your life!'

The quiet insistent words were not ones that the Primus Pilus understood, but he stopped and turned. A woman, diminutive, slender, with long brown hair and chestnut brown eyes looked intently at him and held her bow, poised and ready to shoot.

Gallus exhaled with relief. 'I thought you were not going to come. I was nearly a dead man there.'

A slight smile appeared on her face, in the midst of her concentration.

'Marcus, you have cheated death before and now you have cheated it again; and I am sorry, we have taken every care not to be seen. It has not been easy, but I did not nurse you and allow you to grow into my heart only to abandon you when you needed me most.'

Gallus nodded and smiled warmly in spite of his predicament and she whispered loudly towards the tent flap. 'Callard, Kea, Gawen!'

All three stepped into the tent and she flicked her head towards Gallus.

'Marcus needs untying.'

Callard and Kea unsheathed their swords, hidden under their cloaks, and cut the ropes, while Gawen stood watch at the flap.

'I did it, Gwalian. I said I would. I told him to his face. That is why I am here and that is why he has sent Secundus to kill me.'

She looked across to him, smiled more broadly now, with eyes of affection and said, 'I knew you would do it, but now we must leave before we are found.'

Marcus turned to his old friend. 'Secundus, there is another way. Let us go. We will slip away unseen and you will never see me again. Where I am going, no Roman will find me. You will be safe and so will I. Here, take my dagger. See, it has my initials on it. Tell him that the job is done and that Marcus Trebius Gallus is dead and will trouble him no more.

***

The sky was a mix of light blue and wispy, high blown clouds as the weather had turned crisp and clear. Traces of ice from the morning frost hung on bushes and in the puddles on the path.

Morlain and Artur sat at their favourite place on the edge of the hill of Marghros, wrapped in furs against the cold. They looking down at Tamara as she wound lazily and languidly toward Ictis and the entrance to the Mor Pretani. Steam tumbled from their mouths as the warmth of their breath touched the cold morning air.

Beside them stood a large oblong stone with a series of simple circular carvings at its centre and with freshly trampled soil all around it. It had been dragged to the top of the hill by Steren Uskis and a team of horses two days previously and then lifted with ropes and dug into position by all who had survived the siege of Menluit. It stood in memory of those who had given their lives and fought the brave fight to maintain freedom and the right to self-determination in the land of the Dewnan.

'It was right to place the stone here wasn't it, rather than at Menluit?' Artur said.

Morlain looked up briefly and smiled before looking down again to her writing.

'Yes, it was, on this high point, at the centre of Tamara's valley, where all can see how we honour the sacrifice that those who gave their lives have made.'

Artur breathed in deeply and looked out across the valley, thinking about all that had been lost and all that had been won. Good friends and brave companions fighting together against aggression and unprovoked attack. As he gazed towards Ocean, Marrek's song of defiance, the song of the Dewnan filled his mind.

> *Forth the Dewnan brave and true*
> *We shall not submit to you!*
> *Stand with us for freedom's voice*
> *Sing with us our song of choice!*

After a while, with thoughts of sacrifice and victory still prominent in his mind, he turned his attention to what she was doing.

'Can you write in this cold air?'

The cloth, wrapped around her hands, still allowed her fingers to grip the quill, while she leant on a wooden board. Ink in a wool-lined pot sat on the ground beside her as she scratched words intermittently onto the parchment.

'Yes, I must; so much is lost and I have much to do to replace all that I can remember.'

'That will take a while. Rest now, and talk to me.'

She looked back at him. 'We have our lives together to talk to each other, but first I must concentrate and write a new story.'

'Oh yes?'

'I have written the title, do you want to see?'

'I do. Morlain, will you teach me how to read and to write?'

'I will. The King should be able to read, so let us begin with this.'

She handed the parchment to him. He took it and looked at the shapes on it.

'What is the meaning of the shapes?'

'They say, "The Story of Artur".'

He looked at her now. 'It is our story, not just mine.'

'Yes, it is, but the future of the Dewnan, our home and this Sacred Land is with you and other Arturs yet to come; and the story has begun.'

Artur looked towards Ictis, thinking about what she had said, and then a movement caught his eye. A small group were coming up the hill. He peered intently. Now he was certain.

'Look, it is Kea and Gwalian, Callard and Gawen, and Marcus is with them. They are back!'

'And all of them here, which means they have done it... told Caesar. He has failed and he and his Romans have met their match in Artur of the Dewnan!'

'Who would not have achieved anything, without Morlain Priestess of the Pretan.'

She looked into his eyes, smiled, put the parchment down and jumped up.

'Come on, let's go and meet them.'

The End

author's note

There has always been a separation in these islands, between the people of the Ocean and the Estrenyon, who are continental in their origin. Blood and DNA, much intermingled now, marked them as distinctive. Long before any English and Celtic divide was recorded, the people were different and came from a different place, and the label of the Celt has no basis here – except in its designation by the Welsh antiquary, Edward Lhuyd early in the eighteenth century. Nineteen hundred years before, in the first century before the Common Era, no one in these islands would have called themselves Celtic.

The Ocean People lived by, traded on and undertook voyages of discovery along the Atlantic seaboard. They venerated the celestial bodies, the Ocean, land and their ancestors. Over centuries and millennia, they left their mark in cairns, barrows, dolmens, brochs and sacred landscapes. They built with stone and wood and lived in fortified rounds and hill and clifftop promontory settlements. They dug for tin, copper and silver and innovated to create a strengthened, more durable bronze. And they knew the wider world, through engagement with traders who came from near and far in search of *kassiteros*; covertly, secretively, protecting their source and trade of this highly valuable commodity.

The Greek geographer and explorer, Pytheas of Massalia voyaged to 'Belerion' and to 'Ictis' in the fourth century BCE and wrote about it in *On the Ocean*. Then, in the first century BCE, another Greek, Diodorus Siculus set down his *Bibliotheca Historica,* and was almost certainly drawing on the observations of Pytheas, when he wrote:

"The Inhabitants of Britain who live on the promontory called Belerion are especially friendly to strangers and have adopted a civilised way of life because of their interaction with traders and other people."

In this first extract from *The Chronicle of the Dewnan*, the suggestion is that this interaction – a connection with lands around the warm sea, through Massalian Greeks, Phoenicians and all the way back to Mycenaean Greeks – was long established before Pytheas undertook his voyage.

But it is the writings of Julius Caesar, in his *Commentarii de Bello Gallico,* that most closely align with the events described in *This Sacred Land.* His commentary, in response to rebellion and the need to maintain Roman law and 'the law of nations', is seen differently from the perspective of the Dewnan, the Veneti, and all those who got in the way of the Roman legions or were simply fodder in a much bigger power play. Furthermore, the assertion here is that the reports Caesar sent home from the front may not perhaps have been the whole truth about his intentions or the actions he took.

At the outset of *This Sacred Land,* the Dewnan and their Veneti kin are at their lowest ebb. Centuries of retreat and consolidation have reduced trade and led to the slow eclipse of their way of life. This has been brought about by gradual Estrenyon creep, the looming threat of the Roman legions and an apathetic leadership, at least in the case of the Dewnan, which has left them diminished and in need of a hero and a saviour. Artur, named the 'son of the bear king' and inheritor of the Dewnan myth of wise Orsa, is that hero. Orsa was the protector of the ancient Great Wood, a symbol of simplicity, purity and days of origin before their world was sullied by expansion, war and defeat. This first Artur, King of the Dewnan, inspired by Morlain's guidance and support, sets a precedent for others to follow – future Kings who would also be allocated the title, utilise the name and build the potency of the legend and its ability to meet and repel invasion.

The Dewnan are a confederation of tribes, led by a high 'King', to whom the other lesser tribal chieftains or lords give varying degrees of allegiance. The Estrenyon regard all of the Dewnan as a lesser tribe and a throwback to a bygone age, who are small in stature and with dangerous beliefs in magic and equality between male and female. They call them Dumnoni, an inferior 'dark and earthy' people. A name passed on to the Romans in the first century of the Common-Era – and so into history.

In *This Sacred Land*, reference is also made to the Kernovi, but this should not be imagined to be a modern-day Cornwall equivalent. Not yet. The heartland of the Dewnan in the first century BCE is the valley of the Tamar. This is on both sides of the river and along the Fowey and Camel and surrounding coastal areas. Here is the centre of trade and where connections with distant lands were most strongly formed. The Kernovi are the furthest west, and by contrast, insular; more concerned with local obsessions than wider engagement, despite their metal-based wealth. Still, the King of the Dewnan provides a useful buffer against Estrenyon incursion and so allegiance is given. But it is the Kernovi, in the end, who will keep the words of the Dewnan alive when all else is lost.

acknowledgements

Three works, in particular, have supported my re-creation of the *Chronicle of the Dewnan* and its first volume extract, *This Sacred Land*:

Commentarii de Bello Gallico, Julius Caesar's writings about his campaigns in Gaul in 56 BCE. Although *The Chronicle* refutes the veracity of his stated intentions and justification for his actions described, the commentary nonetheless provides an indispensable timeframe and contemporary insight into the events that surrounded Caesar's attack on the Veneti. I used Carolyn Hammond's translation (1996) and the introduction, especially on Roman military organisation, and the maps provided were also very helpful.

Rising Ground, A Search for the Spirit of Place (2014), Philip Marsden's journeys across Cornwall. In this book, he describes the land and its features and how they have both inspired and been shaped by pre-history and history – building a sense of place at the heart of daily existence. I thoroughly enjoyed reading and re-reading it. The chapters on Bodmin Moor were particularly inspiring.

Cornish Place Name Elements (1985), Oliver Padel's amazing work for the English Place Name Society (a misnomer for this volume). This was published in 1985 and referenced also in *Rising Ground*. It is fascinating reading and proved invaluable in imagining lost history and filling in the gaps for the place names of the Dewnan.

The work and publications of Barry Cunliffe have strongly influenced my thinking in various ways; for example, on Mount Batten as a likely site of Ictis, on Pytheas the Massaliot and in *Britain Begins* (2012) – even if I have on occasion taken a different view on the interpretation of evidence or events.

I should also mention John Germon's A to Z of Devon dialect, available on archived BBC Devon webpages: (http://www.bbc.co.uk/devon/voices2005/features/devon_dialect.shtml),   which proved very helpful for both finding and imagining words. Most of the dialect and naming are based, of course, on modern or comparatively modern usage of both the

Cornish language and Devon dialect – although the place name elements referred to above are much older.

I have used all of the above and read many snippets and extracts of reading and myriad of internet-based source material and commentary in my research. If mistakes have been made, they are purely my own and I am indebted to all of the input and insight that I have derived from them.

I would like to give particular thanks to Ben Watkins, for detailed advice on content and layout; to Tim Russell for advice on the text, and to the team at I am Self-Publishing. And then to Jackie, Don, Andy, Martine, Steve, Sam, Joe and Penny. Thank you for all your thoughts and input, incredibly useful and very gratefully received – and a special thank you to Matt for his artwork and to Nigel, without whom the Path of Ronan and the very earliest kernel of an idea might never have been conceived.

Finally, to Penny, Joe and Charles – thank you for bearing with me, giving me great insight and comparisons to draw from and helping me to decide when things got difficult – and, of course, for helping me to strengthen the description of that dragon.

In the land of the Dewnan, 2018

connect with
tim bagshaw

Find out more about the Chronicles of the Dewnan and the author, Tim Bagshaw, and sign up for our newsletter at: www.inthelandofthedewnan.com.

Lightning Source UK Ltd.
Milton Keynes UK
UKHW012022250119
336222UK00001B/185/P